Embrace the Grim Reaper

Books by Judy Clemens

The Stella Crown Series
Till the Cows Come Home
Three Can Keep a Secret
To Thine Own Self Be True
The Day Will Come
Different Paths

The Grim Reaper Series
Embrace the Grim Reaper
The Grim Reaper's Dance

Embrace the Grim Reaper

Judy Clemens

Poisoned Pen Press

Copyright © 2009 by Judy Clemens

First Trade Paperback Edition 2010

10 9 8 7 6 5 4 3 2 1

Library of Congress Catalog Card Number: 2008937735

ISBN: 978-1-59058-720-1   Trade Paperback

Poisoned Pen Press
6962 E. First Ave., Ste. 103
Scottsdale, AZ 85251
www.poisonedpenpress.com
info@poisonedpenpress.com

Printed in the United States of America

For my father, Philip Clemens,
who is not afraid of Death.

Acknowledgments

Thanks must go to a group of people who make the world of writing and research enjoyable, and who keep me from making too many mistakes.

The world of martial arts is a new one to me, and one I never would have entered without my friend Jenny Baumgartner. Besides being a blackbelt in hapkido, she is a writer in her own right, and I hope to soon see her books on the shelves. Master Doug Custer is a wealth of information, and very generous with his knowledge. Many thanks to him and his students, who were willing to be guinea pigs for my research. Grandmaster Rudy Timmerman was kind enough to allow me to use his name in the book, and his interest and enthusiasm are gratifying.

John Bellomo, my friend and a talented Fight Director, was instrumental in choosing the play in the book, and in designing the stage combat scenes.

Doug P. Lyle, MD, once again answered medical questions with detail and expediency.

My friend, lawyer Don Witter, answered tough questions, and gave me some great ideas.

My hubby, Steve Smucker, besides allowing me to live a writer's life and squirrel myself away in my office, knows more about cars and appliances than I ever hope to, and always answers my mechanical questions.

My parents, Philip and Nancy Clemens, my first readers

and number one fans, are more of a support than they can ever know.

A huge thank you to my children, Tristan and Sophia, for their interest and for understanding that sometimes I have to "go away to do book stuff."

And finally, to the people of Poisoned Pen Press, you make this crazy business a joy.

Oh, somewhere in this favored land the sun is shining bright;
The band is playing somewhere, and somewhere hearts are light,
And somewhere men are laughing, and somewhere children
    shout;
But there is no joy in Mudville—mighty Casey has struck out.
    —From *Casey at the Bat*, by Ernest Lawrence Thayer

Chapter One

And then Death turned to her and said, "The only reason I didn't take you that day, Casey, was—"

"—it wasn't my time to go. I know. I *know*." Casey shook her head. Looked at the pebbles under her sneakers.

Death gave a warm, throaty chuckle. "No. No, Casey, that wasn't it. Not at all."

Casey closed her eyes. Opened them again. "Then why?"

Death smiled. "I didn't take you then, love, because it's so *much* more interesting this way." Death looked down the highway. "Someone's coming."

Headlights approached, and Casey watched as the two bikes—big Harley-Davidsons—roared beneath the overpass, stopping in the small dry patch at the side of the road. The silence when they hit their kill switches was complete, except for the drumming of the rain on the concrete above them.

The first man eased a leg over his bike and shook his head, beard and braid splattering rain, like a tattooed dog after a bath. He rubbed his eyes, hooked his thumbs in his belt loops, and looked ahead on the road, into the driving rain.

The second man, larger than the first, his bald head and shaven face speckled with raindrops, laughed loudly. "Hoo-eee! That's some dumpin'. Thought they was gonna poke right through my face!"

The first one grunted, turned, and stopped, looking up the stony embankment. "Well, I never. You okay up there, darlin'?"

The bald one jerked around, his eyes finding Casey in the midst of the stones and stumpy weeds. He squinted into the grayness, as if expecting more creatures to pop out from the shadows. "You all alone?"

Casey saw nothing beside her anymore but a sense of something lingering, like the air hadn't quite closed itself behind Death.

"I'm okay," she said.

The first guy gestured at the rain. "Little wet, maybe?"

She glanced at her sleeping bag, dry except for the corner, where drips from a tile in the overpass had created a sodden triangle. Her clothes were dry, as was her backpack. She'd found shelter just in time, as the wayward sprinkles had started falling, blurring the afternoon into a misty smear.

The hairless biker reached into his saddlebags and pulled out a rag to wipe his face, leaving a greasy slash across his cheek. He tossed the cloth onto the bike's seat and used his tongue to work at something in one of his back teeth while he studied Casey, glancing behind him only when a truck roared past in the opposite lane, spraying water as far as the shoulder, just short of the men.

"Where you headed, sweetheart?" the other one said. "Don't see no wheels here."

Tires screeching, the world spinning, metal rending—

Casey pulled her knees up to her chin and rested her arms on them, her head at an angle to avoid hitting the road above her. "Nope. No wheels."

"You hitchin'?"

She shrugged. "Walking. I just follow the road as I feel like it."

He nodded. Looked at the rain. Looked at her. "Well, you want a ride when this rain stops, you got one." He jerked his chin up the highway. "We're headed east. Toward Pittsburgh."

She turned her head. "I guess I could be going that way."

The bald guy studied her a moment longer before shaking his head once, hard, like she was nuts. That was okay.

Casey watched as the two wiped down their bikes. Checked the tires. Pulled the straps on the leather saddlebags tighter, keeping out the rain. Sat on their bikes, their backs to her, heavy boots crossed in front of them at the ankles.

This was not one of those moments she'd considered. Alone by a sleepy highway with two very large, very tattooed men. No idea who they were. No idea what they were like, except they were dressed all in black, one with a skull embroidered on the back of his jacket. She rubbed her eyes with the heels of her hands. The bikers were still there when she stopped.

Gradually the downpour diminished, the thunderous pounding easing to individual splatters, and then to nothing. The sun didn't come out, but the day lightened, the clouds a thin veil across the sun. Casey considered the bikers, and their offer. She felt no animosity from the men. No sense of threat. Was she ready to move on?

Not much here, on the rocky ground along a highway.

She swallowed. Looked at the motorcycles. They weren't cars. Or even vans. Didn't have four tires, or air bags.

And she was really, desperately tired.

"I'll take that ride, if you're still offering."

The bearded biker pushed himself off of his bike. "Sure thing, hon. You can ride with one of us, strap your stuff to the other."

"Thanks." She gathered up her possessions. There weren't many of them. She hadn't even bothered to take out anything but her sleeping bag and a bottle of water. She folded up the damp bedroll and tied it to the top of her backpack, scooting the whole lot behind her down the rocky embankment. When she reached the bottom she eased upward, stretching her sore muscles. A sleeping bag hadn't been enough to protect her bones and body from the hard, uneven surface. She rolled her neck, but stayed aware of where each man stood, primed for self-defense should her sense of their intentions prove wrong.

"I'll take that." The larger man held a hand out for her backpack.

Casey hesitated, then lifted it into his arms.

"We ain't got no helmets," the other guy said. He sat astride his hog, fingers on the key.

Casey laughed under her breath. No helmets and a motor-cycle on a rainy day. Not the smartest method of travel. But then, it probably wasn't *interesting* enough for Death to take her that way.

On the other hand, maybe it was.

She stepped up to the bike, and got on.

Chapter Two

"Not a good day for ridin', huh?" The trucker at the counter laughed, slapping his knee.

The bikers walked past him and the other truckers sitting along the counter, ignoring the obvious comment.

"Order what you want, darlin'," the bearded biker said when they were seated. "S'on us." He yanked a sticky menu from behind the napkin dispenser and slipped a pair of glasses from inside his leather vest.

"No," Casey said. "I'll pay."

He peered at her over his lenses. "You don't look much like you should be turning down gifts."

"Oh, but I should be." She pulled a couple of crumpled twenties from her pocket and laid them on the table. "It's my treat."

Her two new friends looked at each other until the bearded one shrugged and turned back to his menu. "Your call, sweetheart. You want to pay, we'll be sure to let you."

"Thanks."

The bald one grunted a laugh, his eyes on the list of daily specials.

After they'd ordered Casey sighed, letting her head fall back. She was damp, cold, and tired. The patty melt and fries would help. She hoped.

"So," the hairy one said. "Where you headed, exactly?"

Casey brought her head back up, avoiding his eyes. "Somewhere. Anywhere."

"Oh. So it's like that?"

"Yeah."

A voice from the intercom announced a name, garbled with static, and said the shower was available. One of the truckers at the counter stood and tossed some bills by his empty plate before loping toward the back of the truckstop. Casey watched him with longing. A shower. Oh, to be clean, and warm.

The bald biker leaned back in his chair, balancing on two of its legs. "We're going to State College. Harley rally. Welcome to join us."

Casey outlined a design on the tablecloth with a finger. "Thanks. That's…kind of you."

Their food came then, steaming and fragrant. Casey tucked into her meal, forgetting all but the taste on her tongue, and the warmth in her belly. She came back to the present gradually, her eyes meeting those of her companions, their eyes sparkling as they regarded her across the table.

"Um. Hungry," she said.

The bearded one laughed. "Guess so."

She smiled briefly before finishing the rest of her food and downing the large glass of milk.

"I suppose you'll want dessert now," the hairy one said.

"Oh. No. No dessert for me. But you guys…if you want it, you go ahead."

Baldy grinned. "Don't mind if I do." He ordered and devoured an extremely large banana split.

When they'd finished Casey felt full, warm, and even dry. Content.

"You ready to get goin', sweetheart?" Her bearded friend stood beside his chair, a hand on its back.

"Oh. Sorry." She got up and followed them outside, where the men put away their tarps and swung their legs over their bikes, balancing their rides, their feet on the ground. Casey hesitated.

"Everything okay?" Her driver was waiting.

"Sure. I…it's just, I think this is where I get off."

He looked around. "*Here?*"

"Yeah. But thanks. Thanks so much for everything. The ride. The offer. I…it was nice."

He studied her face. Shook his head. "S'your call, darlin', but you know, some of these others…" He waved a hand at the parking lot.

"Yeah. I know."

The bald guy got back off his bike and unstrapped her bag, holding it out to her. "Would'a been fun at the rally."

She took her pack. "Yes. Yes, I'm sure it would've." She attempted a smile.

He sat back down and saluted. "Then good luck, whoever you are. Wherever you're going."

"Thanks. You, too."

"Never did get your name," the other one said.

"No. No, you didn't."

He shook his head, but any more words were drowned in the starting of their engines. Lifting a hand in farewell, he eased his bike back onto the road, his buddy following.

Casey watched them go until they were just specks, disappearing into the gray horizon.

Chapter Three

"Any chance I could hitch a ride for a while?" Casey stood beside the truck, her heart pounding.

The trucker, clean from his shower, hesitated, his foot on the running board. "Where you goin'?"

She jerked her chin toward the road. "That way."

The trucker pursed his lips, his eyes narrowed. "I'm going down southeast. Ending up in West Virginia."

"That's fine."

He shrugged, switching the toothpick in his mouth from one side to the other. "Gonna be a few minutes. Need to fill up on gas, check the tires."

"That's fine. I'll go in and use the ladies' room."

He nodded, and swung himself up into the cab.

The restroom was a typical one-person affair, smelling of industrial-strength air freshener, with a stack of paper towels sitting on the sink underneath the broken dispenser. Casey locked the door and set the backpack on top of the closed toilet lid. Digging through her bag, she found her brush and yanked it through her hair, ripping through rats' nests, bringing tears to her eyes. Slipping a ponytail holder off of the brush's handle, where she kept a collection of them, she pulled her hair back and banded it there, out of her eyes. She should've done that before going anywhere on a motorcycle.

The water from the tap was surprisingly cold, and heated up slowly. When it finally reached lukewarm she splashed it over her face, rubbing her eyes until she saw spots. She finished off with her toothbrush, scrubbing her teeth in circles, the way they taught in elementary school.

So, not perfect, but better. At least she felt human again.

The trucker was waiting for her beyond the gas station, chewing on his toothpick and glancing at his watch.

"Sorry," she said.

He lifted his chin in response. "You can stash that—" he gestured to her backpack "—behind your seat."

She walked around the front of the cab, freezing when she reached the passenger door, staring at the handle. Months, it had been. Many of them.

Door buckling, air bag punching her face, the smell of smoke and rubber and oil, the sound of someone screaming…

"You getting in or not?" The trucker unlatched the door from the inside and pushed it open.

"Yes. Yes, I'm coming." Casey took a deep breath. Held it. Climbed up into the cab, shoving her pack into the space behind her seat before strapping herself in. Only then did she let out her breath in a tightly controlled hiss of air.

Clenching her hands into fists on her lap, she kept her head down, swallowing thickly as the truck pulled into traffic. The air in the cab felt close, and sweat trickled down her scalp as she concentrated on not being sick.

"You okay?" The trucker squinted at her across the seat.

"Yes. Yes, I'm fine."

She would be. *She would be.*

Several miles down the road she took another deep breath and licked her lips. This was a new day. A new day, with Death sitting in the middle of the bench seat, between her and the driver, looking for all the world like a ride in a semi was boring as hell.

Casey raised her head and looked out the windshield.

The road seemed different from where she sat, high above the smaller vehicles, looking down at the drivers' legs as they passed. Once in a while she saw hands, busy with eating or talking or holding a phone. Sometimes even driving. Every so often she glimpsed a face peering up into the cab before she could turn away.

The trucker wasn't talkative. No jokes from him about motorcycling in bad weather. In fact, the only time he spoke was to ask Casey to pull a CD from the glove compartment. A classical one. Beethoven's Seventh.

After a few hours they'd passed through many small towns. Seen many courthouses and schools and churches. Neighborhoods of turn-of-the-century homes. Queen Annes. Victorians. Some repainted in original colors, some broken into apartments. Some just broken. Railroad tracks, taverns, the never-ending array of fast food.

Sometimes Casey would see a factory on the outskirts of town. New ethanol plants, car manufacturers, food conglomerates. This town, the one they were approaching, had an appliance factory. HomeMaker. Casey recognized the brand. Dishwashers. Refrigerators. Stoves. Anything to make your life more convenient. She hadn't used any of them in quite some time now.

"We'll be stopping here," the trucker said. "Need to walk around a little. Get some coffee."

"Sure."

He found an old restaurant, The Burger Palace, with a truck turnaround, and parked out back. "You coming in?"

"In a minute. Think I'll get out and stretch first."

"Don't make me wait."

"I won't."

He left her there and walked across the cracked pavement, up the rise to the restaurant. Casey looked down the street toward what appeared to be the center of town. Glanced at the sky. Still no more rain. And getting on toward late afternoon.

She was tired of sitting.

Climbing back up into the cab—holding her breath in an attempt not to hyperventilate—she pulled her backpack from its crevice, found another crumpled twenty in her pocket, and wedged it into a corner of the CD player. The trucker should find it there.

By the time she'd made it partway down the street, to where she would turn a corner and be out of sight, she looked back to see the truck pulling out of the parking lot, headed her way. She ducked behind a tree to watch him go by.

He didn't even glance in her direction.

The old Midwestern town—Clymer, Ohio—was like many she'd seen already that day. Clean, quaint, but basically deserted. No mad rush of workers making their way home after a long day, or even neighbors talking in their yards. But she did come across an old-fashioned pharmacy, a bakery, a bank, and what looked like a seller of antiques.

A block past the center of town—a stoplight and Walk/ Don't Walk signs—she stopped and stared at a church, its sign proclaiming, "Strangers Welcome," and "Feeling the heat? Try Prayer-Conditioning." Casey let her eyes roam over the thick stone walls and up the front peaked roof to the bell tower. A chill ran through her, and she glanced sideways.

"Beautiful building." Death stood beside her, hands linked loosely in front. "Do beautiful things happen inside?"

Casey shifted on her feet. "I don't know. They could."

"But you're not going in."

"It doesn't look open."

"Um-hmm." A smile played on Death's lips. "I don't suppose you've tried the door."

"Well…"

"I'm just saying…" The smile widened.

"You're always 'just saying.' It would be a lot easier if you would 'just do'." The heat in her own words surprised her, and she swallowed forcefully.

Death's eyebrows rose. "And here I thought I'd done more than enough."

"Oh, you've done plenty."

"But not lately. Not for you."

Casey balled her hands into fists, her arms stiff at her sides.

Death turned to look down the street, at the businesses and homes. "It's interesting to be in this town. It's not unfamiliar to me."

Casey jerked her head around. "What? You mean *recently?*"

Death shrugged. "Why do you think we chose this town to stop in?"

"*We?* What do you mean *we?* I—" A hot breeze hit Casey's face, and she closed her eyes against the hair that had come loose from her ponytail. When she opened them, only a sense of displacement hovered around her.

She spun in a circle, grasping at the space. "You come *back* here. You come *back!*"

But the air, suddenly stilled, remained empty.

Casey rubbed her eyes, hard, and let out a deep sigh. Shaking her head and clenching her jaw, she continued down the street, muttering under her breath. In a few steps she was walking past an old movie theater, the kind with the ticket booth out front under the marquee. And then she smelled it. Something good. Stew, maybe? Or roast beef?

She followed the scent until she came to a place with *Home Sweet Home* painted on the window. She peered in the glass. Long tables, folding chairs…a soup kitchen? She stepped back and took another look at the empty street. Would a town this size have a homeless population? It was hard to imagine. She turned back to the building and tried to open the door, but the handle remained stiff under her fingers. Locked.

Shading her eyes with her hands, she leaned closer to the glass door and searched for any sign of people. She saw only one. A young man, his skin pale under the fluorescent lights, straightening chairs and picking up the occasional piece of trash.

Casey tapped on the glass, and he looked up. Seeing her, he left the chairs and came to the door, opening it. "Sorry. Supper's not for…" He looked at his watch. "Another forty-five minutes. Five-o'clock."

"I'm not here to eat. I was wondering if I might help serve."

He took in her clothes and backpack, ending at her face. She couldn't have deteriorated that much since she'd washed at the truck stop. Could she?

"Well, come on in. We can always use another pair of hands." He held the door open wider, and she scooted past him, noting the fresh fragrance of laundry and something heavier. Cologne. But not a familiar kind. Once inside, the smell of the food was almost overwhelming, and the man's scent was erased.

"What's your name?" he asked.

"Um. Casey Smith."

He nodded, his hazel eyes dancing. "All right, Ms. Smith. Nice to meet you. I'm Eric. Eric Jones." He smiled, exposing perfectly straight and white teeth.

Casey couldn't help but answer with a smile of her own. A small one.

"Actually," Eric said, "my last name's VanDiepenbos, but don't tell anyone. It's too hard for them to remember. You wouldn't believe the things I've been called."

Casey held up two fingers. "I promise."

"Why don't you help me straighten up these chairs, first. Here, I'll take your backpack into the staff room."

She hesitated.

"It'll be safe. Really. We keep it locked all the time. There's even lockers if you want to use one."

With a mixture of relief and anxiety she unloaded her burden and handed it over to Eric. To this young man, at least a decade younger than she ever remembered being.

While he was gone she studied the room. The tables were laid with brightly colored tablecloths. Blue and pink and yellow. Like a birthday party. Vases of plastic flowers decorated every section. Pretty flowers, clean and cheerful. This was unlike any homeless shelter Casey had ever seen.

Eric returned, and together they picked up trash and straightened chairs.

"It's supper only," Eric told her. "We'd like to do more, but it's hard to find enough food for the meals we do, let alone a supply of volunteers. The Missionary church down the street offers lunches on Wednesdays, but other than that people need to fend for themselves."

Casey could feel his eyes on her face, as if gauging her reaction.

"Really," she said. "I'm not here to eat."

She could tell he didn't believe her, but there was nothing she could do about that. "I'm curious…"

"About what?"

"You've got a small town here. I didn't see… Do you have that many homeless people? Folks who need meals?"

He squatted to pull a wadded napkin from under a table. "Not *homeless*, necessarily. But we've added a lot of place settings during the past year. And it's only going to get worse with the plant leaving."

"What plant?"

He stood up. "You're not from around here?"

She shook her head.

"I should've figured that. Sorry."

"What plant?" she said again.

"The one on the edge of town. HomeMaker. It's closing. Moving to Mexico, actually. About a quarter of the employees were laid off last Christmas—nice time for that, huh?—and it's shutting down completely within three months. This town, it's just going to— Anyway, we've got lots more people coming for supper than we had even six months ago. But not any more supplies. People can't afford to feed their families, let alone have anything left over to give away."

"What happened? With the plant?"

He held out a trash bag and she dumped her handful of garbage into it. "The usual. You know. The union wants more money, better wages for the workers. The owners say, 'screw you,' and move to Mexico to get the tax breaks and cheap labor. Nothing new." He tied the top of the trash bag and heaved it over his shoulder. "Come on, I'll put you to work with the food."

Casey followed him through a narrow door into a steaming hot kitchen. A skinny elderly woman stood at a stove in an apron, her hair scraped back into a hairnet as she stirred something in a big pot. Her coffee-colored skin shone in the moist heat, and she wiped at her forehead with her sleeve.

"Loretta, this is Casey. She's going to help out with serving tonight."

Loretta glanced up. "Well, *thank you Jesus,* that's good of her, um-humm. You just make yourself at home, baby, okay? *Praise God!*"

Casey met Eric's eye, and he turned, smiling, to the other person in the room. "Johnny, this is Casey."

Johnny grabbed Casey's hand and shook it enthusiastically, his smile almost as wide as his face. His eyes had the slant of Down's Syndrome, and he stood several inches taller than Eric. He was stockier, too. "Eric always finds nice ladies to help," Johnny said. "I wrap all the silverware in the napkins. Everyday." He waited expectantly.

Casey cleared her throat. "I'm sure you do a great job with that, Johnny."

"Oh, yes, ma'am, I do. I'm the best at it, want to see?"

"Well. Sure."

He bounded back to his station and returned, clasping a smooth bundle of silverware encased in a white paper napkin. "You see? You put the knife at the back, then the fork, then the spoon so they fit together right, and then you put them in the middle of the napkin and wrap the napkin around them. I'm the best at it."

"I can see you're very experienced."

"I'm the best."

"Okay." Eric clapped Johnny on the shoulder. "Better get back to work, buddy. The folks will be here before too long and we want to be ready for them."

"Oh, yes, Eric, yes, we do. I'll get to work. I'll do them all. I'm—"

"—the best at it. Yes, you are."

Johnny smiled angelically, gave Eric a bone-crushing hug, and lumbered back to his spot.

Eric grinned. "I love my crew."

"I can see why."

"Now." Eric clapped his hands together. "You and I can set out the bread." He opened a cupboard and pulled out a dozen baskets. "Line these with those linen napkins over there. You can use that counter."

Casey washed her hands at the large metal sink, then took the baskets and set them in a row, flapping open the white squares of fabric. Eric followed, removing sliced bread from plastic bags and filling the baskets.

"Homemade bread?" Casey asked.

"Day old, from the bakery down the street. Or two days old. Still good. Better than store-bought. Plus, it's free. You want to cover the bread with the extra napkins?"

She did, and they carried them out to place them on the tables, along with economy-sized tubs of margarine.

Movement at the front caught her eye, and Casey saw faces at the glass of the door. "Guests?"

Eric turned. "Yup. It's almost five. Why don't you let them in?"

She went to open the door and stood back as a family of five eased past her, the three young children studying her with an uncomfortable intensity. Casey took another step back. The parents glided by without a glance, their eyes on the floor. Casey peeked out the door, but seeing no one else, shut it and went back to the kitchen, passing the family, who'd seated themselves at the far end of the first table.

Eric stood beside the open refrigerator door in the kitchen. "Here." He took out a tub of peaches and set them next to some spotted bananas on the counter. "Cut these up and arrange them on these trays."

"How—"

"Doesn't matter. Just in slices. You can divide the bananas into quarters, maybe. Leave them in the peels."

"Where are you going?"

"To greet the folks. They're used to seeing me. I like to at least say hello."

"They didn't say anything to me."

"No." He smiled sadly. "They wouldn't. It's been…" He stopped.

"What?"

"Oh. Difficult."

"With them losing their jobs?"

"Sure. Yes. That's been really hard."

There was more, Casey could read it in the tightness of his jaw. But Eric wasn't saying anything else.

Casey watched him go, the stiffness of his shoulders the only other clue of his discomfort. Of some kind of pain.

This town is not unfamiliar to me. Death's face hovered before Casey's.

"Eric!"

He stopped in the doorway, his face turned back toward her, eyes wary. "Yeah?"

"Oh. It's nothing. Never mind." *Yes, Eric, Death told me a few minutes ago that…*

He continued on.

The dining room soon filled, and Casey stayed busy helping Loretta serve the beef and vegetable soup (low on both beef and vegetables), mopping up a glass of spilled milk, and refilling the bread baskets, until the bread was gone. There was even dessert—day old cookies and brownies from the bakery, along with the remainder of a birthday cake. Casey wondered if the bakers got some kind of a tax break with all of their donations, or if they gave out of the goodness of their hearts. Perhaps both.

The guests ranged in age from an infant, still at his mother's breast, to a man so old he needed help guiding his spoon to his mouth. There must have been sixty-five people around the tables, but from the noise level Casey would have guessed fewer. The lack of volume disturbed her, as if these people had no energy left to do anything but fill their stomachs. Had this room sounded like this a year ago? Or before last Christmas? A sudden cry rent the air, and Casey swallowed the lump in her throat as the young mother paused in her own eating to hold her baby over her shoulder and pat his back.

Eric came to stand beside Casey, an empty bread basket under his arm.

"It's nice of his daughter to help him eat," Casey said, indicating the old man, and the woman beside him.

"Oh, she's not his daughter. He doesn't have any family around. She's his neighbor. Brings him along with her every day. Or the days he feels good enough, anyway."

"Where's his family?"

His face tightened. "Left at Christmas, when Karl kicked them out."

"Karl? Who's Karl?"

"What?" Eric blinked. "Oh, Karl Willems. He's the CEO of HomeMaker. Made the final decision to move HomeMaker out of the country."

Families were beginning to clear out now, bobbing their heads and mumbling thanks to Eric as they left. Casey watched him do his best to make eye contact with them, even hunkering down to talk with the kids, one of whom hit him on the head with one of Johnny's carefully wrapped silverware bundles. The mother, horrified, snatched her child from the floor and hustled out the door. Eric saw the last of the guests out and locked the door before heading back toward the kitchen, rubbing his head.

Casey grinned. "Need an ice pack?"

"I'm going to have to ask Johnny to double-wrap the children's forks and spoons. Come on, let's see what he's up to."

They found him standing beside Loretta at the sink, a dishtowel in his hand as he lectured her about silverware and the best way to clean it. Together the two of them had already made quite a dent in the washing. Reassured that things were in hand, Eric led Casey back out to the dining room, where they cleared the tables, wiped down the tablecloths, and began picking up trash.

"Whoops," Eric said, glancing at the clock. "I gotta go. Have something at seven, and I've got ten minutes to get there."

Casey saw with surprise that time had, indeed, flown by. "I'll finish up here."

"You don't have to. I usually do it the next day, like you helped with earlier."

"I don't mind. Really." It's not like she had anywhere to go.

"Oh. Well, all right. Thanks." He jogged to the kitchen and came back out with a duffel bag slung over his shoulder. He paused at the front door, his hand on the latch. "Thanks for helping tonight. It was...fun."

Casey regarded him. "You're welcome. Thanks for letting me be a part of it."

"Loretta can open the staff room for you to get your bag when you're ready." He looked out the front door, then back again. "If you're around tomorrow..."

"I'll try to come back. If I'm still in town."

"Okay. Good." He gave her another one of his blinding smiles, although this time Casey could see the events of the past two hours reflected in his eyes. "See you around, then, Casey Smith."

She nodded. "Mr. Jones."

And he was gone.

Chapter Four

The door locked behind Casey with a snap, and she stood on the sidewalk, her backpack resting on the ground beside her.

When Casey had finished cleaning the dining room, Loretta (*Hallelujah! Praise God!*) had insisted on feeding her before letting her leave. Casey didn't argue. There was just enough leftover soup for the three of them, and even a little fruit. Johnny cheerfully slurped his way through his bowl after bestowing Casey with a set of silverware. She had thanked him solemnly, and he sat next to her so closely she couldn't move her left arm.

"Birthday cake for the nice lady," Johnny said when she was done, handing her a corner piece with a wilted icing flower.

"Thank you. Who's birthday was it? One of the children?"

"Oh, no, baby," Loretta said. "It was Eric's, the dear boy."

"And how old is he?"

Johnny pursed his lips, and Loretta stared at Casey's cake. "Somewhere in his twenties. Or is he thirty now? He didn't want to make a big deal out of it, but he's such a precious child of God we didn't want to miss it. *Thank you Jesus!*"

Casey ate her cake, but didn't ask any more questions.

Now she stood outside after retrieving her bag from the locker room, and for the second time in one day she had a full belly. The air in the darkening evening had chilled, and Casey pulled a jacket from her pack, zipping it up to her chin. She looked back into the building, but the lights were off, and everything was quiet.

Time to find somewhere for the night.

She heaved her bag onto her back and started down the sidewalk. She should've asked the others where to stay, and wondered why she didn't. Forgot. Or didn't want to sound needy. Whichever it was, she was paying for it now as she cast an eye toward the starless sky. She hoped it wasn't about to rain again.

A few blocks down the street she found an enclosed—and apparently unused—bus stop, and she stepped in to look at the map on the wall. An X designated where she stood, but no names, other than streets, gave her any information of which colored square might be a hotel. Giving up on that, she perused the information sheets taped to the wall. Advertisements for baby-sitting, with phone number tabs to pull off, an announcement of a church fish fry for the previous Friday, and a schedule of the local high school's fall sports. There was also a call for garage sale items to benefit the family of a woman named Ellen Schneider, who "left us before her time."

Casey sucked in her breath as she read the fine print below the announcement. Ellen, a resident of the town, had died suddenly the week before, leaving her two school-age children parentless, with no father in the picture. No details about her death. No explanations. Casey gritted her teeth. Death must've been especially bored. A young single mother? Sudden death? Casey's breath came fast and hard, and she pulled her eyes from the poster, concentrating on her heartbeat. *a-One. a-Two. a-Three.*

She forced herself to look beyond the garage sale notice, and continued past a homemade sign depicting a lost cat named Snowball, to yet one more faded announcement, this time for play auditions, held almost two weeks earlier. *Twelfth Night.* A rather strange choice for a dying town. But then, maybe they needed all the humor they could get.

The paper fluttered in the breeze, two of the four corners ripped from the tape, and Casey held it down to read it. Open try-outs, it said. Anyone interested was to come by the Albion Theater one of the two nights. Rehearsals would begin the next week. Which would be last week, Casey thought. She found the theater on the map, its address plainly stated on the announcement. She looked at the sky. Wasn't raining yet. And maybe they were rehearsing. It would give her something to do other than camp out in a hotel room, watching cable and being angry with Death.

It wasn't hard to find the Albion. In fact, she'd already passed it when she first got to town, only she'd thought it was a movie theater. It probably had been, in its earlier days. Posters covered the front windows, with photos of past productions displayed prominently. *The Foreigner, Little Women, Cheaper by the Dozen.* Casey swallowed. Looked away. Found the front door, and went in.

The lobby was dark, with only emergency lights illuminating the open space. Benches lined the walls, and a display stand held an unfinished board showing a few of the play's cast. A stack of loose photos lay on the floor, waiting for positioning on the sign. Community production, Casey thought, the visible headshots just missing the mark of professionals.

Voices seeped through the double doors from what Casey imagined was the theater space. She stood with her ear against the crack, listening for a moment before easing one side open and slipping in.

The musty smell hit her, almost a physical assault, and she closed her eyes, memories cascading through her mind as she stood in the aisle, her hands grasping one of the seats. The voices of the actors drifted over her, underscored by the quiet hum of the house lights, and slowly she regained her equilibrium. Opening her eyes, she slipped into the back row and lowered herself into one of the lumpy seats. Dust motes floated in the light from the instruments hanging on the catwalk, and the distant actors now stood quiet, looking down at the director, a silhouette in the front row.

Casey let the sounds, the smells, and the lights wash over her as she traveled back. Back to life before Omar. Before now. Her muscles tightened in response to her thoughts, remembering the feel of the stage, the thrill of a full house.

The sharp voice of the director snapped her out of her memories, and she broke out in an instant sweat. The director clearly wasn't happy with what he'd seen. His words, plainly heard from where she sat, were clipped and harsh, and the actors stood hunchbacked as they listened.

"I am at a loss," the director said. "I know we are without one of our leading ladies. I know Becca here is filling in, but…" He held his hands up, as in supplication. "Is this really the best you can do?"

Casey sat up in her seat, squinting toward the front of the theater. Was someone sitting with the director? Was there a stage manager, taking down blocking, answering the calls for 'Line'?" Trying to keep the director from actually killing his cast members? No one that she could see. She sank back in her chair to take a closer look at the actors.

And allowed a small smile.

I have something at seven, Eric had said.

He stood on stage beside the female lead, rubbing a hand through his hair as the director spoke. He looked much younger under the house lights than he had at the soup kitchen, where the pain of his constituents was etched into his face. Now his sandy hair shadowed his eyes, and his face was revealed as a smooth white blur. Casey rested her elbows on the arms of the chair, her hands dangling over her stomach as she watched Eric resume his place by a reclining lawn chair, obviously a rehearsal prop.

"Okay," the man in the front row said. "Page twenty-three. Viola's scene with Feste, Toby, and Andrew. See if we can't generate *something* interesting. Come *on*, people. Go."

Casey winced as the woman began speaking. Not exactly Equity quality. But then, the director had said she was filling in, and Shakespeare wasn't the easiest for *any*body, let alone someone in a tiny Midwestern town who'd probably never seen a union production of *any*thing, let alone *Twelfth Night*. The other two actors in the scene offered their lines, a duet of not enough inflection and way too much, but they were young, maybe not even out of high school, and actually better than the woman. Soon it was Eric's turn, and Casey held her breath, wishing she'd left before hearing him, as she'd liked him and wanted to be able to think of him without remembering badly done Shakespeare. But it was too late, and she gritted her teeth, waiting.

As he spoke she sat up straighter. Eric was not only leagues above the others, but equal to the actors she'd worked with in Seattle, Cleveland, and Chicago. She looked around, feeling as if she were on one of those dreadful reality shows, someone waiting in the wings to surprise her with a sudden flash of a camera.

But it was no joke.

Listening with growing surprise and wonder at Eric's quality of acting, she shook her head. Who would've thought, here in… what was the town called? Clymer? And really, what on *earth* was someone with his talent doing in a community production?

Shocked, Casey remained in her seat, not even minding the slaughtering of the language going on around Eric. It was worth it, just hearing him open his mouth. She wondered what the director was thinking. Was he irritated because the others couldn't possibly act to Eric's standard? Was he another talented man, like Eric, who was for some incomprehensible reason here in this tiny town doing community theater? Or was he one of those all-too-common folks who think they know a lot more about theater than they actually do?

The scene played out, and the actors looked toward the director. Casey watched Eric, but his expression revealed nothing. Not anxiety, not hope. Not even much interest. Casey checked out the others, only to see the lack of emotion repeated. The only actor really listening as the director ranted was the younger man playing Sir Toby, his eyes rapt on the director's face.

"Enough for tonight," the director said with a jerk of his hand. "Go home. Go over your blocking. Learn your lines, for God's sake. Do *some*thing." He stood, shoved his notebook into a bag, and before Casey had a chance to react he was striding down the aisle toward her seat. There was nowhere to hide, and the director stopped by her chair, lifting his hands toward the ceiling.

"It's about time," he said. "I thought you'd *never* get here."

Chapter Five

Casey blinked. "Excuse me?"

The director frowned. "I spoke with you ages ago. You'd think you could show up before we all grew old."

Casey placed her feet flat on the floor and eased herself up out of her seat to stand in front of the director, aware of her personal space and how close he was to violating it. "I'm not here for you."

His eyebrows lifted. "Oh, really? Then who, exactly, are you here for? *Those* people?" He jerked a thumb backward toward the stage. "When I get a commitment from an actress, no matter how good she thinks she is, I *expect* her to be here for me. I don't tolerate prima donnas."

Movement behind the man distracted Casey, and Eric peered around the man's shoulder, his face flooding with red.

"Thomas," he said. "She's not the one."

The director stared at her for a few more seconds before acknowledging Eric. "Well, then, who is she?"

The rest of the cast was there now, too, and they all watched her, expressions much more animated than five minutes before on the stage. Eric grinned. "Her name's Casey Smith. She helped out at dinner tonight."

Thomas looked her up and down. "I should've known. I bet you couldn't act your way out of a paper bag, could you, sweetheart?"

A roar filled Casey's head. She glanced at Eric's face, now white, and gave a grim smile. She forced herself to look back at the director. "You don't think so?" She held out her hand.

He sneered at her outstretched palm. "What?"

"A script, please."

"But—"

"Or a paper bag."

The director's eyes narrowed at the snickers from the cast. "Eric?"

"Yes." Eric's face was rigid with suppressed laughter.

"Get the lady a script. And read something with her."

"Sure thing." He turned to the woman he'd been acting with and smiled. "Care to share your script, Becca?"

Becca's face tightened, and she glanced at Casey. "Eric..."

"Come on, Becca. What can it hurt?"

Becca took a deep breath, looked at the ceiling, and reached into her purse. "Here."

"Thanks. Come on, Casey."

Casey eased around the director and accompanied Eric down the aisle to the stage.

"You know this play?" Eric asked.

"Intimately."

He glanced at her with surprise. "Any choice, then, on what scene we do?"

Her lips formed a tight line. "How about the conflict scene with Sir Andrew and Viola?"

"I guess that would be—"

"How are you with fighting?"

He gave a soft chuckle. "You mean in real life or on the stage? I've got experience with both. Although off-stage it's been much less violent." He grinned. "But as you can see, we haven't graduated to using practice swords yet. He—" He jerked a thumb toward the director "—says he's waiting till he's convinced we're ready for the weapons. I think he just doesn't know any fight choreographers."

Casey laughed. "We don't need swords. If I say two left jabs and a half roundhouse before a contact stomach punch, upper-cut, and a sit fall, would that mean anything to you?"

They'd reached the stage, and Eric held back to let her climb the stairs ahead of him. "I'd know what you mean, but without practice I'm afraid I could hurt you."

She waited for him at the top of the stairs. "Oh, I'm not afraid of *you* hurting *me*. You ready?"

He hesitated, then stepped forward. "I guess. Although you've got me a little scared now."

"No worries. Let's show this blowhard a thing or two."

Eric shook his head. "All right. Hey, Jack. Aaron. Come on up and do this scene with us. Jack, you be Toby. I'll read Sir Andrew—"

Aaron, the older of the two kids, jumped onto the stage. "But that's my part."

"Just for now, you play Fabian. Please?"

Aaron shrugged, and grinned. "Fine with me."

"All right. Casey and Aaron, enter from over there. Jack and I will do our lines from here."

Casey followed Aaron to the wings on stage left. Her blood tingled in her veins, and she opened and closed her hands, bouncing on her feet as she listened. Jack began his lines in Sir Toby's drunken fashion. *"Why, man, he's a very devil; I have not seen such a firago."*

Casey closed her eyes and breathed in as he finished his line, as Eric joined in with his rich voice. She let her chest expand and contract, and relaxed completely as she waited for the entrance line. When it came close, she opened her eyes to find Aaron waiting for her to cue their movement.

"This shall end without the perdition of souls," Jack/Toby stated.

Casey and Aaron stepped onto the stage. Casey watched and waited as the others read through the lines leading up to hers. She, as Viola, took in the scene and her opponent, Sir Andrew.

Toby gestured to her. *"There's no remedy, sir; he will fight you for 's oath's sake…"*

Casey waited for the end of the line and began hers. *"Pray God defend me! A little thing would make me tell them how much I lack of a man."*

The scene continued to its ending, with Casey's lines assuring the others that the fight was against her will. Eric pounced, taking two quick left jabs at her face. She ducked, then blocked his roundhouse, aimed at her head.

Getting her balance, she swung at his stomach, making light contact as he let out a whoosh of air fit for an NBA flopper. She finished him off with an uppercut, her hit upstage of Eric's face, while he jerked his head with perfect timing, using the hit to slowly send him backward, where he landed hard on his butt.

Casey stepped over him, raising her foot as if to finish him off, when Jack jumped in with the next line, using a different voice for the character of Antonio. *"Put up your sword!"* He giggled, completely not in character, and Aaron joined right in.

Casey, breathing hard, relaxed her stance and stepped back, holding out a hand to Eric. After a brief study of her face, probably to make sure she wasn't bluffing and was really about to take him down again, he allowed her to help him up. Together they turned toward the house, which sat in complete silence.

Casey paused, blinking at the lights, and closed her eyes as a rush of memories swept through her. The lights. The musty smell. The audience.

Omar's face.

Reuben's…

She swayed, and felt Eric's hand wrap around her arm.

"You all right?" His voice was anxious.

She swallowed and opened her eyes. "I'm fine." She pulled her arm away. "Thanks."

He gestured at the stage behind them. "That was…amazing. I mean… Who *are* you?"

Applause came suddenly from the two actors on stage with her. After glancing at them, Casey put a hand over her eyes and squinted into the house. The woman, Becca, still stood in the aisle, her eyes wide, hands clutching her bag. The director, his face a blank mask, sat silently in the fourth row, his hand under his chin as he stared at Casey.

The young men hollered again. "Bravo! Encore!"

Casey shook herself, and handed Eric the script. "Think I got out?"

Eric's forehead creased. "What?"

"Of the paper bag."

He smiled. "Oh, I'd say you got way out, crumpled it up, and threw it away."

"Good."

She turned and walked across the stage, descending the stairs. She brushed past Becca, but stopped when the woman called her name.

"You will do the part, won't you?"

Casey looked at Becca's face, which was filled with something Casey would've called desperation, if it hadn't seemed over-dramatic. "No. I'm just passing through. The part's yours."

Becca's face crumpled. "But I don't *want* it. I've been waiting for *you*."

That again. "Look. No one here has been waiting for me. *I* didn't even know I was coming."

"But—"

"Please, Casey. Can't you stay?" Eric was standing next to Becca now, his face pleading.

Casey shook her head and ran her fingers through her hair. What was up with these people?

The other actors joined them, their expressions of awe and humor only slightly dampened. The four of them stood in a tight semicircle, waiting, apparently, for her to say she was staying.

"It actually is *my* decision, you know," the director said.

They turned as a whole toward his seat, where he reclined, his hand half covering his face. Slowly he sat up, his hands on the armrests, elbows poking up beside him. He slanted his face toward Casey. "That was very interesting."

She waited.

"You seem to have some experience."

She nodded slightly, not really caring one way or the other what he thought.

"But I'm not sure you're what we really need right now."

The other four actors gasped as one, then let go with a volley of disagreements. The director held up his hand. "Enough." He looked at Casey. "You may go."

"No," Eric said. "Wait." He looked past her, toward the director. "You really are as big an idiot as you appear."

The director's mouth dropped open, but snapped shut as his face clouded. "You have no right—"

"But I do. And you know it."

The director's eye twitched, and he clamped his teeth together. "She is nothing like Ellen. Ellen brought a much more feminine—"

"Ellen's not here." Eric glanced at Becca, who'd made a small whimpering sound. "Ellen was…wonderful. We all know that. But this role doesn't have to be so…so womanly. It can actually use an…earthier feel." He glanced at Casey, probably hoping she wouldn't take that wrong. He put an arm around Becca's shoulders. "Becca doesn't want to do this. She's said so. And here—" He swept a hand toward Casey. "She would be different, but come *on*, Thomas. How could you not see what she just did? She's *perfect*."

Ellen. Casey knew she'd heard that name recently. No. She'd *seen* it. On the notice about the garage sale for her orphaned children.

Casey cleared her throat. "Didn't she—Ellen, I mean—last week…"

"Yes," Eric said. "She died."

Silence again covered the theater, and Casey looked from face to face. Eric's sadness, Becca's discomfort, the two young guys without a clear expression.

And the director's stubbornly held jaw. "She's not what we want."

Eric glanced at the rest of the cast, then back at the director. "Says who?"

The director pushed himself from his seat, held a finger out toward Eric, then let it drop. Stiffly he gathered his belongings—briefcase, coat, umbrella—and put them over his arm. "Fine." He looked at Casey, his chin held high. "Rehearsal tomorrow evening. Seven-o'clock. Don't be late. And try to…" He waved a hand at her clothes. "Clean yourself up a little."

Without another look he swept out the double doors, allowing them to slap shut behind him.

Chapter Six

"I'm sorry," Eric said. "If I'd known you were coming, I would've warned you."

"Yeah." Casey shook her head. "I wish you could've."

They sat on a bench outside the theater, the night air still promising rain.

"Thomas is a head case," Eric said. "He really is."

Thomas. The director. "And you're in his play...why, exactly?"

A smile flitted across his face, and he ducked his head toward the street. "Let's just say it's penance, and leave it at that."

Penance. Casey breathed in the cool night air. "Well, I hope what you did to deserve it was worth every moment. Penance like this would cover a lot."

"It better."

They sat quietly, and Casey eased her head back, her face toward the sky. "What happened? With Ellen? The notice at the bus stop said she died suddenly."

"Yeah. She did."

Casey brought her head down at the pain in his voice. "You knew her well?"

He shrugged. "We were in the play together. She would... she and her kids came to eat supper at the hall."

Casey studied his profile. "There was no husband in the picture?"

He looked away. "It was just her and the kids."

"Were her children there tonight? At dinner?"

"No." He leaned forward, his hands in prayer position between his knees. "They've gone to stay with their grandparents. Ellen's folks. They don't live in Clymer."

Casey nodded, closing her eyes. When she opened them again, she had to force herself not to jump at the sight of Death, who sat on the other side of Eric, picking fluffy buttered kernels of popcorn from a paper bag and chewing them with gusto.

"How did she die?" Casey asked.

Death shrugged, looking at Eric with interest.

Eric's face remained averted. "They say she killed herself."

Casey sucked in her breath.

Death made a face.

"Was she…did she have an illness?"

Eric gave a sad laugh. "Not unless you call unemployment being sick."

"Oh. She got laid off from HomeMaker."

"Right before Christmas. In the first wave."

"And since then?"

He sat up again, still looking at his hands. "She was doing odd jobs, where she could find them. But there aren't a lot here. No one else in Clymer is in the position to hire a cleaning lady or an extra hand at a store. The Burger Palace at the edge of town was about it. Not that she could support herself and her kids with that."

Casey shook her head slowly. A sad story. A *painful* story.

Death stared at Casey with wide eyes, obviously wanting her to ask Eric more questions. But about what?

Eric's face was pale, his lower lip sucked in, like he was trying not to cry.

Casey nodded. "You…cared about her."

"What? Of course I did. I care about all—"

"But she was special."

Eric closed his eyes. "I thought maybe…even with the kids… maybe partly *because* of the kids…we might…" He stopped.

"She was such a strong person. I never would've thought she... But I guess all that doesn't matter anymore, does it?"

"Of course it does." She looked at Death. "Just because someone dies doesn't mean she isn't still important to you."

Death tossed a popcorn kernel in the air and deftly caught it and ate it.

Eric turned his face toward Casey. "You sound like you've had some experience."

Casey grimaced. "Exactly what Thomas said."

Eric gave a small laugh. "Please, don't compare me to him."

"Sorry. Didn't mean to make you nauseated."

He smiled, and glanced at his watch. "Well, it's getting late. Want to go somewhere for something to eat? Or get a drink?"

The two full meals Casey had eaten had more than filled her up. As for the drink...

It had been just before her last birthday. The party with Reuben's colleagues. They'd closed a huge deal and were celebrating. Reuben's boss was happy, standing rounds for the whole crew. Casey had stuck pretty much to the champagne. Reuben to his usual Corona, with lime. Not too much. Nothing excessive.

She'd caught her husband's eye across the room, where he was held captive by one of his team, a loud-talking IT expert, who believed the world would be a better place run entirely by computers. Reuben had tolerated the ideas because the kid knew his stuff. And because Reuben was just that kind of guy.

Reuben had given her that smile. The one that said he was just biding his time before they'd stayed long enough and he could take her home to their bed. She'd worn the red dress, the one he especially liked. She'd raised her glass to her lips, holding his gaze, and had blushed at the thought of what would happen later.

"Thanks," she said now, to Eric. "But I really don't...drink. And I'm not hungry."

"Oh. Okay. Well, then, can I take you to your hotel? Or wherever you're staying?"

She looked at Death. "I don't actually have a place to stay."

Eric sat up, blocking Death from her view. "Really? You want to stay at my place? I've got an extra room, with a futon. But if you don't like futons you can have my bed and I can sleep on the futon."

Casey looked at Eric's face, alive again with helpfulness. "Thanks, Eric, but I think... Is there a hotel or something close by? Something not too expensive?"

His face fell, but he covered it up quickly. "Sure. The Sleep Inn is right out by the highway. Nothing great, but they have beds."

"That's all I need. And a shower."

He grinned. "I'm pretty sure they have bathrooms, too." He swung himself up, off the bench. "I walked today, so we'll have to go by my place for my car."

Casey stood, thinking about Eric's car. "You know, I can just walk to the hotel. It's out by The Burger Palace, right?"

A shadow passed across his face, probably at the thought of Ellen's last job. "It's at least a mile. I can run and get my car, if you want. Bring it here."

"No. No, that's okay." She looked Death in the face. "I really prefer walking. It's more interesting."

Eric looked confused at that, but held up his hands. "Whatever you want. I can walk with you."

"But then you'd have to walk back. You go on home. Really. I'm used to it. I can take care of myself."

He looked uncertain. "Yeah. I've been curious about that."

She'd been wondering how soon he'd ask, how long he could contain his questions about where she'd come from, and why. "Practice tomorrow evening at seven?"

He gave a little smile, apparently seeing through her change of subjects. "And dinner at five, if you want to come by."

"To help."

"To help."

"Okay. I'll be there."

"Good." He looked down the dark street. "You're sure I can't—"

"I'm sure. Goodnight, Eric."

"Well…goodnight."

Casey hefted her bag onto her back and watched Eric walk away. He stopped once, about half a block away, to look back. She raised a hand, and he resumed his walk.

Casey took a deep breath and walked in the opposite direction, stopping in front of Death, who still sat on the bench. "I suppose you want to come along? There will probably be two beds."

Death looked after Eric, who was just disappearing around a corner. "But it won't be nearly as fascinating as if you'd gone home with him."

Casey shook her head. "You're impossible."

"No. Not impossible. Just picky. Have fun at your cheap hotel."

And Casey found herself standing in front of an empty park bench, the breeze blowing an empty popcorn bag to the ground.

Chapter Seven

Death was right. The hotel certainly wasn't interesting. Gross, maybe, but not interesting. Casey lay in her own sleeping bag on top of the covers, far removed from the sheets, which apparently hadn't been washed after someone with lots of dark curly hair had slept there. The cable TV wasn't working, and the air conditioner made such an awful racket Casey wouldn't have heard the Second Coming if it happened right outside in the parking lot. The temperature in the room really didn't need lowering, either, so Casey turned off the malfunctioning equipment.

By the time dawn broke and light began seeping through the too-small curtains into the room, Casey had gotten only a few hours of sleep and had had enough of counting the little dots on the lowered ceiling. She got up, moved enough furniture around she could just manage her morning routine of calisthenics and hapkido techniques, took a quick shower in barely heated water, and headed out, hoping nothing too disgusting had crawled into her backpack while she'd slept.

The sky was brighter than the day before, and Casey doubted rain was in the forecast. It would be nice to be dry for at least a little while. She stopped at the desk to ask the sleepy, barely-out-of-high-school attendant where she might get some breakfast, and he directed her across the street to what she'd assumed was a closed diner, not having seen any cars there earlier. But inside the restaurant she was pleasantly surprised at the light and the cleanliness—both a nice change from The Sleep Inn.

After a good mushroom omelet Casey brushed her teeth in the bathroom and asked the cashier if there was a library anywhere close. He assured her there was, right downtown, and Casey headed back the way she'd come the night before.

Her path took her past the bus stop where she'd seen the fliers. She stopped to look again at the notice of the benefit for Ellen's family. A garage sale. A fitting event for a struggling community. Probably not a huge fundraiser, but something these folks could afford.

Walking on, Casey took one turn and soon stood at the doors of the library. Closed. The schedule on the window said the library would open at eight-thirty. Casey checked her watch. About eight. She slid the bag from her back and took a seat on the bench outside the front door. It wouldn't hurt her to sit for a while. Her night's sleep certainly hadn't been the greatest.

But by the time she was roused by the jingle of the doors being unlocked she was ready to move again. The librarian, a young man almost as wide around as Casey's right leg, opened the door with a smile. Casey was careful not to knock into him as she passed. The slightest touch would likely break a bone.

"Visiting town?" the man asked. Stacy, it said on his nametag.

"Yes. Could I use one of the computers?"

Stacy sat behind the counter. "Do you have a library card within our system?"

"No. I'm from out-of-state."

"All right. How about a driver's license?"

She did have that, but she hesitated. "You hold it as collateral?"

"That's right. It's the only way I can allow you to use a terminal."

Nothing new. "Okay." She took her license from her wallet and handed it to him, watching as he set it in the slot for Computer #1. So no written record of her library visit. Good.

"That's your station, right there," Stacy said, pointing. "If you need anything else, please let me know."

Casey thanked him and took her place at the computer. Going on-line, she first checked her e-mail. A gmail account. Non-traceable, and entirely non-geographical. She found the usual smattering of spam, which she deleted, but not much else except the usual note from her brother. This time it was brief: *Call me. Ricky*

She sighed. He couldn't ever just write what he wanted to talk about.

No other e-mails needed her attention, as she never gave out her address. How the spammers found her, she never knew.

Clicking out of e-mail, she typed in the name of the other site she had memorized. One that repulsed her, but drew her at the same time. Taking a deep breath, she hit Enter.

Pegasus.com came up immediately. Bright colors, flashy advertisements, End-of-Season sales announcements for the new line of hybrid cars. Of course lots of space describing their all-star rating for gas mileage.

Somehow, there was never anything about mechanical malfunction, accident rating, or the way their cars burst into flame upon impact. Nothing noting any pending lawsuits.

Suddenly dizzy, Casey rested her head on her hand and took a deep breath. *Breathe in, breathe out. In. Out.*

"Ma'am? Are you all right?" Stacy's voice held a tinge of panic.

Casey lifted her head and managed a small smile. "I'm fine. Thank you. Just tired."

"If you're sure…"

Casey put her head back on her hand, this time tilting her face away from the inquisitive librarian and toward the monitor. Could Stacy see the screen? She snuck a peek toward him. No. Wrong angle.

Casey focused her attention on Pegasus, going to the bio for the company's owner, Dottie Spears. Same smile, same glossy hair-do. Same exact photo as last time. Casey clenched her jaw, making the same unfulfilled promise she always made—to never go to that web site again.

A crick in her neck called her to sit up straighter, and again she regretted her night at The Sleep Inn. Leaving the Pegasus web site behind, she typed in parameters to find a bed and breakfast in Clymer, if there was such a thing. And there was. One. The Nesting Place.

Hmm. Sounded a bit out there, but it was the only place in town, and the pictures of the renovated Queen Anne looked appealing. Casey grabbed one of the scrap papers and sharpened golf pencils from the basket by the computer and wrote down the address. It was worth a try.

In the midst of writing, she stopped. Did she really want to get involved in this town? In that play? In the soup kitchen?

She wasn't sure.

Tucking the paper into her pocket, she went back to the search engine and typed in Ellen... What was her last name? She pictured the garage sale announcement. Ellen Schmucker? Snyder? *Schneider.* She hit Return.

A wide array of Ellen Schneiders filled the screen, and Casey realized she'd made the search too wide. She added the words, "Clymer," and, "Ohio," and tried again.

This time it became clearer, and she was presented with several articles from local papers about the untimely death of the young single mother of two.

WOMAN FOUND DEAD IN HOME

FORMER HOMEMAKER EMPLOYEE
DIES BY OWN HAND

SINGLE MOTHER LEAVES
CHILDREN TO STARVE

Casey frowned at the tabloid-style headlines, and clicked on the first article, dated the earliest.

Ellen Schnieder, 31, was found dead in her home yesterday afternoon when her neighbor, Mrs. Bea Tilly, stopped by to ask about the

Schneiders' dog. "I've never seen Griffey in such a state," Mrs. Tilly told this reporter. "He's always such a calm little fellow. It was like he was trying to tell us something."

And it seems he was. Entering her neighbor's unlocked front door, Mrs. Tilly found Griffey's owner slumped onto the kitchen table, an empty coffee mug and a spilled bottle of prescription pills in front of her. "All I could think was that I needed to do something before the children came home," Mrs. Tilly said. "They didn't need to see that."

They didn't. By the time Schneider's children were released from school, law enforcement had closed off the scene, and the new orphans were in the custody of their grandparents. The Schneiders, Ellen's parents, were unavailable for comment.

"I've never seen anything like this here in Clymer," Police Chief Denny Reardon said. "I can't comment on what happened, but can assure you it is under investigation."

The town of Clymer is eager for answers. "It's horrible that she could do this, if it really is what it looks like," Clymer resident Becca Styles said. "Everyone loved Ellen, she was so level-headed, so the idea that someone like her could make this choice is scary."

Casey looked up from the screen. Becca Styles? Could this little town have more than one Becca? Probably not. And with the small population it wasn't that strange that Becca would be quoted. Especially if she and Ellen were involved in the theater together.

The article finished with a promise for up-to-date news, and Casey moved on to the next.

FORMER HOMEMAKER EMPLOYEE
DIES BY OWN HAND

When HomeMaker CEO Karl Willems performed
last December's lay-off of more than fifty
employees, he knew it would be rough. What
he didn't expect was for one of his former
workers to commit suicide. "Ellen Schneider
was a wonderful woman, and a hard worker,"
he said. "I always thought she would be one
to land on her feet."

Unfortunately, such was not the case.
Overwhelmed by her climbing debts, lack
of employment, and the pressure of raising
two children on her own, Ellen Schneider,
a thirty-one-year-old single mother, of
Clymer, Ohio, allegedly took her own life
two mornings ago while her children attended
school. "It's a sad, sad thing," Chief Denny
Reardon said at this morning's press con-
ference. "This town has been through some
rough months, and this will only make it
harder."

When asked for details of Ms. Schneider's
death, Chief Reardon said only that she was
pronounced dead at the scene, apparently
from an overdose of her own prescription
sleeping pills. More information, he said,
would be coming.

Casey sat back, swallowing the bad taste in her mouth. With
a flick of her finger on the keyboard she wiped the article from
the screen, and sat staring at the library's home page.

Did she really want to take this poor woman's spot in the
play?

"Miss, um, Kaufmann?" Casey jerked around to see the
librarian at her elbow, her driver's license in her hand. "I'm sorry,
but your time on the computer is up, and we have someone
waiting."

Casey blinked and glanced around. While she'd been working
the library had gotten busy. Well, as busy as it could in such a

small town. And there were only three computers for the patrons. "Oh, sorry. I didn't realize…"

"No problem. Feel free to come back later."

Casey grabbed her bag, took one last look to make sure she hadn't left anything on the desk, and accepted her license back from Stacy, glad it still bore her birth name, rather than her married one. Stacy, if he ever got curious, wouldn't have much to go on. She hadn't lived in the licensing state for years, and her social security number was not on it. She nodded at the man waiting for the computer and pushed out the library doors into the bright mid-morning. She glanced at her watch. Almost nine-thirty. Too early to find the bed and breakfast. If she decided to stay.

A mother with a toddler in a stroller went past on the sidewalk, heading across the street to a small park. Casey watched them, an ache spreading through her chest. Benches and a few picnic tables sat under two big trees, and Casey made her way over, settling at the picnic table farthest from the play equipment. Digging through her bag, she pulled out a cell phone, one that was paid ahead, with a number that would die a quick death when she'd used all the minutes and bought a new phone.

She punched in a number she knew by heart.

"Hello, Wilson's Catering, may I help you?" The voice, as always, made her smile, but also brought tears to her eyes.

"Ricky."

He paused. "Casey? Where are you?"

She gave a half laugh. "How are things?"

"Oh, you know, the usual. Paying your bills, gathering your mail, having a builder repair your roof."

"What? What happened?"

"Storm. That big maple in the front yard dropped a load on your porch."

"Oh, no. The tree?"

"Gone. I'm sorry, sis."

Casey pushed on her lips with her fingers until she evened out her breathing. "The house?"

"Taken care of. Had a few prospective buyers go through, but no offers. The realtor's still hopeful, but I don't know…"

"You're not really trying, are you?"

"Now, come on—"

"Ricky."

"All right. I'm not pushing it. But I have it listed with an agency, okay? I just…" He hesitated. "You'll be back sometime, and wish you hadn't sold it. You know you will."

"I don't know that. In fact, I'm sure I won't."

"But Casey—"

"Enough. Tell me other stuff. How's Mom?"

"As well as can be expected."

"Ricky—"

"She worries. You know she does. She's not used to the idea of women striking out on their own, with no place to call home. Well, I mean you have here to call home, of course, if you only would."

Casey sighed and rested her elbows on the picnic table, dropping her head back to look at the leaves above her. The happy screams of the little toddler pierced her heart.

"*They've* been here," Ricky said.

Casey sucked in her breath, sitting up. "When? Which ones?"

"A few days ago. Came to *my* house. Said they'd given up on yours. The same two as always. The woman with the bad dye job and the guy with the face." The face with the unusually asymmetrical look. Like it had belonged to two different people, and been molded onto one skull.

"What did they want?"

Ricky snorted. "What do they always want? To know where you are, of course. And what your plans are in regards to Pegasus."

Casey concentrated on her breathing, trying to calm her racing heart. "Did they threaten you?"

"No more than usual. Said their lawyers would be contacting yours. Like that's anything new."

"Did you tell them—"

"That you have no interest in pursuing the case? That they were legally forbidden to contact you? Of course I did. I always do. But do they listen?"

"I'm sorry, Ricky."

"I know. And really, you know I don't mind helping out. I just wish…"

"Yeah. Me, too, bro."

They sat quietly for a few moments.

"More papers came in the mail," he finally said. "Stuff for you to sign."

"You know where to take it." Her lawyers. The only ones who ever knew approximately where she was.

"Sure you won't come home?" Ricky asked. "Or at least let me come to you?"

Casey swallowed hard. "I can't. You can't. Not yet."

Ricky sighed. "Is there *any*thing I can do for you?"

"You're already doing it."

"But, Casey. What are *you* doing? Are you really…are you okay?"

"I'm traveling. I'm looking."

"For what?"

"God only knows." She looked up, and almost jumped off of the bench.

"I know, too," Death said. This time, rather than popcorn, Death licked a melting chocolate ice cream cone.

Casey frowned. "Love you, Ricky. Thanks for everything."

"But Casey—"

"I gotta go. I'll call again soon."

"Soon as in tomorrow? Or soon as in next month?"

"As soon as I can, Ricky. Take care of yourself." She pushed the off button on the phone, keeping her eyes on the screen for a few more moments, as if she could keep her brother there with her. "What do you want now?"

Death waited for Casey to lift her eyes. "Just checking in. Seeing what's going on."

"You're not afraid you'll scare the children?"

Death licked the ice cream and glanced over at the playground, which now held a small playgroup of kids. "They aren't scared of me." Death waved at a small boy in the sandbox. The boy waved back.

"He can see you?"

"Of course. Only people who aren't afraid of me can actually see me."

Casey studied the parents. "So to the grown-ups, I'm sitting here talking to myself."

"They're probably as scared of you as they are of me."

"But they can see me."

"Of course. You're not a mythical figure."

"Mythical?"

"Legendary. Supernatural. Call me what you like."

"A pain in the ass."

The corner of Death's mouth twitched up. "Not to everyone."

"You realize you interrupted a perfectly good phone conversation with my brother."

"Nothing keeping you from calling him again."

Casey licked her lips and looked at her phone, caressing the screen with her thumb. Nothing but homesickness, which would only get worse the more she spoke to him. She shoved the phone into her jacket pocket.

"So what now?" Death asked. "You going to hang out here in the playground all day?"

Casey glanced over at the mothers, seeing that one held a baby in her arms. Casey jerked her head away. "No. I'm done here."

"What I thought. But this town? You're going to stick around here for a while?"

Casey shrugged. "You got a better idea?"

Death ate the last bite of ice cream and gestured all around. "Clymer, Ohio. Who knows? It could be interesting."

Interesting. Casey sighed. That word again. When all she really wanted was a spate of plain old ordinary days.

Chapter Eight

The Nesting Place was beautiful. Casey wouldn't have been surprised to see flocks of birds fighting for control in the canopy of oak, maple, and sycamore trees. As it was, the yard—at least a double lot—was filled with shady woodland paths, and the freshly painted Queen Anne house sat like a blossom among the flowerbeds. Casey looked down at herself, glad she'd taken that shower at The Sleep Inn, no matter how quick and unsatisfying it had been.

A four-door Honda Civic sat by the curb, its keys in full view on the driver's seat, so Casey figured someone was home. Or the inn had a guest who was about ready to check out.

Up on the porch the inside door to the house was open, with a screen door allowing a view into the heavily decorated foyer. Casey listened for any sound signifying that someone was home, and hearing nothing, pushed the doorbell. No response. Casey held her hand over her eyes and peered into the dark hallway. "Hello? Anybody home?"

Footsteps sounded on the hardwood floor. "Coming, coming!" Casey heard the voice, but no person became visible until a few seconds later, when a swath of red billowed toward the door. "Is it locked? No? Come in, darling, it's open."

The vision in scarlet swept the screen door open, her smile wide as she pulled Casey in by her wrist. "No need to ring, our door's always open."

Casey stood frozen, speechless at the sight of this woman in a voluminous blood-red robe, her hair almost as bright, but much more orange. Her lipstick matched her hair, and heavy black lines outlined her eyes.

"Uh," Casey said. "Thank you."

"Were you looking for something, dear? Or someone?"

"Well, I was looking for a room."

"This early in the morning? You're done hiking for the day?" She took in Casey's burden with a practiced glance.

"Actually, I just came from a hotel and would like something… cleaner."

"Ah. The Sleep Inn? Whoever steered you there…" She waved a brightly manicured hand. "But no matter, we certainly have a place for you. No one else staying at the moment. Follow me and I'll take you there directly. Lillian!" She yelled into the recesses of the house, startling Casey.

"My partner," the woman said in explanation. "Keeps the books, you know." She led Casey toward the winding wooden staircase in the central hall. "Oh, well, you can do the paperwork later, when you've had a chance to settle in. I'll take you up."

The second floor was as grand as the first, with shiny oak trim, high ceilings, and brocaded wallpaper. Casey struggled not to feel hemmed in, and was heartened by the natural light allowed through the tall windows. The woman led her down the hallway to an open doorway.

"Here we are, darling. How would this suit you?"

Casey stepped into the room. Decorated in dark greens, the room appeared surprisingly open, with a large window on each of the two outside walls, and a skylight in the slanted ceiling. The queen-sized bed was covered with pillows and a ruffly cover, and a roll-top desk graced the corner. A comfortable looking chair sat by a small table at one window, with a full bathroom on the other side.

"It's lovely," Casey said. "How long is it free?"

"As long as you want it. How long do you think that will be?"

Casey set down her bag and walked over to a window, peering down into the yard. "I'm not sure. It could be just a night or two. Or it could be several weeks."

The woman blinked. "Well, I must say that's refreshing. A young woman with a mind of her own. You just let us know day by day if we're to freshen up your room, or if you'll be leaving us. We tend to be pretty flexible here."

"Thank you." Casey turned to the woman. "If your partner's name is Lillian, what's yours?"

"Oh! I never said, did I? It's Rosemary. But you can call me Rosie, or Rose, or even Mary, if you like. I'll answer to anything, almost. Just don't call me crazy!" She gave a loud, hearty chuckle and placed her hand on the doorknob. "I'll leave you to make yourself comfortable. Whenever you feel like coming down we can take care of the messy signatures and those awful money matters. Take your time."

She swung the door closed behind her, and Casey was alone.

Except not completely alone.

Casey put her hands on her hips. "And who are you?"

The fat, long-haired cat on the bed blinked sleepily, stretched, and lumbered off the mattress to go stand by the door. Casey walked over and unlatched the door, opening it wide. "Go on, then."

The cat stared at her a few more moments before sauntering into the hallway. Casey shook her head. A cat. Like she needed to be dealing with one of those.

Casey turned around, and sighed with frustration. "*What?*"

"This place is much nicer." Death sat exactly where the cat had been.

"So glad you approve."

"Are you making a commitment?"

"To what?" But she knew.

"Clymer, Ohio."

Casey stalked to her bag and yanked the zipper open, spilling the bag's contents onto the floor.

"Eww," Death said.

Casey turned her back and began throwing laundry onto a pile. "I'm not making any commitments. I'm just…seeing what happens."

"Eric's cute."

Casey jerked up. "I do not care if Eric Jones is *cute*."

"VanDiepenbos."

"Whatever. It doesn't matter what he looks like. Or what his last name is." She grabbed her bag of toiletries from the floor and marched into the bathroom, where she plopped it onto the counter.

"He's nice, too," Death called from the bedroom.

Casey stalked back in and flung a pair of socks onto the dirty clothes. "So what? There are all kinds of nice people."

"Ellen was nice."

Casey stopped, sinking down onto her heels, running a hand over her face. "That poor woman. I wish…" She shook her head.

"What? That you could've taken her place?"

"Of course not."

Death hesitated, but let it go. "Eric seemed surprised she killed herself."

"He did, didn't he?"

"Said he didn't think she would've done it."

Casey grabbed her bag and stood up. "No one likes to think someone they know would commit suicide." She took the back-pack and stashed it in the wardrobe.

"No. No, they don't. Sometimes it's even hard for me."

Casey snorted. "Right."

"Hey, who do you think I am?"

"Death."

"Well, yes, but who else?"

"You mean, like, the Grim Reaper?"

Death nodded.

"I don't know. It's not like I've studied it."

"Uh-huh."

Casey rolled her eyes. "Okay. Azriel, the Angel of Death."

"Also known as the hand of God."

"Whatever. Thanatos? Isn't that one? And La Muerte. And the Fourth Horseman of the Apocolypse."

Death's nose wrinkled. "I don't like horses. Any others?"

"L'Ankou?"

"Very good. But I'm thinking of nicer names. Like Eternal Rest. Or the Gatherer. Or the Help of God."

"Trying to make yourself into something good?"

Death smiled gently. "But Casey, I *am* something good. Maybe I'm not always welcome, or arrive always at the right time, but I'm not ultimately bad."

"Yeah, well, tell it to the judge."

Death pointed toward the ceiling. "Believe me, I have."

"Fine. But what's your point?"

"My point is that I'm not the easy way out. But then, I think you know that, don't you?"

A rush of emotion hit Casey, and she doubled over, arms crossed over her stomach. She fell to her knees onto the laundry pile, tipping over onto the carpet. Her head filled with the sound of static. *The smell of burning rubber...the sound of wrenching metal...the sting of tears...the ache of her breasts as she gazed into the silent coffin...*

No. Death was not the easy way out.

But sometimes, God knew, it would've been welcome.

Chapter Nine

"Lillian?" Casey peered around what seemed to be the kitchen door. She'd been drawn downstairs by the smell of food, and it was coming from the other side of that doorway.

The woman standing over the stove took up about a quarter of the space Rosemary had, and her clothes and hair lacked the shock value. Her smile, however, was just as wide. "Come in, come in. You must be our new guest."

"Yes. Casey."

"Well, Casey, are you hungry?"

"Actually, I am." She had fallen asleep on her floor and awakened an hour later with a kink in her back, and a growling stomach. After a quick face-washing, she'd made her way downstairs.

"You're welcome to have lunch with us," Lillian said. "I know it's a bit late for it, going on one-thirty, but it's hard to find time for eating when there are so many other things to do." She waved her over to the table. "Rosemary will be here in just a minute. She's at her hapkido class."

Casey let go with an involuntary laugh.

Lillian smiled. "Yes, I know. She doesn't exactly look like a martial artist, does she? But she's passionate about it." She lowered her voice. "I think, however, her classmates try to avoid partnering with her during sparring. Having her step on your toe—let alone falling on you—can be hazardous to your health."

"Helloooo!"

Lillian straightened, the grin still on her face. "She's home."

Rosemary filled the doorway, resplendent in her Dobak, her hapkido uniform. "Ah, there's our new guest! You should ask her to lunch, Lillian."

"I already have."

"Of course you have. Come, my darling. Sit!"

So Casey sat at the little table, barely big enough for three, and ate an egg and cheese sandwich with way too much pepper.

When they'd finished, and Casey had heard the entire history of the house (part of the Underground Railroad, don't you know!), their partnership (known each other since grade school!), love lives ("I'm a widow, and Lillian's a *divorcee*"), and just how long it took to renovate the room she was staying in (way too long), Casey sat back and tried not to imagine the pepper coming back up her esophagus and making her sneeze.

"Is there a Laundromat somewhere close I could use?" she asked, when she could get a word in.

The two women looked at each other, brows furrowed.

"There's the one on Wilson," Lillian said.

"Or Second Street." Rosemary tapped her chin with a finger. "If it's still open."

"But really," Lillian said, "the closest one would be—"

"—in our back room." Rosemary smiled, and Lillian crinkled her eyes at Casey.

"Oh, but I couldn't—"

"Oh, but you could." Lillian patted Casey's arm. "We insist."

Rosemary stood and began clearing dishes. "And we also insist that you use our bicycle while you're our guest. You'll need it to get to play rehearsal."

"What?" Had she mentioned that?

Lillian leaned toward her. "It's a small town, remember?"

Casey sighed. "Thanks. I'd love to use your bike."

Rosemary, at the sink, peered over her shoulder. "You'll have to get the tires pumped up down at the gas station. No one's ridden it for a while."

"Sure. Thanks. And thanks for lunch." Casey got up and took her plate over to the sink. When she'd done that, she hesitated. "When's the next time you go to a hapkido session, Rosemary?"

Rosemary grinned. "Whenever I want. But probably not today."

Casey put her hands in her pockets. "Any chance I could tag along?"

Rosemary's smiled broadened. "Of course. Do you know something about it?"

"Yeah. Something."

"I'd love to have you join me. How about tomorrow?"

"That would be great. Thanks." Casey turned to leave.

"You're taking Ellen's place in the play."

Casey halted in the doorway and looked back. Both women faced her. She wasn't sure which one had spoken. "I guess I am."

Lillian nodded. "That's good."

"Is it?"

Rosemary thrust a pan into the full sink. "This town needs something like *Twelfth Night*. Needs some laughter."

"But about Ellen. It's terrible."

"Of course it is, darling." Was Rosemary crying, or had she splashed herself?

"We loved Ellen," Lillian said. "The whole town did."

Eric did.

"We just couldn't believe it, when we heard."

Rosemary spun a metal spatula in a wide arc, sending bubbles to the floor. "We *still* don't believe it. She wouldn't leave those kids."

Casey bit her lip. "You don't think she killed herself?"

"Of course not!" The spatula was really moving now. "Just the thought that that sweet girl committed suicide is…is…"

Lillian moved to the other woman and put an arm around her shoulders. "Shh, Rosemary. Quiet down, now."

Rosemary's face went red, and her lips trembled. Carefully, she set the spatula in the water, wiped her hands on the towel beside the sink, and took a deep breath. "I'm sorry."

Casey shook her head. "There's nothing to be sorry about."

"Yes, there is," Rosemary said. "There most certainly, *certainly* is."

Chapter Ten

After lunch Casey walked upstairs to put her dirty laundry in the basket Lillian had loaned her. On her way out she stopped in the doorway to look back at the room. There was nothing to say she even existed. Her bag was stashed away, her bathroom supplies were in the medicine cabinet, and the bed was as smooth as if it had just been made.

"I don't understand why you don't have any pictures."

Casey ground her teeth. "I wish you'd stop sneaking up on me like that."

Death leaned against the doorjamb, sucking on a lollipop. "And what's with all the junk food lately?"

"What? You afraid it's going to kill me?"

Casey bit back a reply and pushed through the doorway.

Death stepped out of her way. "So why don't you?"

"Why don't I what?"

"Have any pictures?"

Casey stopped at the top of the stairs. "I don't need pictures. I have all the images I need."

"They can't be very nice ones."

"They're fine."

"If you say so."

Casey looked back. "What do you want me to do? Sit around all day and stare at photographs? Wish they were back here, with me?"

Death pushed off of the doorjamb, meandering down the hallway, looking at the antiques spaced along the wall. "You already wish that."

"Of course I do. Having photos would just be worse."

"If you say so. Where are you going, Casey?"

Casey looked at the laundry basket. "Where do you think?"

Death peered into the pile of dirty clothes. "About time, too. I was beginning to think I'd have to keep my distance because of the smell."

Casey started down the stairs. "Why don't you go bother someone else for a while?"

"Aw. I'm beginning to think you don't want me around."

"I would've gone with you willingly before. But you obviously have other plans in mind. Now you're just annoying."

"Casey?" Lillian's voice floated up the stairs. "Are you talking to me?"

Casey looked up toward the second floor. Death gave a small, mocking bow, and walked back into Casey's room.

"No," Casey called down. "Just talking to…the cat."

The fat cat stared at her from a bench on the stair's landing, whiskers twitching, eyes wide.

Lillian came into view. "Oh, that's Solomon. He likes to get to know our guests. Don't you Solly?" She ran a hand over the cat's head, and he nipped at her hand. "What's the matter with you, boy?"

Casey indicated the laundry basket. "Thought I'd get this started, if that's okay."

Lillian left the cat. "Of course. Right through here."

She led Casey through the living room—a huge flat-screen TV set incongruously on the far wall, amongst Victorian furniture—into a sunny room at the back of the house. Painted yellow and surrounded by large, uncovered windows, the room pulsed with life and light. A door led to the outside and stood open, letting in the cool afternoon air. Casey blinked at the brightness.

"Everything you need is above the washer in this cupboard." Lillian opened a little door to reveal various bottles and jugs. "Use whatever you like."

"Thank you."

Casey waited for Lillian to leave, but the older woman sat on a small chair in the corner. Casey set her basket on top of the dryer and began tossing her clothes into the washer, the silver HomeMaker symbol on the glossy white finish catching her eye.

"I'm sorry about earlier," Lillian said. "With Rosie."

Casey stopped, a shirt in her hand. "Like I said before. Nothing to be sorry about." The shirt joined the rest of the clothes in the washer.

"This past week has been very difficult for her. For the whole town, of course, but Rosie's taken it very hard, and she tends to wear her heart on her sleeve."

"Were she and Ellen close?"

Lillian didn't respond, and Casey turned to see her staring out one of the windows, her hands clenched in her lap. Casey went back to sorting.

"We offered to keep the children, you know," Lillian said. "Ellen's parents aren't in the best of health, and we have plenty of room. But everyone thought it better if the kids weren't...if they were with their own family." Her voice was brittle.

Casey finished up with the darks, measured out the detergent, and began the cycle. "Eric VanDiepenbos—do you know him?—was pretty close to her."

Lillian's head jerked away from the window. "Oh. Oh, yes, poor boy. He's had a hard time of it all. We had hopes... But with his family being what it is, there wasn't much chance of anything happening."

Casey opened her mouth to ask what she meant, but Rosemary bustled by the windows of the room and burst in the door with a handful of flowers. "For our table. Aren't they lovely?"

Lillian's face lit up. "They are. Let's go find a vase."

And Casey's chance for questioning was gone. She followed the women into the kitchen, where Lillian was pulling a vase out of the china cupboard.

"I'm going to take the bike downtown, if that's okay."

Rosemary looked up from her flowers. "Of course, dear, you go right ahead. It's in the shed out back. The door handle sticks a little, so you have to jiggle it."

"Thanks."

Casey actually had to jiggle the handle quite a bit to get the door open, but she eventually won the struggle. The bike, an old Schwinn three-speed, sat enmeshed in cobwebs and trinkets, and she had to work to rescue it from what looked like the detritus of many years. Perhaps from before these women had even owned the place.

By the time she had the bike in the yard she was smeared with grease and dust, and spidery silk clung to her clothes. She left the bike in the shade and went back inside.

"Oh, my," Lillian said.

"Yes. Would you have a rag I could use?"

Rosemary laughed. "And a bucket for soapy water. You'll find everything you need in the garage."

"Not the same shed?"

"No. We actually *use* the garage. Just go in the side door."

Casey followed her directions and went into the garage. She flipped on the light. And stood staring at the shiny Pegasus Orion. One of those supposedly hybrid SUVs, huge on promise, not so big on follow-through. Twice as big as the company's cars. Black, with brand new tires and not a speck of dirt, the SUV squatted there, like a predator. Casey pressed back against the door. In all of her dreams, she'd never have thought those women inside would have something like this...

Standing in her spot, she tore her eyes from the vehicle and searched for the promised bucket. There it was, on a shelf, just down the wall. She scooted sideways for several feet, until she could reach out and snag the pail. Inside it were a jug of car wash, a sponge, and Turtle Wax. She didn't think she'd be waxing the bike, so she took out the little container and tossed it back on the shelf.

A few steps back along the wall she could feel the door behind her. Turning the knob, she spun out of the garage, and stood outside, breathing deeply. She let out a nervous sound, some-where between a laugh and a moan. The idea of Rosemary, with her bright red robe and orange hair, at the wheel of the Orion was enough to give her something to think about for a while, something to take her mind off the idea of a Pegasus vehicle so close to hand.

The bike cleaned up pretty well, and Casey was able to get the grease stains muted, if not completely off her pants, and the spider webs removed from her shirt. She rinsed out the bucket with the hose and set the sponge in the sun to dry before walking the bike down the lane and toward town. She hoped the tires would survive the trip, as flat and old as they were.

They did, and she found a free air pump on the side of the filling station, a ten-minute walk from the B & B. The rest of the bike needed a little attention, however, and she spent a few dollars for a can of WD-40 to spray the chain, paying the middle-aged attendant who seemed to be manning the station on his own, and squeezed the brakes several times to loosen them up. She took a couple of minutes to ride slowly around the parking lot, and was soon convinced the bike was ready to roll.

The town was quiet, as it was the evening before. The occa-sional car passed Casey as she pedaled around the streets, but she saw only two people outside, both walking briskly, with their heads down. No young parents occupied the playground—probably taking the opportunity for their children's afternoon naps—and Casey met no other bikes.

Casey rode past Home Sweet Home, even stopping to peer inside, but the interior was dark. There were still a couple of hours until Eric and his crew would be getting ready for their subdued dinner crowd.

The church down the street stood just as silent as the day before, and Casey didn't stop. Instead, she continued down the block of shops, where she found a bike stand. She parked the bike, considering briefly that she didn't have a lock for it, and scanned the stores. Only a few of them seemed to actually be open for business. The bakery, of course. And the antique shop. And, on the corner, Wayne's Pharmacy.

She went in.

A bell tinged when she opened the door, but no one came running. The check-out counter stood empty. She assumed someone was actually watching the place, but from the looks of it she was pretty much alone. Slowly she walked up and down the aisles of wrapping paper, Willow Tree angels, and summer toys on clearance. Eventually she found the personal items aisle, where she stocked up on sunscreen, toothpaste, and Band-Aids. The pharmacy section had the vitamins she used, and she grabbed a small bottle.

By the time she made her way back up front to the check-out, the cashier was behind the counter.

"Becca?"

The woman she'd last seen at play rehearsal glanced up from wiping the glass countertop. She smiled, looking surprised, but pleasantly so. "Casey, right? So you didn't leave town?"

"Not yet."

"I'm glad. You'll be at rehearsal tonight?" She looked down at the countertop, then back at Casey, obviously trying not to appear too eager.

Casey sighed. "Yeah. I'll be there."

Becca's shoulders relaxed. "Great. I'll be there, too."

"A smaller role?"

"Bigger one, actually. Just a different kind. I'm going to be the stage manager."

"Oh, good. I was wondering about that. I didn't see one last night."

"We had one. But she quit. She and Thomas didn't get along."

Casey grunted. "Imagine that."

"He's not all bad." Becca grinned.

"I guess there's always hope."

The bell above the door dinged again, and Casey watched as a man in a suit hustled into the store. He nodded at Casey, but continued toward the back, where the actual drug part of the pharmacy stood behind a tall counter.

Casey paid for her items, and Becca was bagging them when the man got in line behind her.

"See you tonight, then?" Becca said.

"Seven-o'clock."

Becca turned to the man. "Hello, Mr. Willems."

Casey hesitated, then took her time checking out a rack of cards at the front of the store. Could this be Karl Willems? The CEO of HomeMaker, who had laid off all of those people at Christmas, and planned to do the same to the rest of them? Casey peeked around the display to check him out.

Handsome in a business kind of way. Gray hair, trimmed close. Tanned skin. Face beginning to show signs of age. Taller than Casey, by at least several inches.

"Yes, good afternoon," he said to Becca.

Becca glanced outside. "Looks like a nice day out there. Is it warm?"

"What? Oh, yes. Warm enough."

Becca rang up his purchase and slid it into a bag. "Will there be anything else today? One of those candy bars you like?"

"Hmm?"

"A Hershey bar with Almonds?"

"Oh, yes, I do like those. How did you know?"

Becca's smile looked forced.

"I don't need one today, though," Willems said. "Thank you."

He took his bag and left, again nodding to Casey as he passed her. Casey stepped out from behind the display.

"He never remembers who I am," Becca said, not looking at Casey. "You'd think after all the times he comes in here…"

Casey shrugged. "Some people are like that."

"Yeah, I know. But it makes it even harder…" She broke off, and went back to rubbing her rag on the countertop.

Casey tried to finish the sentence. "Harder to see him fire people, when he can't even remember their names?"

Becca kept up her scrubbing for a few moments before dropping her hand and looking at the floor. "Not only names. It's the faces, too. He doesn't even remember them."

Casey looked at Becca's face. It was a pretty one. Not one she'd think men would forget so quickly.

But then, some people had a hard time seeing past their own.

Chapter Eleven

Karl Willems was driving away in a black Cadillac STS when Casey got outside. She watched the car turn right at the stoplight, heading out toward The Burger Palace and The Sleep Inn. It was also the direction of HomeMaker. She remembered seeing the building as she and the trucker had driven into town.

Casey strapped her pharmacy bag to the back of her bike with a bungee cord she'd brought from Rosemary and Lillian's garage, and swung her leg over the seat. The factory wasn't far; she'd walked much farther in the recent weeks, and she could use the exercise. Her laundry was probably ready to be switched back at The Nesting Place, but it could wait. She pushed off from the curb and headed out of town.

Once she'd made the turn and gotten close to the hotel she began to see cars. People, too, lunch boxes dangling from their hands as they walked toward her. Their clothes were uniform, each light blue button-down sporting a HomeMaker patch on the left breast. Casey assumed their names were the cursive splotch below the company's emblem.

She eased to the side of the road and pulled her cell phone out of her pocket to check the time. Just after three. Change of shift. She returned the phone to her pocket and resumed riding toward the factory, scanning the faces of the people as they passed. No one she knew, of course.

As she got closer the factory loomed large and white. Not depressing, actually, as she'd expected. The HomeMaker sign on the side of the building—blue and red—shone brightly. No letters with burned-out bulbs. No weeds growing up through cracks in the pavement. She circled the building, skirting the edge of the massive parking lot, avoiding the main flow of the exiting traffic. Well-maintained grass surrounded the building, mature trees lined the borders, and a manmade pond, complete with fountain, graced the open space toward the highway.

The traffic dwindled. Those taking over this shift had already begun work, and most of those leaving were on their way home. Casey braked to a stop close to the front door, studying the cars in the parking lot. American cars, mostly, with a few Hondas and Toyotas thrown in. None of the Pegasus hybrids. Only a few parking spaces held vehicles in the upper echelon of the car world, and those were the ones up front in the reserved spots. The ones designated for Karl Willems—his Cadillac STS—, the Senior VP—a shiny Indian motorcycle—, and the Executive Assistant. That space held a new-looking Acura Integra. Not hugely expensive, but more than the assembly line workers could afford.

The front doors whooshed open and Eric VanDiepenbos exited, his eyes on the sidewalk as he strode toward her.

"Eric?"

He jerked to a halt, his tight expression easing as he recognized her. "Casey? What are you doing here?"

She gestured to the bike. "Trying out my new wheels."

He checked out her ride. "Nice. Where'd you get it?"

"The place I'm staying." She got off the bike and pushed down the kickstand. "I have to tell you your hotel recommendations are now suspect."

He wrinkled his nose. "Pretty gross, huh? But that bike doesn't belong to The Sleep Inn."

"No. I found a nice B & B."

A smile flickered on his face. "The Nesting Place?"

"That's the one."

"You'll like it there. I didn't recommend it last night because it was so late and because…well, you said you wanted something cheap. Are the ladies cutting you a break since you'll be there for a while? At least I hope you will, since the play won't be done for over a month."

Casey bit her lip. "Actually, we haven't gotten around to talking about the price. With me getting there in the morning, and them being busy…"

Eric laughed. "Sounds like them. But you might want to find out the price before you get too settled." He held up a hand. "Not that they'll cheat you or anything. It's just…" He swept a hand at her.

"I know. I don't exactly look like a high roller, do I? But their place is so nice. Clean, even."

He grinned. "It would be." He studied her some more. "I'm sorry. You just don't look like a bed and breakfast kind of person."

She winced. "You know you can't judge a book by its—"

"I know. I'm sorry. I'm being incredibly nosy and rude."

She smiled. "That's okay. I won't take it personally."

"So, in the vein of nosiness…why *are* you here? At HomeMaker?"

"Just curious. I've heard so much about it since I got here yesterday. I wanted to check out the big, bad wolf."

His face clouded. "I guess it's hard to be in Clymer and *not* hear about it."

"It's like any big business. They sort of…take over."

"You sound like you've had experience."

"Some."

They stood quietly, watching as mist blew across the pond from the fountain.

"I hear a happy birthday is in order," Casey said.

He kept his eyes on the fountain. "Not sure how happy it was."

"No. I guess not. But Loretta and Johnny felt good about getting you a cake."

"Yeah, they would." He turned to look at her. "I'm headed over there to get ready for dinner. You coming?"

"Is it time already?"

"Not quite, I guess. But sometimes Loretta and Johnny get there early. I want to make certain they aren't burning the place down."

"Sure, I'm coming." She walked back to her bike, disengaging the kickstand.

"You want to put that in my car?" Eric said. "I'm pretty sure it would fit in the trunk."

"No. I mean, thanks, but I'll ride. It's not far."

"If you're sure."

She straddled the bike. "I'll race you."

He grinned. "You're on." He shot off, sprinting toward his car.

Casey took off down the parking lot, waving good-naturedly when Eric passed her in a dark green Camry. She followed him, catching up as he waited for traffic at the end of the drive, then cruising up onto the sidewalk, now devoid of people.

About a block from Main Street, trailing only by a few hundred feet, Casey ducked down an alley, which she believed would take her behind Home Sweet Home. Pausing at the cross streets to make sure she didn't get hit, she bounced through the rutted, gravel lane, counting buildings and looking for the church steeple.

She found the church sooner than she realized, and skidded to a stop as the alley dead-ended at a cast iron fence surrounding the church's back yard. The grassy area was barely visible through the branches of thick bushes, but Casey could make out some flowers and a pathway among trunks of larger trees.

The gravel lane angled sharply to the right, toward Main Street, and Casey turned her bike quickly in that direction, hoping she could still beat Eric to the kitchen.

"But it's not *fair!*"

Casey froze at the words, the woman's shrill voice traveling easily through the air, along with footsteps and the slap of the church's back door. Casey leaned toward the bushes, squinting through the leaves into the church's garden.

"I don't like it either, Holly, but what was I supposed to do? Eric made it clear what he would do if I didn't cast her. And we have to replace Ellen if we want to do the play."

Thomas. The play's director. Casey grimaced. And he was talking about *her*.

"What could Eric really do? Tell people about your little *problem*? Like they even care?" the woman, Holly, said. Casey couldn't quite make out her face, but could easily imagine the pout that must have been on it. "You've got to tell her to go away."

"I tried. You can try if you want, but you'll get the same response. Everybody else wants to keep her."

The two were close together, the woman's arms crossed tightly over her chest. Thomas stood over her, his posture just as stiff.

"I don't understand why you let Eric push you around so much, Thomas. He's younger than you. And smaller. Why wouldn't people believe you instead of him, no matter what he said? You should just show him who's the boss. I mean, you *are* the director."

"I *know* that, dammit! And he knows it, too. But I can't change who his parents are, can I, or what he knows? Or why he's come back to town?"

Holly snorted. "How about why *you* came back? Doesn't that matter at all?"

They stood glaring at each other.

"I think," she finally said. "That you're just *chicken*. Like everyone says."

Thomas reared back, his face a picture of shock and anger.

"Quite a pair, aren't they?"

Casey jumped, whacking her foot against the bike's pedal. Death stood on the back, feet on the axle and hands on Casey's shoulders, like a ten-year-old catching a ride on a friend's bicycle.

"Who's there?" Thomas stalked toward the bushes, his face dark.

With a growl Casey pushed off, racing down the alley, trying to balance with Death's weight on her back. After the short distance to Main Street she skidded around the corner and dashed the remaining half block to Home Sweet Home, hoping the church's fence didn't have a convenient gate for Thomas to find.

"Thanks a whole lot," Casey said. "Are you *trying* to get me in trouble?"

Death's eyebrows rose. "Who? Me?"

Casey shuddered. "You are so—"

"Casey?" Eric held open the front door and winked. "Glad you could join us."

Casey stepped off of the bike and dropped it against the brick store front, hoping to squash Death against the wall. Death stood suddenly at the curb, shaking a finger at her.

"Yeah," Casey said. "I got detoured."

"Maybe next time. But then, I *was* driving a car."

Turning her back on Death, Casey walked past Eric into the soup kitchen, taking a whiff of the same cologne Eric had worn the night before. This time it was replaced by the smell of pasta, rather than beef and vegetable soup.

"Macaroni tonight," Eric said. "We had lots of government cheese to use up."

Casey followed him to the kitchen.

"*Thank you, Jesus!*" Loretta said. "*Hallelujah!*"

"Pretty lady's back!" Johnny skipped toward her, arms outstretched, a bundle of silverware in each hand.

Ducking to avoid losing an eye, Casey allowed Johnny to hug her, squeezing her so tightly she lost her breath, along with her sense of place.

It was at the funeral. The last time someone had hugged her like that. Not as hard, nor as joyfully. Her aching breasts had sent arcs of pain through her body. Full breasts, and tender, no longer the sustainer of life, but the reminder of life lost. Omar's casket, so small in the receiving room next to the larger box.

Casey's whole life, enclosed in two cases of pine.

"Let her go, Johnny." Eric was laughing. "Ease up, my man."

She almost fell from his arms, grabbing onto the counter for support.

Eric's hand slid onto her back. "Casey? You okay?"

She took a deep breath, eyes focused on the bread knife lying on the counter. "I'm all right. It's nothing." She darted a quick look around the kitchen, expecting Death's face. It was not there.

"Well, you look pale. Johnny, you've got to be more careful."

"No." Casey stood up, her hands flat on the counter. "It wasn't his fault." She attempted a smile. "He's fine."

Johnny stood chewing on his lip, his eyes twitching.

She tried harder at the smile. "I'm glad to see you, too, Johnny. Thank you."

His tight face relaxed, and the smile returned. "See, Eric. You find nice ladies."

"Yes, Johnny, I do." He steered Casey toward a chair and pushed her down into it. "What happened?"

"Nothing." She brushed him away and rubbed her face. "He just surprised me, is all. Now, what can I do?"

Obviously not convinced, he reluctantly set her to work doing what she had the previous night—arranging bread in baskets and cutting up just-past-ripe fruit. She could feel his eyes on her throughout their food preparation, and even when the guests began arriving.

"Eric." She waved him over to the kitchen door from his spot in the dining room.

"What is it? Are you feeling all right?"

"I'm fine. Really. Now pay attention to *them*, not me. Okay?"

Color rose in his cheeks, and he looked away.

"I appreciate it, Eric, but really, they need your attention more than I do."

He let out a breath. "Yeah. I guess you're right. You don't really need help from me, do you?" Without looking at her again, he set to work welcoming the diners.

Casey did what she could to serve, scooping out macaroni, taking away garbage, and refilling water glasses. As she worked and watched, it became even more apparent, this second night, that food was only partly why the people came. The time here in Home Sweet Home served another, perhaps even more important, function. More than filling their bellies.

These people's lives were hard. They'd lost jobs. They'd lost dignity. They'd lost Ellen Schneider. This fellowship, this time together, underscored the reality that they weren't alone. They weren't the only people suffering. Here, in this room, was proof that others were as badly off as they. Some even worse. It wasn't their life, alone, that had been affected.

But this realization wouldn't come through conversation. The people were as quiet as the night before, speaking only when they needed something passed, or to offer a quick thank you after being served. But they were together. They understood each other.

And they had Eric.

Casey watched Eric as he mingled with the people. He, out of everyone, was the central figure. Not in a showy way. But everyone in the room seemed aware of him, turning toward him, searching him out, as one searches out any item of comfort. His concern for the people was evident on his face as he moved from one to another, listening, talking, putting an arm around a shoulder.

What exactly was his connection here? While Eric had questioned Casey about her presence at HomeMaker, she hadn't asked why he was there. Was he an employee? Had he been visiting someone? And what had those other two—Holly and Thomas—meant in the church garden? Who were Eric's parents? And why did they think he had the upper hand?

"*Praise God*, here are the cookies!" Loretta handed Casey a tray with cookie plates, filled with a variety of day-old goodies from the bakery.

Casey took the tray and walked around the tables, leaning in to deposit dessert every so often. The people whispered thank yous, but didn't look up and meet her eyes. She wondered how long she would have to work there before they would be brave enough to acknowledge her presence.

She met up with Eric at the kitchen door. "You okay?"

He shrugged. "Sure. Why wouldn't I be?"

Right.

The diners ate the cookies quickly, and were soon headed home. Eric stood as host at the front of the room, shaking hands and patting the kids' heads. Casey smiled. He should be running for office.

As soon as the door shut, Eric locked it and strode to the kitchen. "Any of that macaroni left, Loretta!"

"*Thank you, Jesus*, there's just enough!"

She pulled a partially filled casserole dish from the oven, and Casey found a couple of bruised peaches in the refrigerator, which she sliced and distributed on their plates.

"Silverware, nice lady!" Johnny thrust a bundle at her.

"Thank you, Johnny."

"I'm the best at wrapping it, you know."

"Yes, Johnny, you definitely are."

They sat at the end of one of the dining room tables, Loretta said grace (*Thank you, precious Jesus!*), and Johnny told them all about a restaurant he'd visited when he was sixteen, and how the napkins were folded like pyramids. Eric made comments at the right places, but Casey could see he wasn't entirely with them.

He finally set down his silverware on his empty plate. "Well, Loretta and Johnny, do you mind cleaning up? Casey and I have a rehearsal to get to." He smiled at Casey, almost erasing the worry from his face.

"Is it that time already?" Casey glanced at the clock. The day kept flying by. And she wasn't exactly looking forward to another meeting with Thomas, or coming face-to-face with this Holly person, who obviously didn't want her around.

Eric stood and took Casey's plate, along with his. "We can clean up before dinner tomorrow. If Loretta doesn't mind wiping down the tables, at least?"

Loretta clucked her tongue. "Of course I'm happy to do that, baby. Jesus wasn't afraid to work, *thank the Lord!*"

"I appreciate it. See you tomorrow, Johnny?"

Johnny jumped up from his chair to hug Eric, and spun toward Casey. She was ready this time, and folded her arms protectively in front of her chest to receive Johnny's embrace.

"See you tomorrow, Johnny."

"See you, nice lady."

Eric walked her to the front door, so he could lock it behind her. He smiled as she passed. "Wanna race again?"

She made a face. "On a full stomach? I don't think so. Besides, I don't want to make you look silly in front of the cast."

"I've still got the car."

"Yeah, but I'm getting a head start, and it's not that far."

He grinned. "What if I told you I'm walking?"

She waved at her bike. "You can have a ride on my handlebars."

He eyed the old Schwinn. "I think I'll pass, thanks."

"How 'bout I just wait for you to lock up, so we can arrive together?"

He leaned against the doorway, his arms crossed. "Scared?"

"Not for me. But I think Thomas is going to be gunning for you tonight, after your show of…whatever it was last night."

He pushed off from the jamb. "Nah. He's too wimpy, when it comes right down to it. And he really has no say in the matter."

"I wanted to ask you about that—"

"So we'd better get going. Just a sec." He trotted back into the building and came out with his bag, Loretta following. "She'll lock up. Shall we?"

Casey walked beside her bike, with Eric on the other side.

"It'll be interesting tonight," Eric said.

"Why's that?"

"Whole cast will be there. You only met some of them last night."

"Aaron and Jack, right? And Becca?"

"Yup. And there'll be a few more. Todd, who does some of the older male roles, and Leila. She fills in wherever needed— acting, props, whatever."

"And will I like Holly?"

Eric froze.

Casey stopped a few feet down the sidewalk and looked back at him.

His mouth was a tight line. "How do you know about Holly?"

Casey shrugged. "That was the detour I talked about. Why you beat me to Home Sweet Home." She explained the churchyard conversation.

He put his hands on his hips and looked at the sidewalk. "No wonder."

"No wonder what?"

"You're curious about Thomas and me."

"Yeah, well, I was curious before that. Last night's rehearsal wasn't exactly drama-free."

He gave a quick smile. "I guess not." He began walking again, and she kept pace with the bike.

"So are you going to tell me?"

"Tell you what?"

"Why Thomas hates you? And why you can tell him what to do? Which might be exactly why he hates you?"

"We don't have time to go into it all right now. Let's just say his family and mine go a long way back."

"And it reaches into today."

He barked a laugh. "More than that. It reaches in, grabs, and strangles until we can hardly gasp another breath."

Casey blinked. "Wow. Sounds…"

"Awful? Yes, it is."

"And theatrical."

"Well…" He held out his hands. "How can I help it?"

"Yes." She glanced at him sideways. "That was another thing I wanted to ask you about. Your acting skills are—"

"Don't say it. Please. I hear it enough from Thomas."

"But you're so *good*!"

He winced. "I asked you not to say it."

"But… I thought Thomas would only tell you you were bad."

He looked away, then back to her. "Do you really think he could?"

Casey had to smile at his discomfort. "I know he certainly *shouldn't*, but from the little I've seen of him, he's not the kind to give out compliments."

The theater came into view and Eric stopped, putting a hand on the bike's handlebars. "It's not that he gives out compliments. Believe me. It's more like he uses it as a weapon. 'Look, Eric.'" His voice was gruff as he thumped Casey's shoulder with a pointed finger. "'You have to carry this show. If it bombs it's because *you* didn't do what you could.'" He shrugged. "You know. Stuff like that."

Casey sighed. "The rest of the actors aren't *that* bad…"

Eric gave her a look.

"Okay. They aren't great, but I've seen worse."

Eric took his hand off the bike and they walked the remaining yards to the theater door. He leaned toward her as she set the bike on its kickstand. "Just wait till you see Holly act."

"Is she—?"

"We'll talk after rehearsal." With a smirk he opened the door and gestured grandly for her to enter.

Chapter Twelve

Someone had been working on the poster of the headshots. Becca, Casey figured, in her new role as stage manager. Eric's photo—a serious black-and-white portrait—was uppermost on the board, with a woman next to him. Holly, most likely, although it was hard for Casey to recognize her from that brief, obstructed glimpse through the church's bushes.

"You ready?" Eric waited at the performance space's double doors.

Casey took a deep breath and let it out. "I suppose. Unless it's not too late to back out."

"Oh, no, no, no. You said you'd do it. I'm going to keep you to your word."

Groaning, Casey eased past Eric into the darkened theater.

"There she is! Our savior!" Holly—for there was no doubt who she was in person—swept down the aisle, her hands outstretched.

Casey backed up a step, bumping into Eric. He put his hands on her back, gently pushing her forward.

Holly grabbed Casey's hands and squeezed them. "We're so happy you've come to join us. It's been such a hard time, with Ellen dying." Her large brown eyes sparkled with tears, and she blinked, allowing one of them to make its way down her cheek.

Casey felt Eric stiffen behind her, and she pulled her hands from Holly's. "I'm glad to help out how I can." She looked beyond Holly to see Aaron and Jack—the two young actors—sitting on the edge of the stage, watching something across the aisle. Casey followed their gazes.

Thomas stood over a woman, apparently getting an earful. Her face spoke volumes of anger, but Casey could only hear the hiss of *sotto voce* conversation. Obviously not things the woman wanted everyone else to hear. Becca stood awkwardly behind Thomas, a notebook clasped to her chest. She watched Thomas and the woman with a somewhat panicked expression, her jaw clenched so tightly it bunched into knots.

"Oh, don't worry about her," Holly said with a dismissive wave. "She's from Racine. They have a theater program there, too, and Thomas had called last week to see if she would come take Ellen's part. She didn't show up until today, and she's not too happy about you." Holly smiled, and a chill ran down Casey's spine.

"Come on, Casey," Eric said. "I'll introduce you to Todd."

"She hasn't met him?" Holly laced her arm through Casey's, turning her back on Eric. "He's a sweetheart. You'll love him. Todd!"

She pulled Casey toward the front row of the theater, where a man sat slumped in a seat. He looked up as they arrived, his eyes half-lidded under the salt-and-pepper hair lying over his forehead.

"This is Casey…" Holly looked at her.

"Smith," Casey said.

Todd raised his chin a fraction in greeting.

"Todd!" Holly huffed, and rolled her eyes. "This is Todd Nolan. Never mind him. He's glad to have you here, too. Believe me."

Todd regarded Holly with disgust, but tempered it once he realized Casey was watching him. Something resembling a smile appeared momentarily on his face, but was gone just as quickly.

"And this is Leila." Eric gestured toward a young woman, who tore her adoring gaze from him long enough to acknowledge Casey briefly.

Casey looked questioningly at Eric, and he responded with barely disguised, almost desperate, tolerance and frustration.

Holly's grip on Casey's arm tightened, and Casey looked up to see Thomas and the woman headed in their direction. Becca trailed behind.

"Thanks for coming by," Holly said to the woman. "It was good to see you again."

The woman pursed her lips and looked Casey up and down. "Hmphf." With that, she turned and stomped from the theater.

Holly's hand dropped from Casey's arm and she took a step away. "Well, thank God *she's* gone."

Thomas transferred his gaze from the departing woman to Casey. He obviously wasn't convinced he'd gotten the better deal.

"Okay, people," he said. "We have a play to rehearse. Does she have a script?" He jerked a thumb at Casey, not looking at her anymore.

Becca handed Casey a book, her mouth twitching. Casey wasn't sure if it was suppressed laughter or discomfort, but whichever it was, Becca didn't meet her eyes.

"We're going to go through from beginning to end," Thomas said. "To get a feel for…Casey…and so she can see what we've done. The scenes we've worked, we'll act out. The ones we haven't, we'll just read. Go."

Becca jumped onto the stage to set the furniture for Scene One, and Aaron swung his feet up, helping Becca move the folding lawn chair into position. Todd eased himself from his front row seat and strode to the side of the stage to ascend the stairs. Casey watched him, open-mouthed.

From Todd's slouched position in the theater she'd had no sense of his true form. But now, as she watched him position himself in the chair—as Orsino, the Duke of Illyria and her character's love interest—she couldn't help but be impressed. Over six feet tall and fit, he moved with a sense of ease. Almost lethargy. Charismatic, maybe not. But good-looking? Absolutely.

A muffled laugh interrupted her thoughts, and she turned to find Eric at her side, Leila close beside him. "He looks good, doesn't he?"

Casey shrugged, embarrassed at being caught staring.

"The problem," Eric said into her ear, "is when he opens his mouth."

And just then, he did.

"If music be... the food... of love, play... on; Give me excess of it..., that surfeiting..., The appetite may sicken..., and so die."

Casey covered her mouth with her hand in the hopes of smothering the laugh wanting to come out.

Eric nodded. "Kind of makes you want to go to sleep, doesn't it?"

Casey spoke through her fingers. "And after only one line."

"It's been a problem at the bank," Eric said. "Where he works. People nod off in the middle of securing a loan. They wake up wondering what papers they've signed while they've been asleep."

A giggle escaped Casey's lips, and Thomas glared over at them. Casey bit her cheeks as Todd continued droning along. Aaron, as Curio, tried to put some life into the scene, and Jack bounced on as Valentine, but Todd's underwhelming aura overtook the stage.

The scene, only two pages, was enough to give Casey the urge to launch into calisthenics, but it was time for her to read. She stood, looking for whoever was to be the Captain.

No one stood with her.

"Where's Lonnie?" Thomas' voice hummed with tension.

Becca jumped up. "I'm sorry. With that actress showing up I forgot to—"

"Call him!"

"Okay. Sorry. Sorry." She pulled out her cell phone and punched in a number from her contact sheet.

Eric stood. "I'll read with Casey."

Thomas glared at him. "We'll see what Lonnie says first. She should be reading with the actor who's actually doing the part."

"Okay. Just trying to be helpful."

From the other side of Eric, Leila studied Casey with narrowed eyes. Casey smiled at her, but the girl didn't return the compliment, turning away with a huff.

They all waited, listening partly to Holly voicing that it was *so disrespectful of their time for Lonnie to be late,* and partly to the disjointed half-conversation Becca was having.

Becca hung up. "He's in Columbus."

"*Columbus?*" Thomas' face went red. "What's he doing there?"

"Um…shopping?"

"*Shopping!*"

Eric burst out laughing, and Casey was tempted to join him, except for her worry that Thomas was about to bust a vein.

"I told you he wasn't dependable," Holly said. "That he'd have other priorities."

Thomas' voice was even and measured. "Does he plan on honoring us with his presence tomorrow evening, Becca?"

"Yes. He said he'll be back in plenty of time for tomorrow's rehearsal."

"Oh, well good. I'm so glad he's thinking of us." He straightened the papers on his lap. "Eric, if you would be so good as to read Lonnie's parts this evening."

Eric stood quietly beside Casey.

"Well, do it!" Thomas waved a hand.

They read through the scene, Casey enjoying the interplay with Eric, and the cast continued on, Leila performing the part of Maria, and Eric filling in where necessary, in-between his scenes as Feste the Fool. Soon it was time for Holly's first scene, and Eric caught Casey's eye. She watched with anticipation as Holly made her way to the stage.

Eric began the scene, Feste engaging Olivia in conversation. Moving smoothly through his speech, he ended with the greeting, "*God bless thee, lady!*"

Instead of answering with the simple, *Take the fool away,* the script called for, Holly paused, took a deep breath, threw out her chest, and pointed off-stage, her face averted. *"Take. The Fool. Away!"* She punctuated this by swinging her arm back to her body and snapping open a fan, hiding half of her face.

"Do you not hear, fellows?" Eric answered, as Feste. *"Take away the lady."*

Casey bent over double in her seat, her hands over her face as she held in the guffaw threatening to explode from her mouth.

"Go. To," Holly said. *"You're a DRY fool. I'll NO MORE of you. Besides. You grow. DIShonest."*

Eric cleared his throat. *"Two faults, Madonna, that drink and counsel will amend."*

Casey snorted through her fingers, then made a show of pulling a tissue from her bag and blowing her nose. For the next few pages she kept her face in her script, desperately searching for her next scene, to renew her acquaintance with it. Unfortunately, her next appearance was in the latter part of that very section, and she would have to read with Holly.

Casey glanced around, thinking that for sure Death would get a kick out of her predicament. But the theater's seats remained empty.

Her lines approaching, Casey went to the side of the stage. If she read from her seat, she was a lost cause. Her only hope of avoiding an embarrassing and potentially violent scene was to lose herself in blocking. She waited for her cue line, took a deep breath, admonished herself to be as professional as possible under the circumstances, and stepped onto the stage.

"The honorable lady of the house," she said. *"Which is she?"*

How she made it through the line—and the rest of the scene—was a small miracle, but before she knew it she was back in the seats, watching Aaron and Jack plot their characters' wicked schemes.

Eric stayed away from her for the rest of the read-through, which was definitely for the best, because Casey wasn't sure she'd be able to hold it together if he so much as looked at her. It was also good because Casey was afraid Leila would break into a snarl and bite her if she went anywhere close to Eric. She'd have to ask him what Leila's deal was, although it seemed obvious the poor girl had a hot and heavy crush on him.

Somehow they stumbled through the rest of the play, stopping only once to get Holly a painkiller from the theater's first aid kit—*Oh, the stress! My head is bursting!*—until they reached the end and Becca sent them on a short break. Casey fled outside, where she paced the sidewalk, taking deep breaths and gritting her teeth. She didn't know if she would be able to go through with it.

If only Reuben were there.

And I, most jocund, apt, and willingly,
To do you rest, a thousand deaths would die.

She stopped, staring blankly at the building across the street. *Oh, Reuben.* He'd been so dashing up on the stage. He could make people laugh one minute, and cry the next. A true actor. As good as Eric. It was as a result of his passion that she'd ended up in theater at all. If it hadn't been for him, she never would've thought of taking her hapkido skills in that direction. She laughed to herself, remembering the first time she'd tried choreographing a stage fight. The poor man playing Long John Silver had thought she was going to actually kill him. She'd probably come closer than anyone liked to think about.

After that Reuben had thought it best she get a little actual theater training. She'd done that, taking a few stage combat workshops and working for a summer Shakespeare company. She was surprised how much she'd enjoyed it. She hadn't expected to. Hapkido gave so much more physical satisfaction. But the thrill of the stage and the response of the audience had called to her...

Footsteps sounded behind her, and she turned, expecting Eric. Her greeting died on her lips.

"You did a good job in there." Todd, the good-looking but lethargic banker, lounged against the side of the bench. "Done much acting?"

"Thank you. Some." She stopped pacing. "And you?"

"Just here." He gave a lazy smile, tipping his head back toward the theater. "Whenever they need a respectable-looking, non-teenager kind of guy they call me."

"Sure."

He pulled a water bottle from his jacket pocket and held it out to her. "Drink?"

"Oh. Thanks." She twisted open the top and took several swallows, thirstier than she'd realized.

Todd opened a second one and took a few genteel sips. "You here because of Eric?"

"Eric? Oh. Well, sort of." It was true. If it hadn't been for him, she most likely wouldn't have agreed to do the part. In fact, she would've left the theater the night before after hearing the others perform, and Thomas wouldn't have discovered her at the back of the room.

"I hear you're a fighter."

She glanced up.

"Aaron and Jack. They told me about last night's rehearsal."

"Oh, that." She shrugged. "I've done some stage combat choreography."

He took another swallow, eying her over his bottle. Casey averted her gaze, squeezing her drink in her fist.

"So where did Eric find you? Or are you one of his theater buddies from the good ol' days in Louisville?"

She looked back at him, wondering if she dared ask what those good old days consisted of. But Todd's expression was shuttered.

"I stopped in at Home Sweet Home."

"The charity supper? You were there?" His face went hard, and he drained his bottle before tossing it into the trashcan beside the bench.

Casey itched to pluck the bottle out of the barrel and find the nearest recycling bin, but knew that wouldn't make her any friends at the moment. "Is that a problem?"

"No. Of course not. Why would it be? It's a good place. A good thing."

The door opened and Becca stuck her head out. "Ready to get started again?"

Todd took a quick breath through his nose and held out a hand toward the theater, his eyes focused somewhere just beyond Casey's shoulder. "After you."

Casey screwed the lid back on her water bottle and walked past him, wondering why the mention of Home Sweet Home had made him break out into such a sweat that a bead of it was rolling down the side of his face.

Chapter Thirteen

"So you survived."

Casey shook her head and swung her leg over her bike, ready to head back to The Nesting Place, since rehearsal was over. "Barely. And you didn't help."

"Me?" Eric placed his hands over his chest, his eyes wide with innocence. "What did I do?"

Casey gave him a light punch to the shoulder. "Telling Holly she was beginning to get the hang of it was hardly beneficial."

He grinned. "What? You suggest I give her criticism? You think she would listen?"

"No. I guess not."

"Besides, Thomas would kill me."

"He's that protective?"

"Of his position as director. Not of Holly."

Casey looked back toward the theater, not wanting to be overheard. "You sure about that? He was looking at her pretty possessively. Although I did notice he was wearing a wedding ring."

Eric snorted. "Like that matters to him."

Casey crossed her arms over her chest, her feet flat on the ground, balancing the bike under her. "Okay. Spill. You have to tell me what the deal is with you and Thomas."

"Oh. I have to, do I?"

A quick glance showed Casey he wasn't angry. But he suddenly looked tired.

"Come on," she said. "I'll walk you back to your car."

"Eric!" Leila came skipping out of the theater. "You said we could go out for a drink, remember?"

"Not tonight, Leila, okay? Another time."

Leila looked at Casey, her feelings evident on her face. "Fine. Another time."

With a huff she swung her hair off of her shoulders and stomped to the green VW Bug across the street. Eric didn't say anything as she snatched her keys from the driver's seat, revved the engine, and screeched away, her taillights shining brightly in the night.

"Well…" Casey said.

"Come on," Eric said. "Let's go."

He began walking and Casey followed on the opposite side of the bike.

Eric held up a hand, then dropped it. "Like I said, Thomas' family and mine go way back. Our fathers went to school together."

"Here in Clymer?"

"No. I wasn't from here, originally. I moved here when I was eight, when my father got a job. Thomas and his family came shortly after, for the same reason."

"Jobs with HomeMaker?"

"Yes. Anyway, Thomas was just a year ahead of me in school. I know he looks older, but I think it's the beard. He cultivated that to appear more sophisticated."

Casey gave a short laugh, and Eric grinned. "I know. I didn't say it *worked*. But he does his best."

They walked for a few more paces in silence.

"Were you friends?" Casey finally asked.

"No." It came out as an exclamation. "We never were. I'm not sure why, exactly. Our dads were together all the time, and our moms… But he always seemed to think we were in some competition. Girls, grades, basketball. You name it, we were against each other. I didn't even *like* basketball."

"Or girls?"

He laughed. "Oh, I liked them fine. At least, after about seventh grade. But they always seemed to like Thomas better."

Casey glanced at him. "Seriously?"

"Sure. He had that brooding, artistic thing going."

"What? And you don't? You've got more artistic sense than he'll ever have."

He smiled. "Well, thanks. But that took a while to come about. I had no interest in theater at all during school. My mother forced me to sing in the choir, but that was as far as my artistic endeavors went. Back then, I was just…all I tried to do was fade into the background."

"How come?"

He shrugged. "Different reasons. The main one being I was probably the shyest kid in town."

"No."

"Time changes things."

"I guess. And was it just time that changed you?"

He kicked a stone from the sidewalk and shoved his hands into his pockets. "Maybe partly. But it was also Charles Dickens."

"*Dickens?*"

"Well. Sort of." He gave a chuckle. "The musical version."

"You mean *Oliver?*"

"You got it. The high school English teacher, who directed the plays, for some unknown reason decided it was the show to do for the spring musical my junior year."

"And you tried out?"

"No way. I wasn't about to go anywhere near that thing. The closest I would get would be if my mother bought tickets and forced me to go see it. I left the leading man thing to Thomas. He was much better suited to it, being the handsome extrovert."

"So what happened?"

He made a face. "I wasn't exactly large in high school."

"You mean like now, at your hulking five ten?"

"Hey, I can act taller." He stopped, puffing out his chest and raising his shoulders.

Casey rolled her eyes and continued walking.

"Anyway," Eric said, catching up to her, "I was small, blond, and sang in the choir. Good enough for the director. She began a campaign on my mother to get me to do the show."

"Not your dad?"

"No way. My dad would never have agreed to it. It was my mom that had to be convinced. And she was, eventually."

"Your dad didn't stop it?"

Eric pinched his lips together. "My dad didn't have anything to say about it by that time."

"How come?"

"Because he and my mom got divorced when I was twelve. He really didn't have much to do with my day-to-day life after that."

"I'm sorry."

He kicked another stone. "That's the way it was. And my mom couldn't resist the director. She was convinced I secretly longed for the stage, and dragged me to rehearsal. And that was that. I took one step on the stage and never wanted to leave." He pointed down an alley a block before Home Sweet Home, and Casey turned her bike with him. "It was like I'd found my true calling. My mother was right."

Casey followed him around the back of the buildings to the few parking spaces behind the soup kitchen. "Yes, she was. It's obvious."

He stopped at his Camry. "To make a long story short— although it's been plenty long already—Thomas wasn't exactly thrilled I broke into his domain. It's been a battle ever since."

"But you didn't stay here in Clymer."

"No."

"Did Thomas?"

"He didn't, either."

"And you both went to Louisville? Actors' Theater, maybe?"

He glanced at her sharply. "How did you know—"

"Todd. He said you'd been there."

"Oh. Sure. Those were…interesting times."

"And you both came back."

He opened his door and stepped into the lighted triangle between it and the car. "We did."

"Why?"

He picked his keys up from the driver's seat and studied them, singling out the fat one that would start the car. "Different things. It was just…time." He slid into the driver's seat. "See you at dinner tomorrow?"

"Sure. Four-o'clock?"

"Around there. We'll probably be having pizza. I'm making a trip to the Pizzeria in the next town tomorrow afternoon. They save their mistakes for us and freeze them until they have enough for a meal."

"That's nice."

"Want to come along? Except you can't drill me with questions the whole time."

Casey thought about the day, and how it would stretch out in front of her, with the constant temptation of her cell phone, Ricky being only a call away, and the library, where she could log onto the Internet and the Pegasus web site. "Sure. What time?"

"You promise? Only friendly conversation?"

She smiled. "I promise."

"Your fingers aren't crossed?"

She held them out in front of her, fingers splayed open. "I promise."

"Okay, then. I'll pick you up at The Nesting Place at two-thirty."

"Great. I'll be ready."

He shut his door, turned on the car, and reversed out of the parking space. Casey backed up to get out of his way, and bumped into Death.

"I don't know," Death said. "You're spending a lot of time with him."

"So?"

Death smirked. "Like I said before, he's awfully cute."

"Yeah? Well, you're not."

Death gave a shocked gasp. "Now *that* was unnecessary."

"But true."

"You do realize, love, that you can't hurt my feelings?"

Casey sighed. "I know. But it won't kill me to try."

Death cocked an eyebrow.

"Will it?" Casey asked hopefully.

"Nah," Death said.

"Yeah," Casey said. "That's what I thought."

Chapter Fourteen

The evening was chilly, and Casey was glad she'd worn her jacket. Clouds covered whatever moon would've been out, and she shivered in the darkness as she pulled onto the street of the B & B, glad when she could park the bike by the garage and head for the house.

Something flickered in her vision, and she looked across the yard. Was that a *fire*? Her breath caught, and her heart skipped a beat. *This isn't the same. This one smells of hot dog*—burned *hot dog—not oil and gas and rubber.* She placed a hand over her chest, resumed breathing, and slowly picked her way up the dark pathway toward the flames

"Oh, good! Here she is." Rosemary smiled, her face black and orange in the flickering campfire light. "Pull up a stump, dear."

Casey found a stash of the stumps under the awning of the house and dragged one over to the circle of stones.

"Have a stick." Lillian handed her a metal grilling pole. "Hot dog or marshmallow?"

"Um. Hot dog. At least to start with." Casey was surprised at the growl her stomach emitted. A roasted hot dog actually sounded great. Better than it should. "Is that what I'm smelling?"

Rosemary laughed. "Sorry. That was me. Dropped one too low in the flames and it caught on fire."

"I didn't know hot dogs could do that."

"Oh, yes. It was quite spectacular."

Lillian handed Casey a hot dog and watched as she lowered the stick toward the fire. "You know how to do this, I assume."

"Of course she does," Rosemary said. "What child never roasted a hot dog?"

Casey swallowed. She could think of one. He never got the chance.

"So." Rosemary talked around a bite. "How was play practice?"

Casey turned her stick. "Fine."

Rosemary stared at her. "*Fine?* That's all you're going to say?"

"Leave her alone, Rosie," Lillian said. "Can't you see the woman's starving?"

Casey looked up from the flames. "No, it's all right. What do you want to know?"

"Everything. Who was there. What did you do. Did Holly throw a temper tantrum. Did Leila actually drool on Eric. You know. The usual."

Lillian giggled. "Maybe Thomas threw the tantrum."

"Or Todd."

"No, Todd would never expend that much energy."

"And he's not really the type to throw one." Rosemary took another bite of her hot dog, deep in thought. "Aaron and Jack are young enough, the sweet babies, but they have better control of their tempers."

"No, their mother would never stand for it."

Casey's hot dog sizzled, and she turned it again, the underside beginning to turn brown. "Aaron and Jack are brothers?"

Rosemary's eyebrows rose. "Of course. Not twins, but close enough. Their mother had barely birthed Aaron before Jack came along. Not sure what the woman was thinking."

Lillian snorted. "It wasn't what *she* was thinking."

Rosemary let out a guffaw of agreement, and the women exchanged a knowing look, as if all men in the world followed the same example.

"So how did Holly treat you?" Rosemary polished off her hot dog, her eyes bright.

"Before or after the actress from the other town left?"

Rosemary let out a quiet screech. "That awful woman who was in *Hello, Dolly* last year? What was her name?"

They looked at Casey, and she shrugged. "Have no idea. Nobody bothered to introduce us."

"No," Lillian said. "They wouldn't."

"About Holly..." Rosemary said.

Casey grimaced. "She was perfectly nice—overly welcoming, even—until the woman left. After that she dropped me like a stone."

Rosemary humpfed. "That's just Holly. How Ellen ever put up with her..."

"They were friends?"

"As much as Holly can be friends with anybody. Selfish little brat. She'd call Ellen at all hours, claiming she had a crisis and needed another woman to talk to. Ellen would always agree to see her." She sighed. "But then, that's just how Ellen was. She'd invest more time than she should in someone like Holly, just to have it thrown in her face."

They were quiet for a few moments, watching the fire.

"I'm surprised that other actress even showed up," Lillian said. "But she probably heard about..." Her voice caught. "... about the open part and came to snag it."

Casey pulled her hot dog from the fire. "Actually, Thomas called her last week to see if she would come."

"Last *week*?" Rosemary's face went red, visible even in the firelight. "But Ellen only..." She stood up abruptly, her napkin fluttering to the ground, and hustled into the house.

Lillian looked at the ground.

"I'm sorry," Casey said. "I didn't mean to—"

"It's not you. You know that." She looked up. "You need a bun. Here." She pulled one from the bag on the neighboring stump. "And toppings. We have the usual—ketchup, mustard—and this wonderful relish we do up every fall. India relish. Red and green tomatoes, red and green peppers, onions… All from our garden."

"I'll try some of that. Thank you."

Lillian's face was a blank mask as she made up Casey's hot dog on a bright green partitioned tray. Besides the relish she lined the dog with the ketchup and mustard, and even a few onion strips. With a final twist, she deposited a handful of nacho chips in ones of the compartments.

Casey took the plate from Lillian, but the other woman didn't seem to hear her thanks.

"If you'll excuse me," Lillian said, standing and brushing off her pants. "I'm going to check on Rosemary."

"Of course."

Lillian stood with more composure than Rosemary had done, wadding up her own napkin and tossing it into the fire. Left behind, however, were the rest of the supplies.

Casey looked down at her plate, figuring her appetite would be gone. But the hot dog did look good. Smelled good, too. She took a bite, relish and ketchup dripping down her fingers.

It tasted fantastic.

When she was done, her hostesses still hadn't returned. She considered roasting another hot dog, but contented herself with popping an untoasted marshmallow in her mouth and breaking off a piece of the Hershey's chocolate.

"You're not supposed to eat them separately."

Casey didn't even need to look back at the food to see who had addressed her. "Well, you go ahead and make your own s'more. I'm not doing it for you."

Death plopped down on the stump next to her. "And here we were getting along so well."

Casey shook her head, looking into the flames. "Wouldn't you be more at home in there?"

"The fire?" Death huffed. "Not all dead people enter eternal flames, Casey. In fact, very few of them do."

"Is that so?"

"Would I wear flammable clothes otherwise?"

Casey stood and began cleaning up the food, placing the bottles and extra hot dogs in the picnic basket on the ground next to the stump. "Ellen Schneider."

Death pulled one knee up into clasped hands and rocked back to look at Casey. "What about her?"

"Did she really kill herself? Or are her friends right? Did someone else do it?"

Death didn't answer for so long Casey thought she was being ignored. "I asked you a question."

"I heard you, child. But I can't answer you."

Casey balanced the marshmallow bag on top of the condiments in the basket and stood over Death. "Can't, or won't?"

Death looked up at her. "It's not that I'm being mysterious. Or even stubborn. I really can't tell you."

Casey backed up and sat on Rosemary's stump, holding the basket on her lap. "But you're *Death*."

"Exactly. I come when the soul is ready to depart. You might not believe me, but even I don't know exactly when someone's going to go. Especially when it's unexpected. When someone is ill and fading away to a certain demise, I get the message to be prepared. I can be present and ready. Even when it's quick—" Death snapped. "I can be there almost instantaneously. But when it's a death that wasn't preceded by illness, and drags on for a bit, well, I get there as fast as I can, but not always fast enough to know what happened, because the soul isn't ready to go until that last moment, when there's no hope left."

"So Ellen—"

"—had some time before I got there. The overdose…it was a mortal one, of course, but it took several minutes to get to that state. Long enough that whoever killed her could get away before her soul was ready to go." Death held up a hand. "Not that I know there was someone else. But if there was, well, they got lucky."

"And if she did it herself?"

"I wasn't there to see. But that kind of death…I can imagine a woman doing it to herself. But forcing someone to overdose… well, that's extremely rare, and hard to do."

"I guess you would know."

"Yes." Death's voice was gentle.

The silence of the night, punctuated by crackles from the fire, covered them, and Casey looked at her hands. "Were you there?"

Death didn't pretend not to understand. "Almost immediately. When it happens so fast…"

The crash, the rush of the airbags, stumbling out of the car to get Omar from the back seat, the exploding flames, the flying door carrying her back, away from her family…

"Did they suffer?" Her voice was husky. "I remember… I remember the screams…"

Death leaned over, placing one hand on Casey's knee, the other under her chin, forcing her to look up. "It's over now, Casey. They're at peace."

"But *then*? Did they suffer *then*?"

Death studied her face. "You really want to know?"

Her chest constricted. "I *have* to."

Death took a breath, looking upward, then finally turned back to Casey, cupping her cheek with gentle fingers. "It was a short time, Casey. Very brief. They felt panic, disbelief, shock of pain. But then it was over. It's *still* over. They'll never feel pain again."

Casey's eyes blurred and she gripped Death's fingers, cold on her cheek. "Then *why*? Why couldn't you take me, too? Why leave me to…" She pulled away and staggered up from the stump, her hand waving wildly above her head as the picnic basket crashed to the ground, scattering food and plates. "To *this*?"

Death looked around at the campfire, the trees, the food. The locusts sang above them, and the flames popped, sending up gusts of white smoke. "This isn't hell, Casey, honey, no matter what you may think. Someday perhaps you'll see."

Death stood and Casey lunged forward, falling, latching onto Death's wrist. "Take me. Please take me. You *know* where they *are*."

Death looked down at Casey, who trembled, her knees in the dirt, smudged tears lining her cheeks, dotting her shirt. Death knelt in front of her, gently extricating her fingers and pulling her close, patting her back. "Hush, daughter. Listen. Listen to the night. Quiet now."

And shielded in Death's embrace, Casey's tears slowed, until all she could feel was the cover of the darkness.

Chapter Fifteen

Casey awoke to birdsong. It sounded awfully close, as if the bird had gotten into her room. She squeezed her eyes shut and raised her arm to cover her exposed ear. The trilling pierced her stuffy head, and she considered taking the clock from the night table and flinging it toward the feathered trespasser.

And then she remembered.

She opened her eyes, a struggle, as they felt puffy and sore. The campfire was out, only a thin line of gray smoke escaping from underneath the ashes. Casey's face was cool, but the rest of her remained surprisingly warm. Upon taking stock, she realized that not only was she warm, but her head lay on a pillow, and she was covered with a heavy blanket.

She sat up. The picnic basket and its contents were absent, as were the hot dog sticks. The stumps still sat by the ring of stones, but no one occupied them, and Death had gone off to wherever Death went after leaving Casey. To make someone else miserable, Casey figured.

Casey's shoes were lined up beside the blanket, and she tugged them on before slowly standing and folding the blanket. Holding the blanket and pillow, she took a deep breath and let it out, trying to ease the tightness in her chest. She gritted her teeth.

Damn Death, anyway.

She picked her way through the yard to the laundry room, where she eased the back door shut and left the pillow and blanket on the table beside the basket of her clean, folded laundry.

Either Lillian or Rosemary had finished up the clothes she'd forgotten about. She winced. She'd have to have them add a little to her bill.

A look out the back window showed the campfire ring looking almost cheery, with the speckled sunlight dotting the stumps, and the grass surrounding it. She rubbed her eyes, picked up the laundry basket, and stepped into the kitchen.

A note, folded and propped on the counter, had her name scrawled in sparkly purple pen: *Casey, dear, sorry we couldn't carry you in. You're too much for two old ladies! Help yourself to breakfast, whatever you like. We're out grocery shopping! Lillian and Rosie*

Shopping? How late had she slept? A glance at the clock assured her it wasn't yet even eight-o'clock. The women, she guessed, were early risers.

From the color of the ink and the swirl of the script on the note, Casey figured Rosemary had done the writing. And there was no bill accompanying it. With a small smile she left the note, set down the laundry basket, and opened the refrigerator to see if they stocked any orange juice. They did, and she drank a small glass. Somehow food just didn't seem inviting.

After placing her glass in the sink she gathered her laundry and went upstairs, where Solomon the cat sat at her door, waiting for her arrival.

"Well," Casey said. "What do *you* want?"

He blinked slowly, like he'd just been awakened from a nap.

"You want to go in my room to sleep some *more?*" She turned the knob and pushed open the door, but Solomon stayed sitting. He stretched his neck as far as he could from his spot, ears angling, whiskers twitching.

Casey stuck her head in the door, half-expecting to see her usual visitor, but Death was either hiding or absent. "No one there, cat. Go ahead, if you want."

But Solomon brought his head back and huddled on his haunches, blinking up at her.

"Fine. You can't say you weren't asked." She went into the room and closed the door.

The bed, still perfectly made, looked inviting after her night on the ground, but Casey stepped past it to the wardrobe, where she found a pair of shorts, which she exchanged for her jeans. She used the empty space in the room to do her morning calisthenics, and was soon sweating, dripping onto the nice carpet. After her three hundredth sit-up she allowed herself to pace the room, stripping as she made her way to the bathroom. A shower was definitely in order.

After a long time under the steaming water, Casey felt at least partially rejuvenated and put on clean clothes, again avoiding the temptation of the bed. Although what she was to do until two-thirty, when Eric would be picking her up, was beyond her.

She spent a few minutes putting her clean laundry in the wardrobe, but was soon at a loss for further chores, so she grabbed her jacket and opened the door. Solomon, hunched on the floor, made a move to go into her room, but stopped at the threshold, hissed, and turned, trotting down the stairs.

Casey watched him go, wondering if Lillian and Rosemary would have the same reaction. Rosemary had come up with her the day before and all had seemed fine, but Death had yet to visit. It would be interesting to see what happened when the women came up to tidy the room.

Casey followed Solomon's path downstairs, but the cat was out of sight by the time she got to the landing. She shook her head and went out the front door, avoiding the campfire area on her way to get her bike.

When Casey mounted the old Schwinn, the tires squished alarmingly, having deflated overnight. She hopped off. Ride, or walk? And where was she even going?

Not wanting to destroy what was left of the tires, she pushed the bike back to the gas station, where she again made use of the air pump. She checked out the tires as she did so, and decided that if she was really going to use the bike as her transportation, she should invest in a new set. She wondered if the garage attached to the gas station had any bike tires, or if she'd have to have Eric take her somewhere that afternoon.

"Hello?" She stood in the little store section of the station, surrounded by cold drinks, packets of candy, and cigarettes. No one manned the cash register, and she couldn't imagine anyone could hear her calling with the radio as loud as it was, pulsing out an amplified hip-hop beat. A door led to the garage part of the building, and she stepped through it, her fingers in her ears.

Workboot-clad feet stuck out from the bottom of a rusty Ford F150, tapping to the rhythm of the song. No one else appeared, so Casey took a look around the space. Tires adorned the far wall, among them a few that looked like they might fit Rosemary and Lillian's old bike.

Taking the chance of scaring the mechanic, she walked over to the side of the car where his head should be and squatted down. "Hello?"

Still no response.

Getting up, she went to the other side of the car and tapped one of the protruding feet with her shoe.

Both feet shot up, banging the thighs of the man on the undercarriage of the car. In a moment, he scooted out from underneath, on his wheeled lorry.

"Sorry," Casey mouthed at him. Then, "Aaron?"

The man—or kid, really—grinned up at her, then leapt off the pallet with surprising grace. He held up a greasy finger and trotted over to a shelf, where he punched a button on the sound system. The silence in the garage was staggering.

"Hey, Casey." He sauntered back toward her, wiping his hands on a rag. "Sorry about the music. It helps the day go quicker."

"Sure. But can you hear afterward?"

He laughed. "Most days. Although sometimes I pretend not to hear when Mom asks me to do something really nasty."

"Um-hmm."

"You're not going to ask me to do something really nasty, are you?" He looked suddenly like a child, waiting to be told he must clean out the litter box.

"Absolutely not. All I want are some bike tires."

"Oh." His relief was palpable. "That's easy." He walked over to the wall, gesturing for Casey to follow. "What size do you need?"

"Not sure. But I have the bike outside."

"Let's see." He changed directions, headed toward the front of the shop, and outside. His eyebrows rose at the sight of the bike. "Not exactly brand-new, is it?"

"Nope. It's just what Rosemary and Lillian had in their shed."

Understanding lit his face. "No wonder, then. But the tires are standard. Why don't we bring it on in." Grabbing the handlebars, he steered the bike into the garage and put it up on a rack. In no time at all he'd placed a tire iron under the rubber and stripped the tires from the rims. "Rims look good. The tires are just worn out. Rubber *and* tubes." He glanced at the clock. "It'll only take me a few minutes, if you want to wait."

"That would be great. Unless you need to fix the truck first."

"Nah. This won't take that long. Have a seat…" He looked around for something not occupied by tools, papers, or greasy rags. "Hang on." Disappearing into a small office, he returned with a battered folding chair. "It's not pretty, but it's clean."

Casey smiled. "If only I could say that much for myself."

His eyes narrowed playfully. "I don't know. You look pretty clean to me."

Casey barked a laugh, and Aaron turned to pick new tires off the wall, which he held up to the bike. "Look good?"

"Perfect."

He set to work, whistling.

"So have you worked here long?" Casey watched his black-smeared fingers, marveling that she hadn't noticed them at rehearsal.

"Since I graduated from high school."

"And that was what? Last year?"

He glanced back at her. "How young do you think I am? I've been out three years."

"And you came here right away?"

His ears reddened, and Casey could see his jaw bunching. "Pretty much. I'd thought about college…" He shrugged. "But that didn't exactly work out."

Casey wanted to ask why, but wasn't sure she should be that personal. After all, she'd known the kid a total of two days. If you could call the little she'd seen him "knowing."

"And Jack? He's your brother, right? A year younger?"

"That's right."

"Does he work here, too?"

He was quiet for a moment as he spun the front wheel of the bike. "No. He works down at HomeMaker."

"Really?"

He stopped the tire and moved to the back one. "For now, anyway. We were surprised he lasted through Christmas." He turned to her. "You heard about that?"

"I heard."

"Well." He was back at the tire. "Somehow he got missed when the lay-offs happened. His whole section did. But it really doesn't matter. He'll be out of a job come a month or two, anyway."

"Any ideas for where he'll go next?" Not college, apparently.

Aaron shook his head and gestured at the garage. "Not here. The owner can barely afford me, let alone another guy. It's just me and him, and when he's not here…" He shrugged. "We do what we can. It's not like folks have the money to be doing work on their cars unless they absolutely have to, anyway."

All of which explained the unmanned cash register at the front, and the one guy she'd found at the station the day before.

"Do you get other customers? Other than from town?"

"Some."

"People who work at HomeMaker?"

He looked at her sharply. "A few."

"The CEO?"

He snorted. "Karl Willems bring his car here? I don't think so. He'd never trust us smalltown hicks with his precious Cadillac."

"What about Rosemary and Lillian? Do they bring their car here?" The Orion in the garage looked undriven, but that could've been from the care.

"Their old Civic? When it needs it. But they don't drive that much, and Civics don't need a lot of work, so…" He plugged an air compressor onto the back tire's air valve and gave it a pump. In a few seconds he was done and swinging the bike down from its perch. "Good as new."

Casey wondered about the Orion, but didn't want to bring it up in case the ladies did, indeed, take it elsewhere for service. "Thank you, Aaron. What do I owe you?"

Aaron wheeled the bike back to the front of the garage and stepped behind the cash register, where he scribbled on a receipt pad. "Two new tires, plus installation." He ripped off the sheet and held it out to her.

She pulled some bills from her wallet and placed them in his hand. "Keep the change, okay? I *am* allowed to tip you?"

He blinked. "I guess. No one's ever tried before."

She smiled. "There's a first for everything."

"Thanks."

"You're welcome. And thank *you*. Now I won't have to come down to the air pump every morning."

"Too bad. I could use the company."

She mounted the bike, enjoying the feeling of the firm tires. "Just because I won't need air doesn't mean I can't come by."

"Sure. And I'll see you at rehearsal tonight, anyway. Right?"

"Right. Now—" She tilted her head toward the garage. "Back to your hip hop."

He grinned. "Until the next customer scares me to death."

She waved, and pedaled the bike out to the road.

When she looked back, Aaron was gone. She could already hear his music.

Chapter Sixteen

Casey took her time riding down the town's streets, unoccupied as they were by cars or people. The architecture was impressive—or, it would've been a hundred years earlier. Her tour made it clear that The Nesting Place wasn't the only pretty Queen Anne in town. Just the only one whose owners could afford to refurbish it. Many of the houses she was seeing appeared to be divided into multiple apartments, with more than the town's fair share of undrivable cars sitting either in driveways or corners of yards. Even if a home was single-family, it lacked the finished look of Rosemary and Lillian's inn.

That's not to say there weren't homey touches. A pot of flowers here, a tarnished *Welcome* sign there… The people of Clymer may have been hurting—financially and otherwise—but they hadn't forgotten those little details. She couldn't help but wonder how it was Lillian and Rosemary could afford to have their place looking the way it did.

Casey pulled up to a stop sign, where she dutifully stopped and looked both ways. She held her position, waiting for the cop car, coming from her right, to either pass or make a turn. Instead, it pulled to the side of the road, and a middle-aged man got out of the driver's side.

He nodded and sauntered her way. "Nice day for a bike ride."

Casey got off of the bike and put down the kickstand, freeing her hands and balancing herself on the balls of her feet. It wasn't that she expected the police officer to attack her, but sitting on her bike felt too precarious. Although she probably *could* take him if he came after her, as he wasn't any too young and she would have the element of surprise. Besides, he was tiny. She had an inch and twenty pounds on him, at least.

The cop looked her over, from behind what looked like prescription sunglasses. "May I ask your name?"

"Casey Smith. I'm staying at The Nesting Place."

"Ah, yes, of course."

Like he hadn't known that.

Casey remembered the articles she'd read about Ellen's death. "The chief of police, I assume?"

"That's me. Denny Reardon. Grew up here. Probably'll die here, too." He angled his head toward the cruiser. "I was out for a little ride myself. Checking things out. Don't suppose you'd care to join me on a little jaunt?"

She glanced at the car. "No, I wouldn't."

His eyebrows gravitated upward.

"But thank you." Casey put a hand on the bike's handlebars. "I prefer bikes."

"I see. Any particular reason?"

"Saves gas."

"Um-hmmm." He jingled something on his belt as he made a show of looking down the street. "Something you're finding interesting in our town, Ms. Jones?"

"Smith," she said. She tried to gauge his tone. Was he accusing her of something? Or just naturally curious? Or paranoid? "I'm just traveling through."

"But getting awfully involved, meanwhile."

"The play, you mean?"

He took off his sunglasses, pulled out a handkerchief, and cleaned the lenses, breathing onto them and smearing the fabric across the glass. "Sure. Sure, that's what I mean."

"Yeah, well, that just sort of happened. I wasn't planning on staying in town that long."

"I see. And you know people here? Eric VanDiepenbos? The ladies at the bed and breakfast, perhaps?"

"Not before two days ago."

He nodded some more. "And where did you come from two days ago?"

"Detroit."

"Motor City. Tigers fan, are you?"

"No. I like the Rockies, myself."

He looked at her sharply. "You're from Colorado?"

"No, but they've got lots of young, handsome players."

He kept his eyes on her, sucking his cheeks to his teeth. Eventually he said, "So you like handsome young men?"

"Sure. Who doesn't?"

The corner of his mouth twitched. "There's some who say you came to town for Eric."

"Really?"

"And some who say you came to town for HomeMaker."

"HomeMaker? Why?"

"I suppose you'd have to tell me."

She frowned, wondering who exactly the chief had been talking to. She asked him.

"Oh, just this person and that person. You know. A variety."

"So there must be more theories."

He grinned a little. "Of course. You're FBI, come to check out our failing factory, or you're the opposite, and *wanted* by the FBI. You're a traveling journalist, documenting your experiences, you know, like that guy, what's his name, Charles Kuralt. Some even say…" He gave her a steady look. "You're the long-lost sister of Ellen Schneider, come to get revenge for her death."

Casey swallowed. "But I thought she killed herself."

"That's right, but something had to drive her to it, isn't that right?"

"I guess." She picked at the wrap on the bike's handlebars. "Any chance she *didn't* kill herself?"

The chief gave her a long look, then slowly placed his sunglasses back over his eyes. "It's been officially ruled a suicide,

Ms. Smith. The autopsy confirmed she died of an overdose of her own sleeping pills. She sat down with a few cups of coffee and just about emptied the bottle. No bruises saying someone forced her to take them. No needle marks saying someone shot her up with something. All of the evidence points away from there being anyone else involved."

"No fingerprints?"

He snorted. "Been talking to your friends at The Nesting Place, have you? They'd like me to call in favors from the governor to get Ellen's entire house taken apart and analyzed."

"But fingerprints are simple."

"Yeah. And these simple prints are telling us *no one else was involved.* I really don't think there's any point in bringing her death up again, questioning how it happened. People here have enough to worry about these days, without thinking that maybe Ellen was murdered." He held up a hand, forestalling her response. "I wish to God she hadn't done it, Ms. Smith, but facts are facts. Nothing we can do will change them, and it's not worth getting everybody all riled up over something that's not true, or even likely."

"Her kids might think differently."

"Her *kids* are ten and seven. I really don't think it matters to them one way or the other, does it?"

"You *don't?*"

"Either way, they're orphans."

"Yes, but one way she chose to leave them, and the other she didn't. I'd say that matters a lot."

"Ms. Smith, that might matter to some people. Her family, sure, I can give you that. Her friends, like your hostesses at the bed and breakfast. They've made no secret of their feelings. Her *boyfriend...*" He looked at her meaningfully. "But somehow, Ms. Smith, I don't see that it should matter a whole lot to *you.*"

"But—"

"Good day, Ms. Smith." He began the trek back across the street, but stopped when he reached his cruiser, turning to her as if struck by a sudden thought. "And you know, I find myself hoping one last theory about you is true."

"Really? And what is that?"

"That you're a gypsy, and you can only stay in one place a few days at a time, or poof!" He splayed his fingers upward. "You evaporate."

Casey watched him, her mouth open, as he opened his car door and slid into the seat. With a slight wave he accelerated through the intersection and drove off.

"Now *that* is a rude little man." Death stood in the middle of the street, drinking a Slurpee and watching the police car turn a corner and disappear from view.

Casey crossed her arms. "So. Will I?"

"Will you what?"

"Evaporate?"

Death walked over and pinched Casey's cheek with fingers icy from the drink. "Hardly. Chief Reardon doesn't know anything about gypsies."

"Really? And you do?"

"Of course. And gypsies do *not* evaporate."

Casey sighed. "So much for that idea."

Death took another loud slurp and took off the drink lid, stirring the ice with the straw. "Gypsies do, however, get arrested and convicted of crimes they did not commit."

Casey jerked her head in the direction of the police car.

When she turned back around, Death was gone.

Chapter Seventeen

Casey was pedaling slowly, trying to bring her heart rate back to normal, when a strange vibration came from her jacket pocket. She glanced down. *What in the world?* Oh. Her phone. She'd forgotten to remove it the day before.

She braked and stopped, one foot on the curb. Yanking the phone from her pocket, she scanned the face for the incoming number. Ricky. Of course. He could've gotten her information when she'd called yesterday. His catering business was sure to have Caller ID.

"Ricky?"

"They were here again. At my house. The lady with the hair, and the guy with the face."

"What? When?"

"Just now. And that's not all. *She* was with them."

"She? You mean…" He could only mean one person. Dottie Spears. The CEO of Pegasus. "What did she want?"

"Same thing Hair and Face wanted yesterday. To know where you were."

"But for her to come—"

"Something must've happened."

He was right. He had to be. "What did you tell them?"

"What I always tell them. The truth. I don't know where you are, where you're going, or how to get in touch with you. Except that was a lie, of course, since we're on the phone now and I do know your e-mail address. Not that you check it very often."

"Are they gone?"

"Of course they're gone."

"I mean *gone* gone. Have you looked outside?"

She could hear his sigh over the phone, and the rustle that meant he was moving.

"Okay. I'm looking out the front window. There's nobody there. No cars, either. Except mine and—"

Casey waited. "And?"

"Nothing."

"Oh, no. You're not doing that. Who's car is there?"

"Casey…"

"It's not that awful girl from work again, is it, Ricky? What was her name? *Jewel?* Please tell me it's not."

"And if it is?"

"I guess I'll have to come home after all."

"Aaaah, so now I know the secret. I think I *will* have to call her again."

Casey put a hand to her forehead. "So it's not her?"

"It's not her. But back to the reason I called—"

"You're okay?"

"I'm fine. It's not like these people are dangerous or anything. Just annoying."

Casey wasn't so sure. The guy with the face…well, that face wasn't any too forgiving. "Just promise me you'll be careful."

"Of what? Incoming lawsuits?"

"Ricky…"

"All right, all right. I'll be careful. Whatever that means."

"It means—"

"I *know* what it means. I'm not an idiot."

"Are you sure?" Casey squeezed her phone. "This number will be in your records now. I'll have to get rid of it. You do realize they can track cell phones?"

"You called me yesterday."

"At *work*. Not on your personal phone."

"Oh. That's right. But if you get rid of the phone how am I supposed to—"

"By e-mail, like usual."

"But you have to promise—"

"I can't promise anything."

"—that you'll check your e-mail more often. Okay? That's all I'm asking."

Casey blew a stray hair from her eyes. "Once a day."

"At least."

"*Once* a day."

Ricky grumbled something she couldn't hear.

"And Ricky? Check on Mom, will you?"

"You think they'll go after her?"

"They're bugging you. They've gotta think Mom knows where I am, even if you don't."

"I'll check as soon as we hang up."

"Thanks. And hey, if you find something out about…about Pegasus, let me know, okay?"

"Same goes for you."

"I'll tell you."

"Good."

A few seconds of humming phone service hung in the air between them.

"So…"

"Thanks for calling, bro. I appreciate the heads up."

"You're welcome. Now come home."

Casey smiled sadly, gripping the phone tightly to her ear. "As soon as I can, Rick. I promise."

"Well. I guess that's about as good as I can expect. Love you, sis."

"Love you, too."

She held the phone to her ear long after he'd hung up, listening to the dead air.

Chapter Eighteen

Dottie Spears hadn't started out as a horrible person. At least not when Casey had met her. She'd been sympathetic and kind, her iron hand at Pegasus showing only when one of her underlings said something insensitive in Casey's hearing.

But Casey's lawyers hadn't trusted the woman, even at the beginning. In fact, they'd gone so far as to call her a slimy, bottom-dwelling, daughter-of-a-snake cannibal. And that was just for starters.

Casey had wanted to believe the best. Had actually been in too much shock and misery from the loss of her family, not to mention her own injuries, to notice when Dottie said things that might've been out of line. Such as suggesting it would be easier for Casey to just forget the whole thing and go on with her life, rather than fight the fight with Pegasus.

Casey hadn't *wanted* to fight the fight. Had sincerely thought it would be best to leave it all, so she could just fade away, spending her days in the darkness of her bedroom, with her blanket over her head. But her lawyers hadn't felt that way. Neither had Ricky, or her mother. They said she had to keep her head up. Go on with it all to show Pegasus that they couldn't get away with their faulty mechanics. To keep anyone else from losing their family.

But Casey could honestly say she hadn't cared at the time. Hadn't cared that an entire fleet of hybrid cars and the people in them were headed for catastrophe. She didn't care about *anything* at that point, other than the fact that she was alive, and didn't want to be. In fact, she wasn't convinced any car other than hers had had the same problem. Hers was a freak. An almost impossibility. Dottie Spears had told her so.

But as the months went on, as Ricky and her mother forced her to survive, she began to realize that something wasn't right. The CEO of the company who killed her family shouldn't be allowed to come to Casey's house whenever she wanted, bearing plates of cookies. Sure, there was the possibility the woman actually cared, but as time went on Casey could see the reality of that was even more remote than the chance her car really was the only faulty one.

Casey finally agreed to take them on.

It wasn't pretty. None of it was. Dottie Spears' change from sympathetic friend to lethal opponent was so fierce it gave Casey nightmares. As if she needed any more of those. At least these involved claws and teeth, rather than flames and explosions and the screams of loved ones.

Casey didn't want to go to court. Didn't want photographs of her mutilated husband and son plastered across the courtroom, and therefore the nightly news. Didn't want her family to become the poster children of vehicles gone awry. Didn't want to sit in the witness stand at the mercy of Dottie and her legions of lawyers, who claimed Reuben had been drinking too much before they'd gone to pick up Omar that night…

She also didn't want to look like the crazy woman, going after a scapegoat Pegasus for millions to make up for her dead family. Because nothing could make that up. And nothing is what would happen if she came off looking like a money-hungry bitch.

So they'd fought it in boardrooms. Closed doors, keeping out the media. Hammering away at a resolution that should please them all. All except Casey, who would be pleased only when she received a pass to that eternal haven, where she would meet up with Reuben and Omar.

She hadn't gotten that.

Casey, now back at the library under stick-thin librarian Stacy's watchful eye, had forced herself to return to the Pegasus web site. Not that they would have anything worthwhile there. She would have to look elsewhere for whatever had spurred Dottie Spears' visit to Ricky. The woman still looked the same… if the on-line photo was up-to-date. The same as yesterday. The same as every day Casey looked.

Shaking her head, she brought up a search engine and typed in "Pegasus," plus the date. If anything new was happening, it should be in the day's news. She scrolled through the hits. Stock prices—still growing. Car dealerships—mostly the company's own, with their trademark "personal green touch." A question and answer site, where Pegasus owners took turns praising and criticizing their new rides. Nothing controversial, that Casey could find. Nothing new.

She expanded her search to include the entire month of September and received more of the same. Paging down, she scanned the headlines, looking for anything different, anything other than the Pegasus propaganda and useless "how do I take out the middle drink tray to clean it" questions.

She found it on page four. "Man Dies in Fatal Crash." Pulse pounding in her temple, she read the article, which described the fiery inferno that engulfed a fifty-two-year-old man on his way home from work in Clear Lake, Iowa. He was driving a Pegasus car, same model and year as Casey's had been. He left a wife and two college-aged children, and had been a large-animal veterinarian.

Casey laid her face on her fists, her breath coming in short, shallow gulps. How could this happen? Pegasus was supposed to—

"Everything okay?"

Casey's breath caught, and she rounded on the person at the next computer, her voice a hiss. *"No, everything is not okay!"*

Death glanced around, eyebrows raised, before leaning toward Casey. "So you found it?"

Casey jabbed a finger at the article. "How long have you known about this?"

"Let's see, when did it happen?" Death looked at the computer screen. "Two weeks ago Thursday, right? Yes. I've known since then."

Casey turned back to her computer and closed her eyes. "You kept this from me—"

"Ma'am?" Stacy the Librarian hovered at her elbow. "Um, is everything all right?"

Casey took a deep breath and let it out before looking up at him. "I'm sorry. I just found out some...bad news."

"Oh." He looked at the computer screen. "Anything I can help with?"

"No."

He backed up a short step.

"No, I'm sorry." Casey held up her hand. "But thank you. I'm...fine. I'll go in a minute."

Relief washed over his features, quickly replaced by a professional mask of helpfulness. "Okay. Well, let me know if I can do anything for you."

"I will."

She watched from the corner of her eye as he made his way back to his desk, and avoided his gaze as he glanced back at her.

"You get me in more trouble..." She talked without moving her lips.

But Death was gone.

Casey found the "forward this article" button and e-mailed it to Ricky. He needed to know Pegasus had fresh worries. And had possibly violated the agreement they'd hashed out in those boardrooms so long ago.

Chapter Nineteen

"They were supposed to fix those cars, Don," Casey said. "Every one."

"I know." Her lawyer's voice was even and quiet. "It was my understanding they did."

"Well, apparently they missed one. And the guy's dead."

"Okay. Tell me where to find the information."

Casey did. "It shouldn't have happened, Don."

"No. No, it shouldn't have." Casey could hear him ruffling some papers. "I'll make some inquiries."

"Have they been there?"

"Who?"

"The Pegasus people. Have they been bothering you?"

"No." He sounded surprised. "Why would they?"

"Because they're trying to find me. They won't leave Ricky alone. And I'm afraid they'll go after my mother."

"What are they doing?" Don's voice wasn't so quiet now. "It was part of the agreement. No contact. You would both keep up your end of the settlement, and that was supposed to be that."

"Yeah, but the agreement just talked about me. No contact with *me*. It didn't say anything about Ricky or my mom."

The silence on the phone was ominous. "Leave it to me, Casey. I'll take care of it. And besides, if they're trying to find you—which they shouldn't be doing in the first place—what exactly are they going to do if not *contact* you?"

Casey wasn't sure she wanted to think about that. "Ricky said he was going to send you some more papers for me to sign. You should get them in a day or two."

"What are they?"

"Don't know. But I'll give you an address soon, where you can send them."

"Where are you now?"

She smiled. "You and Ricky. You just won't stop, will you?"

"Hey, a guy's got to keep trying, doesn't he? One of these days…"

"Yeah. One of these days it won't matter anymore." She looked across the picnic table toward the playground, where this time two fathers played with the children. She swallowed the large lump in her throat. "And don't bother trying to call me back at this phone number. Ricky already called it from home, so I'll have to ditch it."

"Casey—"

"They're not going to stop, Don. They'll keep looking till they succeed, and I really don't want to find out what they want."

"It can't be—"

"Thanks for everything. I appreciate it."

"You're welcome. But Casey…take care of yourself, okay? Do you need money?"

Casey laughed. "Don, you're the one who signed that agreement with Pegasus. You *know* I don't need money."

He sighed. "I know. But it's the sort of thing one is supposed to ask."

"Well, you don't have to ask me. Good-bye, Don."

"Good-bye. And Casey?"

"Yeah?"

"Call again soon."

She pushed the off button and considered the phone. How such a small piece of equipment could betray her… She got back on her bike, taking a last look at the fathers and their kids. Reuben had never gotten to play with Omar at a playground.

Never taken him to a ball game. Never got to hear that universal first word. *Da-da.*

She pointed the bike toward the highway, and began pedaling.

Chapter Twenty

Several trucks sat in the over-sized parking lot of The Burger Palace. Casey looked around to make sure none of the truckers were in their cabs, and picked the trailer with the most remote license plate. Oregon. After carefully wiping the phone of all personal information, phone numbers, and fingerprints, Casey threw it on the cement several times, until the screen was cracked and it would no longer turn on.

She picked up a few stray broken pieces, then ducked under the truck, searching until she found a crevice where the phone would be neither discovered nor dislodged any time in the near future. She stood back up, glancing around again to make sure she hadn't been spotted, and rode quickly away, not looking back.

The diner, across the street, had a few cars in the parking lot, and Casey realized she was hungry. The benefits of the orange juice had long gone, and her appetite had, for no apparent reason, returned. After seeing the article at the library, she'd been convinced she wouldn't ever eat again.

She parked the Schwinn along the side of the building and went in the front door, inhaling the rich diner aromas of coffee, hash browns, and grease. The sign told her to please seat herself, so she chose a place at the front window, where a little of the autumn sun stole across the table.

"What can I get you?" The young waitress—Kristi, by her nametag—didn't chew gum, and she wore low-slung black pants under her pink-and-white striped diner uniform shirt. No fifties diner look for her.

"Is there a daily special?"

"Breakfast is pumpkin pancakes. Lunch is shredded chicken sandwich and mashed potatoes. You could have either."

"Oh." Casey picked up her menu and perused the lunch items. "I'll just have a hamburger. Fries. Cole slaw."

The waitress took the menu and stuck it under her arm. "Anything to drink?"

"Lemonade?"

"Sure. I'll be back in a minute." The girl flashed her a brief smile and left in a wake of hair product smell that rivaled the coffee.

Casey sat back in the vinyl bench seat and looked around the diner. Not a busy lunch crowd, but then, she was early—more like the brunch crowd—and the people of Clymer didn't seem to have a lot of extra money for the luxury of someone else's cooking. An older couple sat in the corner booth. A single man at the counter. No one she knew. Which wasn't at all surprising.

She looked out the window, across the parking lot, and saw the corner of the main HomeMaker building. She leaned forward, toward the glass, to take in more of the factory, and wondered again what had happened to Ellen Schneider. Had she been killed? Or were her friends just wrong when they said she wouldn't do such a thing as kill herself?

"Mind if I join you?"

Casey looked up, expecting her usual companion, but was pleasantly surprised to see Todd Nolan, the banker, standing beside her table.

"That would be fine. Have a seat."

He did, and the waitress was soon at the table, setting down Casey's lemonade and allowing Todd to put an arm around her waist.

He smiled. "How's your day going, sweetheart?"

The blood in Casey's veins went cold, and she calculated how quickly she could reach over and suppress his carotid artery, sending him to sleep. Or perhaps she should just kick his shin under the table.

Kristi rolled her eyes and stepped away from his arm. "Daaaad, not in front of the customers." She looked sideways at Casey. "You two here together?"

Casey let out the breath she'd been holding, and allowed her body to move back into normal "at ease" mode. His *daughter*.

Todd grinned at the girl. "She's in the play. Casey, right?"

Casey nodded.

"I just met her last night."

Kristi still didn't seem so sure. "Mom know?"

"That I'm in the play? Of course she does."

Kristi opened her mouth to say something else and Todd patted her leg. "The usual, okay? And not too much salad dressing this time?"

She cocked her hip at him and flounced away, leaving him to chuckle. "You have kids?"

Casey's throat closed, and she grabbed her lemonade, taking a deep swallow, but choking on the sweet drink.

"You okay?" Todd looked ready to perform the Heimlich, his palms flat on the table, his elbows up, to propel him from the bench.

She set her glass down and wiped her mouth with her napkin. "I'm fine. Thank you."

He nodded. "No kids, I take it?"

"No."

He glanced at her hand. "Married?"

She shook her head.

"Kristi's my oldest. Got two more in high school. All girls." He smiled. "Whenever they start talking about shopping I get out as quickly as I can."

Casey cleared her throat. "And that's why you're here today?"

"No. I'm working today, at the bank, and just felt like coming by and seeing my girl." He winked. "My wife is taking the day to clean the basement, so I'm glad it's a workday, to be sure."

He sank down a bit in the bench seat, as if making himself comfortable for a good long stay.

Casey eyed him over her glass as she took another sip of lemonade, remembering his reaction when she'd mentioned Home Sweet Home. That bead of sweat rolling down his face.

"So what are you doing in Clymer?" Todd asked, interrupting her thoughts. He wasn't sweating now, and he looked so relaxed his eyelids drooped, as if he were about to fall asleep.

Casey ran a finger down the side of her glass, drawing a path in the condensation. "Just traveling through."

"By yourself?"

"It works."

He shook his head slowly, as if not sure what to think of her. "You on vacation? Took time off?"

Casey looked away. "I don't have a job right now."

"So how do you afford traveling? Family money?"

Casey's breath caught. *Family money.* She pressed her fingers to her mouth. He didn't know how right he was.

"Sorry," he said. "I get nosy about money. Goes with the job."

Casey didn't say anything, keeping her hand up, staring out of the window until her breath came back and she could talk without her voice shaking. "So," she said. "Tell me about the play."

"*Twelfth Night*?" Todd's eyes opened wider. "We just read through it last night."

"I don't mean the play itself. I mean the people involved. Why you're in it."

"Oh." He shrugged. "What I told you last night. They needed a guy my age, so they called."

"It's basically the same group each time?"

He sniffed, flicking a hand over the tip of his nose. "I don't know. It depends who's in town, I guess. Before Eric and Thomas came back we were a little hard-pressed for good people, but we got by. Holly's in everything—well, as long as there's a role for someone she thinks is attractive enough—and Becca likes to be involved. Leila…well, if Eric's in it, she's somewhere close by."

"Aaron and Jack?"

He grinned again, a slow smile. "They like the plays. Keeps them out of trouble."

Casey picked up her fork and twisted it in her fingers. "How about Ellen?"

"Ellen?" His face went white, then red, before returning to its usual color. "She was good. She enjoyed the plays."

"I'm sorry," Casey said. "I shouldn't have said anything."

"No, no, it's all right. She was—" He stopped and leaned back as Kristi arrived with the lunches.

She set Casey's hamburger platter down, then slapped an enormous salad in front of her dad, followed by a bottle of dressing. "There. Put on your own dressing if you're going to complain." With another narrowed-eye look at Casey, she stalked away.

Todd winced.

"Should I sit at another table?" Casey asked.

"No." He held up his hands. "No, if anybody moves, it should be me. But there's no reason for it. It's fine."

They looked over at the counter, where Kristi was scrubbing furiously with a dishrag, her eyes shooting darts toward their table.

"You sure?" Casey wasn't.

"I'm sure." He tipped the bottle to drip dressing onto his salad.

Casey slid the pickles off of her hamburger and placed them on the side of her plate. She didn't think she should ask him to resume where he'd left off talking, as it obviously disturbed him.

"Tell me about Eric," she said instead.

A glob of salad dressing landed on his salad, and he tried to scoop it back up with a spoon. "I'm not sure what was going on with them."

"Who?"

The tips of his ears went red. "Eric and Ellen. Isn't that who we were talking about?"

She blinked, then filled a few seconds putting ketchup on her plate. She dipped a fry and held it. "I guess so. But I was just wondering about Eric—why he left, and why he came back."

"Oh." He let out a breath, a smile flickering across his mouth. "That's easy. He left, going down to Louisville, to get away from his family. And he came back to deal with them."

Casey held the fry halfway to her mouth. "To deal with them? What do you mean?"

"Well, his dad's not exactly the most popular guy in town, so Eric had some major fences to mend."

"People don't like his father? Why?"

"Why do you think?" Todd gave a half-hearted laugh. "Because he's getting ready to put this entire town out of work."

Chapter Twenty-one

Eric's father was *Karl Willems?* The CEO of HomeMaker? The man who saw Becca's pretty face and didn't *remember* it?

Casey sat astride her bike outside the diner, a bag of leftovers dangling from the handlebars. Once Todd had hit her with that bombshell, she'd lost her appetite again. He'd finished up his salad, his natural lethargy kicking in so they didn't have to talk, and left his daughter a huge tip, paying also for Casey's lunch.

It made sense, Karl being Eric's dad. It explained Eric's feeling of protectiveness of the townspeople, his disdain for Karl Willems, and even his presence at HomeMaker, when Casey had ridden over the day before. It *didn't* explain why he hadn't told her. But then, she could make a guess at that.

Sliding her doggie bag to the middle of the handlebars for better balance, Casey thoughtfully rode toward the B & B. Poor Eric. He comes home, most likely to try to ease some of the pain his father has caused, only to fall in love with a HomeMaker employee who subsequently is fired, and then dies. Whether she committed suicide or not wasn't irrelevant, of course, but whether it was by her own hand or someone else's, the end result was the same. The tricky part was that if she *did* kill herself, not only was that hugely horrible, but it meant that Eric's father had essentially killed her.

Casey shook her head, but stopped quickly, as it made her wobble, and she hit a pothole, sending her almost into the path of a car traveling toward her. A Bug. She stopped before she crashed into the curb.

Leila screeched to a halt and glared at her through the windshield. She rolled down her window. "Why don't you watch where you're going?"

"Sorry." Casey held up a hand. "Lost control for a second."

Leila looked in her rearview mirror, but no one was coming. "What are you doing here, anyway?"

Everyone was so concerned about that.

"Just had lunch at the diner."

"I don't mean that. I mean here in Clymer. We don't need you."

Casey sighed. "I'm just traveling through."

"Well, then, why don't you keep on going? We'll find someone else for the play. That lady that was there last night."

Casey nodded. "I appreciate the thought you've put into it."

The girl frowned, obviously not sure whether Casey was being sincere or not. "Eric just lost his girlfriend, you know."

"Yes."

"So it's not fair, what you're doing."

"What am I doing?"

She rolled her eyes. "Going *after* him, of course. You should just leave him alone."

"I'm not—"

But a car was coming, and Leila gunned her engine, her tires squealing as she raced away. Casey wondered if the girl knew how to drive without burning rubber.

Letting Leila go with a shake of her head, Casey's mind went back to the blow she'd just been given. *Eric was Karl Willems' son?* It just didn't seem possible.

Casey took a turn up an alley she thought would be a shortcut back to The Nesting Place. But she'd turned off a road too early, and the alley deadended at someone's garage. Turning around, she took the next road to the left, and rode on the sidewalk until she found the next alley. This one went through farther, taking her behind Home Sweet Home, and eventually past the theater.

The theater. Where she'd felt closer to Reuben than she had in some time.

She jerked to a stop, made a U-turn, and pedaled back toward the Albion.

The parking spaces in the back were empty, and the heavy steel door was locked. She walked her bike around to the front of the building and parked the bike just off the sidewalk, underneath the marquee. These doors were open.

Stepping into the lobby she took a deep breath, wallowing in the familiar smells of dust and old wood. Newer theaters might have better technology—although not always—but nothing could beat the atmosphere of a space that had seen a multitude of performances. No matter that this place had shown movies for years. It was still a performance space, where people came to escape from reality, if only for a couple of hours.

The theater was dark except for one blue light on the stage, lit to prevent people from falling off the edge in the dark. Casey walked down the aisle, running her hand along the tops of the seats, until she stood before the stage. The polished wood on the stage floor was smooth under her fingers, and she placed her palms face down, searching for any soul, any life that had been left by actors in bygone days.

She propelled herself onto the stage, landing easily on the balls of her feet. She jumped up and took that into a spin, parrying across the stage, remembering choreography from one of her best attempts at stage combat. *Romeo and Juliet.*

A pencil lay in the dusty wings of the stage, and she grabbed it, holding it up like a sword.

"Draw, if you be men."

With a yell she threw herself toward center stage, parrying, slicing, stabbing, spinning, twirling, feinting…until her breaths grew deep and fast, and sweat stood out on her face. A flat slap at Abraham, a thrust toward Balthasar…

"*Part, fools!*" she said as Benvolio. "*Put up your swords; you know not what you do.*"

She twisted her arm, her pencil beaten down by Benvolio's sword, and stood in the center of the stage, imagining the lights on full. Ambers, and blues, and yellows. She closed her eyes.

And heard a door open.

With a few strides she was behind the curtain. Why she felt the need to hide, she wasn't sure, but the urge was so strong it was almost suffocating. The curtain bunched at the side of the stage, and she squeezed behind the folds, wincing at the thought of her body oils touching the expensive fabric.

"So, this is your new digs?" The voice was raw. Unrefined. Too close. "Not as nice as the last, but hey, not everything can be Derby City."

"It suffices." Thomas. Casey would know that voice anywhere now.

"Oh, it suffices. Hear that Bone? It *suffices*. Glad you haven't lost those big words since coming back to Buttfuck, Ohio."

"Taffy…"

"Oh, sorry, Thomas. *Sorry*. Didn't mean to offend your *sensibilities*."

They were silent for a few beats.

"So, Tommy boy," Taffy said. "Is it here?"

"No, it's not here, Taffy. I told you. I don't have it."

"But you're getting it."

"Soon. I *told* you."

"Oh." Taffy laughed. "You told me. That's right. Ain't that right, Bone?"

A muffled grunt. Bone, Casey guessed.

"I sure hope it's coming soon, Tommy, because some people are getting a little concerned that it's taking so long. They want us to make sure it's not that you've forgotten."

"You don't have to threaten me. Or send other people after me, for God's sake. My word is good."

"Oh, your word is good. Too bad your luck ain't good, too!" He laughed again, a full belly laugh this time. The laughter quickly died out, to be replaced by the same raw timbre as before. "And we're not sending other people after you, Tommy boy. If you've got me and Bone, who else do you need?"

Thomas was silent.

"I asked you a question," Taffy said. "You need reminding other than me and Bone? You need someone else? Cause if you do, we can arrange that."

"No, Taffy. No, I don't. I just thought…"

"What?"

"Nothing. Nothing, Taffy. I'll get it for you. Soon."

Taffy grunted. "So why don't you show us your office?"

"I don't really have an—"

"You've got to be kidding me. No office for the hotshot director?"

Casey peeked out the edge of the curtain, and saw the man Taffy on the audience level, looking over at Thomas. Thomas faced away from her, so she had a good look at the other guy. Big. Thick. Uncomfortable. She watched him as he talked, his eyes narrowed at Thomas, even while his voice held its mocking tone.

Gradually, however, Casey's focus shifted as she noticed movement on the other side of the stage. Another man. Bone, probably. Walking slowly around the stage, peering into the wings, stopping between each of the legs, the partitions made by narrower curtains to hide the rigging and actors before their entrances. Slowly he made his way across the back of the stage, looking up at the flyrails, and back toward the exits. She couldn't see his face, as his back was to her, but she could see his outline. Lean. Strong. Hungry.

Casey eased back behind the curtain and concentrated on stilling her body. Her breathing was silent, and her heartbeat slowed, pulsing…pulsing…pulsing…

She heard a footfall. A bare whisper against the wooden floor. She kept her calm, watching for the edge of her curtain to twitch. She prepared herself, easing her weight onto her right leg, deciding which way she'd attack. A quick kick to the inner thigh to debilitate, then a sprint to the exit.

She wasn't proud.

She held the pencil in her fingers, point up. A weapon, if necessary. She hoped she didn't need it.

And then she could sense him. He stood on the other side of the curtain. Listening. Breathing. Sensing.

Casey gripped the pencil. Clenched her teeth.

"Bone! Let's go. Tommy boy here's given us his word. We have to trust him, don't we? At least for another day?"

Casey felt the man's distraction, and his hesitation. She waited, blinking as if in slo-mo, her eyes focused on the curtain for any sudden movement. But then his feet scuffed the floor. He stepped away.

"Come on, Tommy boy," Taffy said. Casey heard what must've been a slap to Thomas' shoulder. "Get me out of this musty hole. I'm gonna be sneezing all the way back to L'ville. Bone!"

A few moments more, and Casey heard Bone jumping lightly from the stage. Casey eased down so her head was on the floor, and peeked out the crack under the curtain. The three men were making their way back up the aisle, toward the double doors. When they reached them, Taffy opened the door, gesturing grandly for Thomas to precede him. He stepped in front of Bone, following Thomas. Bone hesitated in the doorway, and turned to look back at the stage. Casey froze, narrowing her eyes so the blue light wouldn't reflect on them.

Bone pivoted slowly on his heel, taking in every inch of the stage.

And then he turned around, and left.

Chapter Twenty-two

Casey waited fifteen minutes, and then five more, before easing out from behind the curtain, staying in the shadow of the wings. She walked quickly to the back exit and pushed the bar, heaving a sigh of relief when the door opened. She scooted out the door and peered around the corner of the building. No one there. Feeling conspicuous in the daylight, she walked normally toward the front of the theater. She sensed no one waiting, and found herself to be correct. Looking up and down the street she didn't see Thomas' car or any others that looked out of place.

Grabbing her bike, she left, pedaling hard. It was difficult to concentrate on riding the rest of the way back to The Nesting Place, what with watching out for the men, and Eric's paternity resurfacing in her mind.

She found Lillian and Rosemary finishing their lunch. She looked at them, trying to get her mind around the domestic vision of food and conversation with the image of Thomas and the men still resonating in her mind.

"Hungry, dear?" Rosemary asked.

Casey held up her bag. "Already ate. Can I put my leftovers in your fridge?"

"Of course," Lillian said. "Wherever there's room. Just move things around how you need to."

Casey found a spot on the bottom shelf, beside a bag bursting with Romaine lettuce. She closed the door and stood there for a moment, thinking.

"If Karl Willems is Eric's father," she said, "then why is Eric's last name VanDiepenbos?"

Rosemary's mouth dropped open, and Lillian's napkin fluttered to the floor. Casey went over to retrieve it. Lillian took it back, but averted her eyes.

"I think you'd better have a seat, darling," Rosemary said.

Casey pulled out the third chair and sat.

Rosemary cleared her throat. "When Eric was twelve, he and his mother left his father."

"Right. He told me that. Or at least that his parents got divorced."

"Did he also tell you he swore never to speak to his father again?"

"Um. No."

"Well, as his mother didn't really want to talk to her ex-husband anymore, either, she really couldn't find fault with it. And when she took back her maiden name, well, Eric took it, too."

"So VanDiepenbos was his mother's name?"

"Exactly. He's always been closer to her than to his father, but even with that..." She shrugged.

Casey understood. "Even with that, he left town. To get away from his father."

"Sure, partly. Also partly to go to college. But he stayed away long after that. Some because there's really not much theater here in Clymer—" she gave a little snort "—but also because he just needed to get away from the stress of being Karl Willems' son. Even if you'd never know it from watching."

Casey was trying to digest all of this when Lillian abruptly stood up and left the room.

Casey sighed. "I'm sorry. I didn't mean to spoil your lunch."

"No, no." Rosemary patted her arm. "You did no such thing. And then," she continued, "Karl remarried about a year ago. Eric thought it was best if he came back to make sure his mother was still being taken care of, and just stayed on when everything began happening with HomeMaker. Thoughtful of him, but unnecessary, really."

Lillian returned with a piece of paper. "I think it's about time you filled out our paperwork, Casey." She laid the form on the table.

Casey's face went hot. "I'm really sorry. If I said something—"

Lillian put a pen down beside the paper. "Just fill it out, sweetheart."

With a trembling hand, Casey picked up the pen. She hadn't meant to make them mad. Were they going to kick her out? She'd thought they were getting along well. It served her right, allowing herself to get close to people again. Trying to come in here and dissect a town that had gone on by itself for many years before she'd arrived.

Sighing, Casey lifted her pen to the paper, reading the letterhead. And stopped. *The Nesting Place*, the page said. *Rosemary Pond and Lillian VanDiepenbos, Proprietors.*

Casey gasped, the pen falling from her fingers, and looked over at Lillian, who'd resumed her seat. "*You're* Eric's mother?"

The side of Lillian's mouth twitched. "I am. And proud to be."

"But that also means—"

"I was married to Karl Willems. Yes. I'm not quite so proud of that."

A burst of laughter came from Casey's mouth, and she slapped a hand over her mouth. "I'm sorry. That was... It's really not..."

"I know, dear. It *is* a surprise." She slipped the paper out from under Casey's hand.

Casey grabbed for it. "I really do need to fill that out."

"There's plenty of time for that," Rosemary said. "Now, I'm going to hapkido. Are you coming along?"

Casey had forgotten the invitation. She glanced at the clock, and then at Lillian. "I'm meeting Eric here at two-thirty, to go get food for tonight's supper. I need to be back by then."

"Oh, we'll make sure of it," Rosemary said. "Now, come along. I think I have something you can wear."

Casey slid her chair back. "No need. I have my own."

Rosemary smiled. "Of course you do. Can we leave in ten minutes?"

Casey stopped in the doorway. "Lillian, why didn't you tell me before? That you're Eric's mother?"

Lillian looked down at the table. "Eric's parentage has brought him nothing but problems. I didn't see any reason to muddy the waters. Especially since..." She stopped.

"Since you didn't know how long I'd be sticking around."

Lillian shrugged.

Casey went upstairs to her room, half expecting Death to be there, gloating about Casey's newfound knowledge of Eric, but the only one around was the cat, who sat on a chair across from Casey's room, staring at the doorknob. Casey shook her head and entered, glad she had the place to herself. Going straight to the wardrobe, she pulled out her Dobak and set it on the bed. She put her hair up in a knot, tucked her Dobak under her arm, and went back downstairs.

Rosemary joined her in the front room several minutes later, already wearing her uniform. "I don't like to bother with changing there," she said. "It's much easier this way."

Casey shrugged. "But don't you get your car all sweaty on the way home?"

Rosemary laughed. "Honey, I don't work *that* hard. Now, come along."

Casey stood beside the Civic, focusing her thoughts, telling herself she could actually get in the vehicle.

"Are you feeling all right, sweetheart?" Rosemary watched her over the top of the car.

Casey took a deep breath and opened the door, jerking back at the sight of Death in the back seat, waving a jaunty hello with a bottle of Mountain Dew. Casey ground her teeth, gave Death a good glare, and slid into the passenger seat. She ignored the back seat and thought of other things, such as the fact that Lillian's connection to Karl Willems made sense of some things, like how the women could afford the renovations on the house, and that enormous Pegasus Orion in the garage. Although she had yet to see the ladies drive it, or even acknowledge its presence.

Rosemary plucked her keys from the driver's seat and slid one into the ignition. "We shocked you with that one, didn't we? Lillian's relationship with Karl really isn't one she talks about."

"I can understand." A thought struck her. "Is that why people didn't think Ellen's children should come live with you?"

Rosemary's lips tightened. "Yes. Not that it should make any difference, since Karl is not a part of our lives at *all...*" She turned the key.

"Rosemary."

"Yes?"

"Does no one here lock their cars?"

Rosemary laughed. "What?"

"You. Eric. Leila. You leave your car keys on the driver's seat."

"And?"

"Well, anybody could take them."

"And do what? Drive the car to the other side of town, where everyone and his mother would know whose car it was?"

She had a point.

They drove through Clymer, Casey keeping a lookout for Thomas and the two men. There was no sign of them. Rosemary, oblivious to Casey's interest in passing cars, drove several miles over the speed limit toward the interchange at the highway. When they got parallel to HomeMaker, Rosemary made a show of pulling her visor to the side window, blocking her view.

"It's not the people, of course," she said, "that I'm trying to avoid. Other than the one. But just seeing that place makes me want to throw things."

Casey held her hands in her lap and said nothing, trying not to think about the fact that she was heading onto a highway in a car. Especially a car that was careening along with no respect for traffic or speed.

"Ellen was such a sweetheart," Rosemary said, sighing. "We really thought she and Eric... But of course it's not to be. He'll have to find someone else." Her eyes flicked toward Casey, who leaned back in surprise.

"Oh. Well. He's pretty young, isn't he? He has lots of time."

"Um-hmmm." Rosemary looked back at the road. "And I think it will take him a while to get over Ellen. This past week he's had a hard time of it, and I don't see it getting easier any time soon."

"Yes," Casey said. "It takes a while."

Rosemary gave Casey another speculative look, but Casey turned to gaze out of the window. The Ohio soybean and corn crops were just about ready for harvesting now, golden in the fields. Tomatoes, red and ripening, dotted the lush green rows. Thousands upon thousands of plants, waiting for harvest.

"If Ellen didn't…take her own life," Casey said, glancing into the backseat, at Death, who was actually paying attention. "Who would've? It sounds like everyone liked her."

Rosemary blinked quickly, and raised a finger to her eye. "There was no reason *not* to like her. She was kind, honest, a good worker… Not that most people weren't who got laid off, but someone in her position…"

"Which was what?"

"Administrative staff. They let about half of them go at the same time as the assembly line got cut."

"So she worked in the front office?"

Rosemary's knuckles whitened on the steering wheel. "Right outside the door of the man we don't like to talk about."

"She was Karl Willems' *secretary*? And he *fired* her?"

"No. No, she wasn't his secretary. She was just one of his 'office girls,' as he called them." Rosemary frowned. "I'm pretty sure he knew her name. At least she said he called her 'Ellen' once."

Casey gripped her thighs, trying to come to terms with this man who had no clue. She shook her head, looking straight ahead, and then stopped. "But why?"

"Why what?"

"Why would Lillian marry someone like him?"

Rosemary smiled sadly. "She's not so young anymore, you know."

"She was when she married him."

"Right. And he was, too. Young and funny and smart…"

"You knew him then?"

Rosemary gave a chuckle. "Oh, I sure did. Knew him very well."

"Don't tell me you're Thomas' mother?" She looked back at Death, who grinned impishly.

"Thomas?" Rosemary said. "Thomas Black, the play director?"

"Yes. Eric said his parents and Thomas' were good friends."

Rosemary let out a whoop of laughter and slapped her hand on the steering wheel. "Oh, goodness, no. If I'd been Thomas' mother perhaps he wouldn't be the man he is today."

"You mean he'd be nice?" *And not connected with nasty members of society?*

Rosemary hooted again. "Oh, Casey, darling, you're killing me." As soon as the words left her mouth she sobered, sighing and brushing a hand across her forehead. "I'm sorry. I'm so sorry. The things I say…"

"It's just an expression. You didn't mean anything by it."

"Hmphf."

They drove in silence for a few minutes.

"So how *did* you know Karl Willems when he was young?" Casey finally asked.

"Oh," Rosemary said. "You know. He's my brother."

Casey's shocked reply was cut short as Rosemary swung off an exit, spinning around the ramp with dizzying speed. Casey couldn't speak, as she was concentrating on hanging on and not throwing up.

They drove through quiet smalltown streets until Rosemary pointed a scarlet fingernail at an old brick building. "There it is. It doesn't look like much, but it's cheap rent, from what Mr. Damon tells me." She grinned, and rocketed into a parking space in front of a dusty window with an understated sign proclaiming,

"Cole Damon Hapkido." Casey unlatched her fingers from the dashboard, gathered her things together, and got out of the car. Death remained seated, as did Rosemary.

"You coming in?" Casey asked Death.

Rosemary let out a whoosh of air. "I need a minute to catch my breath."

Death just smiled.

Casey shut her door and waited by the front of the car until Rosemary joined her, leading her to the door of the building. "C'mon. I'm dying to introduce you to my teacher."

Looking back, Casey could see Death, now in the driver's seat, giving her a double thumbs-up.

Chapter Twenty-three

Casey and Rosemary climbed the creaky wooden steps to the third floor, passing an old-fashioned weight room and a dance academy full of trophies, dance clothes, and waiting mothers.

Finally, on the third floor, Rosemary entered a large square room. The wooden floor was covered with a mat, along with a cluster of children in Dobaks and protective head gear. A man stood over them as they sparred in pairs.

"Our teacher," Rosemary sighed.

The man, tall and thick, wore all black, including his thick black belt, and his feet were bare. His long black hair lay against his back in a ponytail, pulled away from his broad face. Curly hair sprouted from the V of his jacket, and Casey could feel his confidence from across the room.

Casey smiled to herself. *So that's why Rosemary comes here.*

"The changing room is over here." Rosemary skirted the mat, showing Casey to a wooden door. "Anybody in there?" Without waiting for an answer, she flung it open, revealing a teenaged boy, complete in a Dobak, a red belt wrapped around his waist.

"Sorry!" Rosemary said. "You're done, right?"

He scuttled out.

Rosemary waved Casey in. "All yours."

Casey shut the door behind her and locked it, breathing in the smell of the *dojang*. Sweat. Effort. Composure. She changed, hanging her clothes on a hook on the wall.

Walking barefoot back into the classroom, she eyed the other students who would be participating in the class. The children were done now, one black belt student helping to remove their helmets and foot protection. On the outside of the mat stood several adults in hapkido uniforms—two more men with black belts, a few teenage boys with various colored belts, and Rosemary, resplendent in her yellow belt, one level up from the white Casey was wearing.

"If you're not experienced at this you can just watch," Rosemary said.

"Oh," Casey said. "I'll be all right."

She looked away to find the instructor studying her from across the room. She kept eye contact, and he moved, catlike, across the mat to stand in front of her.

"My friend," Rosemary breathed. "Casey."

He tipped his head in a bow. "Cole Damon."

Casey bowed back. "A pleasure to meet you, sir."

"Is this your first time?" He indicated her white belt.

"I have some experience, sir."

"I see." He waited for her to explain.

She didn't.

"Welcome to our class," he said. "Participate as you are able."

"Thank you, sir."

He bowed again and walked to the front of the class.

"Aaaah," Rosemary sighed.

"Two lines," Mr. Damon said.

Casey bowed to the mat before following Rosemary to the back row, where she took the far right hand corner, the spot for the lowest belt.

"*Chung Jah*," the instructor said.

The class turned to the American flag and dropped to their knees.

"*Kukki-Eh Dehe Kyong Ye*," he said.

They bowed to the flag.

"*Wonki-Eh Dehe Kyong Ye*."

They bowed to the Association flag.

"*Kwan Jang Nim Ke Kyong Ye,*" a black belt said.

They turned and bowed to the instructor.

"*Yu Dahn Jah Kyong Ye,*" a colored belt said.

They bowed to the black belts.

"*Sooriun Guht,*" Damon said.

They began.

Casey worked through the jumping jacks, push-ups, sit-ups, and squats on auto-pilot, her body taking over for her brain. She dropped, jumped, crunched, and stretched, and only when Damon instructed them to stop did she realize the other colored belts were watching her with something that resembled fear.

Damon, standing in front of the class, was not afraid. A smile tickled the side of his mouth. He sent them to do kicks by the wall, and Casey was glad to evade his eyes. Trying to put him out of her mind, she concentrated on the swing of her legs, and the force of her kicks.

After a few more strength-training exercises, Damon called for the extra mats. Casey, as the lowest belt there, helped Rosemary and the teenage boys pull the cushioning to the center of the room.

"Forward rolls," Damon said.

They took turns at corners, rolling one after the other, until he changed instructions. They moved from front rolls to side rolls, from backward rolls to side falls. Damon stopped them. "Dives."

He crouched down on the edge of the mat.

"Oh, lord," Rosemary muttered. "I hate these. I always end up doing push-ups."

This time was no exception, as her dive over Damon ended with her walloping him in the side. She moved over to the side for her consequence.

Damon peered up at Casey, from where he waited. She ran to him lightly, diving over him and rolling into a crouch without much effort.

"Another," Damon said.

One of the black belts joined him on the floor, on the far side, and the line went through again, diving and rolling. Rosemary, after another failed attempt, joined the two on the floor.

"Now," Damon said to Casey.

She dove and rolled.

"Another," Damon said, adding another student to the line.

They dove.

"Another," Damon said.

Five on the ground. Only Casey, a black belt, and one of the coloreds left to go.

The black belt dove, nicking his fellow black belt with a foot. He dropped for push-ups. The colored belt pretty much crushed the last in the line, and headed for the floor.

"Go," Damon said.

Casey breathed in. Breathed out. Ran. Dove. Rolled into a squat.

Damon sat up, looking at Casey. "Man in the Middle."

A black belt stepped into the center of the mat, while the rest took places around the edge. One of the other black belts went after the middle man with a kick. The middle man fended him off, taking him to his knees. Another attacked, ending up on his face. Rosemary stepped up, her fist out, and the black belt gently lowered her to the mat.

Damon nodded at Casey. She attacked from the side, a kick to the black belt's ribs. He grabbed her leg, flipping and pinning her. She hopped up.

Each student took a turn defending against attackers. Finally, it was Casey's turn. She stepped to the middle, arms loose at her sides, nerves tingling.

She heard the first one coming from the back, felt his arm coming around her throat. She positioned her hip under his waist, lifted, and flung him to the ground, circling around, ready for the next.

He came from the front, fist to her face. She fended off the punch, twisting his arm to take him down.

Another from the back, who ended up on his side.

From the front.

From the side.

Rosemary came at her, eyes sparkling, and Casey twisted her to the floor.

Finally, it was Damon's turn.

He struck without warning, an open hand to her jaw. She parried his arm away, punched twice in his ribs, deflected his arm with her elbow and swung it backward, enclosing his wrist in her hand and twisting his arm. He dropped to his knees and she pulled him forward, spinning him to the ground, a knee on his shoulder, his hand twisted backward, his face in the mat.

He slapped the mat twice with his free hand.

She let go.

He stood, that same smile on his lips, and bowed slightly. Casey bowed back.

"Drink," he said.

The others peeled off, toward the drinking fountain, but kept their attention on Casey and Damon, who stood eye to eye on the mat.

"You have studied before," Damon said.

"Yes, sir."

"You wear a white belt."

"Out of respect for your *dojang*, sir."

He nodded. "Where did you study?"

She hesitated. "At a reputable school, sir."

"Yes. I see that." He bowed again. "A drink."

"Yes, sir."

She hadn't brought a water bottle, but found an old drinking fountain in the hallway.

"What was *that*?" Rosemary screeched in her ear.

Casey shrugged.

"You didn't tell me you were a *black belt*."

Casey stood up, wiping her mouth with her sleeve. "It's white today."

Rosemary guffawed. "Don't you *give* me that." She put a hand to her forehead. "*You've had some experience*, you told him. *Some experience* meaning you've taken on the likes of Bruce Lee?"

"Bruce Lee doesn't practice true hapkido," Casey said.

Rosemary rolled her eyes.

Casey walked back into the room and bowed to the mat before stepping on.

"Techniques," Damon said. "Pair up. Taylor." He spoke to a black belt. "You're with her." He indicated Casey.

"Yes, sir."

Casey and her partner didn't so much practice techniques as spar, working each other through various forms and patterns. Sweat ran in rivulets down Casey's face as she circled, struck, and parried, and her jacket clung to her back. She could feel the moves coming back, as if they'd never left, as if she'd been keeping them at bay for just this moment.

"Enough," Damon finally said. "*Hyung.*"

Casey sighed, shaking out her limbs, and lined up in the back row, where she'd begun class. All eight students began the forms, patterns of movement memorized and practiced time and again. By the fifth form only she and the black belts remained, all of them moving, striking, blocking...dancing together.

When they'd finished the patterns the rest of the belts joined them, and they repeated the bowing ceremony, bowing to the flags, to Damon, to the black belts. Casey stood, walked off the mat, and turned, bowing to it.

"I know your teacher," Damon said quietly.

She looked up.

"Doug Custer and I studied together under Master Timmerman."

She cleared her throat, wanting to run. It had been a mistake to come here.

"Your secret is safe," Damon said. "Whatever it is."

She looked at the floor, then back at his piercing eyes. "How could you tell?"

"That you have a secret?"

"That I studied with Master Custer."

He smiled. "You spread your fingers on your palm strikes. You circle after an attack. The signs are there."

Casey laughed under her breath. "I guess I'm not as smart as I thought I was, coming here."

He shook his head. "He will not know I have seen you." He cocked an eyebrow at her. "If that is what you wish."

"It is."

He glanced at the white belt. "It doesn't work for you. If you come back, wear your real belt."

"Yes, sir." She bowed, and stepped away.

"Casey."

She turned back.

"You have a talent not many possess. You must realize that."

"Thank you, sir."

He looked at her a moment longer before dismissing her with a nod.

She escaped to the dressing room, but it was locked. She stood in the corner of the waiting area, arms crossed, looking at the floor, until the three black belts emerged. One paused, but she eased past him, into the changing room, where she closed and locked the door. She dropped to the bench and clutched her hands together between her knees, to keep them from shaking.

Damon knew who she was. If not entirely, or completely, he'd recognized her form. Her essence. When she stopped shaking enough to stand she changed quickly, left the room, and headed down the stairs and out to Rosemary's car without a backward glance.

Rosemary soon followed, peering at Casey over the top of her car. "*You…*" She shook her head.

Casey looked away, the confidence of the classroom fading as she considered getting back into the car.

"So what do you think of Master Damon?" Rosemary asked.

Casey puffed out her cheeks. "He's too smart."

Rosemary laughed, the tinkling sound echoing from the buildings. "Smart?"

"He is."

"Of course he is. But more than that…" She leaned over the car, lowering her voice. "He's a *dreamboat*."

Casey looked at Rosemary, at her eyes sparkling under her orange hair, and shook her head. What some women wouldn't do for a man.

Chapter Twenty-four

"Hey, Casey."

"Eric."

He sat on the front porch with his mother, his fingers tapping the arms of the rocker. When Casey got to the top of the steps, he stood. "So. Are you ready to go?"

"In a minute. Let me take this upstairs." She indicated her Dobak, which lay damp and smelly in her arms.

"Here," Lillian said, holding out her arms. "I'll wash it."

Casey looked down at it. "You're sure?" And to Eric, "I really should take a shower."

Lillian smiled. "It's not the first time I've seen sweaty clothes."

Eric shrugged. "Or that I've smelled sweat."

"Well, okay. Thanks, Lillian. I appreciate it."

Lillian took the bundle. "Now you two go on. Don't want to keep the pizza folks waiting."

Eric held a hand out for Casey to precede him. She went down the steps, then turned around. "Thanks, Rosemary. That was…good, I guess."

Rosemary smiled. "Oh, it was good for me, too."

"Yeah." Casey shook her head, laughing. "I guess so."

Rosemary gave a hearty chuckle and plunked down in Eric's rocker. "Toodleoo. Have a fun time!"

Casey shook her head and walked the rest of the way to the Camry, where Eric was waiting in the driver's seat. Casey gritted her teeth, opened the door, and forced herself to sit.

She was traveling in way too many cars these days.

She shut the door. "I hope you're a better driver than Rosemary."

"Oh, much better. But then, most people are."

Casey had to agree.

They pulled away from the curb, and Casey lifted her hand to the two women, who waved from the porch. She rested her head against the headrest, closing her eyes.

"I'm sorry," Eric said.

She kept her eyes closed. "For what?" Although she knew.

"For not telling you. You know, about my family…" His voice drifted off.

She rolled her head to the left and looked at him. "You didn't *have* to tell me."

"But—"

"What have I told you?"

He glanced at her. "You mean about yourself?"

"Yes."

He bit his lip, thinking. Finally, his face cleared, and he smiled. "That your name is Casey Smith."

"Right. Anything else?"

He gave a little laugh. "Not a thing."

She turned her head back to center, looking out the windshield. "So see? Nothing to be sorry about."

They drove quietly for several minutes. Eric really was a much better driver than Rosemary. Casey found herself drifting off.

"—and that's what confuses me."

Casey blinked. "I'm sorry. What?"

"Were you sleeping?"

She made a face. "I didn't have the greatest night."

"Yeah. I heard. But then, I guess you're used to sleeping on the ground." He looked at her expectantly.

"Sometimes. But their ground must be extra hard." She didn't need to tell him it wasn't the ground that caused the problems. She glanced into the back seat, but Death wasn't there. "So what were you saying?"

"That Ellen's…death… That she wasn't without hope. In fact, she was determined to get through it all. Had actually told me just the evening before that everyone would soon be working again."

"At HomeMaker?"

"I'm not sure. But I thought that's what she meant."

"But how?"

He shrugged, his mouth forming a hard line. "She never got to tell me."

They went around a corner and Casey pulled down the visor, the sun having momentarily blinded her. "Not a hint?"

"Just that things weren't as bad for us as we all thought they were."

Casey flinched. Well-meaning people—at least *they* thought they were well-meaning—said the same to her during those first several months. She wasn't sure how they thought things could be any *worse*, but she never bothered to ask.

"So did she mean things weren't as bad at HomeMaker itself? Or just within the town?"

"I really don't know, except she wasn't exactly happy about it. I mean, she was happy the town would be working, but something about it upset her."

They rode in silence again, but this time Casey didn't fall asleep.

"My dad never tells me anything," Eric said.

"About work?"

"About *anything*. He used to."

"Before you went away? Or before your parents got divorced?"

He flicked her a glance. "Some when I was little. But he seemed to think, later on, that HomeMaker was something I'd be interested in."

"I thought you'd sworn never to talk to him again."

He shrugged. "I was twelve."

"So what he told you—did you want to hear it?"

He leaned to the side, resting his left arm on the door, driving with his right. "That's the thing. The stuff he'd tell me…"

"Like what?"

"I'm sure you can guess. It was all about the money. It *always* was."

"That's not what Rosemary says."

"What?"

"She says he started out funny and sweet. And something changed him."

"Yeah. A whiff of the green stuff."

Casey nodded. "Could've been that."

"It was." His face was still. Stony.

They were in town now, a slightly larger town than Clymer, boasting a whole row of restaurants, rather than the few Clymer had. The Pizzeria came up on their right, and Eric pulled around to the back of the building. "Want to help carry?"

"Of course." Casey undid her seatbelt, and got out of the car.

Eric tossed his keys on the seat and popped open his trunk before rapping his knuckles on the metal back door of the building. It opened with a scrape against the gravel.

"Hey, Eric." The woman, whose badge proclaimed her the shift manager, shoved a wedge under the door with her shoe. "We've got lots of pizzas for you today. A new kid came on board and can't for the life of him remember what to put on a Veggie Special."

"Well, thanks for hiring him," Eric said, grinning. "Oh, this is Casey. She's been helping out at Home Sweet Home."

The woman put out her hand, looked at it, and brushed it against her pants, leaving a floury smear. Casey took it when she held it back out. "Good to meet you."

"Likewise. So, come on in." She led them to a large refrigerator, shelved with vegetables, meats, yeast, and what looked like an entire twenty pound wheel of cheese. In the back corner was a freezer section, and when the manager opened that door, they saw three stacks of large and medium-sized pizzas, waiting for a purpose.

Eric whistled. "Wow, you aren't kidding. Your new kid must've been screwing up bigtime."

"Enough for two meals for your people, maybe."

"At least. We might have to throw a block party." He held out his hands. "Load me up."

The manager placed the first stack on his arms, almost up to his chin. "You got it?"

Eric mumbled something and did a three-point turn to exit the refrigerator.

Casey stepped up for the second load.

"You're not the same woman he came with the other week, are you?"

Casey blinked. "No."

"Didn't think so." She placed a few boxes on Casey's arms. "She told me she didn't think they'd be taking our pizzas for much longer. That I'd have to find a new charity. You know anything about that?"

Ellen. "No. I don't know anything."

"Seemed pretty sure of herself. Stopped talking when Eric came back in, and winked at me. Guess she didn't tell him." She gave Casey the rest of the stack.

Casey took out the load, lowering it gently to the trunk of Eric's car, on top of a clean tarp. Eric returned with the final boxes. They eyed their treasures.

"The folks always enjoy our pizza suppers," Eric said. "This week they might have it two days in a row."

Casey wasn't sure those people were in a position to actually *enjoy* anything, but she didn't say it.

With a wave the manager closed the back door, and Eric eased the trunk shut. "Mission accomplished. Shall we take it home?"

Home Sweet Home.

They got back into the car and Casey strapped herself in. *I'm almost getting used to this again. Riding in a car.*

"Smells good, even frozen," Eric said. "Make you hungry?"

She shook her head. "No."

"Yeah. Me, neither. I haven't been…it's been hard to eat this last week."

Casey remembered those days. No appetite. Ricky and her mother begging her to eat. Dwindling down to skin and bones. When she finally realized Death wasn't about to take her, she began to force it down. No taste, no appeal. Just sustenance.

"You do what you have to do," she said.

Eric cast her a curious glance, but didn't pry.

"You brought Ellen here," she said. "To get pizzas."

"Yes. Why?"

She told him what the manager had said.

Eric frowned. "So she really did think… Why didn't she tell me the details? What was she waiting for?"

"Maybe she only thought she had things figured out, and was waiting for confirmation."

"But what could it have been?" His voice was strained.

"Something with HomeMaker. It had to be."

Eric clenched his jaw. "If something was going on, there's at least one person who should know."

"But will he tell you?"

He gripped the wheel, his knuckles white. "I'm not going to give him a choice."

"Okay. Good. When are you going to ask him?"

He glanced at the clock on the dashboard. "If we get these pizzas in the refrigerator fast, we'll have about an hour before dinner set up."

"I can stay and get things started. That way you won't have to hurry back."

He gave her a startled look.

"What?"

"You won't come with me?"

"To talk to your father? Why?"

He shuddered. "He just…if I go by myself he'll shut me out. Or say he's too busy. Or something."

"But if I'm there he won't talk. He doesn't know me. He certainly wouldn't remember seeing me in the drugstore."

"You saw him?"

"Briefly."

They traveled in silence for several minutes, and soon they were in town, parking behind Home Sweet Home.

"Please?" Eric said.

Casey closed her eyes and pushed her hair back from her face, holding her head in her hands. She let them drop. "All right."

Together they crammed the pizzas into the refrigerator. Eric scrawled a quick note to Loretta, telling her to only use the number of pizzas necessary for one night, and that they would be back as soon as they could. He taped it to the front of the fridge.

"Okay," he said. "Let's go face the big, bad wolf."

"Grrr," Casey said.

Chapter Twenty-five

The inside of HomeMaker wasn't what Casey expected. Instead of a loud, chaotic atmosphere, smelling of chemicals and metal, what she and Eric walked into felt like the heart of an expensive hotel. Thick carpet, soft furniture, and what looked like original artwork on the ivory-painted walls. The receptionist, a middle-aged woman with gray hair curling gently around her face, sat behind a heavy wooden desk, wearing a headset. The name tent on the desk said, "Gloria."

Her face lit up when Eric walked in. "Mr. Eric! So good to see you. What brings you here today?" As she spoke she rifled through her appointment calendar. "I don't see you down for anything. Was someone to meet you in your office?"

His *office*?

Eric's face reddened, and he avoided Casey's eyes. "No, I was…is Mr. Willems in?"

Not his *father*, Casey noticed. But *Mr. Willems*.

The woman checked her phone console. "He's on a call right now, but he should be off soon, and he doesn't have anything else until the end of the day. I'll let his assistant know you're here. Should I also introduce your friend?" She looked meaningfully at Casey.

"Oh, um, this is Casey Smith. She's working with me at Home Sweet Home, and she's in the play."

"The play!" Gloria clasped her hands to her chest. "And how are rehearsals going?"

"Pretty well. We've had to…adjust."

Her face fell, and her mouth worked, as if wishing she could take back the question.

"Casey here is…filling in," Eric said. "She's an amazing actress."

"That's wonderful," Gloria said, offering Casey a wry smile. "I'm glad you could help out."

"Me, too," Casey said. Although she wasn't sure it was actually true.

"Oh!" Gloria said. "The light's off. One moment." She pushed a few buttons and talked quietly into her headset before turning to them. "You can go right on back, Mr. Eric. Nice to meet you, Ms. Smith."

Eric led Casey to a large door beside the desk. "You want to go first, or shall I?"

"Oh," Casey said. "Definitely you."

He gave a small laugh, but Casey knew he wasn't actually amused.

"Eric," she said quietly, as they went through the door. "You have an *office* here?"

"I told you. There was a time he thought I'd be interested…"

He led her into another room, this one with several desks, only two of them filled. Casey couldn't help but wonder which had been Ellen's.

The women at the desks looked up, each brightening at the sight of Eric, their eyes flicking briefly—and curiously—toward Casey.

"Hello, Yvonne. Kathy. How are you?"

Both said hello, they were fine.

"So, we're here to see my… Mr. Willems. We were told to come on back."

The women's demeanors changed at the mention of their boss, and they became suddenly more businesslike. Yvonne, the one closest to the door with Willems' name, stood up. "Yes, that's right…" She walked quickly to Willems' door, her shoes quiet on the carpet. She knocked lightly, and at his summons slipped into the office, holding the door closed loosely against her back. She came back out, her face a mask of professionalism. "He's ready for you."

"Thank you." Eric touched her shoulder lightly as he passed.

Casey pinched her lips together in a smile at the woman, but it wasn't returned.

Karl Willems was waiting for them in a high-backed office chair, elbows on the chair's arms, his fingers together. He watched as they walked across the expanse of office—at least fifteen steps just to reach the chairs in front of his desk—and pursed his lips as Eric pointed Casey to one seat, and sat himself in another. The desk was empty, save for pens and a metal letter opener in a wooden holder, one notebook, and a large crystal paperweight, with a butterfly forever doomed to display itself in death at the center of the cube.

"So." Willems looked hard at Eric, and even harder at Casey. "What brings you here?"

Eric swallowed audibly, and Casey leaned forward, offering moral support. He didn't look at her. "We've got some questions."

"All right, but first aren't you going to introduce your associate?"

Not friend. *Associate.*

"Oh, sure. This is Casey Smith. She works with me at Home Sweet Home."

"Ah, I see." His eyes narrowed as he turned to Casey. "Do you come from one of those large mission conglomerates? Go around the country to make sure the charities are functioning properly?"

Casey blinked. "No. No, I have nothing to do with that."

"Then…?" He spread his hands. "You're not one of the townspeople. I do know that."

"I'm—"

"She just moved here, Karl." Eric's face had turned hard. "She's not *from* anywhere."

Willems' lips twitched. "Really? Just dropped out of the sky?"

Eric shook his head briefly. "We're not here to discuss her, Karl. We're here to discuss—"

"Yes, what exactly *are* you here to discuss?"

He hadn't moved from his seat, but watched his son over the tips of his fingers, his eyes flashing. From amusement or anger, Casey wasn't sure.

"Last week," Eric said. "Before Ellen....died...she told me that things weren't as bad as they seemed. That everyone would soon have a job again."

Something flickered in Willems' eyes, but it was gone before Casey could determine what it meant.

"And you thought she meant here at HomeMaker?" Willems' voice was even. Smooth. Cool.

"Where else would she mean? It's not like any other big companies have moved in."

"No, they haven't. HomeMaker is all there is. It's too bad the union didn't remember that when they were making their demands."

Eric gripped the arms of his chair. "So what did she mean, Karl? How was HomeMaker going to give all of the jobs back?"

Willems regarded him for a few moments before leaning forward, placing his elbows and forearms flat on the desk. "You said yourself she didn't actually say it was HomeMaker she was talking about."

"No, but—"

"I can assure you, *son*, that things here have not changed. The books don't look any better, and the negotiations are over. The union lost."

"So no jobs are coming back?"

"And those still employed," Karl held out a hand, as if indicating the workers in his domain, "will soon be looking elsewhere. The girls in the front office, the assembly line, the drivers...all gone. We'll probably need to retain a few of the security guards to keep an eye on the building until we know what to do with it, but other than that…" He held his hands out again, in a gesture of helplessness.

"Ellen never talked to you?" Eric's voice was strained.

Willems smiled briefly. "Not about bringing back the jobs. At least, not within the past month."

"But she wouldn't—"

"Lie? Make you hopeful for something that's not going to happen? Take her own life?" He smiled sadly. "I would've hoped the answer to all of those things was 'no.' But it wasn't to be."

Casey's muscles tensed, and she fought back the words coming up her throat. How long would it take for her to round the desk—or simply jump over it—and punch that smirk off the man's face? Or simply pummel him with his own paperweight?

Death appeared suddenly behind Willems' chair, hands clutching the handle of a large scythe, the kind pictured in so many images of the Grim Reaper. The scythe was raised, poised to slash down, to take the life of Eric's father. Casey froze, her thoughts returning suddenly to the room, and the conversation.

"So is that all? " Willems said, not knowing how his life hung in the balance. "You came here with the empty words of a woman who knew nothing of the inner workings of this business." He indicated Casey with a tilt of his head. "And with another woman so new to this town I've never seen her before?"

Casey swallowed, trying to ignore the tableau before her. "But you have seen me."

Willems pulled his head back, as if surprised she could actually speak. "No. I haven't."

"Oh, yes," Casey said. "At the pharmacy the other day. You were picking up a prescription. One you pick up frequently. But you chose not to purchase a Hershey Bar with Almonds, even though it's your favorite. That's too bad. You never know when a chance for something sweet will be your last."

Death looked hopeful, raising the scythe a little higher, as if to strike.

Eric sat as still as his father, both men looking at Casey as if she'd actually attacked the man the way she'd wanted to.

She stood. "Come on, Eric. He's obviously not going to tell you anything. This is a waste of time."

Willems stayed seated, his eyes flashing. "Who *are* you?"

Casey's eyes flicked to Death, whose disappointment was evident.

"I am no one," she said. "But the people of this town…*they* are the ones that must be reckoned with. The ones whose faces you should see each night, the ones whose names should roll off your tongue, with sorrow that their lives have taken such a turn. And those who have died? It would be better if you wouldn't claim to know what they knew. The dead have a way of speaking the truth."

Narrowing her eyes, and giving Death a nod, Casey spun on her heel, and left.

Chapter Twenty-six

"My God," Eric said, seeming to mean the words as the prayer they were. "What was *that*?"

They were in his office, where he had pulled her after their exit from his father's presence. He'd shoved her onto a small couch, where she now sat shaking, her hands clutched together in her lap.

"I'm not sure. But aaah…" She shook her head once, hard. "He was so…so…"

"Infuriating? Pompous? Disgusting?"

Casey let out a short laugh, and Eric relaxed, sitting beside her and running a hand through his hair. "Wow, were you scary. It was like you were somewhere else for a minute. Or you'd been possessed by something. Shakespeare, maybe." He smiled stiffly.

Casey couldn't smile back, remembering the image of Death standing over Eric's father, waiting for Casey to lose control… She had a hard time looking at Eric, his eyes concerned and full of trust. "I sort of was. But I'm back now." She stood up and walked to the window, looking out. "There's something."

Eric came to stand beside her, joining her at the window. "What?"

"No, not out there. In here." She turned, indicating the room, the building. "He's hiding something."

Eric snorted. "He's always hiding something."

"Something about what Ellen said. I think she was telling you the truth."

"Of course she—"

"I don't mean she wasn't lying. I never thought that. I mean she was *right*. There was something that could've gotten these people their jobs back."

Eric tensed. "You really think so?"

Casey remembered that flicker in Willems' eyes, that split-second sign that there was a secret. "Yes."

Eric's face hardened. "Then we have to find out what it is. And we have to find out before..."

"Before it's too late and this place is closed down for good."

He nodded.

Casey looked at his desk. "What's on your computer?"

"The usual. Production details. Payroll. Employee records."

"Do you have access to everything?"

"I'm not sure."

"Find out."

He seated himself at his desk and turned on the computer. "I haven't used this in weeks."

Casey paced the office. "Ellen's desk."

He glanced up, his computer making the beeping and humming noises of booting up. "What about it?"

"Has it been cleaned out?"

"I'm sure it has. She left here months ago." He looked toward the door. "But we can check."

"I wouldn't know what to look for on there," Casey said, indicating Eric's monitor. "I'll go through Ellen's desk. If that's okay."

Eric's face had gone a bit gray with the past hour's events, but he stood and went to the door. "I'll need to tell Yvonne and Kathy. They won't like it, probably, but if I ask they won't make a fuss."

Casey followed him out to the office, where he explained to the two women that Casey would be searching Ellen's desk. He glanced nervously toward his father's door. "What are his plans the rest of the day?"

Yvonne didn't even have to look. "Nothing. I mean, he has no appointments. He could leave any time. If he sees..." The worry was easy to read on her face. She wanted to keep this job. Even if it was only for three more months.

Eric turned to Casey. "Maybe we'd better wait. Come back later."

She considered it. "But if there's anything there..."

"He's not going to do anything with Yvonne and Kathy sitting out here."

"And if he waits until they leave?"

Eric exhaled loudly, running a hand over his face. "If he comes out here he's going to be angry."

"He's already angry."

The two women were looking at them, fear apparent on their faces. Eric spoke to them gently. "She needs to look. It won't take long."

Yvonne grabbed a stack of papers. "I have things for him to go over and sign. I can keep him busy for about five minutes. Six or seven, maybe, at the most."

That would have to be enough.

Casey motioned Eric back to his office and stayed out of Willems' sightline as Yvonne knocked, opened the door, and entered, closing the door with a soft click. Kathy pointed out Ellen's desk and Casey raced to it, immediately turning on the computer. While it booted up she opened the drawers, beginning with the top middle and moving methodically down each side.

There was nothing there. No folders, no memos, not even a stray Post-It note. Quietly she slid each drawer out of its slot, looking under and over it, feeling into the space. Nothing.

She turned to the computer, searching for anything remotely personal. Again, nothing. The hard drive had been wiped clean of everything but boilerplate forms, the word processor, and the company logo. She glanced at the clock. Five minutes had already elapsed. The doorknob to Willems' office turned, and she ducked behind the desk.

"He'll be busy a few more minutes," Yvonne said quietly, once the door was closed. "That's all I can promise."

Casey sprang back into the seat and went to the search engine's history. Cleared. The bookmark column—empty.

Growling under her breath she flicked the computer off, slid the chair in place, and went to Eric's office door. "Thank you," she mouthed to the women.

They acknowledged her gratitude with obvious relief.

Eric looked up as she entered his office and closed the door behind her. "Anything?"

"Zip."

His shoulders sagged. "Nothing here, either. At least, that I know of. This stuff isn't exactly… I mean, I'm an *actor*."

Casey swiveled, leaning her hip on the desk. "It's too much to ask for it to be that easy. Is there any point in your looking further?"

Eric rested his elbows on his desk, his fingers twisting his hair until he looked like a mad scientist. He flicked a thumb toward the two secretaries. "If they knew something that would save their jobs they would have told somebody. Right?"

Casey rubbed her eyes with one hand, the other hand keeping her balanced on the desk. "Probably."

Eric sat back, checking his watch. "We need to go. Loretta and Johnny will be waiting." He stood up and pushed in his chair. "There's nothing here." His hands gripped the back of his chair. "Nothing but the livelihoods of hundreds of people in this town."

He looked at her bleakly, and Casey felt the sudden urge to smooth his hair and take him in her arms, comforting him. "Come on," she said, instead. "Let's go do the little we're able to. Thanks to you they'll at least have full bellies tonight."

He stood for a moment, head bowed, knuckles white on the chair. Finally he looked up, gave a ghost of a smile, and held out a hand. "Shall we?"

As they left he turned to look at his office once more, as if seeing what it could have been, before turning off the light.

Chapter Twenty-seven

Eric was right. The people really did seem to enjoy the dinner. Somehow just the sight of pizza rounds on the table made the room more festive. Not laugh-out-loud, party favor kind of festive, but a more subdued hum of contentment. Children took huge, sticky bites, cheese stringing from their mouths, while adults wandered from pizza to pizza, trying out varieties of Veggie Special. A few of the pies even featured pepperoni, that coveted pizza foundation.

To complement the main course, Loretta had tossed up a salad of slightly wilted greens, garnered from neighboring grocery stores for cheap, and the diners had their choice of several kinds of generic soft drinks. All the room needed, Casey thought, was a clown to pop out of the kitchen and perform bad party tricks.

"Nice," she told Eric at the kitchen door.

He didn't say, "I told you so."

The cheery atmosphere lasted until the pizza was gone—except for one forlorn piece missing half of its cheese—and the two-liter bottles were empty. Napkins lay strewn on the tables, and tomato sauce dotted the floors and the children.

But then reality came crashing down, and the look of quiet desperation began to leach back into the adults' eyes. The children, oblivious to the changing emotions, continued to skip or run around the room until their parents snagged them and pulled them, protesting, out of the building.

Eric closed the door behind the last of the diners, sagging against it. "At least," he said, picking up on their last conversation, "it was nice while it lasted."

Casey stooped to pick up a ragged piece of pepperoni, flattened to the floor. "You gave them a respite. You always do. It's important."

He didn't look at her, but shoved himself from the door, calling toward the kitchen. "Loretta! Is there enough left for supper tomorrow?"

"*Praise God*, there's plenty!" Her face, shiny with perspiration, appeared in the opening to the kitchen. "There's even enough for us each to have a couple of pieces tonight. *Hallelujah!*"

Eric waved her off. "I don't need any."

Loretta gasped, a hand to her chest. "I believe you do, young man, *thank you, Jesus!* You will sit down and eat the pizza our good Lord has provided for you. *Amen!*"

When Eric seemed ready to argue, Casey sat down across the table. "You're no good to anybody if you faint from hunger."

"But this pizza is for—"

"It's ready now, and she said there's enough for tomorrow." She tipped her head toward the front door. "They aren't hungry now."

Eric looked at the ceiling, took a breath, and let it out. "Fine. But I'm not going to enjoy it."

Casey blurted out a laugh, and though he fought it, Eric had to smile.

"Eric got us pizza!" Johnny bustled out from the kitchen and shoved Eric into his seat. "Pizza and the nice lady!" He beamed at Casey before dropping onto a folding chair.

Loretta brought out part of a Veggie Special, and the four of them made quick work of it, along with bowls of the wilted lettuce. Casey wouldn't have said she actually enjoyed it, but it was pretty good.

They cleaned up as much as they could before heading out for rehearsal, Eric quiet as they scrubbed tables and mopped the floor. Johnny and Loretta did their part in the kitchen, Loretta singing gospel songs, Johnny talking in streams about silverware, tomato sauce, and nice ladies, their dual monologues punctuated with the sounds of clanking dishes.

Casey worked with Eric, filling trash bags and brushing crumbs from the table. The sounds from the kitchen served as a comforting background, and she wasn't aware she was listening to the words until she heard Ellen's name.

"She was a nice lady, too," Johnny said.

"*Umm-hmmm, Praise God,*" Loretta sang, right in rhythm with her present melody.

"But I didn't like that man. He didn't look at my silverware."

"*Praise Jesus.*"

"I'm glad he doesn't come here anymore."

"*Thank the good Lord.*"

Casey jerked upward, listening, the trash bag held out in front of her. What man? She looked at Eric, but he either didn't hear the conversation, or was pretending not to.

"Why did he stop coming?" Johnny's voice was high with question.

"Don't know, baby. Maybe Eric knows, *thank you, Jesus.*"

Maybe Eric did know, but he wasn't saying.

"About that time," Eric said suddenly, thrusting a last wad of soggy napkins into the bag. "I'm going to go wash up."

Casey tied the bag, watching Eric go. By the time he was ready, she was waiting at the door.

"Drive or walk?" Eric said, still not looking directly at her.

"Oh, walk, definitely."

So they set out. Casey had been hot when returning from the *dojang*, so she had forgotten to grab her jacket at The Nesting Place afterward. She wished now that she was wearing it, and hugged her arms to her stomach.

"Cold?" Eric hesitated on the sidewalk.

"I'll be fine. We'll be there in a minute."

They turned the corner, leaving Home Sweet Home behind.

"So why doesn't Leila work with you at Home Sweet Home?"

Eric didn't answer.

"I mean, she obviously adores you. I'd think she'd want to help out with the soup kitchen, since it's important to you."

He glanced over at her, obviously uncomfortable.

"Sorry," Casey said. "None of my business."

They walked in silence for a bit.

"First of all," Eric said, "Ellen worked there with me. That cramped Leila's style." He gave a little smile.

"That makes sense."

"But most of all…it's that her family eats there."

"Oh. But…"

"I know. Leila drives the cute little car. Not exactly cheap. But she bought it with her own money. She's not about to sell it now. Besides, I don't know how much equity she has in it, and how much is loans."

"So coming to Home Sweet Home would be awkward. Because of her family."

"Very."

They walked a little further.

"Where does the money come from?" Casey asked.

"What money? Leila's?"

"No. To fund the dinners. The food's not all for free, and the building would cost something, for rent and utilities."

Eric made a face. "Well…"

"You fund it, don't you?"

He shoved his hands into his pockets. "Someone has to."

And if someone had a rich father, it made it a lot easier. Especially if that someone felt the money he had was at the expense of the poor.

"It's a good thing," Casey said.

"Is it?"

"You know it is."

The theater came into view.

"So you didn't have to borrow any money to start it?"

Eric looked at her. "No. Why?"

"It's just…yesterday, here at rehearsal. I was talking to Todd and mentioned Home Sweet Home. It seemed to make him very uncomfortable."

Eric frowned. "It should."

"Why?" Although she was already forming a picture of Todd at the soup kitchen, not appreciating Johnny's silverware. From the way Todd's ears had lit up at the mention of Ellen, Casey figured he'd been busy appreciating something else. And his daughter had known. Or had at least suspected.

They reached the theater before Eric could respond, and other cast members were arriving, greeting them.

Aaron, Casey's mechanic from the morning, held the door for her. "How's the bike?"

"Doing great. Thanks to you."

"Oh, that's so sweet." Jack pinched Aaron's cheek, taking advantage of the open door to slip by him into the theater.

Aaron batted his hand away, but his brother was out of reach before he could actually latch onto him. He scampered after him, chasing him into the foyer and through the double doors.

"What's this?" Eric asked, his face reflecting relief at the subject change.

They walked toward the doors where the boys had disappeared. "Aaron saved me from flat tire syndrome."

Eric still looked confused.

"He put new tires on my bike. Or, your mother's bike."

"Oh. That old thing is my mother's?" He held open the right-hand door.

"From her garage, remember? Which reminds me…" She walked through, but waited for Eric in the aisle. "What's the deal with the Orion in the garage?"

"Take a wild guess."

"It's your dad's."

He snorted. "Might as well be. He gave it to my mom. Thought it would make her less mad at him when he got remarried and took away our old house."

"I don't suppose it worked."

"Would it work on you?"

They reached the front of the theater, where Aaron and Jack sat side by side on the edge of the stage, still pestering each other. Becca crouched in the second row of seats, scribbling madly in her notebook, and Todd lounged in the first, feet stuck out in front of him, back slumped into the seat. It looked like he was asleep. Or, more likely, pretending to be. Leila, watching for Eric, scowled at Casey before practically gluing herself to his side. Casey didn't see Thomas, or the two men who'd been threatening him.

"You must be Casey."

She looked up to see a smiling face, white teeth against a dark tan. "Yes."

"Lonnie." He grabbed her elbow and led her to a seat, where he pulled her down beside him. He gazed at her, sparkling blue eyes beneath the bleached blond—almost white—hair, his smile growing wider. "Tell me everything."

She glanced back at Eric for some help, but Becca had snagged him, and now their heads were bent together, Becca gesturing wildly. Leila hung back slightly, obviously unsure whether she was supposed to be included in the conversation.

"Oh, you don't need to tell me about *him*," Lonnie said. "It's written all over his face."

Casey blinked. "What?"

"That he's madly in love with you."

"No."

"I can see it."

"But it's only been a week since Ellen—"

"I know. I *know* that, but sometimes the heart does strange things, doesn't it?"

Casey forced herself not to look at Eric. "He's not—" she held up a finger to forestall Lonnie's protests "—but if he *were*, it would just be because he needs something to fill the void."

Lonnie patted her hand. "Okay, you can tell yourself that." He studied her face. "But then, you look like you've confronted the void yourself, haven't you?"

Casey opened her mouth to reply, but snapped it shut when she realized Lonnie was no longer paying attention to her.

He craned his neck toward the back of the theater. "I wonder where Thomas is?"

Casey looked around. "And Holly."

"Oh," Lonnie said. "*That* makes sense, all right."

"What? They're together?"

Lonnie laughed. "You'd think so, wouldn't you? But no, it's not that way with them. At least, not that anyone knows about. Her husband would *kill* her. Or him." He considered this, a hand on his chin. "Perhaps that wouldn't be such a bad thing."

"Holly's married?"

His face lit up. "Didn't you know?"

She shook her head. "I've been here a total of three days. And not even quite that."

He leaned toward her, his eyes twinkling. "Then would it surprise you to hear that Holly is none other than your erstwhile lover's stepmother?"

Casey froze. "Holly is married to *Karl Willems?*"

Lonnie glanced over her head, but Eric apparently remained unaware of their conversation topic, for he continued. "He married her a year ago. Caused no end of scandal, of course, with her being so much younger, and him being, well, *him.*"

Casey rubbed her temples. What *else* hadn't Eric wanted her to know?

"Anyway," Lonnie said with a squeeze of her arm. "Holly's late sometimes because she likes to make a grand entrance. You know, that we all missed her so much, but she 'was detained by an important phone call,' or something else vague and ridiculous." He rolled his eyes.

Casey squinted up at him from between her hands, remembering Holly's fit the day before when Lonnie hadn't shown up. "And Thomas lets her get away with that?"

Lonnie shrugged, releasing her arm and sinking back into his chair. "What's he going to do? It's not like we have anybody *else* to do her role." He eyed Casey sideways. "No matter how much we do or don't like her performance."

The doors to the back of the theater slapped open, and Thomas barreled down the aisle, his face a picture of barely controlled fury. Aaron and Jack stopped poking each other and jumped to their feet, Becca clutched her notebook to her chest, and even Eric backed up a step, almost stepping on Leila.

"Oh, boy," Lonnie said in Casey's ear. "Looks like we're in for it tonight." His voice sounded almost gleeful. "I hope I'm not the one he takes it out on. But then, that could be kind of fun, in a perverse sort of way."

"Lonnie!" Thomas bellowed.

Lonnie jumped, then shot an amused glance at Casey.

Casey took another look at Thomas and leaned back to avoid his glare as he checked out Lonnie's clothes. "Done with your *shopping?*"

Lonnie grinned. "Thank you so much for asking, Thomas. I did manage to find some great deals." Thomas' hands curled into fists, but Lonnie took no notice. "I found a sweater that would've been *perfect* for you, but unfortunately they didn't have it in your size."

"*Lonnieeeee…*" Thomas' voice was a growl.

Lonnie held his hands up as if in surrender. "Sorry. *Sorry.* I won't do it again." He looked innocently at the director, blinking woefully, until Thomas turned away. "Until the next end-of-season sale," Lonnie whispered. Casey glanced at him, and he pinched his lips together, trying not to laugh.

"Becca!" Thomas' voice was very quiet, but filled with steel. "Where are we starting today?"

To Becca's credit, she stuttered only once in response, and had the stage all ready to go. Any more arguments were forestalled until the next break.

Casey worked through her scenes, pleasantly surprised at Lonnie's talent, especially since he was playing her character's brother, Sebastian. She found herself a bit shy when on stage with Eric, and tried to avoid him between scenes. If Lonnie was right about Eric, she'd have to watch her step. The last thing Eric needed was for her to crush his feelings, no matter how misplaced they were. Besides that, she didn't need any more of Leila's wrath to come her way.

Holly made her grand entrance about a half hour late, but they barely noted her arrival. She sat sulking in the seats until Becca called her, and even then she needed some extra coaxing to get on stage.

They stumbled through several scenes before break, and Casey escaped to the bathroom, where she stayed until Becca called them back.

"You okay?" Eric joined her, several rows back from the stage.

She didn't look at him. "I'm fine. Thanks."

She was spared further conversation by being summoned to the stage, where Thomas kept her busy every moment. When the end of rehearsal finally arrived she cast about for thoughts of how she might get out of walking home with Eric.

"Casey!"

She stopped in her tracks, as did the rest of the actors.

"Everyone else," Thomas said. "Shoo!"

Shoo? Casey smothered a laugh, albeit a nervous one.

Eric hesitated mid-aisle, and Leila ran into him.

"Go ahead," Casey said. "I'll see you tomorrow."

"I can wait."

"Really. No reason for you to wait. I'll be fine."

His face set into stubborn lines, and he went out the doors, Leila on his heels. Casey sighed, figuring he'd be outside when she was done, although maybe Leila could convince him to go out for that drink he'd promised her. She turned back to Thomas, who sat in his seat, tapping his pencil on his closed script. She glanced up at the darkened stage, wondering if they actually were alone, but got no sense that Taffy and Bone were anywhere in the building.

She looked back at Thomas, but stayed facing the stage. "Yes, Thomas?"

He didn't stop the pencil, and looked steadily forward. "Casey, I want to know who you are."

She stood still, the rhythm of the pencil almost hypnotic. "Who I—"

"Your real last name, for one thing." He grabbed the pencil, stopping it, and looked over at her.

"I told you. It's Smith."

He stared at her, unblinking. "You're going to stick with that, are you?"

"Yes." Her body began its defensive routine of relaxing muscles and deeper breathing. The aisle was on an incline, which could be tricky, but she could compensate. If Thomas came after her, he'd be down in an instant. He didn't have a clue.

"Then how about where you came from? Let's start with that."

She looked at him. "West."

"West. I see. And that would be west as in Iowa, or maybe California? Or perhaps you're thinking the Wild West, in which you are the female version of the Lone Ranger?"

"Just west."

"Ah." He looked down at his script again, laying his hand flat on it, studying his fingers, or perhaps the ring on the fourth one. "Is there a reason you don't want people to know?"

"Is there a reason you need to?"

He was quiet for a moment, looking at his hand, which he brought up to brush over his face. Then he stood, slowly turning toward her and stepping out into the aisle. Casey took a deep breath through her nose.

"I don't know who you are," he said. "Whether you're coming from Hollywood or Broadway, or…other places…because obviously your career—or part of it—has been this one we share." His voice was low. Even. "But I'm telling you now. If you're here to cause trouble for me, it's going to be bad for *you.*" He watched her. "Do you understand?"

"What kind of trouble do you think I'm here to cause?"

His eye twitched. "If you don't know, I'm certainly not going to tell you, am I?" He took a step toward her. "But I am going to tell you this. What you're up to…I'm onto you. I know what you're doing. And when I catch you at it…" His lip rose, and Casey flexed her fingers, ready. But when he moved, it was toward the stage, backing up, still facing her.

"You can go," he said. "And when you do, you tell your *friends* this. Thomas Black is not afraid of them. And if they think sending a…a scrawny little woman to do their dirty work is going to change things, they can think again. I'm doing the best I can, and when I have what they want, I'll get it to them. It should be soon. You tell them that."

Casey stared at him.

"Go on. Give them the news. I'm sure they'll be glad to hear it."

Casey watched him for a moment longer before turning and making her way up the aisle, feeling his eyes on her back with every silent step, ready to turn should he come after her. She went out the double doors and stepped to the side, leaning back on the wall. Out the front door she could see Eric, waiting for her on the bench. Leila was nowhere in sight.

Obviously Thomas was in something over his head. The men expected something from him, and from what she'd heard, it was most likely money. It could've been something else, drugs, maybe. But she'd put *her* money on cash. Did Thomas think she was in league with Taffy and Bone? Or some other entity? Another group of bad guys. Or law enforcement.

She stepped back to the double doors, putting her eye to the crack between them.

Thomas stood with his back to her, hands flat on the stage, his head lowered. As she watched he pushed himself up, ran his hands through his hair, and turned around, straightening his shoulders and grabbing his briefcase before making his way up the aisle.

Casey quickly walked out the front door, attempting a smile as Eric stood to meet her.

"What did he want?"

Casey hesitated. Should she tell him about the two men? Did he already know about them? Or should she let Thomas deal with his own problems without making Eric feel more involved, or even responsible?

"Oh, nothing much." Casey looked up at the sky, clear that night. "He just wanted to talk about how he perceives my role."

Eric gave her a questioning look, but didn't push it.

"Where's Leila?"

He shrugged. "Gone. You still want to walk home alone?"

She jerked her thumb to the right. "My place is this way, and your car is the other. I'll be fine."

"If you're sure."

She glanced back at the theater, where Thomas remained, probably watching her through the large windows. She repressed a shiver.

"I'm sure," she said. "You go on home."

Eric nodded, his eyes darting toward the theater. "All right. You'd let me know if…"

"I'm fine, Eric. He just wanted to talk about…things."

He looked at her for a long moment, then stuffed his hands in his pockets and looked away. "All right. Goodnight then, Casey."

"Goodnight, Eric."

He strode away, head bent, back arched.

Casey turned and walked as quickly as she could in the opposite direction.

Chapter Twenty-eight

Rosemary and Lillian were still sitting on the porch when Casey got to The Nesting Place. They must have moved at some point since the afternoon, because Rosemary was now in her normal clothes—if a bright purple velour tracksuit with rhinestones could be called normal—instead of her Dobak. Her phone was at her ear. "Yes, dear, she's home now. Safe and sound. All right. Goodnight, sweetheart."

Casey gestured at the phone. "Eric?"

"He just wanted to be sure..."

Casey shook her head and turned, looking out at the street over the railing of the porch. "He didn't have to worry."

"I know that. You have no trouble taking care of yourself."

Something in her voice made Casey turn. Rosemary had reached across to Lillian's chair and grabbed her hand, and their hands hung there now, suspended between them.

"What?" Casey said.

Rosemary shook her head, her lips a tight line, and Lillian looked down at her lap.

"Did something happen?"

Lillian's head rose slowly. "No. No, honey. Not since last week." The lines on her face stood out in exaggerated hills and valleys, shadowed by dim porch light.

Ellen, ultimately, had not been able to take care of herself.

Casey took a step forward. "Ellen said the people here in Clymer would soon have work again."

The women exchanged a look, and Rosemary cleared her throat. "You know about that?"

"Eric told me." One of the few things he *had* told her. "At least that's what he thought Ellen meant." She looked at the women, so fragile in their wicker chairs, holding onto each other, facing their pain as a duo. She hated to cause them more. But they knew things. They had to. And if she could get it out of them, she might be able to make some sense of things.

She pulled a chair around in front of them and sat forward, her elbows on her knees. "You don't think Ellen killed herself."

"No," Lillian said, her eyes sparking. "We *know* she didn't. She wouldn't have. We told Chief Reardon—"

"I know. I talked to him." Her face burned as she remembered the conversation, and hoped her anger wasn't apparent in the darkness of the porch. "Ellen told Eric—and the manager of the Pizzeria—that a change was coming. People would be working and there would be no reason for Home Sweet Home to continue serving meals. Eric and I…" She hesitated, hoping the women could take what she had to say. "We went to see Karl."

Lillian inhaled sharply, and Rosemary's eyes flashed in the contours of her face. "And he patted you on the head and told you everything was fine?"

Casey could see that that kind of behavior was nothing new. "Pretty much. He basically said Ellen couldn't possibly have been talking about HomeMaker, and that we should let her—and the factory—rest in peace."

Lillian yanked her hand from Rosemary's, made as if to stand, but sank back into her chair. "That *man*…"

Casey chose her words carefully. "We searched Ellen's desk and Eric's computer for any clue to what she'd been talking about, but there was nothing." She looked at Rosemary. "What did she tell you?"

Rosemary shook her head, her mouth a straight, tight line. "Nothing more than what you know."

"It's important, Rosemary."

"Don't you think I know that?" The words came out harsh and sharp, and Rosemary closed her eyes, visibly getting herself under control. "I'm sorry. I'm sorry, darling. I didn't mean—"

"It's fine. Really. I understand. I wouldn't ask if I didn't need to." She took a breath, looking out over the porch railing, then back at Rosemary. "I need to look in Ellen's house."

Rosemary met her eyes. "You think she hid something there."

"It's possible. It's also possible that if someone did…kill her… that they found it and took it with them. But there was no sign of anyone ransacking the place, was there?"

"If there had been," Rosemary said, "it wouldn't have looked like a suicide. And they needed it to."

The horror of those words hung in the air.

"There was nothing to make anyone think otherwise," Rosemary said. "One coffee mug on the table. Her own prescription from Wayne's Pharmacy, just the fingerprints that would be expected…"

Casey spoke gently. "Do you have a key to her house?"

Rosemary looked at Lillian, who had checked herself out of the conversation. "We do."

"And may I use it?"

"It will help Ellen? Her children?"

"I think so." Casey sat up straighter. "And possibly the whole town."

Rosemary thought for only a few moments. "Of course you may use it. Do you want it now?"

"No. A light in her house would only cause people—" like Chief Reardon "—to come see what was going on. I'll have to wait until morning." And hope their visit to Willems didn't spur any other late-night visitors to Ellen's house. But then, if they'd already cleared out what they wanted, they wouldn't be back. On the other hand—

"Actually, maybe I will take it now."

Rosemary studied her face briefly before rising from her seat. "I'll go get it."

Casey looked down at her clothes. Jeans. Dark blue shirt. About as inconspicuous as anything she had. They would have to do.

Rosemary returned, and Casey held out her hand.

"I'll drive you," Rosemary said.

"No. I mean, thank you, but it would be better if I walked. And went alone."

"But—"

"Please."

Rosemary didn't like it, Casey could see, but eventually held out the key ring, a miniature Shamu, from when Seaworld still had a home in Cleveland. Casey took the key, but Rosemary didn't let go of the charm. "You'll be careful?"

"I'll be fine. There's no alarm, is there?"

"Who can afford one of those in this town? Besides, we don't need them." The irony of her statement hung in the air between them.

"Okay." Casey looked at Lillian, who still wouldn't join the conversation. "And Rosemary?"

"Yes, darling."

"Don't tell Eric. The last thing he needs is to be in Ellen's house, doing this."

Rosemary's face tightened, but she nodded.

Casey shoved the key into her pocket and stood on the top step. "So. I guess it would be good if I knew where exactly Ellen lived."

Chapter Twenty-nine

Ellen's house stood dark and silent. Casey waited in the backyard, in the shadow of the garage, by the alley that ran behind the row of homes. Casey had biked past this house before being confronted by Chief Reardon that morning. She had had no idea that the house belonged to Ellen—hadn't even taken any special notice of it—and wondered if that was why the chief had been suspicious. But even if that were the case, he must have been keeping tabs on her to even notice where she was riding.

The houses on either side of Ellen's were mostly dark, as well. The one to the right had a light on in an upstairs room on the far side of the house, but the downstairs looked quiet. From the other, on the opposite side, came the bluish flickering of television from the side window. Casey hoped the occupants would be glued to whatever inane program was on so they wouldn't notice her entering Ellen's back door.

She didn't see any dogs in either backyard, waiting for an excuse to charge from a corner, barking. Perhaps people would think the dogs were chasing a squirrel, but...

The breeze blew gently, teasing wisps of hair across her face. The air was warmer tonight, but still Casey felt chilled. The home of a dead woman, whether by her own hand or someone else's, wouldn't exactly be Casey's choice for a place to hang out. But if Ellen didn't kill herself, her children—as well as her friends, parents, and Casey herself—needed to know.

Keeping to the shadows, Casey slowly made her way to the back door. No dogs barked. No gravel crunched under her feet. She eased open the screen door—which squeaked too loudly—got out the key, and opened the door. Stepping inside, she closed the door quietly.

To her chagrin, the back door opened directly into the kitchen. The room where Ellen Schneider had lost her life. Casey breathed through her mouth, trying not to picture the woman in the chair, or the pill bottle. She flipped on the flashlight Rosemary had given her and, keeping it low, checked out the room.

Everything was clean. Sparkling. The kitchen looked scrubbed from top to bottom. No sign that anyone had died there. Or that anyone had lived there, for that matter. No dishes in the sink, no crumbs on the counter. She opened the fridge, bathing herself briefly in the light. And no food in the refrigerator.

She closed the door and stood, sensing the atmosphere. Only the usual nighttime sounds. The hum of the refrigerator beside her. The ticking of a clock. Nothing to say there were any people present.

"Kinda spooky, isn't it?"

Casey spun around, the beam of her flashlight impaling Death to the back door. Well, not impaling, exactly, as the light traveled through Death without any sign of actually hitting anything.

"You are *impossible*," Casey hissed.

"No. Oh, well, maybe for *you*." Death moved to stand by the chair where Ellen had died. "Such a shame, you know?"

"Yes," she whispered harshly. "I *know*. Now are you going to help out here, or just be a nuisance?"

"Oh, you know me." Death disappeared into the next room.

Casey moved slowly around the kitchen, hampered by the necessity for using the flashlight. She opened drawers and cupboards, checked the empty freezer, and sifted through canisters of flour and sugar, which hadn't been removed with the rest of the perishable food. She discovered Ellen's junk drawer and took some time going through it. Nothing but loose batteries, expired coupons, rubber bands, and lidless pens. No notes, photos, computer disks, or anything that could possibly be compromising or informative.

Confident she'd searched every possible hiding spot, she moved on to the living room. Death sat on the sofa eating a caramel apple, feet up on the coffee table. Casey took a moment to stand to the side of the window and peer outside. Nothing moved. The television still flickered at the neighbors'. No additional lights had been turned on.

Satisfied that her presence was as yet undetected, she began another search, this time under sofa cushions—asking Death ever so politely to *please* move—inside the TV console, inside DVD cases, and inside the pottery pieces on the decorative shelf. Nothing there, and nothing behind the curtains.

She stifled a yawn and glanced at her watch. Almost eleven. Not that late, but with the sleep she'd been getting it felt much later. She'd have to speed up.

With Death lurking in the doorway, crunching happily, Casey rifled through the medicine cabinet and detergent-scented linen closet in the bathroom. Nothing. She walked down the hallway, pausing at a child's bedroom. A boy's. Sports wallpaper, with a life-sized football player taking up most of one wall, and a Cleveland Indians bedspread. She stepped into the room. "Would a mother hide incriminating evidence in her child's room?"

Death considered this. "Perhaps if it were something that wouldn't explode, smell, or catch on fire. On second thought, forget the smell thing. Ten-year-old boys aren't exactly odorfree."

Casey decided Ellen wouldn't have risked it, and left, thinking she could always come back if she didn't find anything else. She was moving toward the bedroom at the end of the hallway when she heard a door open. She snapped off her flashlight and froze, glancing back at Death, who had, of course, disappeared. A light came on in the living room, spilling toward her, and she tiptoed backward, entering the bedroom. Her sight, having adjusted partially to the darkness with her use of only a flashlight, allowed her to see the layout of the room. Moving quickly but silently, she walked to the far side of the room and crouched behind the bed, her heart beating so loudly she was afraid whoever was out there would hear it.

Padding footsteps reached her ears, and she waited, holding her breath, as they came directly to the bedroom. The overhead light flipped on.

Casey blinked sudden sweat from her eyes and hunched even farther over her knees, trying to peer under the bed at the same time she tried to become invisible. The person hesitated in the doorway, but soon walked in, feet scuffing on the carpet. A drawer opened, and Casey could hear the person displacing clothes. A huff of disappointment, and then another drawer, followed by more searching.

The person went through four drawers before turning to the closet, fortunately on the other side of the room. Another light clicked on, and Casey listened to boxes being pulled from a shelf and opened, and hangers scraping along the pole as clothes were gone through.

Casey's legs were cramping from her curled-up position, and she gritted her teeth against the pain. Why hadn't she found a hiding place where she could stand up, ready to defend herself? As it was, she'd be lucky if her legs would hold her when she finally got up. This was no position from which to fight.

Taking advantage of the next exchange of one box for another, Casey slid her legs backward, so she was lying flat on her stomach. The cramps eased, and she winced as the blood began to circulate again. She placed her hands flat on the ground by her shoulders, ready to propel her upright.

The closet light went off, and the intruder sighed loudly. A man, Casey thought. The closet door shut, and the footsteps came closer to the bed. Casey tensed, ready to rocket upward. The bed sagged as the man sat on its edge. Casey longed to look up over the top, but he was so close. She held her position, trying to see his shoes under the edge of the comforter, in case she recognized them. All she could see was a dark heel. Nothing revealing.

The man sighed again, and the bed squeaked as he stood up. Casey squinted, trying to slide under the bed and at the same time see the shoes as he turned around. It was hard to tell, the fringes of the comforter disguising the shoes.

Suddenly, she was no longer looking at shoes, but at knees, and then a face as he looked under the bed. His eyes went wide and he fell backward, yelling and propelling himself toward the closet, crab-like.

Casey jumped up, her hands out in front of her. "Eric! I'm sorry. I'm sorry."

He stared at her, his feet splayed out in front of him, his back smashed against the closet door. His eyes bugged from his head, and he breathed in labored gasps. "Holy *shit*, Casey! Are you *trying* to give me a heart attack?"

"I said I'm sorry. And I was pretty close to a heart attack myself."

He pulled his knees up and looked down at his pants. "At least I didn't wet myself. I don't think."

Casey circled the bed and sat on it. "What are you doing here?"

His eyes narrowed. "I could ask you the same thing."

"I'm looking for what we didn't find at the factory."

His clasped his hands around his knees. "Yeah. Me, too. I knew where she kept things…" He gestured toward the closet. "But there's nothing there but photographs and old love letters." His face flushed, and Casey looked away, trying to spare him some embarrassment.

"And then," he said, "I thought maybe under the bed. I didn't get very far under there." A smile flickered on his face.

"Yeah. Sorry about that." Casey knelt down by the bed. "Nothing under here except these." She pulled out a pair of fluffy blue slippers.

Eric's face crumpled for a moment, but he regained his composure. "She liked those. Even wore them to rehearsal one time."

Casey returned them and sat back on the bed. "So where else do we look?"

"Where have you checked?"

She recounted her path. "I didn't check the kids' bedrooms because I thought she wouldn't hide anything there. What do you think?"

He considered it. "She wouldn't if she thought there was any way it would hurt one of them. But…" He shrugged. "If it was a great hiding place…"

Casey stood. "Well, then, we'd better look." She hesitated, then held out a hand.

He took it and pulled himself to his feet. "What if it hadn't been me?"

She swallowed, not liking to think of Karl Willems or Chief Reardon discovering her crouched behind Ellen's bed. "I don't know."

He nodded. "Come on, then."

Working by regular light was much easier than by a thin flashlight beam. Riskier, too, but she figured Eric wouldn't be getting in trouble for going through his old girlfriend's house.

Each taking a side of the older child's room, they went through the stash of clothes, toys, and books. Nothing. Casey reached just a little farther, into the back corner of the closet. Her hand wrapped around a carrying case. She brought it out and unzipped the cover.

"Look at this, Eric. From when we were kids." A Walkman, complete with the foam-covered earphones that never stayed on.

Eric gave a small grin. "Yeah, that was Hunter's. He won it at his grandmother's Christmas bingo."

Casey waited for more explanation.

"Ellen's mom gathers garage sale type stuff, or things she gets from the local thrift store, or Dollar Store. The cousins—there are six of them, counting Ellen's two—play Bingo, and when they get a bingo they can pick something from the pile. Hunter picked the CD player, but stopped using it when he got an iPod for his birthday. I guess…I guess Ellen never bothered to get rid of it."

Casey looked down at the player. It sure brought back memories. Saving her baby-sitting money until she had enough to buy her own, the pride she felt leaving the store. The first time she dropped it, and from then on it would skip… She popped the player open, somehow expecting to see a CD of one of her old favorites from her youth. The Cars, or Huey Lewis and the News.

"Eric." Her voice sounded strangely calm.

She held up the CD player, showing him the contents. The CD-Rom, a generic one from the store, had no title. Nothing scribbled on it in black sharpie. But it wasn't a regular CD, and if Hunter had a bootleg music CD, he most likely would've made sure he knew what was on it.

"Eric?"

He and Casey both jerked up at the sound. Someone else was in the house.

Casey took the CD from the player and shoved the Walkman into its carrying case, tossing it back into the corner of the closet. She closed the door and nodded to Eric.

He left the room. "Yeah?"

"I saw your car out there."

It was a man's voice, and Casey thought she recognized it.

"What are you doing here so late at night, son?"

Great. It really was the chief of police. Casey looked around for a CD cover, but finding nothing shoved the CD itself into the waistband at the back of her pants, pulling her shirt over it.

"Just looking around, Denny. I couldn't sleep."

"Uh-huh." It was quiet for a few moments before Casey heard movement toward Hunter's room. Chief Reardon filled the doorway—as much as a guy his size could fill it—and regarded Casey with a mixture of surprise and resignation. "And what are *you* doing here?"

"Keeping me company." Eric pushed gently past the chief and came to stand beside Casey. "It's not easy coming here, you know."

"Yeah. I know." He put his hands on his hips and looked around the room. "And the reason you're in Hunter's room?"

"He wanted me to get something. Mail it to him." Eric's voice was surprisingly even.

"Really? And what was that?"

"His Pokemon game." Eric snatched the game disk from the desktop. "He took his GameBoy, but left this by mistake."

Casey tried to look unconcerned, and prayed desperately that Hunter really had taken his GameBoy, and it wasn't sitting in full view on the desk.

"I see. So you're about done here, then?" The chief kept his eyes on Casey as he talked, the message in them clear.

"We're done," Eric said. "Thanks for checking in."

"Neighbors called. Said someone was over here looking around. They thought it strange that the person didn't turn on the lights, but seemed to be going around with just a flashlight."

Casey looked steadily at the chief.

"Well, as you can see," Eric said. "We've got the lights full on."

"Yes. But it makes me wonder who else might've been here."

Eric made a non-committal noise. "That is curious." He turned to Casey. "Well, shall we go? Now that we got what we came for?" His eyes were asking the question—*Did she have it?*

Casey nodded. "Sure. Let's go."

Chief Reardon stood aside to let Eric pass, but moved his shoulder back into the doorway when Casey approached. "Interesting to see you here, Ms. Smith."

"And you."

"I suppose you remember our conversation earlier today."

"Of course."

"That's good. I wouldn't want you to think I forget about folks who are new to town."

Casey met his eyes. "Oh, I would never think that. Chief."

He held her gaze for a few more moments before turning so she could pass. Eric looked at her with some confusion, but she gave a small shake of her head, moving past him toward the front door.

"See you later, Denny," Eric said.

Casey didn't hear the chief reply. And she didn't look back. All she wanted to do was get far out of his line of sight.

Chapter Thirty

"Okay," Eric said, driving away from Ellen's house. "I am officially freaked out."

Casey didn't answer, feeling enough the same way she was afraid her voice would show it. Instead, she closed her eyes and concentrated on her breathing, trying to ignore the fact that she was, once again, in a car.

"You have the CD?"

She opened her eyes and pulled it out from the back of her pants, wiping it on her shirt. "Got it. Shall we listen to it?"

He looked at the disk, licking the sides of his mouth. "I guess. That's what we got it for, right? And maybe…" He hesitated. "Maybe it's nothing. Maybe it really is an album—or a movie— Hunter got off the Internet."

"Sure, it could be." But Casey knew it wasn't. She could feel it. She slid it into the CD player.

Nothing.

"So it's not audio," Eric said. "It's a DVD. We have to watch it."

Casey ejected it from the player. "Where should we go?" She really didn't want to go to Eric's place, just the two of them, this late at night. "How about your mom's place? They've got that great TV."

He grimaced.

"Oh," Casey said. "Another present from your dad?"

"Irritating, but true. And I have to admit Mom and Rosemary have really enjoyed it."

"Unlike the Orion."

He grinned. "What Orion?"

The lights were still on at The Nesting Place, and the women came hurtling into the foyer at the sound of the front door.

"Oh, thank goodness you're all right," Rosemary said, crushing Casey in a hug. "You were taking so long. And you." She pointed at Eric. "What are you doing here?"

Lillian hung back from the group, her eyes shadowed, waiting for Eric's response.

He cleared his throat. "Um, Casey and I sort of…met up… at Ellen's house."

Rosemary frowned. "You went there."

"Yes."

"On your own."

"Yes."

She shook her head. "And you found Casey going through Ellen's things."

"Well…" He glanced at Casey. "She sort of scared the crap out of me, but I'm over it now."

Casey held up the DVD. "We found something."

The women's eyes locked onto the disk.

"We *think*," Eric said.

"Well," Rosemary said. "Let's watch it. Or is it something to listen to?"

"Watch, we think."

"Then come along."

Together they trooped into the parlor, where Rosemary held out a hand for the disk, then ceremoniously placed it in the DVD player. She remained standing, her eyes on the screen. Casey stood beside her, with Eric on the other side of the TV. Lillian alone sat, but pulled the ottoman close so she could be within their little circle.

An image came suddenly onto the screen. HomeMaker. A wide-angle of the parking lot. The picture, a date at the bottom which said the footage was two weeks old, narrowed slowly, coming to rest on the first row of cars.

"There's Karl's car," Eric said. "And Yvonne's. And that one... it's mine."

"Whose are the other two?" Casey asked.

"Don't know." He looked down at Lillian, but she shook her head.

"Wait." Casey pointed at the car on the far right, one of the two unidentified ones. "There's somebody in there. Two people."

They all leaned toward the screen, as if that would help them to see more clearly.

Rosemary let out a sound of exasperation. "It's impossible to tell who it is."

"Maybe they'll get out of the car." Casey hoped so, because otherwise this was a bust. "Here they come."

A man got out of the driver's side and crossed around the back, opening the passenger door. He held out his hand and a woman took it, stepping from the car.

Rosemary narrowed her eyes. "Who are they?"

Eric shrugged. "Never seen them before."

They walked into the building, leaning on each other, the man's arm around the woman's waist.

The picture switched suddenly to the inside of the office, and Yvonne, Karl's secretary, whom Casey had met earlier that day—came into view, as seen from the vantage point of Ellen's desk. The image was lopsided, as if the camera were strapped to something, or set in a place that would be hidden, perhaps by the computer. The date was the day following the footage of the parking lot.

"What are we looking at?" Eric said. "I mean, other than the office?"

"Karl's door." Casey pointed to the left of the screen, where the door was clearly visible past Yvonne's left shoulder. "Maybe somebody's in there who will be coming out soon."

"Is there sound?" Rosemary got the remote and turned the volume up. They heard the generic sounds of air-conditioning, computer keyboarding, and the occasional comment or question from Yvonne to Kathy.

Minutes passed in which they watched Yvonne work on the computer—words flying across her screen as she typed—talk on the phone, and file papers.

"How did Ellen get this?" Eric asked. "She certainly wasn't working there anymore."

Casey considered it. "Either she got someone else to plant it, or she snuck in and placed it herself, using a timer to start filming when she wanted. Is there someone who would help her with that?"

"Here we go," Rosemary said. "Look." Karl Willems' door opened.

Yvonne looked up at the open door, and even as she continued working smiled up at Karl.

No, she wasn't smiling at Karl. She was smiling at the person behind him, who came through the door directly on the CEO's heels.

It was Eric.

Chapter Thirty-one

Eric's face grew even whiter than before. "*Me?* Why was she taping *me?*"

Rosemary paused the disk and looked from Lillian to Eric. "Okay. What is going on?"

Lillian sat like stone on her stool, looking at the wall, somewhere past the television console. Eric shook his head repeatedly, in short bursts, as if rejecting the image on the screen.

Casey placed a hand over her mouth and closed her eyes. Had she been completely wrong about this whole thing? Was Eric somehow involved in putting the townspeople out of work? Or in killing Ellen?

No. She couldn't be wrong.

But then, Death was awfully anxious for her to befriend him.

"Eric," she said, "you've got to think back. What happened that day? What were you doing there? Why were you talking to Karl?"

He ran his fingers through his hair roughly, pulling it into peaks, as he had done in his office. "I don't *know*. When was it?"

They looked at the date on the screen, jittering slightly on the frozen image.

"Two weeks ago this past Tuesday," Rosemary said. "Ten-forty-three AM."

Eric's hands remained on his head as he thought. "I don't know. I don't *remember*."

"*Think.*" Casey wanted to shake him.

He sighed loudly. "There was a day I went to talk with Karl about COBRA. You know, the insurance for the workers once they're laid off. And severance packages." He thought some more. "I went once to ask why I hadn't been copied on some memos. I had to find out from people at dinner—Home Sweet Home—that the move to Mexico had been pushed back two weeks." He looked up at Casey. "But I don't know which day that would've been. Maybe if I went home and looked at my calendar…"

Casey sat back on her heels and looked up at Rosemary. Rosemary's hair, usually so cheerful and bright, looked out-of-place now over her lined and pale face. Lillian, still seated on the ottoman, kneaded her hands on her lap, chewing her lip.

Casey stood. "Let's watch the rest of the footage."

Lillian turned so quickly she almost lost her balance. "So we can see more of *that*? Accusations against Eric?"

Casey waved a hand at the television. "There was no accusation. Just a film of him coming out of Karl's office. If we keep watching, maybe we'll see something that would make more sense."

They all looked at Eric. He took a deep breath, his nostrils flaring. "Yes. Okay. I know there was no reason for her to be filming me. I want to know what else there is."

Casey nodded, and waited for Rosemary to press Play on the remote. When she didn't, Casey stepped forward, pushing the button on the machine.

The footage went back into motion, with Yvonne watching as Eric and Karl left the picture. Her face was expressionless, her smile disappearing the instant Eric was gone. She grabbed a notebook and pen and stood. Karl Willems swept by the table and she followed, disappearing into his office.

Casey looked sideways at Eric as he watched, wondering what he was feeling. Sorrow? Surprise? Perhaps even guilt? She didn't like to consider that.

A few minutes of footage passed with only the office sounds, the image framing Yvonne's desk and Karl's door. Soon the door opened and Yvonne came out, her face stony, her posture stiff. "I'm going out for a minute," she said.

Kathy said that was fine.

Yvonne dug in her purse, pulled out a pack of cigarettes and a cell phone, and left. The image held on the empty desk. Rosemary, focused again on the task, fast-forwarded until Yvonne was back in her seat. There were several more minutes of keyboarding, which Rosemary fast-forwarded, until Yvonne reached for her phone. Rosemary rewound to just before the movement.

A beep sounded over the speaker, and Yvonne leaned over to grab her handset. She glanced up, toward the front of the office. "Of course. Thank you." She replaced the phone and stood, waiting for someone. They could see by her face when the person appeared, for it became slightly more animated, although still professional. "Good morning, Mr. Nolan."

Eric glanced over at Casey. *Todd?*

It was Todd, and he didn't wait for Yvonne to lead him to the door, surging past with an energy Casey hadn't yet seen in him.

Yvonne was able to sneak past him at the last moment in order to open the door, but Todd pushed directly by her and into the room. Yvonne stood there for a few seconds before stepping back and shutting the door. She looked over at Kathy with an expression of surprise, and sat back at her desk.

Ten minutes later—fast-forwarded by Rosemary—Todd came out of the office, banging the door open against the wall, startling Yvonne. She jumped up from her chair, hands out in front, as if to defend herself. Todd stormed past, his face mottled with rage. He brushed so near to Yvonne's desk that papers fluttered, and she reached out to hold them down. As soon as Todd was gone she hustled to Karl's office, where she spent only a few seconds inside before coming back out and shutting the door behind her, leaning against it, her eyes closed.

After almost half a minute Yvonne walked back to her desk, where she sat and placed her hands on the desktop, hesitating there for several beats until pulling her chair back up to her desk.

"Is there more?" Lillian's voice was small, and quiet.

Rosemary pushed the fast-forward button, but all they saw was Yvonne at her desk, everyone leaving for lunch, and the same routine in the afternoon. No more visitors. Eventually everyone was gone, and the camera stopped filming.

"Well," Eric said. "At least taping Todd makes more sense than taping *me*."

Casey sat on the love seat. "Ellen must've known he was coming by at some point, but didn't know when. I still don't get it. Sure, we saw he was angry, but how does that help us?"

Eric dropped into a chair. "It shows that Todd and Karl had a fight."

"Yes, but…" Casey looked at Rosemary, and then Lillian. "*Karl's* not the one who died. If he had been, then perhaps Todd would be a suspect, based on this. But Karl's alive and kicking."

"Unfortunately," Rosemary muttered.

"It's got to have something to do with the lay-offs." Eric laid his head back on his chair. "Why didn't Ellen just *tell* me? Instead of…" He jutted his chin toward the TV. "Of *that*."

Casey considered his words. "Maybe she was still gathering evidence. She didn't want to say anything until she had it all pieced together. If we think of this video in that way, it makes more sense. It's not everything she knew, but just a part that would make sense with other information."

"So where's the other information?" Eric banged his hands on the arms of his chair. "This doesn't look like anything that should've gotten her killed."

Lillian gasped, and Rosemary strode quickly to her side. "What is it?"

Lillian's mouth opened, then shut, and she stood up, almost knocking Rosemary aside. "I think…" She rushed from the room.

"Lillian?" Rosemary bustled after her.

Eric rolled his head so he was looking at Casey. "This makes me feel like puking, too."

"Oh, me, too."

Casey blinked, and somehow refrained from exhaling with disgust at the sight of Death, one hip perched on the back of Eric's chair, eating a chicken leg.

"It gives me motion sickness, you know," Death said, waving the drumstick. "Watching TV. I really can't take it."

Casey closed her eyes.

Eric leaned forward, his elbows on his knees. "I wish I knew what she was trying to tell me…"

Casey wanted to go comfort him, but couldn't make herself move closer with Death looking over his shoulder. Besides, if what Lonnie said about Eric's feelings was true she really needed to—

"So what now?" Death took a bite of chicken, using a sleeve to wipe barbecue sauce from where it had dripped onto the chair.

Casey could feel her stomach turning.

"Eric."

Death was gone, and Lillian hesitated in the doorway, a box in her hands. Rosemary stepped up beside her, her hand on Lillian's shoulder. "This…" Lillian came closer. "This was from Ellen. She'd given it to me to keep for…for your birthday. With everything that's happened, I just…I forgot about it."

Eric's eyes locked onto the package, a small box with shiny red paper and a gold bow. "What is it?"

Lillian shook her head, her eyes bright with tears. "I don't know, sweetheart." She held it out, but he didn't reach for it.

"Oh, come *on*," Death said in Casey's ear. "Take it already."

Casey made a shushing motion toward the empty air around her, which she turned into a stretch when she noticed Rosemary watching her.

Slowly Eric reached out and took the package, turning it over in his hands. "It hardly weighs anything. Are you sure there's something in it?"

Lillian's mouth twitched. "She said you were sure to like it. In fact, she said it would probably be the best birthday gift you ever got."

Rosemary huffed. "Then she didn't know about that birthday trip to see the Harlem Globetrotters when you were ten."

Eric gave her a sad smile. "I guess I should open it, then, if it's that special."

Rosemary nodded. "No need to save the paper."

Eric ripped the shiny wrapper from the container, which wasn't a jewelry box, but about that size. He stared at it for a moment before gently lifting the lid. He looked down at the contents, then up at the women, his face a picture of confusion.

He held the box out to Casey, and she gazed down at a perfect, silver key.

Chapter Thirty-two

"It's not a car key," Rosemary said.

Lillian shook her head. "Or a house key." She'd recovered from her earlier malaise, and stood by the end table, holding the key up to the light. "It's too small. And thin."

"A safety deposit box?" Eric asked. "At the bank? That would fit with the footage of Todd."

"No," Casey said. "Those are heavy. Thick."

"Yeah. I knew that."

"Bike lock?" Rosemary said.

Casey laughed. "Who locks their bikes? You folks don't even lock your cars."

"Or a lock for a locker room."

Casey considered that. "Like at a gym, to protect her purse while she worked out. Was she a member somewhere?"

"No gym membership." Eric was certain. "She didn't have the money."

"But it could be a portable lock she used somewhere else."

"It almost looks like a diary key," Lillian said. "Like little girls have, to write down who they have a crush on, and how horrible their hair was that day."

Casey looked at Eric. "Did Ellen's daughter have a diary?"

"I don't know. If she did, she'd have it with her at her grandparents, I would think. I really don't want to go back to Ellen's house to check."

"Call her," Rosemary said.

"Now?"

"Why not?"

"It's the middle of the night, that's why not. I'll call in the morning. If it's waited this long, it can wait a few more hours."

Casey felt suddenly tired, and looked at the clock. "It is almost two. I need to go to bed."

Lillian seemed not to hear her, but Rosemary sketched a small wave. "Me, too, darling. I'm about done in. Eric, why don't you just stay here tonight. We've certainly got the room. Eric?"

"Huh?" He blinked. "Oh, sorry. I'm zoning out."

"That's settled then. The lighthouse room for you."

"Oh, good." He yawned. "I like that one. Is the white noise machine still in there?"

"With the button set to ocean waves. Off you go."

Eric didn't look like he could get out of his chair. Casey hesitated, then offered her hand to pull him up. He lurched out of the chair, stopped from falling only by Casey grabbing his arms. He stepped back. "Sorry."

Casey patted his elbows and headed toward the stairs, Eric padding along behind her. Solomon greeted them at the upstairs landing, where he sat directly across from Casey's room.

"He want in?" Eric asked.

Casey shook her head. "Watch."

She opened her door, and Solomon arched his back, his tail growing to twice its normal size. He hissed, spat, and raced down the hallway.

"Whoa," Eric said. "What are you keeping in there?"

"Oh, you know. Creepy things."

"I guess so." He looked down toward the other rooms. "See you in the morning, then." He stopped at the second room and opened the door. Solomon scampered inside. "Well," Eric said. "Seems *I'm* not creepy."

Casey snorted, and went into her room.

"I am *not* creepy." Death perched on the window seat. "I'm *impressive.* Scary I can take. Or frightening. Even immobilizing. But I am not *creepy.*"

Casey ignored this and walked into the bathroom, slamming the door.

"I can still see you, you know!"

"So shut your eyes."

A minute later Casey opened the door. "Don't you have someplace else to be?" she said around her toothbrush. "Isn't someone dying somewhere?"

"Oh, Casey, you refuse to understand, don't you? I can be in more than one place at a time."

Casey spat into the sink. "You're getting that annoying tone of voice again. Your patronizing one."

"If I could only be one place at one time I'd never get everything done. Like Santa Claus."

"You are *not* like Santa Claus." Casey's throat tightened. She had never gotten a chance to decide whether or not she'd let Omar believe in Santa.

"That's true. Santa's not real. But in every other sense we are the same."

Casey got a T-shirt from the wardrobe and went back behind the bathroom door to undress and pull it over her head. "Yeah, you're so jolly and happy. And like to dress in red."

"I can't help it I look best in black."

"The sleigh with flying reindeer?"

"My coach has white horses. And while I don't like them, I have to admit they can fly."

"Delivering presents?"

Death laughed. "What's better than receiving your eternal reward?"

Casey stalked back out to the bedroom and yanked down the covers on the bed. "Now listen. I am going to get good sleep for the first time in three days. No bad dreams. No interruptions. You leave me alone."

"I'll just sit here quietly."

"No, you won't. You will go away and let me sleep in peace. For once." She climbed under the down tick and pulled it up to her chin.

Death came over to the side of the bed and reached out to touch Casey's face. She flinched.

"Come now, child. You know you like me."

"Liking you and wanting to go with you are two entirely different things. And since you refuse the one, I certainly won't do the other."

"Now you're getting confusing."

"So go bother someone else who will make it easy on you." She reached over and turned out the lamp by the bed.

And waited. There was no sound. No movement.

"Are you still there?" she finally said to the room.

No response.

She snuggled further down into the bed, sighing with pleasure at the feel of the clean sheets and soft mattress. The hum of the furnace made her cozy and warm, and she wrapped her arms around a pillow, pulling it to her.

When she was almost asleep, her breathing even and her body relaxed, she felt it. A whisper of breath, a sigh, floating past her cheek.

"Reuben?" she whispered.

There was no answer.

Chapter Thirty-three

A ray of sunlight snuck through the side of the curtain and pierced Casey's eye. She groaned, rolled over, and tried to go back to sleep. It didn't work. She opened her eyes all the way and saw the clock. She sat up. "Ten-thirty!"

She lay back down, her head swimming. The smell of something delicious hovered in the air around her. Bread? Sausage? She couldn't quite tell. Her stomach rumbled.

"Okay, okay."

She pushed down the covers and swung her legs over the side of the bed, giving a huge yawn. Rubbing her face, she walked over to the window and flung open the curtain. A sunny day. No clouds. Just the blue sky against the changing leaves.

Letting the curtains fall back, she examined the room. She was alone. For the moment. She turned back around and hooked the curtains onto the side knobs, allowing the sunlight to fill the room. She did the same with the window on the opposite wall. See if Death could compete with *that*.

She'd always loved Saturday mornings. Nowhere to go. No pressing agenda. She and Reuben had spent most Saturdays sleeping in, waking to a morning of cozy lovemaking, and cooking up a batch of pancakes afterward, which they'd more often than not eaten on their porch, in the shade of the old maple tree. That changed with Omar, of course. Then it became a game of whose turn it was to get up before dawn with their overeager morning person. That trait couldn't possibly have been genetic.

Knowing it was a mistake, Casey went to the wardrobe and pulled out her backpack. Unzipping the inside pocket, she reached in and pulled out the meager contents. The little cap was as soft as a newborn, striped with skinny pink and blue lines against the white background. Tiny, like Omar's head the day they'd brought him home from the hospital. She held it to her cheek. It didn't smell like baby shampoo anymore. Now it smelled like musty camping gear and damp canvas.

The ring hadn't changed. Hooked onto a chain, the gold of the symbol—Reuben's promise to love her forever—shone in the morning light, on top of the penny-sized sun. Casey held the chain and its charms in her palm and closed her fingers, squeezing, the metal edges biting into her skin.

She shivered and placed the treasures back in the pocket. Out of sight.

She closed the wardrobe and stood with her head against the wooden door. It took so much work to breathe. To stand. To think about what was next.

What happened next was her morning workout, a shower, and a quick clean-up of the room, including making the bed. Once those chores were done, there was really nothing else to keep her upstairs.

"Well, if it isn't the sleepyhead!" Rosemary sat at the kitchen table in a bathrobe of royal blue. Fuzzy yellow slippers stuck out from beneath the housecoat, and her hair, now combed, looked less like a circus act than it had during the night, and more like the hairdo of an eccentric middle-aged woman. Half-glasses perched on her nose, she held the morning paper in front of her.

"Hungry, dear?" Lillian stood at the stove, bacon sizzling in the skillet.

"Actually, yes."

"Good." She set a plate in front of Casey and proceeded to load it with toast, eggs, and meat, followed by a large glass of orange juice.

Casey took a drink. "Is Eric still sleeping?"

"Oh, heavens no." Lillian laughed. "He's long gone. Left a note saying he was off somewhere or other foraging for food. Not that we wouldn't have fed him."

"Did he call Ellen's daughter?"

Rosemary didn't look up from the newspaper. "Yes. The key isn't hers."

Not the news they'd been hoping for.

Casey took a bite of egg and chewed while she considered what Lillian had said. "Eric's foraging for Home Sweet Home? I thought he was planning on serving pizza again tonight."

"I don't know, hon," Lillian said, pouring a cup of coffee. "He didn't say."

"Well, I guess I'll find out tonight at supper." She froze, a forkful of eggs halfway to her mouth.

"What?" Lillian stood beside her, coffee pot halted mid-pour.

"Home Sweet Home. There are lockers there. For the staff. Lockers that have actual locks."

Rosemary inhaled sharply. "They would fit the key?"

"They might. Ellen worked there with Eric, right?"

"She did." Lillian sat on the third chair, then bounced up again. "I'll call Eric."

She talked with him briefly, then hung up. "He's on his way."

"To Home Sweet Home?"

"Yes."

Casey looked at her full plate.

"You eat that, honey, and then one of us can take you over."

Casey did eat it, but refused a ride. Instead, she grabbed the Schwinn and rode. Eric's car was already parked behind Home Sweet Home, and the back door was open. Casey left her bike leaning against the wall and went in.

"Eric?"

There was no reply, so she walked through the kitchen to the locker room. Eric stood staring at the lockers. Only one sported a lock. He didn't turn when she came in.

Casey stepped up beside him. "You going to open it?"

"I was waiting for you. Mom called to say you were coming, and I thought…it would be easier with you here."

Casey shuddered. She had been alone when she had found Reuben's stash. She'd been going through the garage, looking for the Pegasus car manual, several months after the accident. She hadn't thought it had been in the car. If it had been, it had been turned into so much ash. So she checked the cupboards in the garage. She hadn't found the manual. But she'd found other things. Car parts, of course. Tools. Nails and screws. Old paint. Ratty tennis balls.

And Reuben's hiding place. An innocuous five-gallon bucket.

The first thing she'd seen had been the letters. Shaking, she'd pulled them out, only to find they held her handwriting. She'd gazed at them with disbelief. Every letter—every *note*—she'd ever written to him. Rubber-banded in a thick stack. Following those were the souvenirs. Ticket stubs, concert programs, take-out menus. And photos. Some photos she'd never seen. Of her, mostly. Photos she hadn't even known he'd taken. Snapshots of her with Omar. Cooking. Mowing the lawn. Even sleeping.

And one from before she'd even met him.

She'd gone cold.

A photo of her, sitting outside her *dojang*. She still wore her Dobak, so it must have been between sessions. She sat on the little patch of grass, her legs underneath her in the butterfly position, her face tilted toward the sun. She'd known right away the photo was from before they'd met, because he'd given her a necklace on their first date, the day following the church social where he'd approached her, saying she was meant to be with him. She'd felt the same, and had put on the necklace with the sun charm the moment he'd given it to her, taking it off only in the shower.

She wasn't wearing it in the photo.

Digging deeper into the bucket she'd found other surprises. Photos of an aging couple, their brown skin wrinkled, mouths missing teeth. Other people, all with Reuben's skin and black hair, but their surroundings of dirt, sun, and adobe huts.

Letters, all in Spanish. From Mexico.

Casey had closed the bucket then. Had stumbled back into the house, where Ricky had grabbed her and led her to the couch. Had finally cried the tears that had so far been evasive.

Reuben's family was dead. He'd told her so. No parents. No siblings. She was his only family. And then Omar. It was just the three of them—

"I'm a little afraid of what's in there," Eric said.

Casey swallowed.

"You're not going anywhere, right?" His voice shook.

She hesitated to answer.

"I mean, right this minute."

"No. No, I'm not going anywhere now."

"Okay." He stepped forward, withdrawing the key from his pocket. "Here goes nothing." He slid the key into the lock, and turned it. The lock popped open. He stood looking at it, his hand on the bottom half, not turning it away. His shoulders went up. Then down. He glanced over his shoulder at Casey. She tried to look encouraging.

"I wish he'd just *open* it."

Casey shrieked, and jumped away from Death.

"What?" Eric jerked away from the locker. "What is it?"

Casey turned away, her hands on her hips, trying to catch her breath. "Nothing. It's fine. I thought…I saw a rat."

"A rat? In here?" Eric turned in a circle, hands up and out, as if a rat was going to jump out at him.

"I was wrong," Casey said. "There's no rat. It was, just a… just a shadow. A trick of the light."

"Oh. Well." He put a hand over his heart. "Don't *do* that."

"Sorry."

He shook his head and turned back to the locker. Casey glared at Death, who'd adopted an innocent look and munched on some dark chocolate M&Ms from a king-sized bag.

Eric squared his shoulders, wrenched the lock from the locker, and flung open the door. They stared.

Casey stepped closer. "What are they?"

"I don't know." Death peered over her shoulder.

"I don't know," Eric said. "Parts for something."

Two little pieces, one white plastic tube-like part with a small metal tab on its flat end, and the other, also of white plastic, that looked like an oversized and flattened nail.

"Something from the plant?" Casey asked.

"I would think so."

They stared at them some more, until Eric picked them up and pulled them out. He walked with them out to the kitchen and set them on the counter. He turned them this way and that, but nothing made it clear what exactly they were.

"Are there serial numbers?"

He shrugged. "Don't see one. That wouldn't help me, anyway. I don't see these things enough to be able to identify them."

"Your computer?"

"It would have a list, but like I said, there's no number."

Death had found an empty spot on the counter, and was shaking out the last pieces of the candy. Casey looked over and made a subtle gesture at the plastic pieces, but Death shrugged, obviously unaccustomed to—or *uninterested* in—appliance parts.

"So how do we find out?" Eric asked. "I can't exactly march into HomeMaker and ask around. Ellen hid them here for a reason."

Casey scooped an empty pasta box out of the trash. "Put them in here."

"And we'll take them to HomeMaker?"

"Nope. We're taking them down the street to our own private mechanic."

Chapter Thirty-four

"It's a door latch," Aaron said. It had taken him about two seconds to identify it. "The two pieces fit together."

Eric frowned. "A door latch for what?"

"A dryer, maybe. At least, that's what I'd guess. Where's it from?"

"We don't know," Casey said, cutting off Eric's reply.

"But—"

"Look, Aaron, we'll tell you when we can, okay? For now, though, can we just…"

"Keep it quiet?" He shrugged, but his eyes betrayed his interest. "I can do that."

"Thanks."

"Aaron," Eric said. "We mean it."

"Can I at least tell Jack?"

"No," Casey and Eric said together.

Aaron held up his hands. "Okay. Geez. I won't say anything."

Casey tried to smile, but was sure she just looked grim. "It's for your own safety, Aaron. Okay?"

"Okay." He let his hands fall. "So this is serious."

"Very."

He made a zipper motion across his lips. "I don't know a thing, and I never saw *that*." He nodded toward the box.

Eric closed the lid. "That's what we want to hear. Thanks, buddy."

They were on their way out when Aaron called, "See you at rehearsal tonight?"

Eric looked back. "We'll be there." He stashed the box behind the driver's seat and Casey reluctantly joined him in the car.

"Now what?" Eric said.

"Now we figure out why she had that particular part in her locker."

"What time is it?"

Casey glanced at the dashboard clock. "A little past noon."

"Good."

"Why?"

"Because the front office people at HomeMaker only work a half day on Saturday."

"So we can go to your office?"

"It sits there empty most of the time. It's time we put it to good use."

They waited in the parking lot of the diner, Casey not at all hungry after her late breakfast, until almost twelve-forty-five before driving over to the plant.

"Karl's space is empty," Eric said. "And Yvonne's. We should be clear." His voice betrayed his anxiety.

"If someone's there, you can fake it. You have legitimate reasons to be here, right?"

"I guess. But I was here yesterday. And the day before. They're going to start to get suspicious that I'm working so hard." He gave a wry smile.

"So you've turned over a new leaf. Gotten interested in Daddy's business."

"And you?"

"I'm new in town. You're just being friendly."

"Yeah. They're sure to buy that." He sighed. "All right. Come on, then."

The front door was locked, which was a good sign. "The line workers go in the back," Eric said. "So they don't need this door. The only ones coming in here are administrators and visitors."

He unlocked the door and went in, punching the numbers on the alarm key pad.

"I'm surprised you remember the code."

"The first thing Karl taught me. He hates getting called away from bed—or a golf game—for a false alarm."

The office was silent. No clicking keyboards, no phones. No receptionist.

Eric unlocked the door to the back and they went in. Neither Yvonne nor Kathy was there. Eric walked quietly to Willems' door and knocked. No response. He tried the door, but it didn't open. "Not here."

Casey let out the breath she'd been holding. "So let's get to work."

In Eric's office, she pulled a second chair around to the back of his desk so she could see the computer screen. He typed in a search for dryer parts, which brought up about a hundred listings.

"Try dryer door latches," Casey said.

He typed it in, and about a dozen lined up on the monitor. "Well, we can rule out several of those."

Seven of those displayed had entirely metal parts, where theirs was all plastic, except for the small piece on what the computer called the "catch."

Casey scooted her chair up closer. "What about the others? Are there dates for when they were manufactured?"

He clicked on the first one. "The ones with the completely metal 'strike' are marked as only special order. The dryers them-selves went off the line ten to twenty years ago. It's amazing anyone would still have one."

"How about the pieces like ours?"

He clicked around. "Looks like the only ones that match and are currently in production are the last three."

"Can we get close-ups?"

He enlarged one of the photos, and Casey reached into the box and pulled out the parts, setting them on the desk separately, beside the computer.

"Is my door locked?" Eric asked.

Casey made sure it was, and sat back down.

"Okay," Eric said. "Let's go through these one by one."

"Ours isn't the same as this photo." Casey pointed at a piece on the computer. "That one, on the catch, it has another metal piece there I didn't see before. On the rear part."

"Right. Next."

They studied the second photo. "Almost the same as ours," Casey said. "But our strike looks…"

"Skinnier."

"Yes, and longer."

Eric held the piece up against the screen. "Nope. Definitely not the same. Here's the third."

It didn't take long to see it wasn't a match either, this one being entirely made of white plastic.

Eric sat back. "You think Aaron was wrong?"

"No. I mean, look at them. It's definitely the same *type* of part. It's just not *exactly* the same."

"So is it from a different manufacturer? But why would Ellen keep *that*?"

"Let's see if we can find it."

They looked them all up. Whirlpool. Kenmore. Sears. Lots of parts that looked almost like theirs, but weren't an exact match.

Eric put his elbows on the desk and rubbed his eyes with the heels of his hands. "I can't look much longer. My head's bursting."

Casey got up and paced. "Okay. There's no record of this part in your computer. No sign of it anywhere else on the web. But…" She stopped and poked at the part. "It exists. It's sitting right here. Could it be a prototype?"

Eric exhaled, letting his head drop back. "Sure. It *could* be."

"And where would we find the schematics?"

He waved at the computer. "Should be in here. Unless the part's so new it hasn't made it in yet."

"Who would know?"

He jerked a thumb behind him, toward the plant. "Someone over there. I mean, *somebody* made this."

Casey nodded. "Jack."

"What?"

"He's still working here. We can ask him."

"At rehearsal tonight?"

"No, we don't want to take this there. Too many people."

"He could be working now. We could find him."

"Huh-uh. We can't go take this into the factory."

Eric sighed. "Of course. You're right."

"You know what shift he works?"

"No clue. But I guess it could be on here somewhere." The computer.

"Doesn't matter. We can just call him. If he's home, we can go see him."

A knock sounded on the door.

With a sweep of his hand, Eric cleared the parts from the desk, dumping them into the box. Casey shoved the box under the desk while Eric clicked out of the screen displaying the parts.

"Yes?" Eric said.

"Eric?" A woman's voice.

Eric got up, scooted around Casey, and opened the door. "Yvonne?"

"I wasn't expecting to see you here again." She looked past him to Casey, who still sat behind the desk.

"Oh, um, I was just showing her around."

Yvonne's eyes flicked to the door, which had been locked, and to the sofa in his office. "Of course."

Eric's face reddened. "I thought you left at noon."

"I did. But I left my book in my desk." She indicated the novel in her hand. "I wanted to read it this weekend."

Eric nodded. "Sure."

They stood awkwardly for a moment before Yvonne stepped back. "Well, I'll be seeing you, then."

"Have a good weekend."

Yvonne hesitated, glancing once more at Casey, before walking out of the office.

Eric put one hand on the doorjamb and circled the other around. "Now there will be all sorts of rumors. I'm sorry."

Casey shrugged. "I've been through worse."

He looked over at her, a question in his eyes.

Casey stood. "So do you want to call Jack from here?"

He watched her for a few seconds before straightening. "Why don't we just go over? It's not far, and I'm ready to get out of here."

She couldn't argue with that.

It took only a few minutes to reach Jack and Aaron's home. On the way, Eric pointed out a gray two-story house. Several beautiful large trees graced the yard, but the shrubs needed trimming, and the yard hadn't seen a mower for just a little too long. Other than that, the place looked well taken care of. Not exactly inviting, but in basically good shape.

"My place," Eric said.

Casey studied it as they drove by. "Nice."

"Yeah." He gave a little laugh. "It'll do. Not exactly House Beautiful, though, is it?"

"You put your time into other worthwhile things."

He laughed shortly. "That's the polite way of saying it needs some help."

"The thing is, I mean it."

He let it drop, and they drove the rest of the way to Jack and Aaron's place, which sat on a street Casey had toured during her bike ride. The house was one of those with a flowerpot on the porch, and a Welcome sign on the door. Cheerful, well-kept. A not-so-subtle difference between their place and Eric's.

Jack was mowing the lawn, but turned off the machine when Eric and Casey got out of the car.

"Hey!" Jack called. "What's up?" He left the pushmower where it had stopped.

Eric held up the box. "We were wondering—"

The screen door on the front porch slapped shut, and Aaron came trotting down the steps. "It's okay, Jack, I got this."

"Actually, Aaron," Eric said, "we need him this time."

Aaron looked at the box. "I was wrong?"

"Nope. You were right. But we're confused."

"I am, too," Jack said, with a grin. "What is it?" He leaned toward the box, as if to see inside the closed lid.

Eric glanced at the neighboring houses. "Can we go inside?"

"Oh! Right. Sure," Aaron said. "Come in."

He led them into the front room, where they stood in a circle around the box. Eric held it out to Jack. "Can you identify this?"

"Sure, it's a box of pasta."

The rest of them didn't laugh.

"Sorry." Jack took the box and opened it. "Oh, it's a dryer door latch."

"I told you that." Aaron frowned.

"Yes," Casey said, "you did. But we need to know exactly *which* dryer door latch this is."

Jack squinted into the box. "Can I take it out?"

"Of course."

He set the box on the coffee table and sat on the couch behind it. Aaron took a place beside him, and Casey knelt on the floor. Eric perched on a close-by chair.

Jack pulled the two pieces out, turning them over in his hands. He looked up at Eric. "It's a HomeMaker piece. For sure. You checked inventory?"

"It's not there. Several that look almost like it, but none with that metal piece." He pointed at the side of the catch.

"Yeah. The ones we're doing now are all plastic." Jack's eyes widened, then narrowed, and he set the pieces down on the table. "Last year. Last *spring*. We made these. And then all of a sudden they were gone, and we were making the all-plastic ones."

"No explanation?"

He shook his head. "None was needed. They bring in the instructions, we make the parts. It doesn't really matter to us what we're making or why. We just put in our hours and come home. Everything goes to the all-mighty HomeMaker, no matter what it is, so what's the point in worrying about it?"

Casey sat back on her heels. "We didn't find it in the computer at all. There were other parts that were either out of production or special order, but this was gone completely."

Jack shrugged. "Don't know anything about it."

"So as far as you can remember," Casey said, "you made this a year ago last spring?"

"Yeah. Don't know how long we made 'em, but long enough it looks familiar. Why does it matter?"

Casey glanced at Eric. He said, "We found this, and got curious."

Aaron frowned again. "But you said—"

"—it could be dangerous. I know. And it could be. So please, neither of you mention this to anybody, okay?"

Jack looked at Aaron, and back at Eric, half laughing. "What is this? *CSI? Law and Order?*"

Eric glanced down at his hands, and Jack's mouth fell open. "It *is*. It *is Law and Order.*"

Casey leaned forward. "Promise you won't tell anyone."

"Except Aaron?"

Aaron punched him on the arm. "I already know, dude."

"But we can talk about it."

"Actually," Casey said, "that would be good. See if you can remember anything more about these." She stood. "We'll take it with us."

Jack picked up the pieces and looked at them some more before placing them back in the box. "There's something..."

Casey closed the box's lid. "What?"

"I don't know. I just think I heard..." He shook his head. "Can't get it. But I'll let you know when I remember."

"Thanks." She stuck the box under her arm. "Eric? Eric." She nudged him with her foot.

"What? Oh. We going?" He blinked, and his eyes focused on Casey.

"Come on."

Aaron and Jack followed them onto the front porch, Jack continuing down to the lawn and the mower. Eric slid into the driver's seat, grabbing his keys from the seat, and Casey opened the back door on the same side, placing the box in the back seat. She shut the door and bent down to Eric's open window. "You okay?"

"Yeah. I just...every once in a while it just hits me, you know? That she's really gone. And now I have to wonder if she's gone because of *that*."

"It's only been a little over a week, Eric. You can't expect to *not* think about her."

He looked away, then fumbled with his keys, putting them into the ignition. "You coming?"

"Where are you going?"

"I was on my way to the bulk food store. Home Sweet Home needs salt, sugar, that kind of stuff."

Casey considered climbing back into the car and accompanying him. "You know, I have a few things to do. I think I'll stay in town."

"You want me to drop you somewhere?"

"Nah. I'll walk. Thanks."

"Okay. See you tonight at dinner, if not before."

She patted the top of the car and stepped back onto the sidewalk. He eased away from the curb, and she waved to Jack. Aaron stood on the porch watching her, his arms crossed over his chest.

Chapter Thirty-five

"So where are we going?" Death said.

Casey gritted her teeth. "*I* am going to the library."

Death made a sound of disgust, focusing on a light blue hand-held computer game, pushing the buttons, turning this way and that with the image on the screen. "You're so boring. The library, play practice, helping at the soup kitchen. Don't you ever do anything *fun*?"

"I used to."

"Oh, don't get that whiny tone again."

Casey walked faster. Death stepped deftly over a raised crack in the sidewalk, eyes still on the game.

"You do realize you could go bother someone more interesting," Casey said.

"Of course. It's just, your *potential* to be interesting is so much greater than most of the others."

"I can't see how that could possibly be."

A car drifted past Casey, and she tried not to show her discomfort. A police car. Not the chief this time, but another officer, wrist bent over the steering wheel as he watched her walk. A few seconds later he was gone, but Casey could feel his eyes between her shoulder blades, a reflection from his rearview mirror.

"See what I mean?" Death said. "That *could've* been something to see."

Casey peeked at the game Death was playing. "What is that?"

"It's called *Gardener's Row*. You plant flowers, or vegetables, and try to keep them watered, weeded, and bug-free."

"And you think *I'm* boring?"

"Hey. Nature is good stuff. And how often do I get to actually grow things?" Death made a face as the game emitted a sound of failure, a crumbling, sucking sound of plants dying and vegetables decomposing. "Unfortunately, I've got a rotten thumb."

"At least you can use your scythe to cut down the stalks when they're dead."

"Har, har. You're a stitch."

Casey walked up the library steps, moving aside to let a mother with two young children pass. The older child, probably about five years old, craned his neck to see what Death was playing. Recognizing the gardening game, he wrinkled his nose and followed his mother, who gave no sign of seeing anyone but Casey.

"See?" Casey said. "Even little kids know your game is lame."

Death sat on the bench. "Well, then, let them play the violent stuff. I get plenty of that in my line of work."

Casey left Death to weeding and entered the library. Stacy greeted her and hooked her up with her usual computer station. She opened the browser and checked her e-mail, remembering her promise to Ricky to check it daily. There were two actual e-mails among the spam. The first, from Ricky: *Mom's fine. Nobody's been there. The realtor's showing your house this afternoon. Hope they hate it. Sent the papers to your lawyer. He called this morning, about Pegasus coming around. Call soon, sis, okay? Love, Ricky. P.S. I gave Jewel a call. She was happy to hear from me.*

Casey shook her head. He knew what he was doing, calling that awful girl. If anything could get Casey back home…

The second e-mail was from Don, her lawyer. *Casey. Your family is fine. Ricky seems annoyed with Pegasus, but not threatened. Your mother has so far been left alone. Got the papers from Ricky. Let me know where to send them, and they'll be off.*

As for the Pegasus car that killed the man two weeks ago, Pegasus claims he didn't return his car for the new piece, so they are not liable. That was about as far as I got. Will keep you posted.

Keep in touch. Don't get too lost.

Don

Casey sat back, looking blankly at the words before closing the screen and typing "HomeMaker dryer door latch" into the search engine. She was rewarded with a long list of places to buy door latches, explanations from home repair gurus on how to replace them, and instructions to fix a door if it isn't latching correctly. She clicked on one of the latter. The basic answer was to put a new latch in, something just about anyone could do on their own. One person said they'd started slapping a large magnet over the door handle to keep it closed during the cycle, and one went so far as to wonder if she should just get a new dryer rather than mess with it.

HomeMaker dryers, along with their parts, were all listed and available. Same latches she and Eric had seen on his computer. Same dryers.

Nowhere could she find anything to indicate Ellen's latch had ever existed. But it did. And Jack was sure it was a HomeMaker product.

Giving up on that avenue, Casey ran a search for the Pegasus car accident from two weeks earlier. There were only a few hits, a couple about the investigation of the accident—which was inconclusive—and the arrangements for the man's closed-casket funeral. Casey e-mailed all of the articles to Don, in case he hadn't seen them.

Inconclusive.

Her family's accident had remained inconclusive, as well. No matter what her investigators tried, they couldn't seem to find the one piece of evidence that would nail Pegasus. She knew it was the manufacturer's fault. *They* knew it was their fault. Why else would they have performed the recall? But there was no way to make them accountable for Casey's accident if they could run rings around Casey's team, and as long as they had the witnesses to say Reuben had been drinking beer the night of the accident. Even if it hadn't been anywhere close enough to make him drunk, or even approaching the legal limit. With his body destroyed there was no way to check, so it was Pegasus' innuendo against her word.

They only thing for sure in the whole matter was that Casey's family was dead.

Casey clicked out of the browser and sat for a moment, staring at the blank screen. Finally, she shook herself, retrieved her driver's license from Stacy, and went outside. Two teenaged boys sat bent over a book on the bench where Death had been waiting. Casey took a peek at their book as she went past, but couldn't see what they were reading, other than the colorful illustrations of a graphic novel.

At least they weren't playing some awful electronic gardening game.

Death was nowhere to be seen, so Casey made her way down the street to Home Sweet Home, where she retrieved her bike. She was beginning to get hungry, but really didn't want to go back to the diner. She rode to The Nesting Place, parking the bike by the garage.

"Ever thought about why they don't drive the Orion?" Death peered through the side window of the building.

"Of course. Have you?"

Death shrugged. "Gas guzzler."

"I'm sure that's a big reason."

"You think there are others?"

"Probably. The main one being it's from Karl. They obviously hate the man, even if he is family."

"What about the money?"

"What money?"

"That it took to buy that thing. That vehicle represents a huge chunk of change."

Casey shook her head. "I hate it when you talk like that."

"Like what?"

"Slang. You should be using Old World English."

"I'm as contemporary as I am old-fashioned, love."

"Don't call me that." She turned away and walked toward the house on the stone path. "Anyway, they use other things he gives them. Like the TV."

Death followed her. "True. But the Orion's worth a lot more. Shouldn't they sell it and use the money for HomeMaker's unemployed?"

Casey stopped abruptly, but rather than bumping into her, Death strode right through her. Casey shivered. "Don't *do* that."

"You're the one who stopped."

"Anyway…" Casey looked back toward the garage. "What if there's some reason they *can't* sell it?"

"Such as?"

"It's still in his name?"

"That would work. But why would he do that?"

"I don't know. In case he wanted it back he could just take it."

She turned back toward the house and squeezed past Death, not wanting to step off the path into the vegetation. "I'm hungry. I'm going in."

Death gazed at the back of the house with a smirk.

"What?"

"Never mind. Go ahead. I'll see you soon."

Rosemary was in the laundry room, a cup of coffee in her hand, staring out the back window.

"Hey, Rosemary. You okay?"

"What? Oh, sure, I'm fine. What did you and Eric discover?"

Casey's stomach rumbled. "Would it be all right if I grabbed something to eat while I told you? You can add food cost to my bill."

"Of course, darling. Let's find you some lunch." She hesitated. "Do you want to invite your friend to join us?"

Casey froze. "What friend?"

Rosemary gestured toward the back yard, where Death still stood, smirking at the window.

"You can...you can see someone out there?"

Rosemary sighed. "Yes. I wish I didn't, but I do."

Casey closed her eyes, suddenly dizzy. "What about Lillian? Won't she care?"

"Oh, Lillian's not here. And she wouldn't care, anyway. She can't see...*that*."

Casey shook her head.

"Go ahead," Rosemary said. "I'll get something ready." She swept into the kitchen.

Casey opened the back door. "I don't want this."

Death smiled and walked into the house. "Of course you don't. But Rosemary is *desperately* interesting."

"She doesn't seem to like you very much."

"She'll warm to me."

Casey wasn't so sure.

"Here you go," Rosemary said as they walked in. "I hope a turkey sandwich with tomato and lettuce is okay."

"Sounds great," Casey said.

"Divine," Death said. "Are they your own tomatoes?"

Casey rolled her eyes.

"They are," Rosemary said. "You can tell, can't you? But then, I guess you can see most things."

"Oh, I'm still learning about vegetables."

That launched them into a conversation about gardening, and mulch, and the benefits of chicken or cow manure, while Casey chewed her sandwich, silently swearing at Death. Could she not even *eat* in peace now?

"So, Casey," Rosemary said. "You were going to tell me what you and Eric discovered." She glanced at Death, her eyes half-lidded. "I assume you know all about it?"

Death nodded, watching Casey with what one might construe as innocence.

Casey glared at Death and told Rosemary about Aaron's identification of the parts, HomeMaker's faulty inventory, and Jack's recognition of the dryer latch. She ended with her unhelpful trip to the library.

"So we really don't know much, do we?" Rosemary said.

"Not enough."

Death pointed at Casey with a potato chip. "I think she should go talk to the banker."

"Todd?" Casey shook her head. "He's not going to tell me anything about HomeMaker's money."

"What if it's not *about* money?"

"What else would it be about?"

"We do have another mystery to solve, don't we? Not just about the unidentified appliance part?"

"Something that has to do with Todd?"

"Something that has to do with *Ellen* and Todd."

"You mean—" She stopped, remembering Todd's glowing ears when she'd mentioned Ellen, as well as his fury on Ellen's footage. She looked at Rosemary. "What do you know about Todd's marriage?"

Rosemary fussed with some breadcrumbs on her plate, pressing them down with a finger, then putting them to her mouth. "I don't know much."

"But what you *do* know?"

"They've been married a long time. They have three daughters."

Casey waited. That was the easy stuff. Even *she* knew those things. "Did he like Ellen?"

"Of course he did. Everyone did."

"You know what I mean."

Rosemary sighed. "I think so. At least, Eric didn't like the attention Todd paid to her. Todd had even begun working at Home Sweet Home."

"He doesn't any more."

"No. He'd stopped soon before she…" She swallowed. "Before she died."

"Did she return his feelings?"

Rosemary looked at Casey, her face grim. "I don't know. She didn't tell him to get lost, which she should've. She was too nice for that."

"Would she have told him anything about HomeMaker? About what she thought she'd found?"

"I really can't see…" She shook her head. "She didn't even tell Eric. She wouldn't have told Todd. I'm sure of it."

Casey wasn't. What if there was a reason for her to tell him? Like money issues for HomeMaker? Or as a trade-off for something else Ellen needed to know?

Casey looked at Death. "I still don't see how going to talk with him will help. He's not going to tell me anything about HomeMaker's finances *or* Ellen. Unless he thinks I know already."

Rosemary stopped, her arm halfway across the table, reaching for Casey's empty plate. "Why would you know things like that?"

Casey snorted. "People are suspicious of me. Thomas Black thinks I'm a spy or something worse, and is convinced I'm here to ruin his life." She remembered Taffy and Bone, the men in the theater, and shivered.

Rosemary snatched Casey's silverware and clicked it onto the plate. "Thomas is doing a good enough job of ruining his life on his own. Messing around with Karl's new trophy wife…" She stood, pushing back her chair with a loud scrape.

"Lonnie didn't seem to think there was anything going on with them."

Rosemary dumped Casey's dishes in the sink. "I hope he's right."

Casey stretched, wondering how she could be feeling so tired when she'd slept so late.

"Honey," Rosemary said, peering over her shoulder. "You look all done in, even with sleeping in this morning. Why don't you go up to your room and rest for a while."

Nothing sounded better. "Can I help with the dishes first?"

"No, no, sweetheart. I've got it. You go." She thrust her hands into the soapy water in the sink. "Washing dishes is…comforting. Besides, I've got help." She looked pointedly at Death, who held up hands in mock horror before standing and collecting the rest of the dishes on the table.

Casey used to enjoy washing the dishes. In fact, she and Reuben used to argue over who got to do them while the other kept Omar entertained. After a night of sleep broken by multiple feedings, a day of diaper changes, and attention never wavering from protecting a baby, Casey had longed for a few minutes of solitude. Precious minutes where all that was required of her was to plunge her hands into the warm water and mindlessly wash the bottles and dishes and baby spoons. She'd often ignored the dishwasher, preferring the manual labor, and the time alone.

How she wished she could have those minutes back. Those night interruptions, that exhaustion that comes from raising an active child.

"Okay, I'm going upstairs."

Casey paused just outside the door of the kitchen to see if she would be followed by Death. Instead, Death stood beside Rosemary at the sink, towel in hand. Casey left, slogging up the stairs, her brain fuzzy. Solomon the cat was nowhere in sight this time, and Casey couldn't blame him. Death wasn't exactly hiding at the moment.

Casey went into her room, took off her shoes, and lay down on the bed. She was awakened sometime later by a weight by her feet. She raised her head.

"Well," Death said. "I've been officially unwelcomed."

"Huh?" Casey rubbed her eyes.

"Rosemary said that while she's not afraid of me, she doesn't want me hanging around."

"And you listened?"

"I'm still here, aren't I?"

"But not with her."

Death lay across the foot of the bed. "I figured I'd come back up here. She won't know."

"Haven't I been unwelcoming? Why don't you listen to me?"

Death leaned on an elbow. "You don't really want me to go away."

"Yes. I do."

"No. You want me to go away and take you *with* me. That's the difference between you and Rosemary."

Casey laid an arm over her eyes. "Who did you steal from Rosemary?"

"I'm not a thief. But it was her husband, of course, that I took. Remember? She's a widow?"

"How?"

"Hiking accident."

"*Hiking?*" Casey lifted her arm from her face.

"Oh, yes. Rosemary and her husband were quite the outdoor adventurers. I know, you wouldn't think it to look at her now, but at one time she was quite the explorer."

"What happened?"

"They were camping. Hiking a trail along the Appalachians. A place they'd never been. He went off in the twilight to gather kindling, and never came back. Rosemary went to look for him and discovered him at the bottom of a ravine. The way he'd fallen had broken his neck. He was dead when she found him."

"But that's *awful!*"

"Rosemary took it well. Said it was a better death than lots of other things. At least it was quick."

Burning up in an exploding vehicle was quick.

Casey scooted up, leaning her back against the headboard and wrapping her arms around her knees, studying this…this *entity* who had become her most constant companion.

It had been in one of the boardrooms that she'd first seen Death. Casey had thought an extra lawyer had joined the team. Hers or Pegasus', she wasn't sure. All she knew was that an extra chair sat at the table. It only took a few minutes, however, to realize that this lawyer wasn't on any team, but spent every second sitting back in the chair, fingers steepled, staring at Casey with… was that *amusement?*

At the first break, Casey had confronted the new lawyer, who stood alone, leaning against the stair railing in the foyer. How dare someone laugh in the face of her pain?

Death only smiled, leaning closer until Casey breathed in… and she *knew*.

In fact, she was ecstatic, holding out her arms to receive Death's embrace. Only that's not what Death had in mind. Ricky had come to her then, concern etched into his face as he stood in exactly the spot where Death had been a moment before. She'd searched wildly around the hallway, but Death had disappeared, leaving her too emotionally distraught to continue with the day's proceedings. Neither team of lawyers had been happy about *that*.

"What?" Death said now, seeing Casey's face. "What did I do?"

Casey shook her head, disgusted with herself, with Death, with everything. "Nothing. You did absolutely *nothing*." She jumped off the bed and grabbed her jacket, heading out the door. "And you'll *continue* to do nothing, you worthless piece of… of…*dark matter*." She slammed the door on Death's surprise, and went downstairs.

Chapter Thirty-six

Casey headed directly out the front door, avoiding any conversation with either Rosemary or Lillian, and took off down the sidewalk. No bike this time. She needed to get back on her feet.

Her feet took her to the door of the bank, apparently with the idea of confronting Todd at his workplace.

It was closed.

She studied the lobby hours printed on the glass, seeing that they'd closed already at noon, this being a Saturday. Shoving down her frustration, she changed direction and strode down to the corner, entering Wayne's Pharmacy.

Becca was behind the counter, wrapping what looked like a birthday present. A girl and her mother watched the process as Becca fashioned ribbons into a festive poof of curls. "Here you go, sweetie. Courtney will be very happy with her new tiger snake."

The girl grinned, hugging the package to her chest, and left with her mother.

"Tiger Snake?" Casey asked. "For an eight-year-old?"

Becca laughed. "It's a toy. You know, those stuffed animals you play with on-line?" At Casey's blank expression, Becca waved away the subject. "You're not here to talk about kiddie toys. What can I do for you?"

"Can you tell me how to find Todd?"

"Todd Nolan?"

"Are there other Todds?"

Becca swept ribbon cuttings from the counter into a trash can. "No. I just…he doesn't exactly seem your type."

"Becca, I'm not looking for a type. I'm looking for some answers."

"About the play?"

"What? No. If I had those, I'd ask you or Eric. No, I have… banking questions."

Becca regarded her with doubt. "Banking?"

"He *is* a banker." It wasn't a lie.

"True."

"And the bank's closed."

"Yes, it would be."

She slid her scissors into a drawer. "Okay. I'll give you directions, but you'd better hope his daughter's not there to see you."

"Kristi?"

Becca blinked. "Yes. How did you know?"

"Met her at the diner."

"Oh. Sure. Anyway, she's not too keen on her dad right now, let alone women he might talk to."

Casey looked around the store, but they were alone. "Ellen, right?"

Becca made a face. "I don't know what it was about her. Eric, and Todd, too. At least Eric was free to do something about it."

"I heard Todd was working at Home Sweet Home."

Becca snorted. "If you want to call it working. From what I've heard he didn't do a whole lot except get in Ellen's way."

"So it's no wonder Kristi was unhappy. What about his wife?"

Becca shrugged. "Todd's wife is…spacey, shall we say? I don't think it would even occur to her to think about Todd being interested in someone else. It wouldn't have occurred to *most* of us. He's too lazy." She gave a half smile.

"But Kristi?"

"She's smart. And she could see exactly what was going on. In fact, she was the one who finally put a stop to the whole thing—whatever there was."

"And that's why he stopped helping at the soup kitchen?"

The door tinged, and Becca turned to welcome the customer, no one Casey recognized. She turned back to Casey. "From what I hear, Kristi gave him the whole get-it-together-or-I'm-telling-Mom speech. He quit that day. I don't think he quite understood what he was getting himself into."

Casey shook her head. "He can't be dumb, if he's a banker."

"He's not dumb. People just sometimes do dumb *things*."

Casey shoved her hands in her pockets. Reuben hadn't been dumb. In fact, he'd been one of the smartest men—the smartest *people*—she'd ever known. But everyone had secrets, and Reuben's just happened to be bigger than most. An entire family, their lives sealed in a five-gallon bucket, kept from her because they wouldn't accept his choice for his wife. She was an American. A *white* American. Who was far from Catholic.

They'd never met her. Hadn't attended their wedding.

Had never met their grandson.

"So you still want directions?"

Casey snapped back to the present, to Becca's question. "Yes. Please."

With Becca's easy-to-follow instructions, Casey left the store and turned toward the gas station, her first landmark.

Reuben's family hadn't come to the funeral. Casey wondered how long it had been before they even knew he was dead, along with his son. The items in his bucket were proof he'd been in touch with them. Had sent them pictures of Omar. Their letters had reflected their response. Their unwillingness to accept the gift of life from someone like Casey.

She passed the gas station, quiet now, only the front office open, the owner visible through the window. He looked up as she went past, sketching a wave. She raised her hand, then turned the corner, the opposite direction. A few more turns and she stood looking at a large two-story house, attractive, a two-car garage, one side open with a Suburban taking up the space.

No one was outside, so Casey went to the front door and rang the bell. When no one answered, she went back down the steps to the side entrance, beside the garage. She knocked.

Footsteps sounded inside, and Todd opened the door. He wore old jeans and a Grateful Dead T-shirt, and was decorated with dust and a spiderweb, which draped over his left shoulder. "Casey?"

"Hi. I was wondering…" What? If he would tell her about HomeMaker's finances? Why exactly he was furious with Karl Willems? If he'd killed Ellen Schneider because she didn't love him? "Could we talk for a few minutes?"

He glanced behind him, down what appeared to be the basement steps. "I'll be back in a minute, hon."

An affirmative response floated up the stairs, and he gestured for Casey to follow him to the kitchen, where he filled a glass with water. "Want some?"

"No. Thanks. Can we go outside?"

He studied her, then gestured to the door. He followed her out, looking around for a place to go, and decided on the bumper of the Suburban. They leaned against the SUV.

"So you didn't get out of basement cleaning, after all?" Casey said.

He grunted. "No such luck."

"Yeah, well, you'll get good behavior points for it."

He laughed, but stopped abruptly. "What do you mean by *that*?"

"Nothing. Just, I'm sure your wife is glad to have your help."

He narrowed his eyes at her, and drained his glass. "What is it you wanted to talk about, Casey?"

She stood and faced him. "You don't get along with Karl Willems."

He raised his eyebrows. "And that's news?"

"I guess not. *Most* people don't get along with him." She considered her words. "What I'm wondering is, is that dislike business or personal?"

He stood up. "Look, Casey, I don't know why you want to know, or, really, who you even are, so I'm not sure why we're talking about this."

"I know. It's very presumptuous of me. But it's important."

"To whom? You? I can't see how. Unless Thomas is right and you really are more than you appear to be."

She let out a short laugh. "So he told you that, too? What is he afraid of?"

"You, apparently."

She shook her head. "Are you, too?"

"I wasn't. Not until you came here, asking questions."

"I'm sorry." She was. "But it's just…I think Ellen's family deserves to know."

He went white, and glanced toward his house. "There's nothing to know. Nothing happened, and nothing was going to."

Casey held up a hand. "I don't mean about you. I mean about…why she died."

He looked down at his glass, and then up again, his eyes pained. "She killed herself. Do we really need to know more?"

"You really believe that? That she…committed suicide?"

He closed his eyes. "It's what they say, isn't it? The cops?"

"Yes. But do you think they're right? Other people think they're wrong."

His eyes opened. "Look, Casey, I don't know why you're here, or why you're asking these questions. I liked Ellen." He glanced at the house. "She was kind, and smart, and…and real. But as for killing herself?" He shrugged. "She was a single mom without any hope for a good job here in Clymer. She was going to have to leave, get help, or…or something. I don't know exactly why she did it. And I wish like hell she hadn't. But I don't know anything to say she *didn't*."

Casey turned away from the pain on his face. She could feel it radiating from him, like heat. "Todd, I don't think she did."

He didn't move.

"In fact, I don't think you do, either. Nobody who knew her well believes it."

He waved his glass toward the sky. "So what are we supposed to do? I'm not a cop. Or a doctor."

"No. But you know things. Things that could tell her story."

"I don't know anything." He looked down at her. "Like what?"

"Like why you went storming into Karl's office two weeks ago. And why you came storming back out."

"What?"

"People saw you, Todd. Was it…did he threaten you? About Ellen?"

"About…" His face wrinkled in confusion, then cleared. "Do you mean…no. *No*. He had nothing to threaten me with. *Nothing*."

"Really?"

"Look. I don't know how to prove it to you. But it wasn't a personal visit."

"But you know which one I'm talking about?"

He set his glass on the bumper and rubbed his face hard with the heels of his hands. "I don't go over to HomeMaker. Hardly ever. If they—*he*—needs something, he comes to the bank. To my office. But that time…" He looked at her. "I went to him."

"About what?"

"Casey, I can't tell you that. I'll get fired."

He would. Of course.

She stuck her hands in her back pockets and looked up at his house. He needed his job. He had three daughters. Property. A wife. "It wasn't personal?"

"No. I swear."

She studied his face. His eyes, piercing hers. "Okay."

"Todd?"

He jumped, looking toward the house. "Coming, honey."

His wife stood in the doorway, a rag in her hand, her clothes just as dirty as Todd's, although her spider web was draped across her hair.

Todd gestured to Casey. "She's in the play. Had a couple of questions."

"Oh." His wife smiled. "The new girl?"

"That's me," Casey said. "The new girl."

"Wonderful. Todd, when you're done talking there's some old insulation that needs to be changed beside the furnace."

He sighed heavily. "Coming, dear."

With a wave of her rag, she disappeared back into the house.

"Well," Casey said, "Thanks."

He huffed. "For nothing."

She shrugged. "Not entirely. See you at rehearsal?"

"I'll be there."

She walked out the lane, wondering what she actually had learned that could be of any importance.

"Casey?"

She turned.

"You want to help Ellen? Really?"

"Yes. Really."

He looked at the driveway, then back up at her. "The reason I was at HomeMaker?"

"Yes?"

"Let's just say it wasn't personal on *my* part. And Ellen had nothing—absolutely *nothing*—to do with it." He turned, and disappeared into his house.

Chapter Thirty-seven

Casey was waiting at the back door of Home Sweet Home when Eric drove up.

He got out of his Camry. "Hey."

"Hey." She went to the car. "Got things to carry in?"

"Well, yes, but—"

She waited at the trunk until he opened it, holding out her arms for the bags of just-un-sellable vegetables and food staples. They took in the groceries and put them away, finding what space they could around the pizzas in the fridge.

"What is it?" Eric asked when they were done. "You learned something. I can see it."

"I think the video might be a dead end." She explained what Todd had told her.

"But maybe it *did* have to do with her," he said. "Todd's either lying or he doesn't know."

"Unless…"

"What?"

"Eric." She made her voice gentle. "Have you remembered why you were there that day?"

He opened his mouth, then snapped it shut. "You really think I did something to Ellen?"

"No, I don't—"

"Because that's just…" He flung his hands outward, and stalked away, keeping his back to her.

She followed him. "I don't think that, Eric. Really. But what if something about your visit was important? You need to remember."

"I know. I *know*." He banged the flat of his hand against the wall, and leaned there, hanging his head.

"Can you at least tell me what Thomas thinks I'm doing here? Why he would threaten me, telling me to leave him alone?"

He turned his head to look at her. "Thomas? He did that?"

"He seems to think I'm a spy."

He sighed heavily. "Lord knows what Thomas thinks about anything."

"I think you know, too."

He pushed himself off the wall, rounding on her. "What do I know?"

Casey readied herself for self-defense, all the while telling herself it was stupid to worry around Eric. "You have something on him, Eric. He knows it. You know it. What *is* it?" She could still picture that man, Taffy, telling Thomas he was being monitored. Should she mention it to Eric? Or would that just put Eric in danger, too?

"Thomas and I have known each other a long—"

"Stop. Just *stop*. You've given me that spiel before. So you've known each other forever. You grew up together. Your dads both moved here to work together. I get that. But what does that *mean*? You feel some sense of…what? Responsibility for him?"

"No, I don't, it's just…"

"*What?*"

"I think he wants out."

"Out? Out of what? Theater? This town?"

He glanced at her. "This town, definitely, but that's not what I meant."

"Then what? It has something to do with money, doesn't it? Large amounts of it?" She couldn't imagine what *else* Taffy and Bone would want.

Eric let out a long sigh, and leaned back against the wall. "I can't… It doesn't have anything to do with Ellen, okay? Trust me on that."

"Are you *sure*?"

"Yes. If I thought it did, I would tell you."

"Would you?"

"*Yes.*"

She watched him for a moment. Did he know enough that he could also be a target of those men? Whatever group was threatening Thomas? Would Taffy and Bone come after him?

"Eric, there's something I think you should know—"

"I know everything I need to about Thomas and his problems."

"But—"

"No. No more. I don't want to talk about it *anymore*." He turned abruptly and walked through the door into the dining area.

Casey clenched her jaw. She hated thinking of Eric in any way other than positive, but how long had she actually known him? Three days? Four? And with them knowing nothing about what had really happened to Ellen, how did he really know Thomas' problem wasn't relevant?

She started after him, but the back door opened and Loretta entered, kissing her fingers and raising them to heaven. "*Thank you, Jesus*, for another day serving you. *Hallelujah!* Hello, baby girl." This last was to Casey.

"Hello, Loretta."

"Pizza again tonight, *Praise God!*"

"Yes."

The door smacked open, and Johnny filled the entryway. "Nice lady!"

Casey smiled. "Hello, Johnny."

He hugged her with abandon, and lumbered off to his station to roll silverware. Casey followed.

"Johnny, Ellen worked here with you, didn't she?"

He slid the silverware drawer out. "Oh, yes, ma'am, she was a nice lady."

"I'm sure she was." She watched as he carefully placed the knife, fork, and spoon on a napkin and rolled it all into a perfect oblong bundle. "Did she ever say anything to you about work?"

"Work?" His face crinkled in concentration. "About silverware?"

"No. No, I mean about HomeMaker."

"Oh, *that* work." He turned backed to his silverware, as if he didn't care to reply.

"*Praise the Lord,*" Loretta said, "Ellen was going to make the need for this kitchen go away, *thank you Jesus!*"

Casey went closer to her. "Did she tell you how?"

"Didn't say much, did she now, poor angel of God, but she was confident in His power, yes she was. *Praise the Lord!*"

"She thought God was going to save the factory?"

Loretta pursed her lips. "Now don't be getting that tone, young lady, although God loves you even so."

"I'm sorry. But I was serious. What made her confident? Trust in God?"

"That's always there, honey. But she was the one doing God's work and helping the meek and poor in spirit."

Casey clenched her fists against her hips. "But *how?*"

"Oh, well now, baby, I'd tell you if I knew, wouldn't I? *Hallelujah!*"

Casey took a deep breath, reminding herself that taking an elderly woman to the mat was really not appropriate. No matter how heartfelt it would be.

The door slapped open again, and Casey's stomach dropped. "Leila."

"Where's Eric?" The girl's eyes sparked with anger—and something else—when she saw Casey.

Casey jerked her thumb toward the dining room. "Out there."

Leila spun on her heel and marched out of the kitchen. Casey followed, stopping in the doorway to make sure Eric wasn't about to get assaulted. She needn't have worried. Leila's only concern seemed to be to find Eric and give him some urgent message. Somehow, Casey had the feeling it was about *her*.

Casey went back to the kitchen and took a couple heads of lettuce from the fridge, washing them and cutting off the brown spots with a knife. Maybe it was time for her to leave Home Sweet Home, at least, if not Clymer altogether. She wasn't getting any answers. Eric was angry with her. Leila was telling secrets. Loretta thought she was a heathen. Johnny had even turned his back on her.

She closed her eyes and leaned on the sink, a wave of dizziness sweeping through her.

"Don't go falling into the sink now," Death said. "You'll cut yourself with that knife."

Casey shook her head, her eyes still closed, and whispered, "No one would care."

"Sure they would. You'd get blood on the lettuce."

Casey straightened, giving Death a good glare. "Thanks so much for your concern."

Death shrugged and peeled a perfect yellow banana.

"What is with you?" Casey said. "First junk food, now the healthy stuff."

"I get bored. And besides, I'm really enjoying learning about—"

"Gardening. I know."

"Casey?" Eric came to stand beside Casey and she blinked as he stood in Death's spot, Death's form shimmering, but staying in place, outlining Eric's body. Eric shivered. "Is it cold in here, or is it just me?" He reached over to shut the door.

Leila stood in the entryway to the dining room, her expression triumphant, arms crossed over her chest. Casey went back to chopping lettuce, avoiding the sight of Death/Eric.

"Um, I'm sorry," Eric said. "I know you're just trying to help by asking me to think of these things. I'll go home tonight and look through my calendar. See if I can piece together which visit to my dad that would've been."

Casey nodded. "Good. That would be helpful."

Leila cleared her throat.

Eric looked back at her, then turned again to Casey, a violent shudder running through his body. He looked at the window, but it was closed. "Why is it so *cold* in here?"

"Go on back out to the dining room," Casey said. "We've got things under control in here."

"All right." He leaned closer. "But that means I've got to deal with Leila."

Casey grinned. "You're a big boy. You can handle her."

He glanced over at the girl in the doorway, who now had her fists planted on her hips. "I'm not so sure."

Casey nudged him out of the way as she leaned over the sink, and he left.

"That wasn't nice," she told Death.

Death shrugged. "I was here first."

Loretta walked past Casey, a stack of pizzas in her arms as she headed for the stove. "Another volunteer for the kitchen, *Praise God!* Did you bring a friend, Casey?"

Casey shook her head, somehow not surprised that Loretta could see Death. "No. This *friend* was just leaving."

Death frowned. "I was?"

"Nice lady's friend?" Johnny turned from his task in the corner and headed for Death, arms open.

"No! Not you, too!" Casey stepped in front of Death, and Johnny's face fell. "I mean," Casey stammered, "my friend has…a cold, Johnny. I don't want you to get it."

"Oh. Sorry, nice lady's friend!"

"Well," Loretta said, pointing at Death. "If you have a cold, baby, you get out of the kitchen. *Praise the Lord* we don't need anyone else getting sick."

"But I'm not—"

"You heard the woman," Casey said. "Get out."

Death frowned. "I'll be back."

"Oh," Casey said, sighing. "I have no doubt about that."

With a final glare, Death stomped out the back door, leaving it flung open.

Loretta clicked her tongue. "With a temper like that, we don't need more help, do we, *thank the Lord?*"

"That's right," Casey said.

For some reason cutting up lettuce got a whole lot more enjoyable after that.

The smell of pizza soon filled the kitchen, and Eric and Leila carried it out to the diners—Leila shooting Casey smug, angry looks—along with the salad and some chips. Leila must have felt so strongly about Casey's presence it was worth it to serve her own family. Casey stayed in the kitchen, helping Loretta and Johnny with dishes and refilling the pizza trays as necessary.

Before long the people were gone and the volunteers were standing around eating the leftovers. Leila didn't leave Eric's side, her demeanor daring Casey to make an issue of it. For the second time that night Casey had to remind herself that martial arts had no place in a charity kitchen.

"Well, it's about that time." Eric said, glancing at his watch.

"I'll drive you to rehearsal." Leila batted her eyes at Eric.

He glanced at Casey. "I'll just walk. Thanks, though."

"Oh, then I'll walk with you," Leila said. "I can leave my Bug parked in the back, can't I?"

Eric looked at Casey. "You coming?"

She smiled. "Why don't you two go ahead. I'll catch up with you there."

Leila's narrowed eyes widened, and she smirked, grabbing Eric's arm. "Come on, Eric, let's go."

With a pleading backward glance, Eric allowed Leila to lead him from the room. Casey listened until she heard the front door open and close.

"You should go, too," Loretta said. "You'll be late for rehearsal, *Praise God!*"

"I'll go in a minute. I just didn't want Leila to kill me before I got there."

Loretta chuckled. "You just take that friend of yours along, babydoll. Then that girl will behave."

A good idea, but there was no way Leila would be seeing Death. Casey was quite confident of that.

She picked up a pizza tray to take it to the sink, but Johnny was already coming at her for a hug, and the tray came up, smashing against her chest. He backed up, and they looked down at the mess, splotches of tomato sauce and cheese clinging to Casey's shirt.

Johnny cried out and grabbed a dishcloth, swiping at the spots, making little sobbing noises.

Casey gently took his wrists, holding them away from her. "It's okay, Johnny."

"I'm sorry, I'm sorry, I'm sorry." He jerked against her hold, wanting to go at the stains with the cloth.

"Really, Johnny." She tried to make eye contact. "It's okay. I'll wash it out."

"Just don't you put that blouse in the dryer until those stains are all gone, baby," Loretta said. "Or they'll be there until kingdom come, Lord willing."

Johnny gasped. "Not the dryer!" He jerked his hands upward, flinging the dishrag, narrowly missing Casey's face.

"I'll spray the spots really well," Casey said. "And I'll double check before throwing the shirt in the dryer. I promise."

"No!" Johnny said, coming at her again with the dishcloth. "Stay away from the dryer!"

Casey again grabbed his wrists, forcing him to look at her, but his anxiety had climbed way past a simple messy accident. "Johnny. It's okay. I'm not angry. The clothes will be fine. I promise."

"No! No!" He jerked and writhed, sudden tears running down his face.

Loretta was there now, laying soothing hands on Johnny's shoulders, praying for God to come and throw his calming presence over their beloved brother in Christ.

"The dryer!" Johnny screeched. "You have to stay away from the dryer!"

Casey shook her head. "Why, Johnny? Why do I have to stay away from the dryer?"

"Because dryers kill people!" he sobbed. "They *kill* people!" He wrenched his arms from Casey's and fell to the floor, grabbing her around her knees. "I don't want you to die, nice lady! Don't die!"

"I'm not going to die. I promise." She stroked his head, smoothing his hair back from his face. "But the dryer, Johnny. Why are you afraid of those?"

"When people use dryers they *die*," he said. "Ellen told me so."

Chapter Thirty-eight

Casey could get nothing more out of Johnny, partly because he was too distraught, but mostly, she thought, because he knew nothing further. Loretta couldn't remember hearing Ellen ever talk about dryers. Just that she had discovered something that could save the factory.

"She was happy about that, *praise God*," Loretta said, "but behind the happiness was something sad, too. Like what she'd found out was haunting her, may she rest in peace."

Which Casey could understand. If the saving of HomeMaker came at the expense of someone's life, Ellen would have to feel the irony, and sadness, in that.

"What do you know about this, L'Ankou?" Casey muttered as she walked to rehearsal. But Death, when wanted, chose not to come. "You really are an ass, you know," Casey said.

The air in front of her shimmered, but nothing materialized.

Rehearsal had already started when Casey slipped in the double doors, and Eric, Aaron, and Jack were on-stage. She scrambled to find her place in her script, glad to see the others rehearsing a scene she wasn't in. Becca showed obvious relief at her arrival, and Casey waved her an apology.

Lonnie squeezed into a seat beside her, his eyes glowing. "And where have you been, our mysterious stranger? I was afraid Thomas was going to blow a gasket when you weren't here at seven. Eric promised you were coming, but Thomas looked ready to pass out until you came in the door."

A glance at Thomas provided only his stony profile, his focus—at least the one he was showing—on the stage.

"Any clue why he was so freaked out?" Casey asked.

Lonnie grinned. "He's really anal about practice time?"

"Somehow I don't think that's it."

"No." He laughed. "Me, either. He never acts that way when Holly's late. Which she is again today."

Thomas turned and glared at them, and Lonnie covered his mouth with both hands. "I guess we need to behave," he said, from beneath his fingers.

"*We?*"

Lonnie pushed his hands tighter to keep from laughing out loud.

At the end of the scene Becca called a break, and Eric jumped off of the stage, making his way toward Casey, Leila close behind him.

"Uh-oh," Lonnie said. "Here comes loverboy. And his lapdog."

Casey smacked his shoulder, then got up to meet Eric. She pulled him to the side, away from Leila, and explained, in hushed tones, what Johnny had told her.

"A dryer *killed* somebody?"

"If Ellen was right. And if Johnny's correct about what she said."

Eric dropped into the nearest seat. "Todd didn't tell you that?"

"No." She sat down next to him. "He said what he and Karl talked about was personal, and had nothing to do with Ellen. But then, maybe he didn't know she knew about it. Speaking of Todd…" She looked up. "Where is he?"

"He was here earlier. Probably went outside for break. So that dryer latch we have—"

"—is somehow connected. It's got to be. I'm sure it's not actually the lock of that particular dryer—at least I wouldn't think so—but it's important." She leaned over and grabbed Eric's hand. "Eric, when you met with your dad that day, was it about dryers?"

"No. I mean, we never talked about dryers. Except in really vague ways about production. Never anything about somebody *dying*."

"Who's dying?"

They looked up at Leila, who stood, hip cocked, beside Casey's seat, her face betraying some kind of excitement.

"Nobody." Eric's voice was flat.

Leila gasped. "Eric, did you not *tell* her?"

Casey looked at him. "Tell me what?"

"Nothing," Eric said in the same flat tone.

Leila's nostrils flared. "So are you taking a break or not, Eric?" She glared at Casey, as if Casey was keeping him from his respite.

Casey stood. "I'm going outside. I need some fresh air." She walked quickly away, not wanting to hear anything else Leila might say.

Todd was not outside.

She waited in the lobby, in the hopes he would come through there before rehearsal resumed, but she was out of luck. By the time Becca was calling for them to return, Todd still was nowhere to be seen.

Casey went back into the theater, only to see Todd slumped in the front row. She moved up the aisle and sat beside him. He looked at her warily from beneath his half-closed eyes.

"What do you know about dryers?"

"*Dryers?*" His face was blank.

"You know, the appliance that dries clothes."

"I know what you mean. I'm not an idiot." He looked around, but no one was close. "What about dryers?"

"Did you and Karl ever talk about them?"

"About *dryers?*"

Casey felt someone's eyes on her, and she looked up to see Thomas staring at her from several rows back. "Yes," she said to Todd. "Did you ever have a discussion about them?"

His expression went from blank to confused. "No."

"Okay. Thanks."

"Casey! Todd!" Becca was gesturing to them. "Act five, scene one."

"Coming." She stood and looked down at Todd. "If you remember anything—"

"I'm telling you, we never talked about them."

Casey climbed the stairs to the stage, Todd following her to join Eric. Eric still hadn't recovered from what she'd told him, if the pallor of his skin was real and not just a trick of the lights. Casey winked at him, and a smile flickered on his face.

The double doors at the back of the theater flung open, and Holly strode in, making her way to the front.

"About time," Thomas growled.

Holly froze. "Excuse me?"

"You're late. Rehearsal began at seven."

She stood there, her mouth gaping, while the rest of the cast looked at each other with shock. Lonnie laughed out loud. Holly and Thomas both rounded on him, and he pinched his lips together with his fingers.

"Um, Act five, scene one, Holly," Becca said. "You'll be on in a few minutes."

Holly swung her hair off her neck and sat regally in a front row seat, her head forward, eyes at stage level. Casey caught Eric's eye, and he made a face.

"Okay, people," Thomas bellowed. "Let's go!"

They got through the scene, and the rest of rehearsal, without anyone blowing up or stalking out. The atmosphere wasn't exactly relaxed, however, and Casey breathed a sigh of relief when Thomas called it quits for the night.

"No rehearsal tomorrow," he said. "Take Sunday off."

"Thank you, kind leader," Lonnie said, then ducked the wadded papers Aaron and Jack threw at him.

Casey was making her way toward Jack, to see if Johnny's news about dryers sparked any memories, when Thomas called her name.

"I need to talk to you."

"*Again?*" Eric said.

Thomas bestowed an angry look on him. "I have the right to talk with my actors."

"Sure, but Thomas—"

"It's all right," Casey said. "You go on. I'll be fine."

"But we need to figure out what—"

"I'll be *fine*." *Shut up about the dryer, Eric.*

Leila was waiting beside Eric, cracking a stick of gum, and did her part in getting him up the aisle and out of the theater.

Becca stood at Casey's elbow, her arms full of notebooks. "Do you need me, Thomas?"

"What? Oh, no. You can go."

She shot a glance at Casey before leaving the same way as the others.

"Thomas…"

"Listen, *Casey*. I don't know who you are. But I know why you're here."

"You do?"

"I'm sorry I ever got involved in it, okay? I'm sorry I ever *went* to Louisville. I'm out of it now. It's over. Done. *Finis.*"

"Look, Thomas, I really don't know what you're talking about. I don't know what you were into—"

His head snapped up.

"—and it's really none of my business. Whatever the deal is between you and Eric, well, that's just the way it is."

"Eric?" His lips formed a tight line. "This is way past Eric."

"I don't understand."

He shook his head slowly. "I wish you wouldn't play it this way."

"Thomas, I'm not playing this any way. I'm telling you *I'm not here for you.*"

He laughed under his breath. "You said that the first day. I wish I could believe it."

"What can I do to prove it to you?"

He stood and gathered his things, still not looking at her. "Nothing. Not anymore. Good-bye, Casey." He strode quickly up the aisle and left, without looking back.

"Weird," Casey said out loud, and followed him up the aisle. His taillights were already shining in the distance by the time she made it outside.

Eric, however, was still there. "Do not tell me to go away."

"Okay."

"I'm walking you home, and I don't want any arguments about it."

She held up her hands. "Okay."

He cocked his head. "You're not going to tell me to leave you alone?"

"No."

"Oh. Well. Good. What did Thomas want?"

She let her hands fall. "He still thinks I'm a spy or a cop, or *somebody*, who's come to reveal some hidden secret about his past."

"Do you know one?"

"Not for sure. Certainly not from anything *you've* told me."

He winced.

"But I guess I wouldn't be surprised if he had a little gambling debt."

Eric's mouth dropped open.

Casey blinked. "I'm right? Really? I'm *right*."

Eric gave a humorless laugh. "No. Not exactly."

"It's not gambling."

"Oh, it's gambling, all right. But not just a *little*."

Casey stared in the direction Thomas' car had gone, then looked back at Eric. "So how *not just a little* are we talking about?"

Eric took a deep breath. "He gambled on horse races. Not just the Derby. But all of them. Whenever he could get away from the theater, and sometimes even when he couldn't. He lost so much money he had to take out loans."

"I'm thinking they weren't loans from banks."

"Hardly."

Casey took a step away, then back. "You're telling me there's organized crime in *Louisville*?"

"I know, it doesn't seem right, does it? But there's a lot of money at Churchill Downs."

She shook her head. "But who does that make me? Someone from the *mob*? Do I look like a leg breaker to you?"

His mouth twitched. "From what Rosemary told me—"

She waved him off. "Does he think I'm from them, or from the cops?"

He shrugged. "Either one would be bad for him."

"I guess so. Poor Thomas."

"Poor Thomas? Are you kidding me?"

She gave a little smile. "Sometimes people get in over their heads…"

He stared at her. "I just can't figure you out."

"Yeah, well. Maybe that's for the best. Shall we go?" She started off in the direction of The Nesting Place, not waiting for him to follow.

"Casey—" He trotted to catch up with her.

"So that's what you have over Thomas? You know about his gambling?"

"Well, partly. That and the fact he's been begging my dad for money. He'd be devastated if people found out about it."

Casey winced. Having to ask Karl Willems for *anything* would be enough to send you into depression. Asking for huge amounts of money would be enough to incapacitate even the strongest person.

"Where's Leila, anyway?" she said, noticing they were alone. "I'm assuming you didn't leave her to walk back to her car by herself."

"No. Todd drove her."

"Bet she wasn't too happy about that."

Eric winced. "No. Not too happy."

Casey stuck her script in her jacket pocket. "Did you have a chance to say anything to Jack?"

"About the dryers? Yeah. I told him, and Aaron, too, what Johnny said. It didn't mean anything to either of them, but they promised they'd think about it."

They walked in silence for a few more steps.

"Casey…"

"Yeah?"

He waited a few more moments, began to speak, then stopped. "Did one of HomeMaker's dryers *actually* kill somebody?"

"I guess it's possible. But you'd expect the culprit to be something electrical, not a door latch. Or something like a heating element that could burn a house down."

"Yeah."

Eric fell silent as they passed under a streetlight and turned a corner on the sidewalk. "I think I remember."

"Remember what?"

"What I was talking to Karl about in that video. I can't imagine it would have anything to do with… It was about Home Sweet Home. I wanted HomeMaker to chip in some money for it. A charitable donation, to help those who had lost jobs."

"And what did Karl say?"

"What do you think? That the company was having enough financial troubles on its own, which was why they're leaving town in the first place. HomeMaker couldn't afford to be sponsoring anything else."

"Of course." No charity for the people he was sending tumbling toward poverty. "Did he give Thomas money?"

Eric shrugged. "I don't know. On the one hand I could see him doing it, since he's an old family *friend*." He spat the word. "But he could just as easily have told him to forget it, and take his lumps like a man."

"It would've been a lot of money, right? Which Karl could probably afford."

"I guess."

"That still doesn't answer why Todd was at his office that day. And why he was so angry. Todd said it was personal. There was no reason he would know anything about Thomas. Unless Karl told him."

"On the other hand, maybe Karl gave Thomas some money and Todd was there to try to talk him out of it. He would know Karl's money dealings better than anybody, although I'm not sure why it would've made him so mad. Unless Karl was using HomeMaker money." He waved his script at her. "Either way, the visit to Karl's office would have nothing to do with Ellen."

"Except that she ate at Home Sweet Home."

"*What?*"

"That's what we were talking about. *Your* visit, and that Karl wouldn't give you any money for your charity. And Ellen ate there."

"*Served* there."

"Okay."

He sighed. "All right. She ate there, too. Along with her kids."

Casey wanted to take his hand. To comfort him.

"*Do it.*"

She jerked away from him and glared at Death.

"Come on," Death said. "Hold his hand. It would be so *cute.*"

Casey shoved her hands into her pockets.

"Aww," Death said. "You are so *boring*. Oh!" Death glanced behind them and raised a fist. "*Yes!* Things are about to get a lot more interesting." Death was gone.

Casey stopped, allowing Eric to get several steps ahead before he turned. "What is it?"

She held up a hand, watching under the streetlight they'd passed seconds before.

Two men came around the corner. Two men she'd seen before, talking to Thomas. Taffy and Bone.

They saw her. And they saw Eric.

Casey's brain shifted gears. Her breathing deepened, and her muscles relaxed, even as her nerves tingled. She stepped in front of Eric. "Can I help you gentlemen?"

They stopped ten feet away. Taffy, as she'd noticed before, had a wrestler's physique. Huge and thick under a loosely fitting jacket and black dress pants. He smiled. "I think you might just be able to, little lady."

"And how would that be?"

He glanced at Bone, who hadn't even a hint of a smile on his feral-looking face. "If you could just tell us who sent you to this tiny little town. The cops? Our...*friends* across town in Kentucky?"

"No one sent me. And I've never been to Kentucky."

He continued smiling, nodding as if she'd said something clever. "That's what Mr. Black told us you'd say."

"Thomas?" Eric's voice had gone tight, and high.

Casey waved at him to shut up, not turning from the men. "It's the truth."

"I see. I guess your definition of truth is different from ours."

"I guess so."

He was talkative. Very large, and very talkative. Casey figured he was already deciding how quickly he would take her down if she didn't comply. His overconfidence was obvious in his swagger, and in the look in his eye.

Casey breathed in through her nose. To her left sat a car. A Pontiac, blocking the way. To her right sat a row of homes, a few large trees, windows with lights shining, TVs flickering. Behind her, Eric, who didn't have a clue what was about to happen.

The man on the left, Bone, the one who had almost discovered her behind the theater's curtains, he was the scary one. About a hundred pounds shy of his partner, his body was lean and wiry, his face all cheekbone and jaw. His eyes, expressionless above a nose that had been broken and badly reset, watched Casey, while the rest of him remained still. His arms hung loose at his sides, hands open, his feet spread shoulder-width. He had no jacket, and no gun that Casey could see. That didn't mean he didn't have something else.

"I'd like to talk with you a little longer," Taffy said. "Just so's we can get straight exactly what the truth is."

"That would be good," Casey said. "To get at the truth."

Taffy stepped forward, his hand out, as if to shake.

"Eric," Casey said under her breath. "Run away."

"What?"

"*Run!*"

She would've run, too, and with the element of surprise could've outdistanced the two thugs in seconds, but she couldn't leave Eric. Not with these two.

Casey slid her hand into Taffy's, but instead of shaking it she torqued his thumb, jamming the pressure point, bringing him to his knees. As he dropped she jerked up her knee, crushing his nose. He fell forward, unconscious, and Casey grabbed the back of his shirt, and his chin, spinning him down and forward, between her and Bone.

Now Bone was smiling.

"You—" Eric said.

Casey turned and shoved him away. "*Run!*"

This time he listened.

Casey heard Bone coming, but didn't have time to turn before his fist slammed into her kidney. She fell to the ground, gasping, clutching her side, and rolled to the left as his foot came down where her back had been.

She flipped to her feet, her brain fuzzy, vision blurred, back pulsing with pain.

A dog barked and Bone glanced to the side, waiting, but the dog went quiet. Bone turned back, and as Casey brought her hands up, he stepped in to hit her with a roundhouse punch. She jerked away so that he missed her jaw, but his fist caught her lip, smashing it against her teeth. She tasted blood.

He smiled again.

Casey sat back on her right leg and kicked his inner thigh. He stumbled to the left, and she turned to run. With a yell he lunged, grabbing her hair and jerking her backward. She reached up, trapping his hand with both of hers, and spun inside, double-twisting until his arm was behind him in a lock and his head was lowered. She rocked him forward, smashing his head against the Pontiac.

Spitting blood and faint from the kidney pain, Casey knew she couldn't run away. At least not very far. She glanced into the Pontiac.

There were keys on the seat.

Dropping the man to the sidewalk, she stumbled around the back of the car and wrenched open the driver's door, flinging herself inside. She grabbed the keys and poked one into the ignition. Not the right one. She pulled at the ring, but it was stuck.

The passenger door opened, and Bone lunged across the seat. She brought up her foot and kicked him in the face, his nose spraying blood as he shot backward.

"Come on, come on," she pleaded, jiggling the keys.

Abandoning the keys, Casey scrambled to get out of the car, but Bone was up again, shaking his head, rounding the hood. He kicked the door, catching her right forearm and sending it back with a snap. She clutched the arm to her stomach as the door repelled against Bone. He kicked the door again, but she hopped backward, out of the way.

Bone wavered there, his face splotched with red. Casey felt her injured arm with her other hand. She didn't think it was broken. She hoped not.

Bone's eyes focused on her. Noting the curb several feet behind him, Casey aimed a kick at his stomach with her right foot. He stepped back, and she threw a sidekick with her left. He took another step away, and she went after him with a right kick, and then a left backward one. One more front kick, and he stumbled over the curb, falling onto his back.

Casey leapt forward to stomp on his stomach and he caught her foot, twisting it inside. She went with the twist and spun away, circling to face him. He stood up, his face a mask of rage now, his eyes horrible amidst the blood. Casey brought up her arms, the right one throbbing.

Bone grabbed at his ankle and came back up with a blade. He slashed at her and she spun away, but the knife sliced her left shoulder, through her jacket. He came at her again, thrusting at her stomach. She danced sideways, circling away. He was smiling again, his teeth smeared with red.

Casey shook her head, trying to focus. Her right arm throbbed, her left shoulder was staining her jacket red, and blood filled her mouth. She spat again.

Taffy groaned from his spot on the sidewalk, but neither Casey nor Bone broke eye contact. She could only hope she had hit Taffy hard enough he wouldn't actually be getting up, or reaching for his gun.

Bone feinted to her right, and she spun away, circling. Her strength was fading. If Taffy got up, she was done. She couldn't outrun Bone. She was losing blood. Her back ached.

She realized Bone had stopped coming at her. He was waiting. Waiting for her to make a mistake.

With a deep breath she stumbled left and clutched her bloody arm, exposing her neck. Bone came at her with an overhand strike. She reached up and passed his arm down, jamming the knife into his left thigh. He screamed. She pulled the knife from his leg, grabbed it with both hands, and stepped back, knife blade up.

Bone clutched his leg as blood spurted out, soaking his pant leg. Bright red blood covered his hands as he pressed against his thigh, and he yanked off his shirt, winding it around his leg. The shirt didn't staunch the flow, but quickly turned red itself, the blood saturating the material within seconds.

He looked up at Casey, his eyes wild. Casey stayed where she was, brandishing the knife, watching with disbelief as Bone's lifeblood flowed through the tourniquet and down his leg.

He blinked once, with disbelief, and Casey stared into his eyes, her teeth clenched, her breath caught in her chest. He lurched forward, his arms outstretched. She backed up. Her knife wavered.

"Please," Bone said.

He stumbled toward her again, grabbing her shoulder with a bloody hand. She held the knife up, toward his throat. She was ready. But Bone's eyes were glazing over, and his breath rasped in his throat. Slowly he leaned forward, his weight tipping toward her, his fingers clutching her shoulder.

"Please."

Bone dropped to his knees, and Casey stepped away as he fell, his face twisting to the right as it met the ground. He jerked once. Twice. His legs spasmed, and he coughed, blood spurting from his mouth.

And then he was still.

"Oh, God," Casey said. "OhGodohGodohGod."

She fell backward against the Pontiac, the knife clattering to the ground. Nausea hit her, and she leaned sideways over the hood, vomiting onto the car and street. She wiped her face with her sleeve and tried to breathe.

Oh, no. Oh, God, no.

"Casey?"

Casey jerked her head up. Eric stood twenty feet away, his eyes wide. "What—"

The sound of a siren split the air, and Casey sucked in a breath. Of course. Of course, Eric would get the police.

"Eric," she said. "I'm so...so sorry."

She pushed herself off of the car, and ran away.

Chapter Thirty-nine

Lillian cut Casey off outside the back door of The Nesting Place, a finger on her lips. She gasped at the sight of Casey's face. "What—"

"I'm all right." She *was*. She *would* be. "What are you doing?"

"They're inside."

Casey's heart fell. They were here *already*? But where was the cruiser?

"I'm sorry," Casey said. "I never meant to—"

"Shh." Lillian pulled Casey's arm, and Casey yanked it back, her hand grabbing her shoulder, her right forearm protesting the movement. Lillian let go, but gestured her further from the house, into the shadows. "You need a doctor."

"No. *No*. What's happening?"

Lillian raised her hands toward Casey's mouth, but she reared away. Lillian dropped her arms to her sides. "Rosemary's keeping them busy. I said I needed to go to bed, because I wasn't feeling well."

With her glinting eyes and upright posture, Casey could see that was far from the truth.

Lillian jerked a thumb toward the house. "They're insisting on seeing your room."

"My *room*? Why? It's not like I've had time to—"

"I'm not even sure how they knew you were staying here, because I'm sure *you* didn't tell them, but here they are."

"Of course they know where I'm staying. Chief Reardon knew it the first time I talked to him."

"Denny?" Lillian blinked. "But *he's* not in our sitting room."

Of course. Other cops. Detectives. Could be the FBI or ATF if Casey's suspicions about the men who attacked her were correct.

"I don't know who they are, exactly," Lillian said. "But they seem to know a lot about you. Said they're business associates of yours. Rosemary didn't like them from the get-go, because the woman's dye job is simply horrendous."

Casey went cold. "Dye job?"

"Yes. Like she did it at home in a dark bathroom with a generic brand."

Casey swallowed. "And she's with a man whose face looks like—"

"—it was cut in half and smooshed back together by a extremely untalented sculptor."

Casey sank to the ground. They'd found her. And she didn't have to wonder how. That damn *phone*. *Dammit*, Ricky.

"I can't…" Casey said. "I have to go."

"But your arm. Your face."

"Lillian. *I have to go.*"

Lillian stared at her for a few more moments, then sighed. "Okay." She stepped behind a bush and pulled out Casey's backpack. "I hope I got everything. There's no first aid equipment."

Casey's eyes stung.

"Rosemary will keep them busy for a while," Lillian said. "We told them you were out, but that we were expecting you back late. They seem to have settled in for the wait."

Casey dropped her chin to her chest. "I wanted…I didn't want…"

"I know, sweetheart." Lillian squatted, knees popping, and laid an arm over Casey's shoulders. "We'll see you again. And whatever your trespasses, my dear, whatever it is you're running from, we hope you're soon running back."

Casey swiped the tears from her eyes with a thumb and forefinger, and they came away, wet with tears and blood. She wiped them on her pants. "Tell Rosemary…"

"I'll tell her, darling."

Lillian stood and helped Casey back to her feet.

"The bike is there," Lillian said, pointing to the side of the house. "It's yours now, if you can…" She gestured at Casey's arm.

"I can't take your bike—"

"You can. You *will*. Go."

A light flickered in the back room, and Casey jumped further into the shadows. Lillian waited quietly, but nothing else moved.

"Go, sweetheart," she finally said.

"I never paid you."

Lillian laughed quietly. "My dear, you've paid us in more ways than one. Now *go*."

Casey hitched her bag onto her back, wincing as the strap scraped her shoulder, and stumbled to the bike. She swung her leg over the seat and rode quickly away from the house, not looking back, her right arm cradled against her stomach. She didn't reach up again to wipe the tears streaming down her cheeks.

Chapter Forty

It was dark in Eric's back yard. Dark and quiet. A neighbor's garage stood open to the night, the car cold. She rolled her bike into the dark space, where it would sit, camouflaged among the family's bikes, one a tiny pink two-wheeler with training wheels, streamers dangling from the handlebars. No one would notice the old Schwinn before she had a chance to take it.

Hunkered down in the garage, she gingerly pulled her shirt over her head, wincing as the material came away from her sliced shoulder. The blood had begun to clot, and the wound started bleeding again as she tore the fabric from her arm. Ripping the shirt with her teeth, she awkwardly tied a strip around her arm to staunch the bleeding.

She unzipped her bag, pulled out a dark, long-sleeved shirt, and eased it over her head. A rake hung on the wall just above her, and the nail was long enough to accommodate her pack, as well. She hefted it up, snagging the nail. The bag was inconspicuous there. Just one more thing, amidst the tools and sports equipment.

Casey looked at her bag. At her bike. She should just go. Just leave. Take off into the night. But even if she did, even if she somehow avoided the cops in Clymer, could she live with that? Could she live with letting Ellen's death be branded a suicide? Could she let Eric wonder forever what had happened—either with Ellen or Bone and Taffy?

Besides, there was no guarantee she could avoid the cops, traveling on a bicycle.

Casey stepped carefully from the garage. There was no good hiding place for her in there. She considered Eric's yard, with its shrubbery, but knew it would be a foolhardy spot to wait for him to come home. His house was the same. Even if she could find a way in, she would be discovered when someone—whoever it was—came to hunt her down.

But what if she didn't find a way *in*.

The houses on either side were dark, and Casey could see no tell-tale signs of activity. No dogs had as yet noticed her presence, and she was hopeful none would.

She eyed the trees around Eric's house. Not huge. But large enough. Sticking to the shadows, she made her way to the side of the house, where a mid-sized maple grew only feet from the building. With a leap, she grabbed onto a lower branch and walked her feet up the trunk until she could swing herself up to straddle the branch. She lay against the tree limb, gasping, focusing past the pain in her arms and back. She had to move. She grabbed a close branch and eased herself upward, climbing until she was level with the roof.

The branches here weren't thick, but were at least as round as her legs. Leaning forward onto her stomach, she shimmied toward the roof of the house, the wood bending under her weight. The branch cracked with a loud pop, and dropped several inches. She froze, waiting to plummet to the ground, but the branch stopped, whether by its own strength or the support of another. When she was sure it was done moving she inched forward again, the branch bending until she was within reaching distance of the roof.

The limb cracked again, and with a lunge she grabbed onto the edge of the roof and scrabbled upward. The branch flicked back up, as if she'd never been on it.

Casey looked around the roof for a good spot, and scooted on her stomach to the opposite side, the driveway side, where she could see when Eric arrived. A chimney sat close to the peak of the roof, and she pulled herself into its shadow, where she brought her knees to her chest, fitting herself into the darkness.

It would take hours for Eric to be done with the police. By the time they finished at the scene and took his statement it would be the middle of the night. Casey settled down for a long wait, aware of the rustling leaves, the sound of faraway dogs, and the occasional car passing the house. Only when her legs began to cramp did she allow herself to move, and then just a minute amount, enough to stop the pain.

She leaned her head against the bricks of the chimney. Her kidney ached. Her lip throbbed. It had stopped bleeding, but she could feel the blood, crusty and already scabbing on her mouth.

The dead man's blood hadn't had a chance to begin clotting.

Casey shook her head. She couldn't think about it. Couldn't think about those eyes, blanker even in death than they'd been in life. The knife, left on the ground beside the Pontiac, holding both Bone's prints and hers. Taffy, who would be waking up in police custody.

Lights danced across the backyard, and Casey brought her head up at the sound of a car pulling into the driveway. She peeked around the edge of the chimney. Not Eric's car. A police cruiser. The doors were opening. Eric was stepping out. Eric and the chief.

"Check the yard," Reardon said to an officer, who climbed out the driver's side. "We'll check the house, make sure she's not hiding here."

Casey eased back behind the chimney. Pulled her knees to her chest. Squeezed her eyes shut, childlike. *If I can't see them, they can't see me.*

Long minutes passed. A breeze blew across the roof, sending leaves past her, skidding across the roof, and she shivered.

She opened her eyes. The officer's flashlight was coming back now. She could see the beam as it bobbed and weaved across the branches of the tree, across the roof, just beyond her toes.

A door slapped open. "Well?" Reardon.

"Nothing, sir. She's not here."

Silence.

"Eric said she ran, sir. She could be long gone already."

Casey could feel the chief's doubts. His inability to believe that she had left town so quickly, leaving no clue as to where she'd gone. "Yeah, well, Eric doesn't know everything, does he?"

Footsteps sounded on the driveway, and the chief's voice was louder. "You know what I want, Eric. She shows up, you tell her to come in. It will be better for her if she tells me the story herself."

"But I told you—"

"You hear what I'm saying?"

A pause. "I hear you."

"Good. We didn't need this, Eric. Our town doesn't need any more death."

"Yes. I know."

Casey held her breath as she listened, and soon the car doors opened, and slammed shut. One. Two. The car eased out of the driveway, the lights flickering against the house and tree. It drove away.

"They're gone, Casey," Eric said quietly. "If you're out there."

He waited for several seconds, then closed the door with a quiet *snick*.

Casey dropped her head to her knees. They were gone *now*. But when would they be coming *back*?

It took them about forty minutes. The car pulled into the drive, and Casey heard one door open, and footsteps up the stairs. She waited. Whoever it was must have rung the doorbell and received no response, because he banged on the door. It opened.

"What?" Eric sounded sleepy, and irritated.

"Just checking in," Reardon said. "To be sure she hasn't come by."

"She's not here." Was that pain in his voice? "Come in and look."

"Oh, I don't need to do that," Reardon said. "I trust you."

Eric laughed.

"Sorry," Reardon said. "Go back to sleep."

The door slammed, and Casey listened to Reardon's footsteps, the car door opening and closing. In a few seconds, they were gone.

She waited an hour this time, and then five minutes more, before crab-walking down the roof. She made her way to the back of the house, where a first-story layer jutted out over the yard. Easing herself over the side, shingles scraping her stomach, she let herself down, dropping into the grass and rolling. She lay motionless for several seconds, waiting for movement in the surrounding yards, gritting her teeth and holding her shoulder. When she saw nothing, she crept to the back door. She was relieved to find the door unlocked.

She entered what looked to be a mudroom and closed the door quietly behind her. Tiptoeing her way through the space and into the kitchen, she went through the house, checking each room on the first floor. Eric was not there.

She climbed the stairs, sticking to the edges, where they were less likely to creak, and paused on the landing. Three rooms. All with wide open doors.

Eric was in the first one. He lay, fully clothed, diagonally across his bed, his mouth open, his face relaxed in sleep. She went in and placed her hand over his mouth. His eyes flew open, and he sat up, pushing her hand away.

"My God, Casey, where have you *been*?"

She sat on the bed, next to him, feeling the warmth of his sleep on the sheets. "I'm sorry. I just…I can't get into this kind of thing with the police."

"*This kind of thing*? Exactly what does that mean?"

She blanched.

"I'm sorry," Eric said. "I'm sorry. It was self-defense. I know that. *They* know that."

"Do they?"

He looked at her for a long moment before climbing out of the bed and going to the window, where he put a hand on the wall and peered out into the yard. He looked fragile in the moonlight seeping through the window. "You do realize you *killed* him."

"Yes. Yes, I do."

"I didn't think—"

"I didn't mean to, Eric. He was just so strong, and coming at me so hard, and so fast."

He turned back toward her. "I know. I told the police."

"But Eric, you weren't there."

"Yes," he said. "I was." The look in his eyes brooked no argument.

"I can't ask you to lie for me."

"You didn't. You haven't. But I know what happened."

"Do you?" She remembered his wild eyes, staring at her across the sidewalk. Across the bodies.

He was silent for a few moments. "I thought so."

He came back to the bed and sat next to her. He took her hand, studying her fingers. She left her hand in his, feeling nothing from him but a childlike fascination as he ran his own fingers along hers.

"Leila knows who you are," Eric said.

Casey froze.

"She wouldn't let it be. She looked and looked until she found you."

Casey pulled her hand from his. "Did she?"

"She used your first name, assuming that, at least, was true. She got the librarian to tell her the name on your driver's license, and the issuing state."

Oh, Stacy, you dumb man.

Eric turned toward her. "And now *I* know. I *know*, Casey Maldonado."

Casey wrapped her arms around her stomach, hugging herself. She stood. "I have to go."

"No!" He jumped up and got between Casey and the doorway. "You can't run away just because I know."

"Oh, really? And what exactly is it you *know*, Eric?"

"About your husband. Your…your son."

Casey hiccupped. "You don't…you can't *know*."

"You can't keep running away, Casey. You've got to face it."

She jabbed a finger in his chest, and he winced, holding his hands up to defend himself. "I have to *face* it? Do you even understand what it is I have to *face?*"

"I thought—"

"They're dead, Eric. *Dead*. They died in front of my eyes. Exploded into a million pieces, while I was thrown clear. Twenty feet away, into a clump of cattails. I should have been in there with them. I should have…"

She feinted toward the door, but he caught her elbow and spun her back, crushing her to him, his arms around her, pinning her own arms against her body. She fought at first, squirming, kicking, trying to take his feet out from under him, but he held fast, not allowing her leverage.

"Let me go!" she cried into his chest. "Let me *go!*"

Eric lifted her off the ground and carried her, still fighting, to the bed, where he fell onto it, holding her beneath him, his height and weight enough to keep her captive, his legs on top of hers, not giving her a chance to get into a position to fight back. She screamed and cried, picturing Reuben, Omar, Ricky, her mother…Lillian and Rosemary, the woman with the bad hair…Eric, and Ellen…even the dead man she'd left on the sidewalk.

Eventually she shuddered, and stopped, her breaths coming in gasps, her face, and Eric's, wet from tears.

Eric kept his weight on top of her, watching her face, until he dropped his forehead gently onto hers. "Can I let you go now?"

"No. No, don't let me go."

So he held her there, his warmth and body trapping her beneath him as she shivered and shook, until she finally, with one last shudder, tapped him on the hip with a finger, one of the few body parts she could move. "Eric."

"Yes?"

"I can't breathe."

He lifted himself onto his elbows and rolled off of her, leaving her flat and deflated. He sat on the edge of the bed, looking down at her, smoothing her tear- and blood-sticky hair from her face. "I'm sorry, Casey."

"Yeah." She closed her eyes. "Yeah, I'm sorry, too." She could hear him breathing, could hear her own breaths matching his. She rolled onto her side, away from him, hugging her sore wrist to her chest.

"I can't do it," Eric said.

She opened her eyes. "Do what?"

"Leave Ellen. I can't let her disappear. I can't let her death be what they want us to think. Chief Reardon never even questioned it. Just believed what the forensic people said."

She rolled back toward him. "We don't have to let her disappear, Eric."

"But what can we do? We have nothing, except—"

"The DVD," they said together.

"I can't go back to get it from your mom," Casey said. "There are…I can't go back."

He nodded, not asking her to explain. "Well, then, it's good you don't have to."

"I don't?"

"Nope. Because I've got it right here. I brought it home after that night at their house."

"You did?" Casey sat up.

"Yes. Come on."

"What about the cops? They'll probably be back. They'll see the light downstairs."

He stopped. "Okay. Wait here."

He was back in less than a minute, sliding the DVD into a player on top of his dresser. "This TV isn't nearly as good as Rosemary and Lillian's, but it should do."

They fast-forwarded through Eric's visit and the minutes of Yvonne typing, until they got to Todd's arrival. They watched his entrance and exit, and fast-forwarded again, through the remaining office footage of Yvonne's office work, all the way to the blue screen.

"Nothing," Eric said.

"Let's watch again."

They did, but saw nothing much more than Karl's door and Yvonne's desk.

"I don't get it," Eric said. He tossed the remote onto the quilt and yawned, rubbing his hand over his face.

Casey picked up the remote and went back to the first frame of the footage, freezing the picture. She sucked in a breath. "Eric."

"Yeah?"

"Look at the picture."

"I'm looking."

"What are we looking at?"

He shrugged. "Karl's door."

Casey shook her head. "What is in the *middle* of the frame?"

He squinted at the TV. "Yvonne?"

"And?"

He sat up. "Yvonne's computer."

Casey started the DVD again and jumped up from the sofa, standing with her face inches from the screen. "I can't read the typing on here. It's too small."

Eric went to the player and ejected the DVD. "Come on. We'll look on my computer."

They left the lights off as they went downstairs, Casey avoiding windows. Eric's computer sat in a messy office, one of the four bedrooms in his house. He put in the disk, and with the media player he enlarged the screen of Yvonne's computer so they could see the typing.

"These are just bills," Eric said. "They look normal. Nothing unusual about paying utility bills or insurance premiums."

"You're sure?"

"No, but I think so."

"Okay. Move ahead."

They fast-forwarded, stopping frequently, moving past payroll and inter-office memos about packing up supplies, announcements telling employees to be sure to sign up for their severance packages, and production lists.

"There," Eric said. "What's that?"

Casey's stomach flipped. She knew the format. She knew it all too well. "It's a contract."

"About what?" Eric said, bending closer to the screen.

Casey noted the names at the beginning of the document: MIKE and PATRICIA MARLOWE.

"This contract is between HomeMaker and these people," Casey said. "The Marlowes." She read further, the hair on the back of her neck prickling. "It says someone died from using one of HomeMaker's appliances." She looked at Eric. "It was a dryer."

Chapter Forty-one

Eric slid the DVD into its sleeve. "So it's true. Ellen was right. Where do we go to find out more? HomeMaker?"

Casey shook her head. "There's surveillance there. We'd be seen for sure." She sighed. "Who would be the best person to talk to?" She held a hand up. "Other than Karl."

"That's easy. Yvonne." Eric chewed his lip.

Casey watched his face go through several emotions. "What?"

"Talking to Yvonne is probably not the smartest thing."

"Why not?"

He closed his eyes and shook his head.

"*What*, Eric?"

"Yvonne is…well, she's married to a cop."

"A cop? Which one?"

He winced. "The one who was here earlier."

"Yvonne is married to the *chief?*"

"No. No, not him. The patrolman."

Casey rested her forehead in her hand. "So how do we talk to her?"

"Do you think he's home? I mean, wouldn't he be out with the chief, at the scene?"

"He could be. He was with him an hour or so ago. But there's no way to know for sure." Casey stood up and paced the room. "What time is it?"

Eric glanced at the computer. "About one-thirty."

"When do the workers take their lunch break?"

"At HomeMaker? Three-o'clock, I think. Why?"

"Is there a way to get from the factory part of the complex to the administrative offices?"

"Sure. There's a hallway that connects them. Two hallways, actually."

"And you have keys?"

He shrugged. "I have a master. I can get into anywhere except Karl's office. What are you thinking?"

"Do the workers go outside during their break?"

"Lots of them. To smoke, or eat their lunches." His face cleared. "We're going to mix in with them, and sneak into the building, aren't we?"

"You up for it?"

"Oh, yeah."

"We'll have to walk."

"*Walk?*"

"If the cops spot your car, we're screwed."

"Right. Besides…" He grinned crookedly. "My car's still back at Home Sweet Home."

Casey grimaced. "Does that mean your keys are, too?"

"Just the ones for the car. Karl would kill me if someone got ahold of HomeMaker keys, so I keep those separate."

"Good. Put on some shoes. And we need light blue button-down shirts. You have any?"

"I'm sure I do. While I'm looking, um…"

"What?"

He touched his lip. "You'd better clean up a little."

Casey found his bathroom, and tried not to be too shocked at her appearance. It was a wonder Eric hadn't fainted when he first saw her. Her lip was swollen to at least twice its size, and blood had spattered across her face and chest. There was even some in her hair.

Not all her own blood, she was sure. She swallowed down the bad taste that rose in her mouth.

She scrubbed her face, being gentle around her lip, and brushed out her hair with a comb she found in a drawer. She also found some ibuprofen, and took a couple of them with water from the sink, hoping they would ease the throbbing in her arms, back, and lip.

Eric knocked on the door. "Here's a shirt."

She took it from him and closed the door again, stripping off her long-sleeved tee. Untying the material from around her arm, she grimaced at the nasty cut on her shoulder. It should probably have had stitches, but after washing it off she used some regular Band-Aids from the medicine cabinet to pull it as closed as she could before wrapping an Ace bandage around her whole upper arm. It was the best she could do.

Stuffing her bloodied shirt in the wastebasket, she put on Eric's. A little large, but she wouldn't complain about that. She twisted her hair tightly and tied it into a knot. Ready. On her way out she hesitated, then stepped back into the bathroom to run water in the sink and wash away any tell-tale blood. She retrieved her shirt from the trash and snatched the bloody washcloth from the sink.

"We'll dump these on the way," she told Eric when she joined him in his dark mudroom. "I don't want the cops finding them here and getting you in trouble."

"I'm already in trouble."

Casey smiled grimly. "You got some dark jackets we can wear over these? And some ballcaps?"

He went back to his room and returned with a black turtleneck, a dark blue sweater, and a few choices for hats. Casey chose the sweater, not wanting the feeling of the band around her neck, and a dark blue Indians cap to go over her hair.

"Eric, how far away does Yvonne live from here?"

"A couple of blocks. Maybe three."

She glanced at the clock. "I think we have time for a detour, as long as we keep it short. It might even make our visit to HomeMaker unnecessary."

"What about her husband?"

"I think you're right, that he'll be with the chief. But if it looks like he's around, we'll split. And you'll need to talk to her yourself."

He looked uncertain.

"You can do it. If you're scared, you just act like you're brave."

He smiled weakly. "I can try."

"Good. Okay, here we go. And here's how we should do it."

After listening to her plan, Eric went out the back door, making an unnecessary trip to the garage in the hopes it would scare out any cops waiting for him. He then continued down the alley. Casey watched from the back window, but after a few minutes was convinced no one was following.

She eased out the door and followed the shadows through the yard and into the alley, where she broke into a jog. She caught up with Eric at the second intersection, and tossed her shirt and the washcloth into a Dumpster.

He glanced at her and she nodded. They were in the clear. For the moment.

It didn't take long to get to Yvonne's house. The windows were dark. No movement, no lights.

Eric's light hair shone too brightly in the dim streetlight, and Casey gestured for him to put his hat on. He made a face. "It's itchy."

Casey didn't respond, and he slid the cap over his hair.

The front of the house was hidden from where Casey stood. "Does Yvonne's husband park his car in the garage or on the street?"

"I don't know. I think they only have a single-car garage, so his might be in the driveway."

Casey eased closer to the back yard of Yvonne's house. She picked up a stick and tossed it into the fenced-off area, ducking behind a tree. When there was no response, she found another stick, a bigger one this time, and threw it closer to the house. No dogs. No movement. No lights.

"Well?" Eric said. "What now?"

Casey didn't answer. The garage was attached to the near side of the house. Sticking to the shadows, she walked along the side of the garage, stopping before she got to the front. She listened, hearing nothing but Eric following too closely, gravel crunching under his feet. Lowering herself into a squat, she peered around the front of the garage, her eyes at knee level.

The driveway was empty, as was the curb in front of the house.

Gesturing to Eric to stay, she eased around the corner, glad to see a small window in the garage door. She peeked in. It was too dark to see anything except what looked like a sedan-sized vehicle.

She went back to the corner. "You know what kind of car Yvonne's husband drives?"

"Not a car. A truck. Don't know the kind."

She nodded. "He's not home."

"So let's go."

She held up a hand. "This is all you, Eric. She knows I'm here, we might as well call the cops ourselves."

He nodded, his face tightening. "And what am I asking her, exactly?"

"What she can tell you about the person who died because of the dryer."

He took a deep breath and let it out.

"You don't have to do this," Casey said.

"Yes. I do." He wasn't looking at her now, but at the door of the house. Without another word he walked across the driveway and rang the doorbell, peering in the window beside the door. He jumped back, the sound of barking filling the night.

A face appeared briefly at the door, and the door opened. "You stay!" Yvonne said, pointing back toward the house. She scooted out the door, closing it behind her. The dogs barked and whined, their claws making high-pitched squeals on the door.

Casey stayed in the shadow of the garage, trying to see without being seen. Even in the dim light she could read the anxiety on Yvonne's face. Eric was gesturing, talking. Casey couldn't make out his words, except for Ellen's name, repeated several times.

"No!" Yvonne finally said, her voice shrill. "No. No, no, no."

Eric stumbled backward, Yvonne's hands out as if she'd pushed him.

"I can't tell you. I won't." She looked around, as if expecting someone to be in the driveway.

Casey pulled her head back, behind the garage.

"Leave it alone, Eric," Yvonne said. "Please. Ellen wouldn't… You have to. It's not… Just *go away*!" She broke off with a sob, and the door opened, then slammed.

Eric pounded on the door. "Yvonne! Yvonne, please! I need your help!"

There was no response, except for the high-pitched barking of the dogs. Eric took one more look at the two heads appearing at the door's window, and lurched back behind the garage. "It's no use, Casey. I'm sorry."

Casey led him back through the neighbor's yard, and into the alley. "Nothing to be sorry about."

"But I didn't find out anything."

"Sure you did."

He stumbled over a rock and righted himself, Casey reaching for his arm.

"What was it?" he asked. "What did I find out?"

Casey glanced back toward Yvonne's dark house, where she was sure Yvonne huddled in the darkness with her dogs, shivering.

"You found out that she's scared. And that changes everything."

Chapter Forty-two

They walked without speaking down back roads and quiet yards, avoiding the homes Eric recognized as ones with dogs. In twenty minutes they were making their way toward the diner, The Burger Palace, and The Sleep Inn. Once they arrived, it was trickier to find places to walk where they wouldn't be spotted. It took them twice as long as it should have to maneuver around HomeMaker's parking lot, and Casey was beginning to worry they'd be too late.

But when the back entrance of the factory came into view they could see many employees still hanging around outside.

"Will they recognize you?" Casey asked.

Eric smiled grimly. "They might. Karl made a big deal of getting me in some corporate pictures. I guess I had the look he wanted."

Casey considered that. "I guess we'll have to take the chance, if we're going to do this. Looks like we can keep our caps on, at least." A lot of the workers she could see were wearing hats. "Where are the video cameras?"

He shrugged. "Never bothered to check."

Casey scanned the face of the building, and saw two cameras. One was high on the wall, to get an overall view of the entryway, and one seemed to be trained on the door. She couldn't spot any in the parking lot. There would be at least one inside the building, she was sure.

"We'll have to leave our dark sweaters here," she said. "I'm glad we can wear these caps, though. Be sure to keep your face down."

They got as close as they could within the shadows before strolling together into the break area, acting like they were in conversation. No one bothered them, or seemed to even notice they were there. They neared the door, and Casey felt like she could breathe again.

"Hey."

Casey froze and turned toward the voice, pivoting on her feet to place her weight on the right one, ready to fend off an attack.

The man held an unlit cigarette between his thumb and forefinger. "Either of you got a light?"

Casey shook her head. "Sorry."

The man grunted his displeasure, but turned to another co-worker to repeat his question. Casey and Eric continued on into the building. Casey didn't look up to search for videos, but she was certain they were there. She hoped Security wasn't looking at the monitors too closely.

Eric didn't hesitate, but headed casually toward the door at the end of the hallway marked Administrative Offices. He put the key in the door and turned it, and before anyone could say anything, they were in the silent, dark hallway, with the door closing behind them. Eric punched the code into the alarm and the access light turned green.

"They'll be able to tell that I was here, when they look," he said.

Casey shrugged. It couldn't be helped. "Let's go."

They walked the length of the hallway, and Casey stopped Eric before he opened the door. "Video cameras? Any idea where they're placed?"

"I know there's one in the lobby, watching Gloria and the front door. I don't think there's one in the administrative offices. My…Karl's big on privacy in the workplace. His own workplace, anyway." He opened the door.

The hallway led directly into the lobby of the building, where Gloria the receptionist sat during the day. They kept their heads averted from the desk, hoping the inmates weren't being seen on the monitors. Eric went directly to the other door, and within moments they were in the main office.

Yvonne's computer was off, as were all of the lights, except for a security lamp on the wall. Casey took a moment to look around, and saw that Eric had been correct. No video cameras. At least none that she could see. She went to Yvonne's desk, sat down in the chair, and booted up the PC.

Eric flipped on one of the overhead lights. "No one can see us in here."

Casey looked around the room. He was right. No windows. How depressing.

"I'm not sure Karl would let Yvonne keep sensitive information out here," Eric said, yanking open one of the desk drawers.

"But we've got to look. And we *know* things are on the computer."

A box came up on the screen asking for a password. Casey looked to Eric, but he shook his head. "I have no idea what it is."

Casey examined Yvonne's desk, and the photos of her family. "What are her kids' names?"

"Joshua and Caitlin, but why would she—"

"It's what people usually do." But not this person, apparently. Casey tried every combination of the names she could think of. "Okay. Husband's name?"

"Jimmy."

No good.

Casey turned with mounting desperation to the final photo on the desk, one of two Doberman Pinschers taking up an entire sofa. They looked a lot sweeter there than they'd seemed back at the house. "Pets."

Eric sighed heavily, his face creased with irritation. "I don't know. How am I supposed to know that?"

Casey grabbed the frame and slid out the cardboard, exposing the back of the photo. "Roxie and Jabba at Christmas." It was worth a try.

Seven long minutes later she hit it with "JoshJabCaitRox."

"Guess Jimmy's the fifth wheel," Eric muttered.

But Casey didn't care about that. She searched the computer for anything that said, "Marlowe."

There was nothing there.

"But we saw it," Eric said. "Right on the screen."

"Well, it's not here anymore."

Casey sat back, looking over the computer toward Karl's door. "We have to get in there."

"I don't have a key."

"I know. But that's where the information is."

"Casey—"

She got up and went to Karl's door, examining it. Assuming there was a way to get in, there was probably an alarm set to go if anyone entered. "You're sure your key doesn't work?"

He came over and tried to put his key in the lock. It didn't fit.

Casey studied the door some more. It was wooden, not steel. She placed her hand on it. It was made of good quality wood, but it was also paneled. The insets would be weak points. All hell would break loose if she did what she was considering, but if they were quick enough...

"Be ready to move, Eric."

"What? What are you doing?"

Casey took a deep breath and sat back on her left leg. She focused on the door, the upper section of the lower right panel, closest to the doorknob.

"Casey..." Eric's voice rose.

She ignored him, and snapped her foot at the door. A loud crack ripped through the office.

"Casey!"

She kicked the door again, and once more, until the panel broke free from the door's skeleton. She pushed the panel out and squeezed her arm through, unlocking the door from the other side. The door scraped open, crooked on its hinges. Casey stood in the opening, surveying the office. No security measures were immediately apparent, but she had no doubt they were there.

"Come on, Eric." She strode into the room and approached the file cabinets along the side wall. They were labeled clearly, and she went for the one holding L-M. Of course there was nothing inside with the name Marlowe.

Eric stood in the middle of the room. "What should—"

"Check his desk."

"The drawers are all locked. But the desk is wooden." He looked at her expectantly.

"I can't kick apart everything, Eric. Here." She grabbed Karl's letter opener from the desk and handed it to Eric. "See what you can do with this."

He stared at it for a moment before going after the lock on the top middle drawer.

Casey turned back to the files. There were too many to go through in the few minutes they had. What else would it be under? *Dryer? Lawsuit? We're Screwed?*

Eric cried out. "Got it!" He yanked the top desk drawer open.

"That was fast."

"Cheap lock."

He rifled through the contents of the drawer and came up with a key, which he shoved into one of the other drawers. It opened. Casey began going through that one while he opened the drawer on the other side.

She flipped through the contents. Folders for insurance, lawyers, Mexico…*Marlowe.* She pulled it out and slapped it open, resting it on the drawer. The top paper was the first page of the contract. The one they'd seen on Yvonne's computer. She skimmed the document, searching for key words. As she read, the room fell away from her, and her blood turned to ice in her veins.

"Casey?" Eric looked at her across his drawer.

She blinked, slowly turning to him. "It was a child."

"A *child?* How old?"

"Two."

Eric stared at her blankly. "A two-year-old was doing laundry?"

"No." Casey shook her head once. Twice. "He wasn't doing laundry." She licked her lips, opposite the swelling.

"Casey, what is it?"

She tried to talk. Cleared her throat. Began again. "He was playing hide-and-seek. He climbed into the dryer. His mother thought she had forgotten to start it, and turned it on. By the time she realized she couldn't find him, it was too late."

Eric's eyes widened as the horror of the story sank in. "Why didn't he just kick the door open?"

Casey swallowed. "The door latch…was defective. It stuck. Even if he had been strong enough to get the door open, if he could've found it while he … he wouldn't have been able to do it."

Eric sat hard on the desk chair. "How can a door latch be defective?"

Casey looked back at the folder. Found a place in the document and underlined it with her finger. "The boy banged against the door, and with pressure from behind, the metal piece on the catch pushed up against the strike, and did exactly what its name says."

"It caught it?"

"So hard it wouldn't let it go. Even when the mother realized what had happened, and was trying to get the door open."

Casey put her elbows on the drawer and dropped her head into her hands. "Loretta said Ellen wasn't happy about the reason people might be able to keep their jobs."

"I knew that, too. But I don't get it. How could this help HomeMaker get people back to work?"

Casey shook her head. "I'm not sure. Unless…."

"What?"

Images swam before Casey's eyes. Board rooms. Teams of lawyers. Dottie Spears shooting daggers at her across the table with her eyes. A contract. *Not* a lawsuit. "A lawsuit wouldn't bankrupt a place like this."

Eric considered that. "Probably not. The amount of money this place goes through in a year…it's more than a lawsuit—even a huge one like this would make—could destroy. And of course there's insurance for this kind of thing. But the publicity. That would be bad."

"I haven't *heard* any publicity," Casey said. "Have you?"

"No. Not a word. I haven't even heard any within the *company*."

"That's why it's a contract. Not an official case. An official case, the reporters would've been swarming the place the next morning. This is the only way to keep it under wraps. "

Eric shook his head. "But why would the family do that? If a company's machine killed my son, I'd want the world to know."

"No," Casey said. "No, you wouldn't."

"I'm sorry. I don't…"

"The mother…she started the dryer. She let her two-year-old *die* in a dryer."

"It wasn't her fault."

"Of course it wasn't. But what is the world going to see if they take this case to trial? They're going to see a negligent mother who didn't know where her toddler was. No matter what the verdict is against HomeMaker, there will be some people who will always see it as the mother, killing her son." Casey let out a shaky breath. "*She'll* always see it that way."

Eric looked at his hands, then back at her. "Do you—"

"No, Eric. No. We are not going there."

"Okay. Okay. Sorry."

He glanced at the clock. "We've been here too long. We need to get out."

"Yes, I know, but…" Casey skimmed the subject lines of other folders in the drawer. Nothing else with the name Marlowe. She looked down at the folder and shuffled through the papers. Behind the contract were numerous memos, letters, statements from doctors… And another contract. This one without HomeMaker's logo. This one said simply, *Karl Willems*. Karl Willems, making his own deal with the Marlowes.

Something behind them rustled, and Casey jumped to her feet.

Willems stared at them from his broken doorway, two security guards in front of him.

"Eric?" He glanced at his son, and then at Casey, his expression hardening. "What the hell are you doing?"

Eric swallowed audibly. Casey moved to get between him and Karl, but he held out a hand, keeping her back. "You weren't exactly truthful with us the other day, Karl."

Karl's lips twitched, and he dragged his eyes toward Eric. "I don't know what—"

"I'm not stupid, Dad."

Eric's hand curled into a fist, hard against his hip, but Casey had no urge to comfort him this time.

"We found it," Eric said. "Him. The boy who died."

Karl nodded, his eyes not leaving Eric's face. "Gentlemen, you may go."

The security guards hesitated, but Karl pushed between them and jerked his head back, an unmistakable gesture of dismissal. "Out. Back to your posts." They left. Karl stepped into the room. "It's not what it looks like, son."

Eric snorted. "And what exactly do you think it looks like? *I* think it looks like you were covering up the death of a child. A death caused by a HomeMaker product."

"Oh, is that what you think?"

"It's more than that," Casey said.

Karl turned to her. "And what do you know?"

"I know how these things work. Businesses and deaths and law suits and confidential contracts."

"I see." He stepped further into the room.

Casey got past Eric this time, and stood between the two men. "Why don't you stay right there?"

Willems regarded her thoughtfully, then nodded. He stepped over to one of the chairs in front of his desk and sat in it, crossing one leg over the other. "You can't have found much. Security called me only ten minutes ago to say you were here."

"Ten minutes for security to get here?" Eric said. "They were slow."

Willems shrugged. "Soon it won't matter anymore."

"Right," Casey said. "When the company moves to Mexico."

Willems shook his head. "It's a shame, but there was nothing else to be done. No matter what some people thought."

No matter what *Ellen* thought, he meant.

Eric sank down onto Karl's desk, his shoulders slumping.

Casey stayed standing. "You're sticking to the story that the company needs to move because of the union's demands?"

"It's not a story."

"Maybe not." She held up the folder. "But this isn't a story, either. At least, it's not a fabricated one."

He hesitated. "That has nothing to do with—"

"A little over a year ago," Casey said. "One of HomeMaker's dryers *killed* someone. A child. Why wasn't there a lawsuit?"

Karl shrugged again. "HomeMaker wasn't at fault."

"Wasn't it?"

"Well, ultimately it could be seen to be. But it's not like HomeMaker purposefully put out a dangerous product. The mother was just as responsible."

Casey's breath caught in her chest, and she forced herself not to smack him. "Was this the first time you knew of a problem with the latches?"

"Of course."

But Casey had seen it again. That flicker in his eyes. "How long before?" she asked. "How long before had the first complaint come in?"

"I told you that was the first."

"And would Yvonne say the same if I asked her?"

"Of course she would."

Casey had seen the fear on Yvonne's face. She would say whatever Karl Willems wanted her to say.

"The boy's death is the real reason you're moving the company to Mexico," Casey said. "If it's actually even moving."

"What?" Eric's voice rose.

"Your fath—Karl has his own reasons for escape, don't you, Karl? How do we know the company's not simply going to cease to exist?"

Eric looked back and forth from Casey to Willems. Willems met his gaze defiantly.

"Dad," Eric said. "*What did you do?*"

"Nothing. I did nothing."

"Yes, Karl," Casey said. "That's exactly what you did." She pulled the second contract from the folder and handed it to Eric. "Take a look at this, Eric. See everything your father didn't do."

Karl made to get up, but Casey stepped forward, crowding him back onto his chair. "You," she said. "Sit."

He sank into the leather seat. "It wasn't my fault. They had no right—"

"Shut up, Karl." Rage burned behind Casey's eyes. *It wasn't my fault. I had no way of knowing such a little thing could cause such an accident. Who would've thought those complaints about the faulty fuel pump could have told us more? Don't blame me, Casey, blame Pegasus if you have to blame someone. How was I to know? I'm just an employee, I do what I'm told…*

"You're the *leader*, Karl," Casey said. "The *Chief Executive*. You're supposed to protect the little guy. The employees. Your customers. Little boys who see a dryer as a good hiding place. If nothing else, you should've protected your *company*."

"The company? What do they care? They would've hung me out to dry in a heartbeat."

"So you decided to make this entire town pay in your place?"

Eric cried out, and Casey looked at him, keeping her position over Karl.

Eric held out the paper. "You *knew*? You *knew* there was a problem with the latches. How many complaints had you gotten? Four? Half a dozen?"

Karl waved a hand. "It was a door latch, for God's sake. A *door latch*. Not the heating element. Nothing electrical. Who would've thought some kid would be dumb enough to crawl inside? And that his mother wouldn't even *notice*? What kind of a mother is *that*? A poor excuse for one, if you ask me."

"And Ellen?" Eric's voice cracked. "She found out about this. About the boy. Did you kill her, too?"

Karl's eyes sparked. "I didn't kill anybody. Not the boy, and certainly not Ellen. What am I going to do, go to her house and force her to OD on her own sleeping pills? Grow up, Eric. Grow up and see that she's the one who did it. Your perfect angel Ellen killed herself. It wasn't anybody else's fault. Not yours. Not HomeMaker's. And it certainly wasn't *mine*."

Casey leaned over and jabbed the pressure point at the back of Karl's jaw. His eyes widened, and she thrust her arm against the side of his neck, cutting off his carotid artery. He slumped over in his chair, but she kept the pressure on.

"Casey!" Eric leapt forward. "What did you do? Is he—"

"He's fine. He'll wake up as soon as I take off the pressure."

"But…but how are you doing that?"

Casey sighed heavily. "It's not hard." She rubbed her free hand over her forehead. "I just…I needed him to stop talking."

Eric glanced down at his father, whose head lolled onto his chest, his mouth slack. "Well, he did."

"And now," Casey said, glancing at the broken door. "We need to leave."

Chapter Forty-three

They didn't bother trying to avoid the cameras this time, as they only had half a minute, at the most, until Karl would wake up. He would be disoriented, which would give them a little more time, but he would soon remember everything that had happened, and be after them with a vengeance.

Casey kept her eye out for the security guards, in case they hadn't gone back to their posts as ordered, but none appeared. Casey and Eric didn't wait around. They ran straight out the front doors and through the parking lot to the neighboring property, where they found and pulled on their dark sweaters.

Once they'd gone a couple of blocks Eric stopped, bending over and putting his hands on his knees. "I've gotta stop, Casey. I'm not made for this."

Casey grabbed his elbow and pulled him upright. "Not here, Eric. We have to keep moving."

With a groan he followed her back the way they had come from town. Casey led him silently through yards and alleys, until they were a couple of streets from his home. Casey's arms were beginning to hurt again. Time for a few more ibuprofen. She wished she'd brought more pills from Eric's house. She pulled down the collar of her sweater and glanced at her shoulder. Spots of blood had leaked through her bandage, onto her shirt. Her lip throbbed, and her head ached.

Knowing it was out of the question to go back into Eric's house, Casey found a dark patch at the back corner of someone's yard and pulled Eric into the shadow.

Eric heaved a sigh. "He knew. He could've kept that boy from dying."

"Yes."

Eric closed his eyes and shook his head slowly. "He was more worried about money. As usual. It would've been expensive to recall the door latches and replace them. Expensive and bad PR."

Casey nodded. He was right. "Karl also could be held personally liable. If he knew about the defective part and didn't stop the production, it could all be put on him. HomeMaker could argue that it was all his fault."

Eric clenched his jaw. "So he gave the company up?"

"Looks that way. It was either close down the company, or he'd get all the blame. Probably go to jail. He made a separate agreement with the family, to protect himself."

Eric looked at her, his expression one of sorrow, and resignation. "So what now?"

She arched her back, wincing at the pain in her kidney, and looked up at the sky, stars twinkling through the leaves of the tree above her. She was tired. She was confused. She needed stitches.

Eric spoke quietly. "At least Karl didn't kill Ellen."

"He says."

"I believe him."

"Yeah. Yeah, I guess I do, too." It had been in his eyes.

"You should leave, Casey."

She turned her head to look at Eric, but saw only the back of his head as he stood facing away from her, his arms crossed over his chest.

"You should take my car and start driving. Get far away."

He was right, of course. She should leave Clymer, with all of its problems, and all of its goodness, behind. Right that moment.

"I can't, Eric."

"Why not?"

Yes. Why the hell not? "I have to know. I have to know what happened to Ellen."

"But *why*?"

When he turned to face her she looked up into his eyes. "Because she deserves the truth, Eric. Her kids deserve it." *And what else do I have to live for?*

He looked away. "But what if the truth is really that she did it? That no one else killed her?"

"You really think she could have? *Really*, Eric?"

He sighed heavily and looked at the ground between his feet. "No. No, I don't really think she could have."

"Then she didn't."

He looked over at her, the corner of his mouth twitching. "And I'm certainly not about to argue with *you*."

She put her hands on her hips and rolled her neck before stepping back into the alley. "Then come on."

"Where are we going?"

She smiled. "We're going to go see exactly what it is Yvonne knows. And we're not taking no for an answer."

He hesitated. "Karl will be out looking for us by now."

"Yeah, well, he can join the club."

They walked a bit, until Casey realized Eric was laughing. She stopped. "What?"

"It's just…you were like Spock. Doing the Vulcan stun thing to Karl."

"Oh. Well. Live long, and all that."

"Yeah."

They kept walking.

Yvonne's house was dark, except for the outside light by the door, which she must've turned on after they left the first time. Her husband's truck was still absent.

"What about the dogs?" Eric said.

"I guess we'll have to hope she doesn't let them eat us." She slipped beside the house, where she'd be hidden when Yvonne opened the door. Eric looked at her to get the go ahead, then rang the bell.

Yvonne didn't answer, and the dogs were silent.

Eric rang the bell again, and knocked on the door. After a few minutes of this, the inside door jerked open.

"Eric? What do you *want*? You're going to wake the kids, and then what are we going to do?"

Casey stepped out, swung open the screen door, and braced the inside door with her foot.

"*You?*" Yvonne said. "They're looking for you." She glanced out at the street, as if expecting a police car to appear.

"Yes," Casey said. "May we come in?"

Without waiting for an answer, she pushed past Yvonne into the house, and found herself pinned to the counter by the two large Doberman Pinschers, snarling and emitting low growls. Casey froze, her hands out in front of her.

"Yvonne, don't!"

Casey looked up from the dogs to see Eric wrestling a cell phone out of Yvonne's hand. He wrenched it away, ended the call she'd begun, and shoved it into his pocket.

Yvonne backed away from him, flattening against the wall. "They said if I saw you again I should call them."

"So they know I was here before?"

"Jimmy came home for something to eat. I told him."

Eric glanced at Casey, who was trying to access her ability to fight two large dogs. Fighting off people was one thing. Dogs were a different story altogether. She glanced at the counter beside her. The only things within reach were the soap dispenser, a dishrag, and a plastic napkin holder. Nothing too promising as a weapon.

"Yvonne," Eric said. "Can you call off the dogs?"

Yvonne hugged her stomach, staring at Casey. Casey had no doubt her swollen lip and bloody shirt did not paint a pretty picture.

"She killed someone," Yvonne said. "She's dangerous."

"She's not dangerous," Eric said. "Not to you."

Yvonne shook her head, her mouth open.

"I won't hurt you, Yvonne," Casey said. "The only reason I…those men attacked me. I had to defend myself."

Yvonne closed her mouth, but her lips continued working against her teeth.

"Yvonne," Eric said. "Please. We just want to talk. Come on. You *know* me."

Yvonne took a few more heavy breaths before holding out her hand. "Only if I can have my phone back."

Eric placed his hand over his pocket. "You won't call them?"

Yvonne lifted her hand higher. "I'll listen to what you have to say."

Eric looked at Casey and she nodded shortly. If Yvonne made the call, Casey would just have to fight her way through the dogs. Maybe she'd squirt them in the face with the anti-bacterial hand cleaner.

Eric reached into his pocket and pulled out the phone. He hesitated briefly before placing it in Yvonne's open palm. She wrapped her fingers around it and pulled it against her stomach. "Roxie. Jabba. Down."

The dogs dropped to their haunches, and their growling turned into happy panting, their tongues lolling from their mouths.

"Bed," Yvonne said.

The dogs trotted to the next room, where Casey could see two large doggie pillows lying side by side. The dogs curled up on the cushions, but their eyes remained on Casey. She shivered, returning her attention to Yvonne.

"Yvonne," Eric said. "We know about the boy."

Her face went blank for only a moment before her eyes widened, filling with tears. "The boy…"

"Come on." Eric led her gently to a chair.

They were in the kitchen, and the closest place was at the table. Yvonne dropped her phone in front of her before laying her face in her hands.

Eric sat next to her. "Yvonne, what happened? What has Karl done?"

She rolled her head back and forth in her hands before jerking it up, her face inches from Eric's. Her eyes were red, and tears spilled over onto her cheeks. "I can't tell. I can't tell you."

"But Yvonne—"

"I *can't!*" She pushed herself away from the table, sending her chair crashing backward. Her face twisted and she grabbed the chair, lifting it off the floor.

Casey stepped forward and wrapped her hand around one of the rungs. "Don't, Yvonne. Please." Casey kept a hold on it, making eye contact, watching as Yvonne's grip slackened, and then relaxed completely.

Yvonne let go of the chair and spun away, leaning against the wall.

"Yvonne," Eric said.

Casey shook her head, and he quieted.

Yvonne's shoulders began to shudder, and soon she was gasping for air, her body heaving. Her hand trailed down the wall as her knees buckled, and Eric jumped from his seat, grabbing her around the waist as she slipped to the floor. He went down, too, and ended up holding her on his lap, rocking her as he would a child. "Shh, Yvonne. It's okay. It's okay."

Tucking her face into his neck, her sobs gradually diminished, until she was taking deep breaths and wiping her face on his shirt.

"Tell us," Eric said gently. "Please."

Yvonne gave one last snort, then climbed to her feet, stumbling into the other room. Casey poised for flight. Eric held out his hand. The sound of Yvonne blowing her nose came from the back hallway, and they heard water running. Yvonne returned to the kitchen, her face blotchy, water spots dotting her shirt.

"I didn't know what to do," she said. "Except keep my mouth shut. He told me...he told me if I didn't, I would be arrested. *Arrested. Me!*" She shook her head with apparent disbelief. "Even with Jimmy being a cop, I could be… Anyway, I couldn't say anything. It was in the contract."

"Why didn't the parents file a lawsuit?" Eric asked.

Yvonne gave a small laugh. "Why do you think? HomeMaker—well, *Karl*—made Mrs. Marlowe think it was her fault. That if she hadn't neglected her son he would still be alive."

Casey made a sound in her throat, and Yvonne glanced at her. "I know. It's awful." She glanced toward the back of the house, back toward the bedrooms. "For any mother to be told that…"

"But why did HomeMaker want that in the first place?" Eric asked. "To avoid publicity?"

"Oh, sure. They didn't want the world thinking they killed somebody. They just wanted it to go away quietly. To pay the Marlowes from the insurance money, sign the confidentiality contract, and have it be over with."

"But something happened," Casey said.

"Yes." Her eyes flicked to Eric. "The Marlowes found out about Karl."

Eric clenched his jaw. "Found out what?"

"That he knew about the door latches."

His eyes met Casey's. So they were right.

"There had been several complaints," Yvonne said. "Nothing big. Just that the latches had jammed. No one had been hurt. But a consumer would put something heavy in, or too large of a load, and the next thing they knew they couldn't open the dryer door. Karl said it was their own fault for filling the dryer too full, and ignored them." She closed her eyes, and swayed on her feet. Eric grabbed her elbow and led her back to a chair.

"Why did Karl trust you to type up the contracts?" Casey asked. "Why put you in that position at all, instead of doing it himself?"

Yvonne looked up at her, and swiped the tears from her cheeks. "Because I knew, too, don't you see? I knew about the earlier complaints. I was already in the position of knowing too much."

"Kathy didn't know?" Eric asked. "She works right next to you. Or...or Ellen?"

Yvonne shook her head. "There were lots of things Kathy and Ellen didn't know. There was no reason to tell them. It wasn't anything exciting. Just...door latches. I mean, we get complaints all the time that never amount to anything, about a lot more serious things."

"But somehow Ellen found out," Eric said. "That's how we knew to even look. She videotaped your computer when you were working on the contract, just a few weeks ago."

"I don't know how she would've..." Yvonne's forehead creased as she thought. "I don't think anybody else knew. The board, I guess, but they don't live around here, and even if they did, it's not like they're going to be telling the employees about legal problems. *I* certainly didn't tell her."

"Lawyers?" Eric said.

Casey shook her head. "Wouldn't tell."

"How about...bankers?" Eric looked at Casey.

Could it be? Todd has sworn his meeting with Karl had nothing to do with the company, that it was personal. But it wouldn't be the first time someone had lied about this whole mess.

Yvonne shook her head. "He wouldn't tell the bank."

"But Todd came to his office—"

"It wasn't about this."

"You're sure?"

Yvonne looked at Casey. "Karl was falling behind on some payments. He'd paid so much money to the boy's family... The bank wanted to repossess some things, but they were in other people's names. Todd was the one who'd approved the loans, and was having trouble explaining to his superiors how he'd made such bad decisions."

Casey almost smiled. The Pegasus Orion. So it was in Lillian's name, after all. Just another way for Karl to save his assets. "Who would Karl tell about the money?"

Eric frowned. "He certainly didn't tell *me*."

Yvonne's face paled, as if there were a connection she feared Casey would make. Casey's breath hitched. "Yvonne, does Chief Reardon know? Is he protecting Karl?"

Yvonne's brow furrowed. "The chief? No, he doesn't know anything."

"Denny?" Eric said. "Why would you think—"

"He's been suspicious of me since I arrived. Like I'm here to cause trouble."

Yvonne gave a short laugh. "That's just the chief. He thinks *anybody* new is here to cause trouble. He knows nothing about this. I swear."

Yvonne's phone rang, and Eric jumped, squinting at its glowing window. "It's Jimmy."

Yvonne bit her lip, then reached for the phone. "Hi, honey. Yes. I'm okay. They're asleep." She listened for a bit as she breathed with her mouth open, her eyes on Eric's face. "It's just…they're here, Jimmy. Right now."

Casey grabbed Eric's sleeve and yanked him toward the door. He stopped, looking at Yvonne, his face filled with betrayal.

Casey jerked him toward her. "Come *on*, Eric!"

With a last look back, Eric ran after Casey into the back yard. She could hear the dogs, barking and whining at the door, their toenails scraping the metal.

"I'm sorry!" Yvonne called as they ran away. "Eric! I'm *sorry!*"

Gritting her teeth, Casey ran even harder, praying Yvonne's door was strong enough to keep those dogs in the house.

Chapter Forty-four

Casey careened down the alley, sprinting through yards and across dark intersections. Eric kept up as well as he could, but his breathing was growing heavy and labored. Casey jumped over a fallen stick, but Eric nailed it, stumbling and skidding along the gravel alley on his hands and knees. Casey ran back and reached to pull him up. He staggered to his feet, spreading his hands to show several imbedded stones.

Casey grabbed his wrist. "Later. We need a place to go, Eric. Not your house. Where?"

He swallowed and scratched his forehead feverishly, as if it would help him think. "Ellen's? No. Mom's…Home Sweet Home…" He brought his head up. "The theater!"

Casey didn't like it. Didn't like it, but didn't know where else to go, other than the parking lot of The Burger Palace, where they could hop on a semi and hightail it out of town.

But the cops had probably already thought of that.

She nodded. "Okay. We can take stock and patch ourselves up there." She looked around. "Where are we?"

"About as far away as we can be."

Of course. "Take us there."

Eric led her back toward the center of town, sticking to dark side streets and yards. Sirens were audible, and two cop cars hurtled past a street over, but Casey and Eric hunkered down in the shadows until they could no longer see the flashing lights. Soon the theater came into view.

Casey grabbed Eric's shirt to keep him in the dark as she scanned the area. No cars in the back, and no lights visible from the few windows. She gestured for him to wait, then snuck toward the front of the theater, staying in the neighboring yard. No cars in the front.

She returned to Eric. "You have a key?"

"Same key ring as HomeMaker. Right here." He patted his pocket.

"Get it out and ready. Is there an alarm system?"

He gave a quiet snort. "Hardly. We're lucky the lock even holds."

"Let's go."

They skirted the parking area and approached the door from the side, sliding along the building. Eric unlocked the door with one twist of the key, and they were inside, closing and locking the door behind them. Casey put a finger to her lips, and they stood listening for several minutes. When all that greeted them was silence, they stepped further into the dark hallway.

"No lights," Casey whispered, gesturing to the windows in the outside wall. They found their way to the stage door, and entered. The blue work light spread its eerie glow across the stage and through the curtain legs toward the back, where they'd entered.

Casey stepped forward and stumbled over a cable. Eric grabbed her arm and she gasped, reaching up to hold her shoulder.

"Sorry," Eric said.

She swallowed. "Where's that first aid kit Becca used?"

"Back here." He led her slowly toward the backstage bathroom, where the kit hung on the wall. He took it down and opened it on the toilet tank.

"Painkiller," Casey said.

Eric popped open a bottle of ibuprofen and offered her a couple. She washed them down with rusty water from the sink.

She grabbed one of Eric's wrists and turned it over to look at his hands. "You need to get those stones out."

"Not until we work on your shoulder."

She sagged onto the toilet seat, feeling suddenly weak.

Eric pulled his dark turtleneck over his head and tossed it aside, a sheen of sweat already forming on his forehead in the tiny, airless bathroom. He squatted in front of Casey, his back pressed against the sink, and helped her pull off her sweater. Once it was off he started unbuttoning her shirt.

"Eric!" She swatted his hand away.

He reached back up. "No time for modesty, Casey. I need to work on your arm."

He was right, of course, and she closed her eyes, gritting her teeth when he slid her shirt off and peeled away the bloodied ace bandage. Without a word he wet a wad of paper towels and swabbed the mess, the towels coming away red. He kept at it until he'd cleaned it all.

"You need stitches," he said.

"Yeah, like I need a hole in the head. You know what will happen if I go anywhere for that."

He shook his head. "Then sit still."

"You are not going to sew me up with costume thread."

"Don't be ridiculous." He rummaged around in the kit and came up with a tube of antibiotic cream, which he spread liberally on the cut. The bandage box held several butterfly strips, which he used to close the wound, and he covered them with sterile gauze pads. There were no ace bandages this time, but he found several extra large Band-Aids, which he placed side by side over the gauze.

He sat back. "That's the best I can do."

"Thank you." She shrugged the shirt back on and buttoned it up, her right hand working slowly, the injury to her forearm swelling her wrist, causing her fingers to stiffen. "Now you."

With the tweezers in the kit she was able to pick out most of the stones from his palms—only a couple were too deeply embedded to reach. When she'd finished, he washed his hands with soap before Casey poured peroxide over the wounds.

He grimaced, but kept his hands under the stream of antiseptic. "What now?"

"Now?" Casey screwed the top back onto the bottle and tossed it into the box of supplies. Her head swam and she leaned forward onto the sink.

"You need to rest," Eric said.

"I can't rest. They'll be coming here eventually."

"The Nesting Place. Mom and Rosie will hide you."

"No. I won't do that to them." Besides, the Pegasus folks had compromised their home.

"There's got to be someone we can call…"

"But *who*, Eric? Who do you trust?"

He clasped his hands together and pushed their sides against his forehead. "I don't know."

"There's no one, Eric. We have to keep moving." She stood, but the movement sent her spinning, and she fell against the wall.

Eric grabbed her waist and held her upright. "Come on."

She lurched out of the bathroom, his arm around her. "Where are we going?"

"You know those Equity cots the union requires theaters to put backstage for weary actors?"

"Well, sure, but—"

"This theater may not be Equity, but I insisted on the bed."

"I can't—"

"Yes, you can." He guided her to another room, where he unlocked the door and pulled the string on a light bulb hanging from the ceiling. "Props, costumes, and a cot. What more could you want?"

She could think of a few things, but had to admit the mattress looked inviting. "Just for a few minutes," she said. "We can't stay long."

He closed the door and pushed the lock on the knob. "You have to rest."

She sat on the cot. Not a very comfortable one, but better than the floor. She studied the room—shelves of old props, a treasure chest at the foot of the bed, a rack of varied costumes. She lay down, struggling to find a comfortable way to lie.

Nothing worked. And she was starting to shiver. "Eric, is there a blanket or anything?"

He grabbed an old army blanket from a shelf—probably from a production of *South Pacific*—and spread it over her. She continued to shiver. He stood looking down at her, then reached up to turn off the light. Without a word, he scooted onto the cot and under the blanket, wrapping his arms gently around her, her arms up between them, trying to conserve what body heat she had.

"Eric…"

"Shh. Just rest." He placed his hand over her mouth, then slid her hat off of her head, pulled her hair out of its knot, and ran his hand over her scalp, rubbing from her temples to the back of her neck. Casey let her head drop back, her nerves tingling as he kneaded her sore muscles. She groaned, twisting her head into his hand, her body arching toward him as his hands brought her closer.

"Casey," he said.

Casey's breath caught in her throat. *Oh. Oh, yes.*

Casey pulled her hands out from where they were trapped between her body and Eric's, and turned them around, fumbling with the buttons on his shirt, desperate suddenly to feel his skin, to feel his heat against her. When the buttons wouldn't cooperate, she yanked his shirt from his jeans, skimming her hand up along his stomach and chest. He rose up just enough she could pull the shirt over his head. The buttons caught at the ends of the sleeves and she jerked the shirt, ripping the buttons from the fabric and forcing the shirt over his wrists. His back was warm, and she flattened her hands against it, pulling him against her.

His hand slid up the back of her shirt, and she shivered, a moan coming from deep in her throat. Eric unclasped her bra one-handed and forced her shirt up, his hand closing over her breast. She reached down to his jeans, unbuttoning the fly and wrenching down the zipper.

He groaned and leaned in to kiss her, stopping at the first touch of her swollen lips, kissing instead her chin, her eyes, the hollow of her throat. Casey moved her hand down to her own fly, undoing the button and zipper, pushing her jeans down over her hips. Eric rose above her, reaching down to free himself from his clothes.

"Reuben," Casey whispered.

Eric froze.

Oh, God. Oh, no. Casey let her head fall back and she gasped.

Eric rolled away and off of the cot, up onto his feet.

"Eric," Casey said.

Eric picked up his shirt and left the room.

Chapter Forty-five

Casey was dressed in a black sweatshirt from the costume rack, her back against the wall, when he returned. "Eric, I'm sor—"

He shook his head. "Don't say it. It was…" He wiped his hand over his face. "What are we going to do?"

"Nothing, Eric. I'm sorry. It's not that I don't—"

"I don't mean about…that." He gestured at the bed. "I mean about everything else that's happened tonight. What we found out about Karl. Breaking into HomeMaker. The cops. You killing that man."

Casey winced at the icy tone of his voice. "You should do what…what you should've done from the beginning. Go home. Let me take the blame. I'll make it out of town on my own. Leave you be."

"Leave me to clean up the mess, you mean."

She looked away.

He paced away from her, and then back, stopping halfway across the room. "Okay. We need to get you out of town. How do we do that?"

Casey thought about her backpack, hanging in the garage close to Eric's house. Omar's little hat. Her wedding ring… "I'll just go. I'm used to running. I'll be all right. But you? What are you going to tell the cops?"

He shook his head. "That I tried to keep you here, but you wouldn't stay." He looked at her from under half-closed eyelids.

"What about Ellen?"

"What about her?"

"You want to know who killed her, don't you?"

He blinked. "It wasn't someone from HomeMaker."

"Probably not."

"Then who would it be? No one would've killed her over anything else. Everyone loved her. Her family, her co-workers, the theater people…"

"You."

He turned away. "A lot of good that does. She's dead, and here I am a week later…" He glanced at the bed, his face red.

"Eric, I miss my husband, too—"

"Obviously."

She stopped. Took a deep breath. "What almost happened… it doesn't make that pain any less. It doesn't mean we love them any less."

"Doesn't it?"

Casey wrapped her arms around herself, trying to quell the shivers that had begun again. She felt her shoulder and was relieved to discover her injury had not reopened. "Eric, don't you want to know what happened to her?"

He shuddered. "I'm beginning to think I was wrong. We were all wrong. Maybe it really was too much for her. She just couldn't take it anymore."

"I don't believe it."

He let out a short laugh. "And what do you know? You never even met her."

"But I know *you*."

"For what? Five whole days? And what does that matter, anyway?"

She stepped forward, close enough she could feel his tension. "Because I know you wouldn't love someone who was shallow. Someone who would leave her kids when the going got rough." She paused. "*You* wouldn't do it. Just like you haven't left me."

He looked away, at the shelves of props, before dropping his head toward his chest. "She wouldn't have," he whispered. "She wouldn't have done it."

Casey stepped around him and looked at his face. "So who *would've?*"

A sound echoed through the theater and into their room, like the scrape of a door opening. Eric reached up and pulled the string on the light, plunging them into darkness.

Casey winced. If whoever it was hadn't known they were there, they would now, seeing the light go off. And Casey couldn't see as well to defend them.

Eric stepped forward, hand out as if to close the door, but Casey held him back, a finger on her lips. She pointed to the wall on the hinge side of the door, and he went to stand there, out of the line of vision, and out of her way. Casey quietly and slowly closed the door, pushed the lock, and stepped further back into the room, where she would be able to see the door if it opened, but the person might not see her in the shadow. She balanced herself on the balls of her feet, body at the ready.

They waited for several minutes, the only sound Eric's ragged breathing. Casey questioned the wisdom of shutting them in the room. She should've scooted out, leaving Eric protected behind the door, herself on the outside. Her judgment, as well as her physical strength, had definitely been compromised by the events of the night.

The doorknob jiggled, and the sound of a key scraping the lock preceded the click of the lock popping. Casey scooted further back behind the shelf of props. The door swung open, hiding Eric from view. The silhouette of a woman stood in the doorway, before she stepped forward and pulled the overhead string. Light filled the room, casting jagged shadows between the shelves, clearly illuminating the cot, the blanket, and the distinct impression that the bed had been used.

Holly stepped forward, her hand reaching toward the blanket. She stopped and pulled back, scanning the room. Casey squinted, making the whites of her eyes smaller, should the light reflect off of them.

"Hello?" Holly's voice was loud in the small room.

Casey prayed Eric would stay silent.

Receiving no response, Holly pulled the blanket off the bed and shook it, as if expecting something to fall out. When nothing did, she dumped it onto the floor and leaned over, smelling the cot. Eyes narrowing, she focused on a section toward the middle of the mattress.

Casey burned with shame and anger at her lack of self-control. She and Eric hadn't completed their lovemaking, but it was certainly possible they'd left incriminating evidence of their encounter.

Holly stood, her face thoughtful. She turned toward the door, toward Eric's hiding place.

"Holly."

Holly spun around, a hand on her chest. "Holy… *Casey*?"

Casey stepped out of the shadow.

Holly studied Casey's face, her swollen lip. "You know everyone's after you. They're saying you killed somebody."

Casey didn't respond.

"You really did, didn't you?"

Casey swallowed. "Yes."

Holly laughed quietly. "Poor Eric thought you were so good. So perfect for this town. For our play."

"It was self-defense."

"Yeah," Holly said, obviously not convinced. "Yeah, I'm sure it was."

Casey took another step forward. "What are you doing here, Holly? It's the middle of the night."

She gave a tight smile. "I heard the sirens, and turned on the radio to see what was happening. It didn't seem like there was any chance of you getting away, with all the cops out. I looked all over for you, and finally thought of looking here. I should have looked here first. I mean, where else would you go? You can't stay at Eric's. Even though it seems like you might want to." She tipped her head toward the bed. "Eric, why don't you come out from hiding? I know you're here."

When he didn't respond she pivoted and grabbed the door, revealing him. "Hello, stepson."

"Holly," Casey said. "What do you want?"

Holly smiled, still looking at Eric. "What do I want? What do you *think* I want? I want life to go back to how it was last year. How it was *supposed* to be when I married the most important man in town."

Eric's face had turned greenish, and Casey hoped he wasn't about to be sick.

She cleared her throat. "Holly, Karl is—"

"—an ass. I know. But he's a rich ass. At least for now. If you two will keep what you've learned to yourselves."

"What we've—"

"I know all about the boy."

Casey gritted her teeth. Of course. Of all people, Karl would certainly tell his *wife*.

"It's a mess," Holly said. "The killer dryer, the parents. The contract. No one was going to know Karl's part in it all. No one *would* have known if you hadn't butted in."

She reached into her purse and Casey leapt forward. Holly spun away, behind Eric, and pressed a tiny pearl-handled gun hard against his temple.

Casey froze, her hands up. "Holly, don't."

"Don't? *Don't?*" She laughed, a high, frightening screech. "Karl came home tonight. Said he found you in his office. Said you'd discovered the dead boy, and were going to reveal his part in it."

"We don't know his part."

"Bullshit. You know it very well. He said you'd figured it out."

Eric's mouth had fallen open, and he breathed heavily through it. Casey met his eyes. *Hang in there.*

There was no way Casey could get to Holly in time to keep her from shooting. Eric didn't have a chance if she pulled the trigger. His head would be gone.

"Holly," Casey said. "We're not going to tell anyone."

Holly snorted.

"Look at me, Holly. Do I look like someone who can go to the police? What do you think they'd say to me if I tried telling them that story? They wouldn't care. All they care about right now is nailing me for the dead guy. And all I care about is getting out of here. I don't want to stick around this town. I don't want any more to do with it."

Holly clenched her jaw. "But what about *him*?" She shoved the gun against Eric's head, forcing him to the right.

"Karl's his *dad*. Why would he do something to hurt him?"

"Oh, come on. We all know what Eric thinks of his dad. He left town to get away from him."

"Sure. But he also came back. He has an office at HomeMaker. Right next to his father's."

Holly's mouth twitched.

"He's not going to tell, Holly."

Eric's eyes stayed on Casey as she inched forward. Casey willed him to remain calm. To watch for a cue, should she have an opening to go after Holly.

"Don't move."

Casey froze as another figure filled the doorway.

Holly gasped. "Thomas?"

He took in the sight of her with Eric, and lifted his own gun, pointing it at Casey. "You killed Bone."

Casey took a slow breath through her mouth. "I didn't mean to."

"Doesn't matter." He stared at her coldly. "You realize what this means?"

He didn't mean that she was wanted for murder. "They'll be coming after you, Thomas."

"I've cost them too much now. Even if I pay them back it won't matter. I might as well have you kill me, too."

Two guns. Two crazy people. Casey didn't like the odds.

"I was never in this town for you, Thomas," she said. "It was never about that."

"It doesn't matter anymore. Karl doesn't have the money to give me, anyway. There's no way I can get them what they want."

Holly's eyes narrowed. "What are you talking about?"

Thomas gave a short laugh. "He didn't tell you, did he, sweetheart? Karl's *broke*. He's got nothing. Not even spare change to get the mob off my back. Some trouble at the factory, and he was using personal money to bail himself out."

Holly's mouth closed, her lips almost disappearing as she clenched her jaw. Karl apparently hadn't told her *that* part of the mess.

Thomas kept the gun on Casey. "Holly? What are you doing here?"

She shook her head. "It's over. It's really over. I did what I could. I thought..."

Casey swallowed. "You thought with Ellen gone your secret—Karl's secret—would be safe. You'd go back to your old life and everything would be fine. Karl would move on to another job somewhere else, and you could play the role you're best at."

"A rich man's wife," Holly said. "It's all I ever wanted to be."

Eric's eyes sparked, then went flat. His hands clenched into fists by his sides.

"How did she know?" Casey asked. "How did Ellen ever find out?"

Holly's lips quivered, and her voice dropped to a whisper. "I thought we were friends..."

"So you told her Karl's secret. That he'd known there was a problem with the dryer latches, but he didn't change them."

"I was scared. Worried. I thought Ellen cared about me."

Casey nodded. "But she cared more about the boy."

"And the other people at HomeMaker. Thought they should have their jobs back." Tears streamed down Holly's cheeks now, and snot shone on the end of her nose. She began to shake, and her grip on the gun tightened. "She couldn't see that the factory was finished. Karl didn't need to be exposed. No matter what he'd done, it was *over*. If HomeMaker hadn't agreed to shut down the boy's family would've brought a lawsuit against the company, against Karl, and nothing would be able to repair the damage. At least this way the workers get a severance package. And they keep their reputations…" She rubbed her nose on Eric's shoulder, keeping the gun in place.

Casey glanced at Thomas. He was staring at Holly, his face filled with disbelief. "You killed Ellen?"

She raised swollen eyes to him. "I had to, Thomas. *I had to.*"

With a primal cry Eric thrust his arms upward, knocking Holly's hand away from his head. The gun went off, and plaster showered the room. Casey snapped her foot at Thomas' hand, knocking his gun to the floor, where it skidded against the wall. He reached for it, and she leapt on him, kicking the gun out of range at the same time she wrenched his arm behind his back, pinning him face-down.

Eric had Holly against the wall, but hadn't been able to dislodge the gun from her fingers. She was turning her wrist, pointing the gun at his head. Casey rolled off Thomas and snatched up his gun, training it on Holly.

"Holly, freeze!"

Holly's knuckles were white as she gripped the gun, and she didn't stop the slow arc toward Eric's head. Casey jumped across the room and threw an uppercut at Holly's arm, sending both guns and Eric flying. Eric regained his balance and dove back toward Holly, knocking her to the ground, squeezing his hands around her throat. She gasped for breath, her eyes popping.

"Eric, stop!" Casey wrapped her arms around his chest, locking her hands together, and pulled back. His grip loosened, and they fell backward, Eric landing on top of her. Holly turned onto her stomach, retching, and Eric ripped himself from Casey's grasp, lurching toward Holly again. Casey grabbed the waistband of his jeans, holding him back.

"Everybody freeze." Thomas was on his feet, breathing hard, Holly's gun in his hand. "Don't. Move." With his free hand he pulled a phone out of his pocket.

Casey eased upward, onto her knees, and Thomas placed his gun a foot from Eric's head, his eyes not leaving Casey's face.

"Yes, hello," he said into his phone. "The people you're looking for? They're at the theater. I have to go." He closed the phone and shoved it back into his pocket. "Now let's all just play nice until they get here."

Holly reared upward, the back of her head connecting with Eric's face, blood splattering across her shirt and Eric's chin. Holly twisted around to face him, her teeth bared, and Eric launched himself out of Casey's grasp, grabbing Holly's hair and pounding her head against the floor.

"Stop!" Thomas screamed. He raised the gun toward Eric.

Casey leaned on her left hand and swung her right foot, sweeping Thomas off his feet. His arm slammed against the floor and the gun discharged, the sound echoing in the room. Blood flew everywhere and Eric jerked to a stop, falling back hard onto the floor. Casey leapt to her feet and grabbed the gun from Thomas, throwing it out into the hallway.

She dropped beside Eric, her hands exploring his body, searching for the wound. "Eric. Eric, oh, God, I'm sorry. Where is it?"

He grasped her hands. "It's not me."

"What?"

Thomas whimpered, and Eric sat up, clutching Casey. Holly's eyes were wide open, as if in surprise. Her face looked perfect. But most of her neck was gone.

Eric leaned away from Casey, breathing fast and hard. Casey placed a hand on his shoulder, waiting for him to vomit.

He didn't.

"Coffee," he said.

"What?"

"The autopsy showed Ellen had been drinking coffee. She thought...she thought she was having one of her talks with Holly. Instead, Holly was putting drugs in her cup. Ellen was trying to be a good friend...and she was being *murdered*."

Casey squeezed his shoulder, and he took several shaky breaths.

"You have to go," he finally said.

Casey shook her head.

"You need to leave, Casey. Get out before the cops come."

"But, Eric—"

"Please. I don't want you to have to— Just go."

She looked at Thomas, slumped on the floor, his face empty, but avoided another look at Holly.

"Eric…" She smoothed his hair away from his forehead, her hands cradling his face.

He put his own hands up, pressing hers against his cheeks. "Good-bye, Casey Smith."

Tears stung her eyes. "Good-bye, Eric Jones."

She leaned forward and touched his lips briefly with hers.

Looking into his eyes one more time she pushed herself up, and ran.

Chapter Forty-six

Casey could hear the sirens coming from every direction.

Ducking out the back of the theater, she raced to the cover of the neighbor's yard, wishing the darkness weren't already disappearing into dawn. Avoiding main streets, she listened carefully for the placement of the sirens, staying clear of them as she ran. Almost more dangerous were the houses, with their windows. The residents of Clymer had to be hearing the morning's activities, and the sight of a woman sprinting through their back alleys wouldn't be something they'd ignore. With a stab of grief she knew she didn't dare try to get back to Eric's block, where her bag waited in his neighbor's garage.

Sticking to the tree lines, Casey made her way toward the only place she could think of. The only chance she had. She prayed the cops had abandoned their post there, thinking they had her at the theater.

She approached the outer part of town more slowly. Just a person walking along the sidewalk. No hurry. No worries.

The Burger Palace parking lot was devoid of cop cars. She could see it even as she approached. The diner had its usual empty lot. She was in the clear.

Slipping in the side of The Burger Palace, she was able to avoid the eye of the girl at the counter and make her way to the bathroom. She locked the door behind her and kept her eyes away from the mirror. Stripping off her shirt, she scrubbed her face and neck, the water in the basin turning pink. Again, blood that was not her own.

After rinsing off her head and rubbing it with paper towels, she ran her fingers through her hair before daring a glance in the mirror. There she was, a clean-faced woman who'd just taken a shower and had come to grab a quick cup of coffee before work. The lip wasn't attractive, certainly, but at least it wasn't bleeding. Not like her shoulder, which had reopened in the fight. She pressed some paper towels against it, hoping it would soon clot again.

She turned the black sweatshirt inside out to hide the blood spatters, wishing she had something else to change into. But it would have to do. She shuddered as she pulled it over her head.

She worked at a few stains on her pants, but her lower half had escaped the worst of the mess, being blocked by Eric's body when it had happened.

Her shoes were clean.

She closed her eyes, shivering. It was time to move on.

The man just leaving The Burger Palace when she exited the bathroom headed toward a truck in the back lot.

Casey followed him. "Hey, buddy. Okay if I grab a lift for a while?"

He turned, his eyes raking over her wet hair, her swollen lip, and her inside-out shirt. He shrugged. "Why not? I could use some company this morning. Wake me up a bit."

"Great. Thanks."

"Any bags?"

Casey's breath caught, and she forced a smile. "Nope. Just me."

"No problem. I need to check something in the back, and I'll be ready to go." He loped toward the rear of the truck.

Casey walked around the front of the cab, hesitating at the passenger door.

"So where are you going now?"

Casey shook her head. "Where do you think I should go?"

Death shrugged. "Somewhere interesting."

Casey took a deep breath through her nose and let it out slowly. "Things have been pretty interesting for the last ten hours or so. Where have you been?"

Death gave a small, sad smile. "I've been right beside you, Casey."

Casey blinked. "But I haven't seen you."

"Why do you think that is?"

Casey took a breath that was half a sob. She closed her eyes and pressed on them with her thumb and forefinger. "I'm so tired."

"I know, sweetheart. I know."

Opening her eyes, Casey looked back in the direction of town.

"They'll be all right," Death said.

"Who?"

"Eric. Lillian and Rosemary. The town. They'll be all right without you. You've done what you could."

Casey looked up at the sky. It was beautiful. Pinks and reds and oranges, heralding the sun. Her bones ached. Her lip throbbed. Her shoulder wound would probably soon leak through her shirt.

She opened the truck door and looked up into the interior. The driver had returned, and was belting himself in. Still plenty of room. Enough for three.

"So," she said to Death, waving a hand at the cab. "Are you coming, or not?"

In the blink of an eye, Death was perched in the middle of the seat. The trucker didn't flinch.

Casey stepped up onto the running board and into the cab. She shut the door. Closed her eyes. Leaned back against the headrest.

"Where you off to?" the trucker said.

But Casey was already asleep.

To receive a free catalog of Poisoned Pen Press titles, please contact us in one of the following ways:

Phone: 1-800-421-3976
Facsimile: 1-480-949-1707
Email: info@poisonedpenpress.com
Website: www.poisonedpenpress.com

Poisoned Pen Press
6962 E. First Ave. Ste. 103
Scottsdale, AZ 85251

LaVergne, TN USA
11 June 2010
185796LV00002B/1/P